Dear Reader:

Kwanzaa is a wonc days, giving honor an before us. If you have Kwanzaa, I know tha in this unique collection will inspire and motivate you to begin celebrating this joyous season from December 26 through January 1.

In my home, we have merged traditional holiday celebrations along with Kwanzaa festivities so that my family and I are truly enriched with the spirit of giving and cultural reaffirmation. It is a chance for us to recognize what is unique and wonderful about our culture, and celebrate thc differences with joy in our hearts. I find that our Kwanzaa traditions give us confidence and purpose to face the year ahead.

In particular, I have enjoyed teaching my son, and all of the children in my life, that each of the seven days of Kwanzaa has a specific meaning and purpose: Umoja (Unity), Kujichagulia (Self-determination), Ujima (Collective Work and Responsibility), Ujamaa (Cooperative Economics), Nia (Purpose), Kuumba (Creativity), and Imani (Faith). On my way home from work, or after an exhausting day of holiday preparation, I look forward to spending time at dusk lighting the Kwanzaa candles and reciting their meanings. This is one small tradition that brings me a great sense of joy and serenity. And these are principles that can guide our actions each and every day, not just during this time of year. (*See back of book for detailed descriptions.)

Kwanzaa's principles, practices, and symbols are specifically geared to building the family and community needs of African-Americans. What draws me most to these celebrations is the opportunity to "call out" the names of friends, family, and other loved ones who have guided me along the way. Recognizing what my grandmother did for me in the past, along with the neighbors who also nurtured me, builds a sense of oneness for me and my family. I leave no one out! And I especially encourage my husband and son to do the same. This ritual enriches our minds, enlightens our souls, and feeds our hearts.

When it comes to feeding the heart, no holiday celebration would be complete without the special foods and smells that remind you of home. I encourage you to prepare some of the recipes in the back of this book to celebrate Kwanzaa (which means "first fruits of the harvest"). Eat them alongside the traditional turkey, stuffing, baked macaroni, and all the rest. I've included several recipes that are easy to prepare and most of all fun to eat! And in the spirit of Kwanzaa, give a gift (zawadi) from the heart. This book or a dish that you've lovingly prepared with a dash of creativity (Kuumba) are excellent choices!

Harambee!

Yanick Rice Lamb
Editor-in-Chief
Heart & Soul Magazine

P.S. Write to me with your unique Kwanzaa celebrations and holiday recipes at:

BET/Arabesque Books
Kwanzaa Celebrations
1900 W Place, NE
Washington, DC 20018

A KWANZAA KEEPSAKE

Bridget Anderson
Carmen Green
Margie Walker

BET Publications, LLC
www.bet.com

ARABESQUE BOOKS are published by

BET Publications, LLC
c/o BET BOOKS
One BET Plaza
1900 W Place NE
Washington, D.C. 20018-1211

First Printing: October 2001
10 9 8 7 6 5 4 3 2 1

Printed in the United States of America

CONTENTS

IMANI
by Bridget Anderson 7

WHISPER TO ME
by Carmen Green 129

HARVEST THE FRUITS
by Margie Walker 255

IMANI

Bridget Anderson

One

Natalie picked up her heavy suit bag and threw it in the trunk of her car. She had enough clothes to last her two weeks. She'd give anything to see the look on Kevin's face when he wouldn't have her to unwrap this Christmas. Two weeks ago she'd ended a three-year relationship that was going nowhere. Men were at the bottom of her list for a while. The last thing she wanted to do was spend her holiday with one.

Her car was gassed up and she had on her comfortable riding jeans. Two weeks in Hopkinsville, Kentucky, should relieve all her stress. Her aunt Polly had invited her to spend the holidays with relatives in Hopkinsville. Since her mother and stepfather were in Germany visiting Natalie's brother for the holidays, she took her aunt up on the offer. She looked forward to spending the Christmas holiday with relatives, then learning about Kwanzaa immediately following, while helping her cousin prepare for the celebration.

Natalie couldn't wait to get out of Atlanta. She sped down the highway in her little Honda wanting to put as much distance between herself and Kevin as possible.

Seven hours later, Natalie pulled into her aunt's

driveway honking her car horn. The cute little two-story white house hadn't changed much over the years. Natalie remembered the green window shutters now trimmed with white Christmas lights. A grin as big as a Kentucky cornfield spread across Natalie's face when her aunt, Pauline Williams, stepped out onto the front porch. She'd always be Aunt Polly to Natalie. The name she called her in her youth. One look at her aunt Polly and Natalie realized how much she'd missed being around her family. Ever since Natalie's mother remarried and moved to Minnesota, Hopkinsville, Kentucky, had become her surrogate home. Most of her relatives lived here.

"Well look at you!" Pauline stood holding the door open for her niece. "Don't you look good."

Natalie walked up the steps lugging her suit bag on one shoulder and a duffle bag on the other. "Hi, Aunt Polly, you're looking pretty good yourself." She kissed her aunt on the cheek as she passed her going inside.

"Honey, I'm so glad you could make it." After closing the door Pauline walked over and gave her niece a big hug.

"So am I, Aunt Polly. I'm glad you invited me." She dropped her bags with a thump, and returned her aunt's hug. The smell coming from her aunt's kitchen made her stomach growl. She'd only stopped once during the seven-hour drive down, for a chicken sandwich.

"Here, let me take your coat." Pauline helped Natalie out of her coat. "You can put your bags in the back bedroom. Wanda should be here any minute now. I told her you were on your way." Pauline hung Natalie's coat in the hall closet.

Natalie quickly went into the back bedroom,

dropped her bags on the floor and glanced around the room. She immediately felt at home. The guest bedroom had a country, sit-yourself-down feel to it. Everything was yellow and blue, from the striped wallpaper to the floral pillows. She closed the door and returned to the living room with her aunt. "How is Wanda? I haven't seen her in so long."

"Oh she's fine. Getting big as a house though. She sits over there cooking for them kids every night, but you can't tell it. One look at her and you'd swear she's eating all the food."

Natalie laughed at her aunt's description of her daughter. Pauline had put on a few pounds also, Natalie noticed. She was a statuesque woman with distinguished features and a stylish, short haircut. However, because of her height, the weight was hardly noticeable. Natalie thought the haircut made her aunt look ten years younger.

Pauline stood across the room with her hands on her hips staring at her niece. "Honey, you'll never gain any weight will you? You look like you're still in high school. You're such a cute little thing."

"Auntie, you've gotta remember, Mama's small, so I'm probably going to be small like her." Natalie looked down at herself. To her, she'd been cursed with not much of a body at all. Everything was small, from her feet to her hands. "I didn't inherit any of the hips in the family. But speaking of gaining weight, I think I smell something that could help." She raised her chin to get a better whiff of the aroma coming from the kitchen.

"Then you come right in here and let me feed you. Honey, if a good wind comes though, it'll blow you away." Pauline led the way into the kitchen.

After both women loaded their plates and sat at

the kitchen table, Pauline cut to the chase. "Okay, what's that young man done now?"

Natalie looked surprised. "What makes you think Kevin's done anything?"

"You're spending your two weeks vacation here in Hopkinsville instead of in Atlanta with that good-looking gentleman of yours. Don't get me wrong, we're glad to have you, but you've never spent that much time here before."

Natalie looked into her aunt's all too wise eyes. There was no fooling her aunt Polly. "We broke up two weeks ago."

"Are you going to be all right?" Pauline asked, before she began eating.

"Yeah, I'll be fine. Our relationship had been on the rocks for months anyway. I just wanted to spend some time with you guys and get away from men for a while. If I don't see another man for a long time, it'll be too soon." Natalie jabbed her fork into her sweet potato.

"Is he the reason for the bags under your eyes? You look like you could use some rest."

"No, that's work. I think they're trying to drive me crazy. Sometimes I ask myself if it's worth it. I needed a mental health break from that place; that's another reason why I came." She continued eating.

"Well, you be sure to try and squeeze in some rest while you're here. Between the shop and my grandchildren, I haven't had much rest lately. I've been feeling a little under the weather. Wanda's working on the Kwanzaa celebration for the family and I know she wants you to help."

"Sure, but I don't know much about Kwanzaa."

"Don't worry, Wanda will tell you everything you need to know. We've celebrated Kwanzaa for the past two years. Believe me, you'll enjoy it. It'll be the most delightful learning experience you've ever had."

"Boy, I should learn a lot this vacation, between working with you in the shop and helping Wanda. Two things I know nothing about." She shrugged her shoulders and smiled at the challenges.

After they finished eating, Pauline stood up to empty the plates and put them in the sink. "You'll love working in the shop. It's my little home away from home, and I love it. It'll be some of the easiest work you'll ever do."

"Well, I'm yours for the next two weeks and I'm sure I'll enjoy myself."

"That's the spirit."

It was Monday morning and time for Pauline's Antiques & Crafts to open its doors. However, Pauline got the chills Saturday night, which turned into a sore throat Sunday. By Monday morning she couldn't get out of bed. Natalie had assured her aunt she could run the shop for one day. *How hard could it be?* she asked herself. If she could handle all the stress of running a retail clothing store in Atlanta, a one-woman antique shop should be a cinch. All she needed was for Wanda to open up and get her started. Wanda picked her up at 8:30 A.M. and drove into town to the antique shop that reminded Natalie of a little gingerbread house.

Natalie had a pleasant morning dusting off old furniture and knick knacks. Things were peaceful until she heard the bell over the door jingle, and knew she had her first customer. Within minutes so many people were in the shop she couldn't keep her eyes on everything. *Where have all these people come from?* she wondered. Her problems had just begun.

She couldn't find any small bags or tissue paper to wrap delicate items in. Whenever she looked up the line was still growing. After the fifth sale, she needed change. All she had under the register drawer were large bills. Now she'd told her aunt she could handle the day, and already things were falling apart.

Suddenly, the bell over the door jingled loudly several times like someone was playing with the door. She looked up and noticed a man backing in the door. From behind he had the body of a perfectly built basketball player. His broad back and shoulders filled the doorway. That tightly muscled behind was covered in a pair of close fitting jeans. Those long legs stopped at a pair of brown cowboy boots. Natalie's eyes traveled back up to his backside as he nudged his way in with a large box in his arms. *My God, who is that?*

As the door closed, he turned around and repositioned the box in his arms. The change dropped from Natalie's hand back into the register. Her customer cleared her throat as she impatiently tapped her fingernails on the counter.

"Sorry, ma'am." She picked up the last of her change and finished the transaction. As the next customer set a small antique lamp on the counter, Natalie's eyes traveled across the room following the Black cowboy as he walked by. He walked back toward her aunt's office.

"Excuse me. Can I help you with something?" she asked, wondering who this hunk was.

"Nope, I've got it. Besides, it looks like you've already got your hands full." He motioned toward the line, which grew longer.

She rang up the next purchase and glanced at him over her shoulder as he walked into her aunt's office. The height, the build, the deep voice, the tight jeans—oh, what a man he was!

Natalie shook her head and groaned inwardly, as she continued working. *Why does such a gorgeous-looking man have to walk into this shop on this very day?* She looked away, reminding herself he was the enemy. *You came here to get away from men, repeat it until you hear it,* she said to herself. Turning, she forced a smile at the next customer, who had been watching her watch HIM.

He walked over and stood next to the counter as Natalie opened the register and realized she had no more small bills, or change. "Excuse me ladies," he said to the women in line. He pushed his cap back a few inches and looked down at Natalie. "You can tell Pauline her lamp parts are here. You must be Natalie? I'm . . ."

As he talked, Natalie eye-balled him a moment, then decided he looked honest enough. She cut him off. "Yes, I'm Natalie and I need change." She grabbed two hundred dollar bills from under the register drawer and shoved them into his hand. "Quick, small bills and change." Whoever he was, she needed his help. They could trade introductions later.

In less than five minutes he returned with her change. She was delighted and grateful. He found bags and tissue paper in the back room. He threw his jacket on the couch, and helped customers with selections and purchases as if he worked there. For all she knew, maybe he did. But her aunt hadn't mentioned him.

Every chance she got she watched him move around the shop. He had the tall and tight build of a basketball player. Her favorite body type. Every time he picked up something, the muscles in his arms contracted and she could imagine them around her. She shook her head to clear her senses and got back to work. When she finally came up for air the shop was empty. After a long sigh of relief, she walked from behind the counter and flopped down on a couch. He joined her.

"Boy," she sighed. "Do they come in droves like that often?"

"Every now and then. Those were charter buses from Louisville. Hopkinsville is sort of the antique capital of Kentucky, and Pauline's is in the middle of Antique Row. Lucky for your aunt you were here today. Normally, if she's not feeling well, she closes shop."

Natalie sat up as she realized she had no idea who this man was. "I'm sorry. Here I've been working you to death, and I don't even know your name."

"Roderick Taylor, but everybody calls me Rod."

They shook hands and Natalie noticed how his huge hands swallowed hers. He was gorgeous. His huge brown eyes seemed to be pulling her in. His smile was warm and inviting, but he seemed to be holding most of it back. To her, his look was more of an inspection of her.

"So, Rod, how do you know my name?" She pulled herself out of his entrancing gaze and relaxed back onto the couch.

"Your aunt's been talking about you for weeks now," he said with a drawl.

"I hauled that box over from Webster Lamps for her. She said her niece from Atlanta was coming in for the holidays. So, I figured the new face in the shop must be Natalie."

In all her twenty-seven years she'd never met a real country boy before, but here he was in the flesh. He sounded like *he* was from Georgia, instead of her. He stretched his long legs out, resting the heels of his boots on the wood floor. Suddenly, she had a vision of those legs wrapped around her body. It had obviously been too long since she'd been with a man. She broke up with Kevin two weeks ago, but hadn't been intimate with him for over three months.

"Do you work for my aunt?" she asked, wondering why he'd picked up the box and pitched in to help her.

"No, I guess you could say I do her favors from time to time. The box was too heavy for her and Webster's doesn't deliver." He shifted himself to the edge of the couch. "Is this your first time in Hopkinsville?" he asked.

"No, I spent a little time here when I was younger. Holiday visits with my parents. But, I don't remember much about the town."

"Then you'll have to let me give you a tour of our little town before you leave. Of course, it doesn't compare to Atlanta, but it's nice."

Natalie noticed how he cocked his head, and said Atlanta like it was a dirty word. "Sure, I'd like that," she replied. She wondered what he had against Atlanta.

The bell over the door jingled as another customer walked in. Rising from the couch with ease, Rod stood over Natalie smiling down at her.

"Well, I better be going. I've got to get back to work."

Natalie sat there awestruck, looking up at him. She reminded herself that he wasn't anything out of the ordinary—just all male. He walked toward the door adjusting his cap forward on his head again. He stopped in the doorway and looked back at her.

"I'll catch you later." He nodded his head and walked out the door.

All she could manage was a slight nod of the head. She couldn't help but follow him to the door to see if he was getting into a truck, or on a horse. He pulled away in a huge black pickup truck.

Two

"Girl, my kids enjoy celebrating Kwanzaa, but we still celebrate Christmas. If they woke up Christmas morning and there weren't any toys under that tree, I'd have three devastated little monsters on my hands."

Natalie helped Wanda wrap gifts for her children. She had two little boys and a little girl named Grachel that Natalie had fallen in love with. The kids were at their grandmother's house for the moment.

Wanda lived in a comfortable two-story brick house in a quiet subdivision of new homes. White Christmas lights and rich green garland gave the house a festive holiday air.

Natalie envied her cousin for all she had. Wanda was blessed with a loving husband, a family, and status within the community. Everyone in Hopkinsville knew who she was. She worked on local town parades, and every type of African-American celebration to be had. Natalie was surprised that Wanda knew as much about Kwanzaa as she did.

"So, Wanda, when did you learn so much about Kwanzaa?" Natalie asked, after wrapping her last gift. She watched her cousin put the finishing touches on a beautiful bow, while she helped herself to more popcorn.

"Believe it or not, it all started with one of Brian's homework assignments."

"You're kidding? He's in elementary school."

"I know, but his teacher sent home a story for him to read and do a book report on. He asked me what Kwanzaa was, and I couldn't answer him. I helped him read the little story and write the report. But after he went to bed, I pulled the book back out and read it again." She took a breather and grabbed a handful of popcorn to munch on.

"Natalie, that little story was so touching. I want my children to know about their African roots. But going to all-white Taylor County School isn't going to cut it. That's the only assignment any of my children have ever had about African-Americans. If we lived closer to town they could go to the city schools. That's where all of the black children in the county go to school. They also have a few black teachers. But Arthur and I wanted to move out here. We need to teach the children ourselves—their family. And I thought I had. I mean, they know who Dr. Martin Luther King is, and Jessie Jackson, but that's about the extent of it. Girl, they thought Africa was one big jungle where Tarzan lived." Wanda shook her head as both women broke out into laughter.

"We're laughing, but so did I until I got into junior high school. I couldn't imagine walking around downtown Zimbabwe, and having it look almost like downtown Atlanta."

"Well, growing up in Atlanta, I'm sure you were exposed to more of your culture than we were here in Hopkinsville. Mama should have moved with your mom after high school."

"I don't know about that, Wanda. Hopkinsville's nice."

"It's okay." She shrugged her shoulders and gave

a half smile. "Well, after reading that book I went to the library and checked out everything I could about Kwanzaa, which consisted of two books and one was more like a pamphlet. So, I went to the bookstore and ordered more books by and about African-Americans. I borrowed Brian's teacher's idea, and now my children read a book a month about or by African-Americans. And I make them give me a report."

"A book a month! Wow, where do you find the books?"

"There's plenty out there now, but if it's a big book, I let them take two months with it. I don't want that to interfere with their school work."

"Wanda, that sounds great. So they must know a lot about Kwanzaa?"

"They learn a little more each year. What I think they like best is making gifts. Girl, wait till you see some of the stuff they come up with."

"I can't wait." Natalie smiled at the thought and couldn't wait to help the children with their gifts.

"Girl, thanks for helping me wrap all these gifts. The kids will be so excited when they come in here tonight and see these presents under the tree."

"Your tree is beautiful."

"Thanks, Arthur and the kids picked it out. And I guess you can tell they decorated it."

Natalie thought the multitude of ornaments on the tree looked good. It definitely had the children's touch. For a moment she felt sad. She wanted a good husband like Arthur, and beautiful, well-behaved children like Wanda's. Kevin's image flashed through her mind. She couldn't have any of those things with him. What she needed was a new man who didn't feel like the world owed him everything.

Someone who could focus on something other than himself for a moment.

"Nat, you all right?" Wanda peered at her cousin from across the room.

Natalie looked up realizing Wanda had been talking to her while she stared into the tree. "Yeah, I'm sorry. What did you say?"

"I said, Mama told me you met Rod yesterday."

Natalie fought hard to stop the huge smile from breaking through, but couldn't, and it lit up her face. "Yeah, he came by the shop and helped me out of a rough spot." She tried her best to pull that smile off her face. For the life of her she couldn't figure out what she was smiling about anyway. He was just a man.

"I'm sorry you got stuck in there by yourself on your first day. But at least you had something good to look at."

The two women looked at each other smiling. "Girl, admit it. That man is fine. I shake my head myself every time I look at him. It don't make no sense for God to make a man look that good. He should have *temptation* written on his forehead."

"He is good looking." Natalie walked over and sat on the couch, tucking her stockinged feet underneath her. "Shoot, I almost forgot I had customers in line when he walked in. Talk about a distraction."

"And believe it or not, he's single."

"Single! A man that good looking doesn't have a woman?"

"Nope."

"What's wrong with him?" Not that she was interested, she told herself.

"Nothing, honey. I don't think there's a woman good enough in this town for him. He used to date this girl who lived in Greensburg for a while. But she moved to Atlanta, and that was the end of that relationship. That boy's not leaving Hopkinsville for anybody."

"Huh, he was a nice little surprise for the day."

"So you like him, huh?"

"I didn't say I liked him," Natalie huffed. "I just met him."

"Yeah, I know. But, I saw the way you smiled when I mentioned his name. He has that effect on women. But not many have an effect on him."

"So what do I care." Natalie shrugged her shoulders.

"He called Mama this morning talking about you."

Natalie sat up, shocked. He was good looking, but she didn't want to be involved with any men right now. She could care less if he looked good enough a blind woman could see. "What did he say?"

"Well he called pretending to be asking about something else. But Mama said he really wanted to know about you."

"He wanted to know what?" He stomach began to flutter. *What could he have been asking about me?*

"Things like how long you were planning to be in town, if you were working all week, and were you participating in the Kwanzaa celebration."

"He asked Aunt Polly all that?"

"Probably not, but she volunteered the information. You know how Mama is. And let me tell you right now, she's crazy about Rod." Wanda walked over and joined Natalie on the couch.

"What are you looking so scared for? Rod's cute."

"I'm not scared of anything. I just don't want to get involved with anyone right now, that's all. Especially not some country boy who thinks he's God's gift."

"Girl, he doesn't think that. It's the women around here who think it. And they all want a piece of him." Wanda pulled her papers out of a folder and laid them on the cocktail table.

"Well, come on, let me fill you in on all the Kwanzaa happenings. We're going to have a great time, and Rod will be participating."

"Wanda." Natalie said her name in a whining tone. She hoped her family wasn't about to start playing matchmaking for the two weeks she'd planned on being in town. When she said she didn't want to be involved with a man right now, she meant it. Especially a man that made her weak in the knees.

It was two days before Christmas and Natalie felt wonderful. The laid-back life in Hopkinsville suited her fine. Everything about the town was so cute and quaint to her. Absent was the stress that came along with a big city, and she appreciated that. She picked up gifts for all her relatives, and couldn't wait for Christmas to be over with, and Kwanzaa to begin. Wanda had loaned her a book to read on the subject. The celebration was being held at the Armory. Wanda had a speaker coming into town, and activities planned for every night. Several church members were helping with the Kwanzaa *Karamu* feast on the thirty-first.

Natalie went to the shop early to help her aunt Polly. She was relieved that her aunt felt better, though she knew nothing could keep her down for long.

"Well, good morning, little lady."

"Morning, Aunt Polly." Natalie looked at her watch. "How long have you been here?" She walked into the back room to put up her purse and coat, then returned.

"Oh, I came in around seven o'clock this morning. Tomorrow is Christmas Eve, and I've got lots to do."

"Well, I'm just glad you're feeling better."

"It must of been some type of bug, because I feel much better today. Besides, I'm too busy to be sick."

"Yeah, those last minute gifts and all."

"Yes, and there's deliveries to be made." Pauline busied herself behind the counter. After a moment she said, "Honey, could you take this sheet and mark down those angel ornaments in the basket over there." She pointed to several baskets sitting at the foot of the shop's Christmas tree.

"Time to start slashing prices. I remember Mama used to love those Christmas sales."

"And I'm sure she still does. Don't bet for one minute she doesn't have them taking her somewhere over in Germany looking for sales." She walked over to Natalie with a red pen.

"Yeah, I hope she's enjoying herself." The one thing Natalie missed most about Christmas was spending it with her parents. Since her parents' divorce, she only saw either of them once or twice a year. Everyone seemed to be living their own lives, ones that didn't include family anymore.

"She is, honey, and so will you. Here . . . mark everything fifty percent off. I hope to move all this stuff before my new shipment comes in. This isn't Macy's so it takes a little longer."

"Aunt Polly, I really love your shop. It's great. I like how you've mixed all these antiques with the locals' crafts."

"Thank you." Pauline looked down at her watch slyly. "Oh, Natalie, I just remembered something. In a few minutes Rod's coming by to make a delivery for me. I wonder if you can ride with him and bring back some pies I ordered for the Kwanzaa celebration?"

Natalie thought for a moment. This was just her aunt's way of matchmaking. She remembered what Wanda had said about her aunt liking Rod. But how was she going to get out of the trip?

"Aunt Polly, I thought Kwanzaa was all about making your own things?"

"It's also about cooperative economics. I buy pies from Mrs. Pennick because she has her own baking business. She's an African-American woman, so I'm within the seven principles of Kwanzaa." Pauline stood with her arms crossed, smiling at her niece.

"Well, Ms. Thing, I see you know your stuff. So, I guess I'm going to pick up pies." Natalie rested her hands on her hips as she cocked her head, laughing at her aunt.

"I sure do." Pauline turned and walked back behind the counter. "Rod should be here any minute."

Natalie shrugged her shoulders and got back to work. What harm could a little ride do? She didn't want to have anything to do with men, including Mr. Taylor. After her disastrous relationship with Kevin, she vowed to lay off men. Still, she figured doing this favor for her aunt couldn't hurt her vows.

An hour later, as she climbed into the truck with Rod she asked, "Just how far is Bardstown anyway?" He held her hand as he helped her into the truck.

"It's right up the road a piece." He pointed ahead of her.

"That tells me a lot." Her aunt had forgotten to mention that little bit of information. All along, Natalie thought Mrs. Pennick lived right there in Hopkinsville, and the ride wouldn't take long. Now she wanted to know how long she had to be confined in the truck with this man.

"I'll have you back before supper, I promise." He started the engine and pulled off. When he noticed her shiver from the cold, he turned the heat up.

The half smile he gave Natalie was just enough to call a smile. Again, she told herself, *I'm only along because Aunt Polly asked me. It has nothing to do with Rod.* She tried to glance at him without him noticing. In his worn leather bomber jacket and cowboy boots, he looked like a rough and tough country boy who probably didn't know how to treat a woman in the first place, she told herself. However, minutes into the ride she was surprised to find she enjoyed his company.

"So, how do you like our little town so far?" he asked.

"I like it, I always have. It's so Mayberryish. Have you lived here all your life?" Feeling a little warmer, she took off her gloves and eased out of her coat.

"Yep, but after high school most people leave."

"Why's that?"

He gave a raised brow grin and said, "This ain't the big city, you know. Not one night club in the whole county. Most of the young people around here don't have much responsibility. Nothing to keep them tied to this place. They can't wait to get out of school, and Hopkinsville."

"So what's keeping you tied here?" Wanda had

told her a little about his parents' tragic death, but she didn't know if he'd share that with her or not.

He looked out the window in the direction of the cornfields. She waited for a response, but he didn't seem to want to give one. She was about to repeat the question, wondering if he'd heard her, when finally he answered.

"I've got responsibilities. About forty acres worth." He leaned forward and turned on the radio. The truck picked up some hiss and crackle, then finally the music of an R&B station from Louisville.

They rode on listening to the DJ's version of a mix of Prince music. Natalie gazed out the window and thought about all the stress she had to put up with in Atlanta. Her life hadn't been stressful until Kevin entered it, pretending to be something he wasn't. A loving, kind, gentle man is what she had wanted, and thought he was. Instead, she got an aggressive, quick-tempered, dictating womanizer. She looked over at Rod who intrigued her. How come such a good-looking man wasn't married? And not only was he handsome, but she could tell he was a good Christian man. He seemed like a man with a good head on his shoulders. The real boy next door type. She finally broke the silence.

"Hopkinsville is absolutely beautiful. Everywhere you look there are fields of luscious green grass, partially covered in snow. It seems so peaceful and quaint. Almost like another world, compared to Atlanta."

"Yeah, I wouldn't dream of living anywhere else. If you want more out of life, the airport's only an hour and a half away. You can take your fancy trip, and return to a nice, peaceful surrounding. I like that." He shook his head as if he were agreeing with what he'd just said. "How long do you plan on staying in town?"

"I'm not sure. Until the first of January or longer."

"You must have plenty of vacation time."

"I took two weeks vacation, but if I stay longer I can call it a leave of absence. My boss knows how stressed I am. She even suggested I take a leave before I left for vacation."

"A leave from Atlanta? The big city where everything's happening?" His surprise came through in his voice.

Natalie ignored his crack on the big city. She'd already gotten an understanding that he didn't like big cities, and especially Atlanta. "No, a leave from being the manager of a retail clothing store. The pressure is unbelievable, besides I needed to get away for a while. My ex-boyfriend went ballistic when I ended our relationship. Somebody had to put some distance between us."

"I'm sorry."

"Oh, don't be. I'm happy. It worked out for the best."

"Ending a relationship can be hard, but you're right, sometimes it's for the best."

Rod made a pit stop at a gas station. Or, rather a gas/bus station/restaurant. A Greyhound sign hung in the window. The house where they made the deliveries was only ten minutes from the gas station.

After stopping at Mrs. Pennick's to pick up the pies, they headed back. Natalie watched how Rod waved at practically every car passing on the two lane road. She wondered if he knew all those people, or if it was a country thing. Whatever it was she decided it was fun, and even waved at a few cars herself.

Back at her aunt's shop Rod helped her inside with the pies. Pauline walked around the shop passing out holiday cookies to her customers. She stopped when she saw the couple come in the door.

"Natalie, dear, you had a call this morning."

Natalie stopped in her tracks. Who would be calling her here? "Who was it?"

Her aunt walked up to her and whispered in her ear. "It was Kevin. He wanted to speak to you, but I told him you were out."

"If he calls back I don't want to speak to him. Did he say how he got the number? I know I didn't give it to him."

"No, and I didn't ask him."

After not talking to Kevin for over two weeks, she wondered why he'd gone through all the trouble to track her down. Whatever he wanted, he'd have to wait until she got back into town. She wasn't going to return his call, and she hoped he wouldn't call back.

As Pauline walked away to greet the next customer with cookies, Natalie hoped Kevin would leave her alone while she was on vacation. Lately, every time she talked to him she developed an upset stomach. Just the sound of his voice made her sick. She could see him lying in the bed with his coworker every time she spoke to him. That wasn't the first woman he'd been with, but she was the last straw. Natalie didn't need a man like that in her life, and she had sense enough to leave him alone.

"Hey, everything okay?" Rod raised his brows in concern.

Natalie hadn't even heard him approach her.

"Yes, just fine." She forced a smile trying to perk herself up.

"Then how come you look like you're upset about something?" He reached out and gently touched Natalie's chin raising her eyes to meet his.

She gazed into his eyes feeling a little embarrassed. For a moment she started to spill her guts and tell him all about her problems, but she came to her senses. *He's a man,* she told herself. *Just like any other man. He's no different from the rest of them. Do what I say, like what I like, build your world around me!*

"I'm okay, believe me. I couldn't be better." With authority she put her hands down on the counter and told herself, *No man is going to get the best of me. I'll live my life as I choose and do what I want to do.*

He let go of her chin after several women walked past the counter. "Okay, if you say so. Thanks for going to Bardstown with me; I enjoyed the company."

"So did I," she confessed, then instantly scolded herself. *So what!* she thought. *I had a good time. Nothing's wrong with that. It's not like I'm saying I like him or anything.*

"Well, I'll catch you later. Tell your aunt I left the signed delivery slip on the register."

"I will."

He stood there staring at Natalie for what seemed like an eternity. She looked back at him, not sure what to say. He finally rubbed his hands together and let out a sigh.

"Have a Merry Christmas if I don't see you till Kwanzaa."

"Oh, you, too. Merry Christmas."

The minute he walked out of the shop she missed him. Natalie had had a comfortable feeling riding around with him most of the day. He let her be herself. He didn't put on airs, or pretend to be somebody he wasn't. The fact that every man she had met in Atlanta lied about who he was, or where he worked, had gotten on her nerves.

With a renewed vigor and spirit, Natalie began walking around greeting customers and helping them make decisions. Wanda even came into the shop to help out. The evening turned out to be a busy one for the shop. Most of the shelves were half empty. She'd sold two pieces of furniture herself today. At closing time she began cleaning up around the counter when the phone rang.

Pauline was with a customer and Wanda had closed herself up in the office counting receipts. Natalie answered the phone.

"Hello, Pauline's Antiques and Crafts."

"So that's where you ran off to."

The familiar sound of a man's voice came over the phone. Natalie felt a constricting knot in her throat as she tried to speak. How in the hell had he found her? And what did he want? She felt her body start to shake.

"How did you get this number?"

"Don't worry about that. When you coming home?" he asked in a stern voice.

"Why?"

"Because I want to see you. We need to talk things over."

"Kevin, I don't have anything to say to you!" She shielded her mouth with her hand, trying to keep her aunt from overhearing her conversation.

"Then I have something to say to you. Baby, I'm sorry. You know how I can't control myself sometimes. I didn't mean to—"

Natalie cut him off. She'd heard that song and

dance too many times. "Kevin you did what you did, and I don't want to talk about it. You obviously have a problem, and I think you need to check yourself out."

"What you mean check myself out? Nothing's wrong with me. You just tick me off sometimes, that's all."

Silence filled the next few seconds. Natalie heard him clear his throat into the phone. She wanted to let him listen to the dial tone, but she knew he'd only call back. Somehow she had to get him off the phone without upsetting him.

"Kevin, I don't want to talk about this while I'm on my Christmas vacation. We can talk when I get home."

"And that's another thing. Why in the hell would you pick Christmas to leave me alone? You know we always spend Christmas together."

"Kevin we broke up two weeks ago. I haven't heard from you once, until today."

"I couldn't find you until today. Look, Nat, we need to talk about this breakup thing. I'm not sure it's what I want to do."

What he *wanted to do!* She'd never asked Kevin if he wanted to break up. The day she ended their relationship she'd caught him in bed with another woman. What on earth gave him the right to say he wasn't sure if he wanted it to end. She'd decided for him.

"Kevin, it's done. We don't need to talk about anything. You've got you another woman. I don't know why you're calling me anyway." Natalie yelled into the phone forgetting about anyone hearing her at this point. He had her about to rupture a vein she was so upset. He still wanted to control her life, tell her what to do, and when to do it.

"She's not my woman—you are." He lowered his voice and tried to sound sexy.

"Not any longer." To Natalie, he sounded like the sleazy, good-for-nothing, pimp-daddy he thought he was.

"You wanna bet? This isn't over until I say it's over. That's what's wrong with you—"

The moment she heard his voice rise, she decided it was time for him to listen to the dial tone. *Click*—end of that conversation.

Three

Okay, so she appears to be interested in me—maybe. Rod drove back to his house after he dropped Natalie off at her aunt's shop. He hadn't stopped thinking about her all evening. She was as cute as a button in his book. So small and feminine. Natalie with the honey-brown skin, big brown eyes, and a permanent address in Atlanta. What did Atlanta have anyway? Why did all the good-looking women have to live there?

He still hated Pam for leaving him and moving to Atlanta. If she'd really loved him, she would have stayed in Hopkinsville. They had planned to marry and start a family. He wanted his children to go to school in Hopkinsville like he did, not in Atlanta with all the drug and gang problems.

"So maybe I should forget asking Ms. Natalie to the New Year's Eve dance?" *She's not the woman for you, so forget her. What you need is a nice country girl. Someone who's content living the country life. Someone like—who?* He hadn't met a woman who turned him on like Natalie in a long time. The minute he saw her standing behind that counter, he'd felt a charge run through his body.

When she had looked up at him with her shoulder-length curls swirling around framing her face, he was instantly attracted. Her body was little and firm. He bet she worked out in one of those Atlanta gyms all the time. When she walked across the room her body screamed, sexy. He'd found it hard to keep his eyes off her most of the day. She had a very attractive, sexy look, but he wondered if she knew it.

After pulling into his driveway, he sat in the car. His eyes were fixed on his house. Another lonely Christmas. His little brother Brandon was spending the holiday at his girlfriend's. So, Thursday he'd probably have Christmas dinner with his uncle's family. They were always kind enough to invite him over whenever he didn't have any plans. He'd have to wait until the first day of Kwanzaa to see Natalie again.

As Natalie helped her aunt cook Christmas dinner, she wondered where Rod would be eating since he lived alone. This was the first Christmas in a long time that she felt as if she'd come home. Plenty of cousins were around and Christmas music filled the air.

"Nat, how many bags of beans did you get out of the deep freezer?" her aunt asked, as she looked into a large pot on the stove.

"Two, I think. Why?"

"Girl, there's not enough beans in here for anybody. Go back downstairs and grab two more bags. That's how you stay so skinny, eating like a bird."

Natalie put down the knife and the sweet potato she was peeling and walked over to the stove. "It looked like enough to me." She peeked into the pot while her aunt had the lid up.

"Enough for whom? You and me maybe. Honey,

we'll have an army over here for dinner tomorrow. Wanda and all her children can eat two bags of beans alone." Pauline replaced the lid.

Natalie wondered if Rod would be part of that army. She didn't want to ask her aunt and get her started, so she let it go. She went back down to the basement and returned with two large bags of frozen green beans. After giving them to her aunt, she continued peeling potatoes.

"Aunt Polly, I can't remember the last time I had a holiday like this. It really feels like Christmas here. Like it used to when I was a little girl, before Mama and Daddy separated."

"Once you kids grew up, your mama never did like to cook Christmas dinner, did she?"

"No, we always went out. We always decorated the house, but then left town until New Year's. Last year I met them in Bermuda. It was nice, but it didn't seem like Christmas."

"Honey, consider yourself welcome here every year."

Natalie looked up when she heard the back door opening.

"Em, em, it smells good in here." Wanda walked through the kitchen with her daughter in tow, and a shopping bag in her hand.

"You need to put that bag down and help." Pauline turned with a tea towel in hand, surveying her daughter.

Wanda ignored her mother and turned to Natalie. "Nat, thanks so much for helping out. Girl, I don't know what I'd have done if you hadn't come to town." She walked past them into the dining room.

"I'm enjoying myself. Never mind that you guys are putting me to work, but I don't mind." She peeled her last sweet potato and walked over to the sink to rinse them off.

"But don't you love all this hustle and bustle at Christmas time? I know I do." Wanda stood in the doorway taking off her coat. Her daughter Grachel ran in past her straight to Natalie.

"I haven't had a Christmas like this in a long time. Aunt Polly and I were just talking about that." She dried her hands and leaned down to give Grachel a hug.

"Aunt Natalie, Mama said you could come live with us if you wanted to. Don't you want to?" Grachel stared up at Natalie with her doe-like eyes.

"Oh, thank you, honey, but I have to go back to Atlanta." Natalie kissed her little cousin, who insisted on calling her aunt.

"For what?" Pauline asked.

Natalie looked up at her aunt, surprised. "Because I live and work there. What do you mean, anyway?"

"You don't like Atlanta, and I know you don't want to keep seeing that old boyfriend of yours. You don't have any family there, and I bet you work all day and read all night."

Pauline was too perceptive for Natalie. "No I don't. I get out from time to time. I'm a homebody, I like staying home for the most part. Besides, what's wrong with that?" She walked over to the kitchen table and sat across from Wanda, with Grachel on her lap.

"Nothing if you've got a good man to be a homebody with," Wanda interjected. "But you don't want to sit around the house weekend after weekend alone. Unless, you're waiting for Kevin to come back into your life." Wanda raised her brows as she took the wrapper off a piece of Christmas candy and ate it.

"He's the last thing I want in my life right now. Believe it or not, I really don't mind my time alone. I work so much that when I get home all I want to do is relax and read a good book." She knew she was also trying to convince herself.

"Yeah, well, it wouldn't hurt to do a little cuddling next to a good man, instead of a good book. Especially on a cold night like tonight. Y'all know it looks like it's going to snow tonight."

Natalie had a vision of her and Rod laying back on a couch cuddling and watching television. They would rent a good movie and buy some microwave popcorn. Maybe after the movie and popcorn they could get a little closer.

"All right you two, help me get these potatoes in the oven and let's start on the Kwanzaa preparations." Pauline walked over to the table with baking dish in hand. "Here, Wanda, work something other than your jaws. Butter these pans up."

Natalie laughed at the interaction between her aunt and cousin. Grachel ran off to watch television while the women finished cooking.

Later that evening Natalie helped Wanda go through her Kwanzaa items. "So what's this?" Natalie held up an old ceramic looking mug.

"That's the *Kikombe cha umoja,*" Wanda responded, taking the cup from her.

"The what?"

"It's a communal unity cup. What you're supposed to do is pour *Tambiko* in the direction of the four winds, you know, north, south, east, and west. That's in remembrance of the ancestors. Then, you pass it around and drink from it as a sign of solidarity. However, we don't actually drink out of it. We use paper cups instead."

"So you somewhat modified things a bit?" Natalie looked over the items sitting on the table.

"Well Kwanzaa's a personal holiday. You can celebrate it however your family wants. Even single people can celebrate Kwanzaa; of course, they modify it differently than someone with children. Like the day after tomorrow, we have sort of a kick off celebration for *Umoja,* the first principle. Then for the next four days we celebrate quietly in our own homes. On the fifth day of *Kuumba* we all come together and feast. And on the last day, called *Imani,* we go back to our homes. But, that's just the way we've decided to do it here. It varies from family to family."

"I think I'm really going to like this." Natalie was beginning to feel a part of something, and she felt better than she had in years.

"I know you will. I'm surprised that living in Atlanta you don't already celebrate Kwanzaa. Especially with such a large African-American population there."

"I know a lot of people who celebrate it, but I've never attended any of the celebrations. To tell the truth, about the only thing I know about Kwanzaa is what I learned on a made-for-television movie. At first, I thought you celebrated Kwanzaa instead of Christmas, until I learned better."

"I think a lot of people get that first impression. But it's really an African-American holiday that pays tribute to the rich cultural roots of Americans of African ancestry. It's not as commercialized as Christmas either."

"Okay, Wanda. Here's the two statues I bought in

Saint Thomas last year." Pauline walked into the room with two black wood carved statues of a man and woman embracing. She reluctantly held them out to Wanda. "And let me tell you now, if you let them kids damage my statues—"

Wanda cut her off. "Mama, don't get started. You know I won't let them touch your statues, let alone break them. I'll set them up on the mantel, where the kids can't reach them." She placed the statues in the shopping bag with her other items.

"Well you better not. I love my grandkids, but if they break my statues, their mama's going to Saint Thomas to get me another one."

Wanda smiled at Natalie shaking her head. "She just had to get that in, did you see that?" Grabbing her mother by the shoulders, she quickly reached over and kissed her on the cheek. "I'll guard them with my life."

"Oh, I know you will. I don't know about you ladies but when I finish dinner, I'm going to bed. Wanda, you need to take Grachel home. It's Christmas Eve. That child should be in bed."

Wanda looked at her watch. "Mama, it's eight o'clock and she's on vacation. She's my little helper tonight. Don't worry, I'll have her in bed before Santa comes."

Natalie's head was like a ping pong ball, from Wanda to her aunt Polly. She wished she had that kind of rapport with her mother. They hadn't spent much time together in the last couple of years, since her mother's second marriage. She missed her mother just as much as she missed traditional family gatherings.

Whenever she didn't meet her family somewhere for Christmas, she'd spent it with a boyfriend. Her Christmases with Kevin weren't traditional, to say the least. All he ever wanted to do was exchange gifts and party with his friends. She was glad she wouldn't be doing that again this year.

Christmas morning came and moved along in a flash. Natalie exchanged gifts with the few relatives she'd purchased them for. She'd brought her aunt Polly a hat from a hat shop in Atlanta. Knowing how Pauline liked wearing hats to church, the gift was more than well received. She had so much fun helping her little cousins play with their new toys. Her brother had been in Germany for two years with a little niece she'd only seen pictures of. She loved children, but never had the opportunity to be around any. Maybe one day she'd have some of her own, she thought.

One thing she noticed and liked about Wanda and her husband, Arthur, was they didn't shower their children with too many gifts. She'd heard Wanda complain about the commercialization of Christmas, and guessed that was why Kwanzaa had become such an important part of their holiday celebration. Each child received an appropriate number of toys and clothes.

Around 4:00 P.M. everyone started showing up at her aunt's house for dinner. They danced around the house to the Temptation's Christmas songs. Dinner would be served at 5:00 P.M. sharp, her aunt warned them more than once. Several of her young male cousins kept popping in and out of the house all morning.

Natalie helped set the three tables for dinner. She counted out the children's places, but wondered who all the adult seats were for.

"There's more seats here than we've got people, why?" she asked Wanda.

Wanda never looked up from positioning the silverware on the table. "I don't know; Mama said set some extras. I think she invited a few friends. You know how that woman is, always opening her home up for hungry people." Wanda smiled up at Natalie and kept working.

Deep down Natalie had hoped she'd say Rod was coming by. She kept telling herself to stop thinking about the man, but she couldn't. Finally, she came to the conclusion that some lucky country girl had probably invited him to dinner.

Minutes later, more guests arrived. More aunts, uncles, and friends filled the house. Everyone brought a dish with them, some even brought gifts.

Wanda found Natalie standing off to the side of the room with her arms crossed, smiling.

"What you smiling about?" Wanda asked her.

"Oh, nothing. This is fun, that's all. I haven't seen some of these people since elementary school, but I remember them." This was like coming home again. Home to a familiar little town she once knew and loved.

"You've been here since then, Natalie, I remember."

"Yes, I have, but I don't remember seeing Uncle Otis the last time I was here, or his children."

"That's because he and Mama weren't on speaking terms for a long time. Something that went back to when they were younger. After we held our first Kwanzaa celebration, Mama picked up the phone and called him"—Wanda snapped her fingers—"and just like that they patched things up."

"Really?"

"Yeah, Kwanzaa really helps to bring families together. In a small town like this you want all your family together, loving and blessing one another. We need each other. No man can do anything by himself."

Natalie gave Wanda a tilted head grin. "And how did you get so wise, honey?" She uncrossed her arms and placed them on her hips.

"Reading, honey. When I find the time, I read everything I can get my hands on. Of course, I don't have to turn in a book report, but I make myself read a book a month also. Hopefully, I get something from them."

"Believe me, you're getting a lot from them." Natalie looked up to her cousin. Wanda was a role model if she'd ever seen one. She only hoped she could be that much of an inspiration for her children when she had them.

"Okay." Pauline walked into the family room banging a spoon on a pot. "It's time to eat, everyone wash up and sit down."

Natalie was the last person to get into the bathroom to wash her hands. She heard the doorbell ring as she walked out of the washroom. Everyone was in the kitchen hovered over the food and didn't hear the bell. She walked over to answer the door wondering who was left; everybody seemed to be there.

When she opened the door, she blinked twice—hard. Rod stood there in a gray cashmere overcoat, with a huge smile on his face. Under his arm were two wrapped boxes.

"Merry Christmas," he said in a deep sexy voice. This man looked good enough to serve for dinner, she thought. And he had dimples! She'd never noticed his dimples before. *Close your mouth girl, and let the man in.*

"You think I can come in? It's kind of cold out here."

"I'm sorry. Yes, Merry Christmas and come on in." She stood aside as he walked in. So her aunt had invited him. As she closed the door she thought, *Damn, he smells good, too.*

"I'll take your coat." She held out her hands for his coat.

He set his packages on the hall table, then took off his coat. "Thank you." He handed her his coat.

He had on a crew neck sweater in the most beautiful shades of brown. Underneath he wore a cream turtleneck. He had brown slacks and loafers to match. Natalie nodded her approval, biting her bottom lip. This man knew how to dress, which only made matters worse. She liked nothing better than a well-dressed man.

"This is for Pauline." He pointed to the small package. "And this one"—he pointed to the larger of the two—"is for you."

"Rod! You didn't have to do that."

"I know, but I wanted to."

"Well, thank you and I'll give this to Aunt Polly. I guess you can go on in and help yourself; they've started." She stood there waiting for him to walk away so she could sneak another peek at him. But he didn't move.

"Are you enjoying your vacation?" he asked.

"Yes, I am. It's one of the best ones I've had in years."

"No kidding?" He looked surprised.

"It really is."

"Well I'm glad you could come to such a small town like ours and enjoy yourself so much."

"Rod, come on in here and get yourself something to eat," Pauline called to him from the kitchen doorway. "I'm glad you could make it."

"I'm on my way." He looked down at Natalie again. "Well, I'm glad you're enjoying yourself. I still want to take you on that tour, if you haven't gone already?"

"No, I haven't. They've kept me fairly busy around here."

"Good, then we've got a date?"

A date! She smiled at him thinking, *I didn't come down here to go on dates. I'm here to relax and get away from men.* "Yeah, we've got a date." *What else could I say?* she wondered. As he walked away, she watched him. He had a body like a model she'd seen in so many magazines—Tyson. She hadn't seen a gym since coming to town, so those muscles must be from hard work. He said he had forty acres of responsibility; he must live on a farm.

When Natalie looked down she realized she was holding onto his coat like it was him. She took the gifts in the living room and placed them under the tree. She'd open hers after dinner. After hanging up his coat, she joined everyone else in the kitchen.

Natalie wasn't sure where to sit. The dining room table was reserved for the elders; she remembered that much. She went into the family room to join Wanda with the children. The card table was full with Wanda's three children and two other children. So, she went back into the kitchen and found a spot at the kitchen table.

Before anyone could eat, her uncle Otis had to say the blessing. Right before he started, a plate was placed next to her. She looked up to see Rod smiling down at her.

"Mind if I sit here?"

"Ah . . . sure. I mean, no, I don't mind." She stumbled over her words. Why did he make her do that? When he looked at her she got tongue tied. She became speechless, and felt dumb. No matter what, she had to fight her attraction to him. Especially once she noticed the way her cousin, Deborah, perked up once he sat down. That girl definitely had her eyes on Rod. Too bad he hadn't seemed to notice her.

Two more teenaged cousins joined them at the circular table for five. Dinner conversation consisted mainly of chitchat, until Rod turned his attention to Natalie.

"Did you help cook any of this?" He pointed to his plate.

"I helped with a few things, but that's about it."

"You mean to tell me you're not a great cook?"

"I wish. I cook, but I can't touch Aunt Polly in that department."

"Oh, you're being modest. I bet you cook really well."

What she wanted to say, she didn't dare say. *I'll have to show you sometime.* Instead she laughed and said, "I make a mean microwave popcorn."

He laughed and replied, "I hope you don't consider that cooking?"

"I'm a woman of the nineties. The microwave is just another oven to me. And anytime you put food in the oven, you're cooking."

They shared a laugh and returned to their meals. Natalie listened as the men at the table talked about everything from cars to sports. She was surprised they didn't get up from the table to find a television.

"Natalie, are you a sports fan?" Rod asked.

"I like basketball. That's about all I can stand to

watch on television." She noticed how Rod kept bringing her into the conversation. He didn't seem to be interested in talking to anyone else.

"Well, we have something in common. I can't stand to watch a baseball game on television, and I catch a football game every now and then, but I love to watch basketball. Who's your favorite team?"

Natalie had to think for a moment. She only watched during the NBA playoffs. "I'd have to say the Bulls."

"Why?"

"I like to see Michael Jordan play."

"Have you ever been to one of their games?"

"No, television is about as close as I've been. How about you?"

"Yeah, I've been to a few. I've got a buddy who lives in Chicago. He has season tickets."

"Boy, it must be nice to have friends in high places."

"He's just a guy who got lucky, that's all. I think he waited for about two to three years on the list for season tickets. We went to college together. He lets me know in advance when he can't make a game."

"Have you ever been to a Hawks game?" Natalie asked him.

"No, I can't say that I have. I've never been to Atlanta either."

"Oh, you have to visit sometime. It's a nice vacation spot."

"Maybe I will, once I have someone to visit."

Natalie looked up at Rod shaking her head. Did he mean her? Did he want to come to Atlanta and visit her? The man was fine, but she wasn't getting into the web again.

Her cousins sitting at the table ended their conversation and Deborah pulled Rod into a conversation with her. She pulled her chair close to his and leaned suggestively on the table.

"So, Rod, tell me something. What did Santa bring you for Christmas?"

Four

Deborah ate and flirted with Rod at the same time. He didn't seem interested. Natalie felt bad for him, considering his efforts to be congenial. Deborah was obviously too young for him. At first, Natalie thought it was cute, but she soon grew tired of her cousin. She kept telling herself she wasn't interested in him, but at the same time she wanted Deborah to shut up so he could continue talking to her.

Finally, one of Deborah's girlfriends arrived.

"Oh, that's my girl Rhonda. Well gang it's been real, but I've got to run." Deborah dabbed her mouth with a napkin. "We're making our rounds today, you know. My relatives' houses, then hers."

"Well, Deborah, we're going to miss you," Natalie said, hoping the whole table got the joke.

"Sure you will." Deborah gave a sexy smile in Rod's direction as she got up. "Rod, maybe I'll see you around later."

He almost choked on his food as he shook his head trying not to laugh.

"Natalie, it was nice to meet you. Now that I know I have a cuz in Atlanta, you'll have to invite me down."

"Yeah, you bet, maybe over the summer." Once her younger relatives found out she lived in Atlanta, everyone wanted to come for a visit. *Thank God, I only have a one-bedroom apartment.*

"Ew, that sounds fun. You can take us to all the clubs."

"You bet!" Natalie smiled at her cousin, trying to remember the last time she'd set foot in a nightclub.

"Bye, everybody." Deborah switched her way out of the kitchen waving back over her shoulder.

After Deborah left, Rod took a drink of water and started laughing. "Man, she's not bashful is she?"

"Just ignore her. She's one of the hottest things around town. I'm surprised it doesn't warm up the minute she walks outside," Marvin said.

"Rod, you better watch out, that girl wants you," James, another cousin, commented.

"Man, she's too young for me. How old is Deborah anyway—sixteen?"

"Fifteen, going on twenty-five if you ask me," Marvin said. "Something better slow that girl down."

"You guys are terrible. Talking about your cousin like that." Natalie had to admit her cousin was a big flirt, but she liked Deborah. The girl just needed to tone down the makeup and perfume a bit.

"Hey, we love her, too, but like Prince says in his song, 'she's a Hot Thing.' " Marvin leaned back in his chair as all the men at the table laughed, except Rod.

Natalie noticed Rod had finished his meal, and was staring at her. Feeling uncomfortable, she reached over for Deborah's plate. "I'm going to clean off the table if you guys are through. Any one ready for dessert?"

"You know I am." Marvin spoke up.

"Here, Natalie, let me help you." They grasped Deborah's plate at the same time from opposite ends. For a moment Rod captured her gaze with his eyes.

"That's okay, I've got it." She carried both paper plates over to the garbage can and threw them in.

"Here, I'll get this one." Rod threw his plate in behind hers.

"So much for all those fancy plates, huh," he commented, while looking at the stack of Christmas plates that lined the can.

"Yeah, well it keeps Aunt Polly from washing dishes all evening long."

Marvin and James grabbed their desserts and left the table. Probably to catch some sporting event on television, she thought. Rod remained at the table looking comfortable and content. Before Natalie knew it, the house was almost empty.

Pauline breezed into the kitchen carrying her coat. "Natalie, we're going to run over to Mrs. Hattie May's house and take her a plate. You two relax and enjoy yourselves." Pauline rushed out of the kitchen, winking at Natalie as she left.

Natalie wanted to run after her. *No, don't leave me here alone with him! I'm afraid of what I'll do or say.* All she could do was look up and watch as her aunt left the room. Too late.

"What do you say we grab some dessert and take it into the family room?" Rod stood up.

Natalie looked up at him with a questioning look on her face.

"I want to check out your aunt's Christmas tree."

"Oh, yeah, let's do that." Maybe she was reading too much into this, she thought. Her aunt probably invited him to dinner all the time. He seemed right at home. He appeared to know all her relatives, and was enjoying himself.

Natalie cut Rod a piece of her aunt's red velvet

mas sale just like all the other stores in town. Natalie was glad to have something to keep her mind on. She didn't want to spend her day thinking about Rod. Last night she'd enjoyed his company very much. They'd talked well into the night about everything from their college days to who sang the best, Whitney Houston or Mariah Carey.

He even helped her clean the kitchen, to surprise her aunt when she returned. Around ten thirty he decided it was time for him to leave. On one hand, she hated to see him leave, but on the other, she wished he hadn't come in the first place. She liked Rod and she knew she had to fight her attraction to him. Several times during the evening, she'd wished he'd pull her into his arms and kiss her.

The bell over the door jingled and she looked up to see several women walking in. She went back to her work once she realized it wasn't Rod. *Now,* she told herself, *forget that man. He lives here in Hopkinsville and you're in Atlanta.* Besides, he could be another Kevin. She didn't really know him. Maybe his country charm was a front, and he was as jealous and unfaithful as the next man. As she thought the words, she didn't believe them for a minute. For the short amount of time she'd spent with him, she could tell he was a good man.

Besides, if her aunt Polly was crazy about him, he couldn't be all bad. Her relatives seemed to like him. Too bad he didn't live in Atlanta, she thought. She told herself not to let her attraction go any further than it had last night. She'd be better off forgetting about him. The less she saw of Rod the better. He didn't walk into the shop all day.

Her aunt closed shop early for the first day of Kwanzaa. Natalie went by Wanda's to help prepare for the opening celebration.

* * *

When Natalie walked into Wanda's house she couldn't believe her eyes. Wanda had redecorated for the celebration. Everything was in the black, red, and green color scheme. The colors of Kwanzaa.

The floral paintings that hung on the walls several days before were replaced with African art. The mantel over the fireplace displayed several carved African statues, including her aunt Polly's. As she glanced around the room she noticed other things she hadn't seen before. A throw had been placed on the back of the couch. She picked it up to examine it.

"That's beautiful isn't it?"

A man's voice came from behind her. She turned to see Brother Johnson, one of the young ministers at First Baptist.

"Yes, it is. I'm trying to see what's on it." She spread the throw along the back of the couch for a better look.

"It's called 'Breaking Bread.' It's a family during their Kwanzaa feast. See that's the child there." He pointed to a figure at the bottom of the throw. Then, he moved to the other end of the couch and held up the throw to give her a better look.

Natalie raised her end also. "Oh, yes, I see it better now. This is beautiful! I wonder where she got this?"

"My sister sent it to her from D.C. A woman in her church makes them."

"I'd love to have one. Could you get me one?" She looked up at him with wide eyes, hoping he'd say yes.

"Sure. I like to practice *Ujima* whenever I can."

"*Ujima,* wait, that's . . . ?" She had to think for a

minute. She'd heard her aunt say it. "Oh, I know." She snapped her finger when she came up with the answer. "That's cooperative economics."

"Yes it is. Is this something you practice in Atlanta?"

Natalie thought for a moment; she couldn't remember the last time she purchased something from an African-American, or lent her support in any way. "No, I can't say that I do. You see, I live on the north side of town, and I'm afraid most of the African-American shop owners are on the south side, or downtown."

He nodded his head and smiled at her. "There aren't any African-American shop owners here in Hopkinsville. But we lend our support to all of the out-of-state shops that we know of. I'll call my sister tomorrow and have her order you one. Just give Wanda your mailing information." He put the throw down, shook her hand, and excused himself.

Still holding her end of the throw in the air, she realized something—he was right. She lived in a town with many African-American shops. And not once had she even checked to see if there were any on her side of town. *I've got to do better. If it was my shop I'd want support,* she told herself.

Now that he'd made her feel like she had so much more to learn, she was eager for the ceremony to begin. She'd only skimmed through the books Wanda loaned her. A picture slowly formed in her mind that Kwanzaa was more than saying affirmations and eating.

She was on her way into the dining room to check out the centerpiece when Grachel ran up to her.

"Aunt Natalie, you gonna come live with us?" the child asked as she grabbed Natalie by the leg and held on for dear life.

"No, honey, but I'm not getting ready to go home yet. We've got a few more days together." She reached down for Grachel's hand.

"You wanna see my room?" Grachel pulled her in the direction of the stairs.

"Yes, I'd love to see your room." Off they went up the stairs.

"Liz, give me your hand." Rod tried to help his great-aunt down the stairs.

"I don't need your help. Hell, I can make it down these stairs by myself. How do you think I get the mail every damn day?" She held onto the rail walking down the front stairs of her one-story house.

Rod worried about his great-aunt. A stroke a few years ago had damaged the right side of her body. But with her white hair pulled into a bun atop her head, she didn't let that stop her. Liz acted like a young woman instead of a senior citizen.

"I'm going to have the mail box moved up to the front porch so you don't have to risk walking down these stairs. What if it's icy out here one morning after a snow storm. How will you get your mail then?"

"I'll call you over to get it for me. I might be old, but I'm not stupid. I know better than to walk out here on ice. And you leave my mailbox where it is. My walk in the morning does me good. I like to get out and see what's going on in the neighborhood."

"You like to meddle, that's all."

"I don't meddle. I see things. Like that young lady that moved into the house on the corner. I don't believe she's married. Not once have I seen a man walk through those doors." She completed her trip down the five steps and held Rod's arm as they walked out to his car.

He could see his great-aunt now walking out to the mail box in her robe, casually looking up and down the street for something interesting. "You know it's not a sin to be single."

"But you've been single for too long. Don't you want a wife and a family? Your mother would want you to be married by now."

"Aunt Liz, when I find the right woman I'll marry her. Now come on, I'm going to be late."

"The damn thing doesn't start until six o'clock and it's only five now."

"I know but once I drop you off I've got to get the truck and swing by the Armory for some chairs. Wanda asked me to bring a few over. She invited more people than she had room for."

"Okay, then help me in the car. Where's that little brother of yours anyway."

"I told you he's spending the holidays in Louisville with his girl's family."

"Oh, yes, I keep forgetting that."

When Rod walked his aunt to Wanda's door, he wondered if Natalie was inside. He started to go in and ask her to ride with him, but decided she was probably helping Wanda. He drove back to his house and exchanged his car for the truck. Driving out to the Armory he couldn't get Natalie off his mind. His great aunt wanted him married so bad, and he'd found the perfect woman. There was only one problem: he didn't know how she felt about him. She was single and didn't have a man, that much he knew. But, she also lived hundreds of miles away. Would a long-distance relationship work? Would she even consider one?

He pulled into Wanda's driveway and hurried inside with a few chairs. As he placed the chairs around the room he looked for Natalie, but didn't see her.

"Oh, Rod, thank you so much for bringing the chairs. Is that it?" Wanda asked.

"No, there's a few more. I'll get them."

"Thanks. Arthur would help you, but he's not here yet. He went to pick up his mother."

"No problem, I've got it." He walked back out to the truck wondering if Natalie had arrived. At least he was sure she'd be here. A quick glance at the cars lined up outside Wanda's house didn't include Pauline's or Natalie's car. Maybe they hadn't arrived yet.

After grabbing the chairs from the cab of his truck, he set them down, and took a deep breath. *Relax, boy, she's just a woman. Something you haven't had in a long time.* But she wasn't just *any* women. Natalie was special to him. Her innocent looking smile turned him on. Especially the way he could tell she wanted to reach out and touch him, but dared not to, excited him. She was attracted to him and he knew it, but he didn't want her to sense it, or she'd probably run the other way.

He picked up the chairs and walked back into the house. The cold air cleared his head, and settled his nerves. He only hoped he could remember his Kwanzaa speech once she showed up.

"Natalie, come here, I've got some people I want you to meet." Wanda stood at the bottom of the stairs as Natalie came down with Grachel in tow.

"We're on our way." She held Grachel's hand as the child hopped down the stairs.

Wanda had invited all of their relatives, and a few

friends. She introduced Natalie to two of her girlfriends, then they walked over to an elderly woman sitting next to their uncle Otis.

Wanda touched the woman on the shoulder to get her attention. "Miss Liz, I want you to meet my cousin Natalie. She's visiting us for the holidays."

"Hello, it's a pleasure meeting you." Natalie shook the woman's frail hand. Her silver hair reminded Natalie of her grandmother.

"It's nice to meet you, too, honey." She smiled up at Natalie.

"Miss Liz used to be Mama's high school teacher," Wanda interjected.

"Now you done gone and told this child how old I am." She rolled her eyes and waved her hand at Wanda. All three women laughed.

"Natalie did you come up with your family for the holidays?"

"No ma'am, I'm single, so I came by myself."

"Well, honey, have a seat for a moment and let's talk before your aunt gets here. You know once she arrives she'll take over and nobody will get a word in edgewise."

Natalie laughed at Miss Liz's description of her aunt, as she sat next to her. She obviously knew Pauline well.

"So, how are you enjoying your visit?"

"I'm having a wonderful time. I think this is the best vacation I've ever been on."

"Now that's really nice. You know"—she paused and looked around as if she had something private to say—"I know just about everybody in this town. I remember when most of the people in this room were born."

"Yes, ma'am." Natalie wasn't too sure what to say

to that, so she let the woman talk and nodded her head.

"Do you know my nephew, Rod?"

"Rod Taylor?"

"Yes, that's him."

Natalie wanted to ask, "Is he here?" She wanted to stand up and look around the room for him, but she controlled herself and kept her seat.

"Yes, ma'am, I've met him."

"Now that's a nice single young man for you. You young people stay alone too long for me. When I was his age I was married with two children. Every woman needs a man, honey, remember that." She smiled as she patted Natalie on the leg.

Not if he's an unfaithful one, Natalie thought. But Miss Liz wasn't talking about Kevin. She was talking about her nephew, Rod.

"You're right, she does. And as soon as I find the right man I'll marry him." *But until then, I'll watch television alone, and listen to my music alone.* She'd have to settle for the men in her romance novels for right now.

Miss Liz leaned over to whisper something to Natalie. She lowered her head to hear what she was about to say.

"Is this old woman bothering you?" Rod's deep sexy voice interrupted them.

Natalie and Miss Liz looked up to see him standing in front of them. Natalie noticed how Miss Liz straightened up and pulled her hand back.

"No, we were having a very good conversation if you have to know." Natalie smiled up at him and noticed something different about him. He'd gotten his hair cut and trimmed his mustache down to a shadow. How could he possibly look any more attractive than when she first laid eyes on him? But he did.

"Who you calling an old lady anyway? You know you're not too old for me to throw you over my knee." She rolled her eyes at him, then turned to converse with Otis.

Rod let out a thunderous deep laugh and pulled a chair up next to Natalie. "I see you've met my great-aunt."

"Yes, Wanda introduced me."

"She's a character isn't she?" He shook his head and peeked past Natalie at his great-aunt. "Look at her . . . she's forgotten all about us and started another conversation."

"I like her." Natalie smiled at him.

Rod looked at her and she felt his eyes staring deep into hers. Here he was, the man she'd been looking for all her life, and she wanted to run from him. Now wasn't the right time, and this wasn't the right place. Why did he have to live in Hopkinsville?

He finally looked away when someone called his name.

"Excuse me, I'll be right back."

Natalie nodded her head as he walked away. She decided to walk around the house herself. Before she got very far, Wanda announced they were ready to begin. She looked back at her seat and someone else had taken it. She also noticed her aunt had joined the celebration, dressed in traditional African clothing. Natalie thought she looked wonderful in her headwrap.

"*Habari gani,*" Wanda said opening the celebration.

"*Umoja,*" everyone said in unison.

Wanda struck a match and lit the black candle in the center of the *Kinara.* "The first Principle of Kwanzaa is *Umoja.* To strive for and maintain unity in the family, community, nation, and race."

Natalie listened to Wanda talk about *Umoja* as she looked around the room for Rod. Had he left the ceremony? She looked back over her shoulder and his great-aunt was still there. Well, he hadn't left to take her home. Where could he have gone, she wondered.

"Now we will have Brother Johnson deliver the Libation Statement." Wanda moved to the side of the fireplace and took a seat.

Brother Johnson lifted the communal cup and poured in the direction of the four winds. Because they were inside, he poured into a large bowl, instead of on the ground. As everyone drank from their cups, he read the Libation Statement.

> "For the Motherland cradle of civilization.
>
> "For the ancestors and their indomitable spirit.
>
> "For the elders from whom we can learn much.
>
> "For our youth who represent the promise for tomorrow.
>
> "For our people, the original people.
>
> "For our struggle and in remembrance of those who have struggled on our behalf.
>
> "For *Umoja,* the principle of unity which should guide us in all that we do.
>
> "For the creator who provides all things great and small."

Natalie drank her punch from the cup. Wanda had told her that no one actually drinks from the unity cup. However, they still passed the cup through the crowd.

Brother Johnson moved on to salute the ancestors as the cup was passed. He started with Marcus Garvey and threw in a few local leaders from Hopkinsville.

Natalie caught a glimpse of Rod standing in the kitchen doorway. He held a book in his hand and appeared to be reading. She realized he was part of the ceremony and had probably been preparing as she looked for him. The butterflies in her stomach began to flutter when he glanced back at her. She wanted to smile, but knew someone in the room would know how she felt about him if she did. Instead, she lowered her head, then crossed her legs as she looked around the room, before settling her eyes back on him.

Finally, Brother Johnson stepped aside and Rod moved in front of the fireplace.

"We are one, our cause is one, and we must help each other, if we are to succeed." He read a quote first spoken by Frederick Douglass. "Tonight I'd like to read to you an excerpt from *Climbing Jacob's Ladder* by Andrew Billingsley."

Natalie sat in awe as she listened to Rod read. He had the gift of a storyteller. There was so much more to this country boy than she had thought. So he wasn't some jock who thought he was God's gift to women. He was a genuinely nice, sweet man. Why couldn't she have someone like him? Someone who lived in Atlanta?

After Rod finished his reading he gestured for the person closest to him to stand and express what *Umoja* meant to him. Everyone in the room stood and said something. When it was Natalie's turn, she stood and expressed what *Umoja* meant to her. She hadn't quite gotten the flow of things yet, so she felt uncomfortable speaking.

"*Umoja* means peace within the family to me. Living harmoniously with your parents, brothers, and sisters. When there's peace in the homes, I believe it's possible to have peace in the community."

She kept her eyes on Rod the whole time she spoke. They locked eyes and she spoke as if she were speaking only to him.

Five

Rod grabbed an armful of firewood from the stack beside the barn, and proceeded toward the house. He didn't know when he'd light the fireplace, but he wanted dry wood inside when he decided to. His dog, Paso, ran circles around his legs barking at him.

"Okay, boy, I know, you're hungry. Let me get inside and I'll fix your dinner." Paso stared at the door rapidly wagging his tail, as Rod opened the door to let him inside. He dropped the wood by the fireplace then went to feed his dog. Paso sat by his food bowl following Rod's every move with his eyes.

"You need me, don't you, boy?" Rod rubbed the top of Paso's head as he passed him. His dog was all he had to keep him company. After opening two cans of dog food and watching Paso chow down, Rod went to get dressed.

He'd already showered for the day, but he needed to shave. Knowing he was going by Pauline's this morning, caused him to pay close attention to his looks. He'd gotten a haircut yesterday after work, but he liked to trim his own face.

Paso appeared in the doorway watching him shave.

"Hey, boy, you want to go by Pauline's with me this morning? Natalie will be there." He lathered his face and turned back to the mirror to shave. "And you know how much I like looking at Miss Natalie. But dig this!" He pointed his razor at the dog. "She likes looking at me, too."

He began shaving the left side of his face, occasionally pointing his razor at the mirror as he talked. "I can see it in her eyes; I know she wants me. Probably about as much as I want her. But what do I do about it? She lives in Atlanta, miles away from here." He rinsed his razor out in the sink, then started on the other side.

"I wonder how she feels about long-distance relationships. We could make it work, if we really wanted to. Yeah, I could visit Atlanta every now and then. It's not like I'd have to live there." He cleaned out his razor and wiped off his face. Paso sat in the doorway with his head tilted, looking at Rod.

Rod tossed his towel in the dirty clothes hamper and started laughing. He looked down at Paso and said, "Damn, I must be lonely—I'm talking to you like you understand me. Let me get out of here and over to Pauline's."

He changed into a clean pair of jeans and a sweatshirt before leaving.

When Rod walked into the shop, Natalie kept her head down going over her figures a second time. She knew they were right, but it was her way of not making eye contact with Rod.

"So, how's Miss Natalie this morning?" he asked, leaning on the counter.

"I'm fine," she said without looking up.

"Um, hum." He stood there tapping his fingers on the counter looking down at her figures.

Natalie looked up with a straight face. "I'm sorry, did you want something?"

Rod stood straight up from the counter. "No!" He stared at her for a moment. Then he leaned back on the counter smiling. "I'm waiting for Pauline."

"She might be out all morning, she had some personal business to take care of. But I'll tell her you stopped by." She tried her best to smile. Being rude and obnoxious wasn't her intent, but she had to put some distance between them.

"No need." He turned around and walked over to the couch across from the counter. "I'll wait for her right here." He eased back onto the couch crossing his legs and spreading both arms across the back of the couch.

Natalie tapped her pencil eraser on the counter as she looked at him. "Do what you like, but you might be sitting there all morning."

He merely shook his head, pouting his bottom lip. He kept staring at her and she knew why. Unable to take his stares any longer, she stacked her papers neatly on the side of the counter and turned her back to him. *Where is a customer when you need one?* she wondered. Pretending to sort Christmas ornaments in a box, she kept her back turned.

After about five minutes of silence the bell over the door jingled. Natalie's first thought was, *Oh good, a customer.* But when she turned around, her aunt Polly strolled in carrying a shopping bag. Natalie looked over at Rod who hadn't taken his eyes off her.

"All morning, huh?" He lowered his arms from the back of the couch as he winked at Natalie.

Natalie crossed her arms and slightly shook her head. Why had her aunt returned so soon? She was supposed to be doing some after-Christmas shopping for her grandchildren.

"I'm telling you, everywhere you go it's so crowded. I didn't even bother to go into Belks." She stopped when she saw Rod.

"Hi, Ms. Pauline, doing a little after-Christmas shopping?"

"Rod! Yes. Honey, I'd forgotten I asked you by this morning." She put her bag behind the counter.

"That's okay, Natalie here was keeping me company." He winked at Natalie, then turned back to Pauline. "Did you want me to run out to Shady Grove for you?"

Natalie wanted to explode. She hadn't said but a few words to him. While her aunt looked through her delivery book, Natalie picked up her box of ornaments and walked into the back office. She made sure to stay there until Rod left.

That evening, Wanda let Grachel light the first green candle as they observed *Kujichagulia.* Wanda relit the black candle. The second principle of Kwanzaa stood for self-determination. Wanda and her husband Arthur discussed how self-determination and persistence helps you to acquire and maintain your identity. The relatives gathered today were fewer than the day before. Only the immediate family was in attendance. After Natalie listened to everyone express what *Kujichagulia* meant to them, she read Nikki

Giovanni's poem "Choices." She wished Rod was there to hear her read.

Sunday morning she saw Rod again at church. Avoiding him there was easy. He sat on one side and she sat on the other. As soon as morning service ended, she slipped out the door and left. She spent her Sunday afternoon thinking about Rod, even though she tried not to.

That evening the family had another quiet observance of the third principle of Kwanzaa: *Ujima,* collective work and responsibility. Natalie had been exposed to one aspect of this principle, but she sat back to learn more. Again tonight she noticed Rod hadn't joined them.

Natalie didn't get into the shop Monday until around eleven o'clock that morning. Life in Hopkinsville was so relaxed and laid-back, she didn't have to be in a hurry to do anything. No stress. Only peaceful living. She helped her aunt with new inventory.

Business was slow, so they had time to price and put out new pieces. "So, tell me what you're wearing to the New Year's Eve dance?" Pauline asked.

"I'm not going," Natalie replied.

"Why not?"

"Nobody asked me. I'm not going to a New Year's Eve dance by myself."

"Honey, you're in Hopkinsville, not Atlanta. It's okay to go dancing stag here. If you wait for one of these guys to ask you out, you might never leave the house."

"Well, I don't know." Natalie sighed.

"If you'd quit treating Rod like he has the plague, he might ask you."

"I don't want to go with him anyway. I didn't come up here to find a man." It was about time she let her aunt know she didn't want to be matched up with Rod.

"Maybe you didn't. But one found you. And I don't believe in coincidences; it was fate that brought you here." Pauline put down the antique ash tray she was about to price. "Natalie, I can see in your eyes that you're searching for something. I know it's not just your family that you miss. You're a lot like your mother. You need somebody to love you. I know you kids were surprised when your mother finally remarried. But, I understood her. She needs love and companionship all the time. Everybody can't handle being alone. She was alone long enough. I see a lot of your mother in you. Don't push men away. It's not true what they say, you know. All men aren't alike."

"I know it. I guess once you get burned it's hard to put your hand back in the fire."

"Don't run from love, honey. It's all in His master plan, and if it's meant to be—it will be."

Natalie thought about what her aunt said once Pauline left for the day. Tonight they were celebrating *Ujamaa*, which meant cooperative economics. Pauline and a few other business owners in town were speaking to a women's group at the community center. Her aunt believed in giving back to the community whenever she could.

Fifteen minutes before closing two women walked into the shop. One explained she'd had her eye on an armoire and needed another look. Natalie showed them the piece of furniture she'd dusted and polished earlier that morning. The cherry armoire was beautiful. As she opened the cabinet doors displaying the inside to the women, she heard the front door open.

Another customer! Man, I'll never get out of here tonight. When she looked past the ladies she almost fell out. It was Kevin! He stood in the doorway in his black leather wrap coat grinning at her. The women turned to see who Natalie had stopped to look at. One lady cleared her throat to get Natalie's attention.

"Excuse me." Natalie shook her head and told herself he wasn't there. He hadn't driven over four hundred miles to intimidate her. She returned to the armoire and explained their delivery process to the customer.

"I really want this armoire. I think I'll bring my husband by over the weekend to have a look at it. Could you ask Pauline to put my name on it, and not to sell it until I can get George over here?"

"Yes, ma'am." Natalie looked back toward the door, but Kevin wasn't there. "If you'll give me your name I'll write it down for her."

The women followed Natalie over to the counter and gave her a name and phone number. "Pauline knows me very well. Just tell her Mrs. Riley wants that armoire."

Natalie walked behind the counter and grabbed a pen and some paper. With shaking hands she took down the information. "I've got it. And thank you ladies for coming in today."

She followed the women to the front door, then flipped over the closed sign.

"Say, your aunt's got a lot of high-priced junk in here."

Her knees shook as she followed his voice. She found Kevin sitting on the couch across from the counter. Fear swept through her as she thought about their last argument.

"What do you want?" she asked in a harsh tone, with her arms crossed.

"What! No hello, hi, Kevin, how you doing? I figured you'd be glad to see me. After all, we missed spending Christmas together, and you know I hate spending Christmas alone."

He sat back on the couch with his legs crossed and his expensive crocodile boot dangling in the air. Dressed in a pair of expensive wool slacks and one of his two-hundred-dollar camel hair sweaters, he made her sick. He looked like every woman's fantasy. She hated the way he made himself at home.

"What's wrong, baby, you're not glad to see me?"

"How did you find me?"

He stood up and walked over to the counter. She backed up as he approached. Slithering like a snake, he leaned across the counter in his coat. "You weren't trying to hide from me, were you?"

"Kevin, I ended our relationship weeks ago. It should be obvious that I don't want to see you again. How did you find me?" she asked again in a harsh tone.

"Look, Natalie, I came up here to talk to you about this breakup thing. I'm not ready to end our relationship. I know I messed up, but . . ."

"Is that what you call it? I call it messing around, and you seem to be addicted to it."

He banged his fist on the counter with a loud sound that Natalie thought would break the glass. "Damnit! I explained that to you. Don't keep bringing that up. I said I was sorry." He abruptly walked away from the counter and around the shop.

"So you left me for Hopkinsville. What in the world are you doing in this little nothing of a town anyway? You need to get your stuff and come back with me."

"I'm not going anywhere with you."

He returned to the counter. "What do you think I drove all the way up here for? My health? You need to close this little dump and go get your clothes. We can talk about it on the way back."

Natalie shook her head and began to laugh. God, had she actually been that naive when she met him? Had he always told her what to do?

"What's so funny?"

"You, if you think I'm leaving with you. I don't know why you came up here, but you shouldn't have. Kevin, you don't own me, nor do you run my life. You can't waltz in here and tell me I'm going home. I'll leave when I get good and ready."

He rested both elbows on the counter. "Look, baby, you know how much I miss you. I had to spend Christmas by myself and everything. I didn't know where you were until I called your boss. Do you know how many messages I left on your recorder?"

There he goes, trying to disguise himself as prince charming. "I doubt that you spent Christmas alone, nor do I care." She looked down at her watch, it was after five o'clock. Somehow she had to get him out of here and get to Wanda's for the observance of Kwanzaa.

"What are you looking at your watch for? It's time to leave all right. Time to leave this town. Come on now, let's go get your bags. We won't get home before one in the morning as it is."

Natalie grabbed her purse from under the counter. "I'm leaving all right, but I'm not going with you. It's time to close shop." She turned off things preparing to close down.

Kevin paced the floor around the counter in silence. He pulled the belt on his leather coat tighter, and turned up the collar.

Natalie walked toward the front door, hoping he'd leave as easily as he'd come. "Well you'd better leave, I have to lock up." She'd put on her short black scarf coat.

Kevin walked toward the door behind her. "Natalie, I'm asking you one more time. Are you coming home with me or not?"

"Kevin, I told you I'm not going anywhere with you." She pulled her purse strap on her shoulder and backed closer to the door. "After what you put me through, how dare you ask me to come back with you. For what, so I can find you in bed with another woman next week?"

He rubbed his chin as he stood staring down at her. "I've gotten all that out of my system now. I'm a changed man, you'll see."

"Changed how Kevin? Maybe you'll be a little more discreet this time?"

"Hey, I said I've changed!"

"Kevin, I don't want to fight with you about women. I don't want to fight with you about anything."

"Don't try to lay the fight on me. You started the fight that night. I was trying to keep you off me."

She turned and reached for the doorknob, and he grabbed her arm and spun her around.

"Natalie, you're going back with me tonight and I mean it. I don't want to discuss it any more, you're mine."

"I don't belong to you . . . get off me." She struggled to free her arm from his grip.

Rod drove through town after work out of sheer curiosity. It was almost five thirty and he knew Pauline's would be closed, but he had to ride by anyway. Natalie hadn't talked to him at church yesterday, and he'd thought about her at work all day. Every since Saturday morning she'd given him the cold shoulder treatment. He took the hint and backed off, but he hadn't wanted to.

During the first night of Kwanzaa they'd shared something special. He gave his words to her and she gave hers to him. There may have been a room full of people, but when he spoke about *Umoja,* he spoke to her. Even the time they spent later that night talking meant something special to him. Natalie was someone special to him, and he wanted to spend more time with her.

As he got closer to Pauline's he noticed the light was still on. He decided to pull up and see why they were working so late. When he parked his truck by the front door, he saw people standing inside the door. As he turned off the motor, he saw Natalie look out the door at him. Then he saw a tall, dark-complected man dressed in all black standing behind her. He got out of the truck slowly, not sure who this man was to Natalie. He didn't want to be walking in on anything he shouldn't. But, when he saw Natalie jerk her arm from the man, he quickened his step.

When he opened the door Natalie seemed to reach out to him. He wanted to grab her and protect her from whoever was harming her.

"Hey, what's going on here?" he asked touching her hand.

"Hi, Rod."

"Sorry, man, but we're closed. You'll have to come back some other time." Kevin let go of Natalie's arm.

Rod ignored Kevin and walked up to Natalie. "Natalie, are you all right?"

"Yeah, she's fine. What's it to you?" Kevin stepped closer to Natalie, pulling her close to him.

"He's leaving." She turned to Kevin and hoped he would leave now that Rod was here. But he didn't move. He pulled her closer to him as he slid his arm around her waist.

"Get off me, Kevin. I told you I'm not going anywhere with you."

Rod was about to explode. This was Natalie's ex-boyfriend she'd told him about. The one who hurt her.

"Look man, I think you'd better let her go and leave—now."

Kevin struggled to hold onto Natalie as she pushed away from him. "This is none of your business, country boy, so I suggest you get your butt back in your pickup and leave."

Now Rod was angry. It looked like he was going to have to teach this city boy a lesson. "Natalie, do you want me to leave?"

"No, you don't have to go anywhere."

That was all he needed to hear. He rushed up to Kevin, causing him to let go of Natalie. If they weren't in Pauline's, he'd pick Kevin up and throw him across the room, but he didn't want to mess up Pauline's shop.

Kevin backed up a few steps as Rod drew closer.

"So what you gonna do, country boy? Fight me for her?"

Rod reached out and pushed Kevin. His arm swung out sending a lamp crashing to the floor, before he followed it. That was the last straw, for Rod.

"Man, you've got one minute to get your butt out of here. Natalie's not going anywhere with you."

When Kevin stood up, Rod pushed him again. Rod stood about three inches taller than Kevin, and outweighed him by about fifty pounds. Rod considered himself too old to fight another man, but if Kevin didn't leave quick he'd reconsider that.

"What are you, her new boyfriend or something? Man, you can't force me to do anything." He stood there straightening his coat and pulling the belt tighter.

"I'll tell you what, pretty boy. If you don't leave maybe I'll beat you to a pulp, then throw you way back in the woods somewhere where nobody will find you for days. If they find you at all." Rod rushed up and grabbed Kevin by the collar of his coat spinning him around.

Kevin fought to push him off. "Man, get your hands off me."

Rod let him go and pointed his finger in his face. "If you don't leave in the next few seconds, you'll lose some teeth, I promise you." He kept advancing toward Kevin shoving him backward.

"Get off me." Kevin swatted at his hand. "I'm leaving." He turned and walked toward the door, then stopped once his hand was on the knob. "Natalie, I'll see you when you get back in town. You have to come back to me some time." He flipped up the collar on his coat and walked out, slamming the door.

Rod rushed to the door after him, but Natalie stopped him.

"Don't, Rod, let him go. I'm just glad he's gone."

Rod watched him get into a convertible BMW and drive off. He banged the door frame with a balled fist. Man, he wanted to hit that guy so bad. When he turned around Natalie was sitting in one of the high back chairs with her head down.

He kneeled down next to her. "Hey, baby, you okay?"

She looked up with tears in her eyes, and it broke his heart. Without saying a word, he pulled her into his arms and held her as she cried.

Minutes later, she sat up and began wiping her tears away. He helped her.

"Don't worry, everything will be okay." He tried to comfort her.

"Until I go back to Atlanta anyway. Sooner or later I'll have to deal with him."

"I thought you two had broken up." He got up and sat in the chair next to hers.

"We did! I broke up with him two weeks before I came to Hopkinsville. Believe me, I had no idea he'd come walking in here today. I was stunned . . . I'm still stunned."

Rod sat back and thought about what could have happened if he hadn't driven by. He leaned forward, resting his elbows on his knees. Kevin wasn't a very big guy, but he still could have hurt Natalie.

"Thank you, Rod."

He reached over and rubbed her knee. "No need to thank me; I'm just glad I happened to ride by."

She closed her eyes and leaned her head back

against the chair. "I can't go to Wanda's like this. I'm a nervous wreck." She looked down at her watch. "It's almost time for the Kwanzaa observance."

"Want me to call her for you?"

"And tell her what?"

"That you're taking a ride with me. We can go on that little tour I promised you. That should settle your nerves."

"I don't know."

"Natalie, I'm not about to leave you alone right now. Do you think he'll come back?"

"No, he's probably gone. Kevin doesn't have much heart. Once he realizes how determined you are, he'll go home. Besides, he probably has some woman waiting for him at home."

"I can't believe he drove all the way up here if he doesn't care."

"It's a pride thing with him. It's okay for him to leave me, but not for me to leave him."

"Man, that's silly."

"That's Kevin. I don't know how I ever fell for him in the first place. God, I must have been stupid." She slapped her forehead and closed her eyes.

"Don't blame yourself. That guy dresses nice, probably talks a good game, and from that convertible BMW, I'd say he has money to burn. You were a couple years younger when you met him, so the material things probably caught your eye."

"Yeah, I guess so."

"Let me call Wanda right quick, and we'll get out of here."

The tour through town was quick. There wasn't much to see, and it was getting dark. Rod filled

Natalie in on a little Hopkinsville history as they rode. With the heat on in his truck she'd relaxed enough to take off her coat.

"Well, that's the city, but I know a perfect place to watch the sunset. Unless you're ready to go home?"

"No, I'm not ready to go home if you don't mind. But I am a little hungry." Right now she felt safe with him, and didn't want to leave him.

"I'm hungry, too. Let's grab something to eat, then we'll watch the sun set."

"Sounds good to me."

After a quick dinner they rode out into the countryside. Natalie wondered where he was going, but didn't ask. She sat back and enjoyed the ride, trying her best to get Kevin off her mind.

"See that over there?" He pointed out her side of the truck.

Natalie looked out at the orange glow of the sun setting. "Yes, and it's beautiful."

He turned into a long driveway, at the end of which a white house sat back off the road. She looked out the window wondering again where they were going.

"This is my forty acres of responsibility I told you about."

Natalie looked out the window at the fields of trees, grapevines, and the huge barn that sat behind the house. The house was nice. It wasn't grand, only one floor, but it had a quaint elegance about it. It was perfect. She turned to look at Rod, as he smiled at her.

He pulled into a graveled parking spot in front of the house and cut the motor off. When he got out of the truck, he walked around to open the door for her.

He took her hand to help her out of the truck. "This is my house; what do you think?"

"Well, it's not your typical bachelor's pad."

Six

Rod picked up a wicker basket sitting in the white rocker on his front porch. He read the note attached and stuck it in the basket.

"They're from my neighbor. Cookies. Want one?" He offered the basket to Natalie.

"Sure, I'll try one. She bakes you cookies all the time?" Natalie imagined a man this handsome had women trying to get his attention all the time.

Rod opened the front door and motioned for her to go in. "No. A couple weeks ago we had a bad storm. I picked up a lot of tree limbs from her yard, because at seventy-two she can't do it herself. Besides, I don't mind. Every time I do something for her, she bakes me cookies."

"Oh," was all Natalie could say after what she'd been thinking. Stepping into the living room she was impressed. The forest-green walls topped with a floral border, definitely had a woman's touch. The sofa, chairs, and tables didn't look like they matched, but had been collected over time, because they meant something to someone. She wondered if everything had once belonged to his mother. The room had a warm comfortable feel to it.

At his invitation she followed him into the

kitchen. He set the basket on the table and reached into the refrigerator.

"Would you like something to drink?"

"No thank you." Natalie walked over and looked out the back window. She saw a basketball goal, and land stretching as far as the eye could see.

Rod walked over and stood next to her drinking a glass of milk. He didn't touch her, but she felt him. She could imagine what it felt like to have his hands running up her arms, and his breath on her neck as he bent to kiss her. But, it was all in her imagination.

"Nothing like this in Atlanta, huh?"

"What?" she asked. When she turned she realized he was standing entirely too close for comfort. *He's a man, girl, remember that.*

"That." He pointed out the window. "Fields of green grass even in the winter time. I love it here."

She looked back out the window, nodding her head in agreement with him. "So, I see you made yourself a basketball court. You any good?"

"I used to be. I'm still good enough to beat Brandon when he comes home."

"Who's Brandon?"

"My little brother. He thinks he's a basketball star. He plays for Western University. When he comes home from school, I have to put him in his place real quick."

They stood gazing out the back window while Rod told her all about Brandon and their parents' death. "You know, you never think your parents will leave you. At least not until you're much older. My parents were hit by a drunk driver at three o'clock in the afternoon, believe it or not. I was away at college and Brandon was in school." He took another swallow of milk, and a deep breath before continuing.

"When my aunt called I was numb. I don't even remember flying home. And because I didn't get a grant or anything, that was the end of college for me. Besides, somebody had to take care of Brandon and the house."

"What about your aunt?"

"She wanted us to move in with her, but I knew we'd loose the house and all this land if we did. My dad worked too hard to get this place for me to let them sell it. So, I dropped out of school and got a job."

"Rod, that must of been so hard?"

"It was. But I've managed to keep the house and get Brandon in college. I don't regret a minute of it."

"Man, I know your parents are smiling down on you. That was such a mature decision to take on all that responsibility."

"Come here, I want to show you something."

He took Natalie's hand and led her down the hallway into the den. She stepped into the county-style room literally oozing with put-your-feet-up comfort. The huge, striped, soft sofa looked like something she could sink into. Several lamps gave the room a soft warm feeling. This room looked really lived in, with newspaper and throw pillows on the floor. She assumed he spent most of his time in here.

The bookshelves were crammed with books and pictures of his family. He pointed everyone out to her. He and Brandon were the only children.

She picked up the picture. "Your little brother's cute. I bet he's a lot like you."

"Believe me, he's nothing like me. Stick around long enough and you'll meet him." He walked over to the stereo and put on some music.

"I had planned to leave on the third of January,

but now I think I'll stay until New Year's Day. I only wish I didn't have to deal with Kevin once I get back." For the life of her, she didn't know why she brought him up again.

Rod stepped closer, taking the picture from her hand. "I wish you didn't have to go back at all. He didn't hit you, did he?" he asked, looking into her eyes with genuine concern in his.

For a moment her breath caught in her throat. He pushed her hair back around her ear. His touch was so gentle and tender.

"No, but I bet he wants to. He's so mad at me right now. And tonight only made things worse." The tears wanted to spill down her cheeks, but she wouldn't let them. She needed to talk to someone, but she'd be damned if she'd cry over Kevin.

"I hope I didn't make things worse for you."

"No, not at all. You helped me more than you'll ever know."

"You want to talk about it?" He motioned for her to have a seat on the couch.

When Natalie sat on the couch, she felt his hand on her shoulder, giving her permission to open up.

"Several months ago I had to attend a conference in Orlando for my job. Kevin called my hotel practically ever hour. When I wasn't in my room, he accused me of messing around with a coworker. I ignored him, but it happened again a few weeks later.

"I finally got tired of his jealous behavior and decided to end our relationship. When I went by his house to talk to him, I found him and one of his coworkers in bed together." She heard her voice shaking as she spoke. Rod put his arm around her shoulders. She fought the tears that were moments away.

"Some men are stupid."

"He slapped me in front of her, and said if I could sleep around, then so could he. But not once had I ever cheated on him, it was all in his head."

"Natalie, it's not safe for you in Atlanta. He's got serious problems. He doesn't follow you around or anything, does he?"

"No. I made it clear that our relationship was over, and I never wanted to see him again. And I hadn't seen him until today. Actually, his job keeps him away for weeks at a time, and I hadn't seen him for three months, until I went by to break up with him." God, she didn't want to cry in front of this man again. But, she couldn't hold it back any longer. She had to release the tension through her tears.

Rod must have sensed how intense her pain was, because he pulled her into his arms just as the downpour began. She tried to stop but couldn't. At first, he let her cry, then she felt his hands caressing her back. He gently caressed her until she stopped crying.

He whispered ever so softly in her ear. "It'll be okay, you'll see."

She eased back from his embrace and looked up into his eyes. He had the eyes of a storyteller. She remembered his reading the first night of Kwanzaa. He looked so serious standing before everyone in that room, just as he did now. Why had she told this man all her business? How did she know he wasn't another Kevin? He reached up and wiped the tears from her face, rubbing his huge hand gently across her face. She shivered at his touch.

He grabbed a tissue from a box on the end table and offered it to her. "Are you okay?"

"Yes, thank you." She knew her eye makeup was

all over her face, and she probably looked a mess. With the tissue she made an attempt to restore her looks.

"Sometimes it helps to cry."

He said it like he'd experienced it, and somehow she was sure he had, even though he looked too tough and masculine for her to picture him crying about anything.

She smiled at him through her tears and realized she had pressed her hand against the wet spot on his shirt.

"I'm sorry I cried all over you." She rubbed the spot with her hand.

He took her hand into his and raised it to his lips, kissing her knuckles. Caught off guard she didn't quite know what to do. Watching him kiss her hand, she sat there in shock and couldn't move. He pressed her hand against his chest and moved in to kiss her on the lips.

Natalie's whole body tingled with delight. She smelled the outdoorsy smell of his aftershave lotion and closed her eyes. In spite of all her resolutions, she wanted him to kiss her. If only for a moment, she wanted to be held and kissed passionately.

Their kisses grew from gentle to ravishing. Her whole body was on fire with desire. She wanted this man in the worst way. She wanted his strong arms wrapped around her. Her back arched at the feel of his hands caressing her breast. His kisses moved from her lips down her neck.

Natalie knew she was losing her head. But God, how she wanted to lose her head right now. She responded to his every touch, wanting more. He unbuttoned her blouse and opened the front clasp of her bra. At that very moment she wanted all her clothes off. She wanted nothing more than to feel his skin against hers. She nearly exploded when she felt his mouth against her breast. Minutes later, he released her breast and raised his lips to her ear.

"Natalie," he whispered. "I want you."

She wanted him, too, but something inside her head went off and she froze in her seat. *My God, you're doing it again! You're getting involved. This is not what you're here for.*

He looked down at Natalie, startled by the change in her behavior. She no longer responded to his touch.

"Are you okay?" His hand was still on her breast.

"No, I'm not." She repositioned herself on the couch as he pulled away from her. *How had she gotten so carried away in the first place?* Her hands shook as she tried to button up her blouse.

"Here, let me get it. I'm sorry." He finished buttoning up her blouse and sat back on the couch.

"Rod, I'm sorry. I didn't mean to lead you on. Right now I'm just confused and real tired."

"Don't apologize, it's my fault. After what happened today, I had no right to come on to you like this. I know you're only in town for a short time and you don't want to get involved. I can understand that." He got up and changed the music in the CD player, then left the room.

Natalie didn't respond to him. He was right. She didn't want to get involved. Or at least, she didn't think she wanted to. She got up and tucked her blouse back into her pants. Walking over to the bookshelf, she scanned his family pictures lined up on various shelves. She heard him clear his throat behind her. When she turned he stood in the doorway holding the basket of cookies.

"They're not so hard now, want another one?"

"No, thank you. I think I'd better leave before Aunt Polly gets worried."

On the ride back into town they were both quiet. Natalie couldn't believe what she had almost allowed to happen. She wondered what he was thinking. Hopefully, he wasn't thinking bad of her. She told herself, *After tonight I can't see this man anymore.* There was no need in her teasing him, knowing she couldn't give herself to him. In a couple of weeks, he'd be nothing more than a fond memory. He deserved someone who would appreciate him for the strong, yet gentle man he was. Someone around on a daily basis.

Rod finally broke the silence. "So, do you have any plans for New Year's Eve?"

"The Kwanzaa feast at the community center, why?"

"I thought you might like to go to the New Year's Eve dance with me at the armory."

"I'm not really up to partying. I'm sorry."

"Sure, don't worry about it, you're not missing anything. Just a bunch of small town folks dressed up and pretending they're going somewhere. Nothing like the fancy dances in Atlanta, I'm sure."

He pulled the car to a stop in front of her aunt's house, and killed the engine.

"I wouldn't know. I don't go out in Atlanta. I'm not a party girl, believe it or not. I'm more of a homebody."

Rod got out to walk her to the front door. The temperature had dropped with the night air. Natalie pulled her coat tighter around her. Rod stood on the porch with his hands in his jacket pockets as Natalie rang the bell.

"Look, I'm sorry about my behavior tonight. I didn't mean to—"

She cut him off. "Don't apologize. I needed your help tonight and you were there for me. I enjoyed the tour and your company. We both got a little carried away that's all."

He smiled at her and shook his head as the front door came flying open.

"Natalie, I've been worried to death about you." Her aunt pushed open the screen door for them. "You two get in here."

"Miss Pauline, I'll let Natalie explain everything to you, I've got to run. Good night, Natalie."

"Good night, and thanks again."

Midway down the stairs he stopped and smiled up at her. "Sure, anytime."

For some reason she didn't think they were referring to the same thing. She stood in the doorway and watched him pull off into the night.

Rod banged his hand against the steering wheel. "Damn, how could you have done that." He'd pushed her too fast, and his timing was off. Tonight was not the night to make a move on Natalie. She'd needed comforting and consoling. He'd tried to be there for her, until she got too close to him. Holding her in his arms like he was, made him want her.

Next time maybe they'd watch a movie, something safe. After he'd gotten a taste of her, he knew there'd be a next time. That is if she wasn't mad at him about tonight. He hadn't wanted a woman like he wanted Natalie in a long time. At first he didn't know if it was all hormones or not, because he hadn't been with a woman in a while. But tonight, he knew that wasn't it. He wanted her to be his, and he wanted to be hers. If only she didn't have to return to Atlanta.

Instead of taking the left turn onto Route 1, he kept straight to his buddy Terry's house. Terry and Rod had played basketball together in high school. He and Terry were the only ones on the team to stay in Hopkinsville. He had to talk to somebody about this woman. He didn't want to give up on her, but he wasn't sure what his next move should be. The last thing he wanted to do was mess up again like he did tonight. Terry was his closest friend; he knew he could talk to him.

"Habari gani!" Wanda addressed the small circle of relatives in her living room.

"Nia!" they responded.

"This afternoon we celebrate the fifth principle of Kwanzaa, *Nia,* which stands for purpose. To make our collective vocation the building and developing of our community."

Tonight Natalie got to light the first red candle. Wanda's family relit the green candles, and the black one. Arthur led the discussion on how we use our purpose to build and develop our communities.

Natalie felt so grateful and appreciative to have family around her right now. She thanked God for sending her to Hopkinsville for the holidays. She hadn't known what she was going to do for the holidays before her aunt called. Germany was out of the question, but staying in town meant dealing with Kevin. It had to be divine intervention that led her here, she thought.

While listening to Arthur speak she wondered what her life direction was. Purpose—did her life have any? Since breaking up with Kevin she'd promised herself to make some definite choices in her life.

For one, she hated her job. The pay was good, but the stress was unbearable. Kevin had told her she'd be a fool to quit. But, she didn't care what Kevin thought any longer. Time had come for Natalie to make decisions for Natalie, and choose her path in life. What she dreamed of was being self-employed. She wanted her own clothing boutique, and one day she would have it. For years she'd saved up enough money to start a business, but hadn't dared to take that plunge.

Natalie listened as Arthur talked about how serving others was his purpose in life. He worked with the youth at his church. Her thoughts drifted away as she pondered over her life. She went to church periodically, but wasn't very involved. However, she did feel good about the volunteer work she did through her job. Plus, she felt good about her school visits for Junior Achievement.

When Wanda stood up to talk about Clara Hale, the woman who started Hale House, Natalie thought about Rod. He helped her Aunt Polly by making deliveries and pickups all for free. She didn't pay him, nor barter with him in any way. Everything he did for her was out of the kindness of his heart. She also liked the way he helped his elderly neighbor just because she needed it.

When it was Natalie's turn to express what *Nia* meant to her she was ready. It was time for her to make some important decisions in her life, and now she felt like she could do so. She told everyone how she planned to give her life more of a purpose, and to stop living from day to day.

* * *

After dinner Tuesday night Natalie sat down to watch a movie with her little cousin Grachel. The child worshiped the ground she walked on. When Natalie sat on the couch with a huge bowl of popcorn, Grachel scooted closer to her. Natalie put her arm around her little cousin while they watched *The Lion King*. A few minutes after the movie started Wanda's son Richard joined them.

Wednesday morning was New Year's Eve. Natalie felt sad knowing she had to leave the next day. For the past week and a half her days had been filled with family and fun. The thought of her lonely apartment depressed her.

She couldn't bring herself to go into her aunt's shop this morning. Memories of Kevin were still there. Instead, she spent the morning with Wanda, preparing the Community Center for the Kwanzaa feast.

Wanda read over the program while Natalie drove to the grocery store. "Man, we've got a full program this evening. I hope we don't run over."

"Why? Do we have to be out of the center at a certain time?" Natalie asked.

"No, but whoever's not going to church tonight will be trying to get to the New Year's Dance. Did Rod ask you to go?"

"Ah . . . yeah. He asked me yesterday, but I'm not going."

"Why not! I thought you wanted to go."

"I thought I did, too, but I don't want to keep leading him on. If I go to the dance with him, he might get the wrong idea."

"What idea? You're leaving town in a couple of

days. What idea could he get, other than you enjoy his company."

Natalie shrugged her shoulders. She really did want to go to that dance. She'd brought a dress with her just in case she found somewhere to go on New Year's Eve.

"Natalie I know he likes you, and I can tell you like him. Girl, I would, too, especially after he sent Kevin running back to Atlanta for you."

Natalie gave her cousin a quick look. She should have known her aunt would tell Wanda about the incident. "So she told you?"

"You know she did. I'm telling you, Rod cares about you. He was ready to kick Kevin's butt for you. I don't even know Kevin, but I don't like him."

"Well, I'll either stay home and watch Dick Clark, or I'll go to church with Aunt Polly."

"Honey, don't sit around and watch Dick Clark whatever you do. Go with Mama to church if you don't change your mind about the dance."

"I'll do something." Natalie had second thoughts about the dance now. She really didn't want to spend the night watching the never-aging Dick Clark again. In the past, she always had her girlfriends to go out with if she didn't have a date.

After the grocery both women went to the Community Center to start decorating. Wanda had brought most of the items she'd used at her house to use at the center. Natalie had on a pair of jeans and a sweatshirt, ready to work. When they walked in several people were draping cloths over the tables, and blowing up balloons.

"Hey, Natalie, I'm glad you could make it. Come help me with this centerpiece." Wanda's friend Angela waved Natalie over to help.

Natalie worked with Angela. They placed the large

straw place mat known as *Mkeka* in the center of the table. Angela set a basket of corn on top of the mat.

"How many ears of corn are in there?" Natalie asked.

"I'm not sure. Wanda said to just fill it up. We're not sure how many children will be here tonight."

Natalie remembered reading that an ear of corn was placed in the centerpiece for each child in the family. She reached in Wanda's bag and pulled out the *Kinara* and the seven candles. After inserting each candle into its appropriate place, black in the center, red to the left, and green to the right, she placed it in the center of the mat.

Angela sat the *Kikombe cha umoja,* the unity cup, on the table. Next to it, she set a stack of plastic cups. Beside them was a large *Mazao* bowl, full of fruits, nuts, and vegetables. Natalie had to help her with this one. Other trimmings were added to the table for color.

"Where'd you get these?" Natalie picked up the red, black, and green linen napkins.

"Some friend of Wanda's made them."

"I didn't know they went with the centerpiece."

"I can tell you've been reading those Kwanzaa books. You can add whatever you like to the centerpiece. Remember *Kuumba* is all about creativity, talent, and imagination. We can set this centerpiece up however we like. Just use your imagination to make it pleasing."

"Okay, yeah." Natalie thought the centerpiece looked beautiful like it was. She didn't change a thing.

"Could you help me hang that banner over by the door?"

"Sure. You know I'm going to be ready for this feast tonight. Especially after I work up an appetite."

They stood on ladders on both sides of the doors. Angela pulled her end higher, causing Natalie's to slip from her hand.

"Hey."

"I'm sorry." With a hand over her mouth, she looked down to see who she'd hit with her end of the banner.

Rod looked up at her as a passing woman pulled the banner out of his box. "Don't worry about it, I know you were trying to get my attention." He winked at her and walked over to set his box on a table.

"If I wanted your attention, I would have called your name." She took a few steps down the ladder and grabbed the banner from the woman. "Thank you." She stepped back up the ladder and finished helping Angela.

Natalie walked around the center helping wherever she could. She managed to avoid Rod most of the time. She noticed him setting up stereo equipment with some other men and wondered why he wasn't at work. Actually, she was still embarrassed about the incident at his house.

"Hello."

Natalie jumped at the sound of his voice, startled when he walked up to her. "Hi."

"Sorry, I didn't mean to startle you."

"That's okay. I guess I'm still a little jumpy. What are you doing here anyway? I thought you'd be at work."

"I took a long lunch break. I've got to run back in a few." With his hands in his back pockets Rod stood talking to Natalie.

"Say, uh, you haven't changed your mind about the dance tonight have you?"

Natalie thought for a few minutes. She did want to go now. Everyone would be there, but her.

Rod looked down at her moving his head from side to side. "She's thinking about it, and the answer is . . . ?"

"Okay, I'll go."

"Great. I'm glad you changed your mind. I really didn't want to go alone. I kind of had my mind set on going with you."

"Oh you did, huh?"

"Yes, I did. If you hadn't changed your mind, I probably would have had to sit through another Dick Clark rocking New Year's Eve party."

"That's what I usually do."

They both laughed.

"Yeah, but they're no fun alone."

"You've got that right."

"Well, I better get back to work. I'll see you later."

"Okay, don't work too hard."

"I never do." He winked at her and left.

Natalie blushed when he winked at her. She stood there grinning as she watched him walk away.

Minutes later Angela walked up to her. "What kind of gift do you think Rod will give you tomorrow?"

"What makes you think he'll give me something?" Natalie was surprised Angela asked her this.

"Girl, I saw the way that man looked at you when he walked in here. Besides I hear you two have been seeing each other."

Natalie wondered how Angela could have concluded that from her conversing with Rod. Even though nothing was going on, somebody was talking about them. "Who told you that?"

"You know how small this town is. Gossip travels fast. I heard you and Rod have been seeing each other."

"Well we're not seeing each other. He comes by and helps my aunt in the shop that's all." She couldn't believe what she was hearing.

"Girl, don't sweat it. Rod's a nice guy. Half the women in this town have been trying to land him. I can't think of one who's ever been invited out to his house."

Natalie looked at Angela with her mouth wide open. How did she know she'd been out to Rod's house last night?

Angela finished positioning the items on the table, then looked up at Natalie. "Hey, like I said, it's a small town."

Seven

"Habari gani?"

"Kuumba," the audience responded.

Natalie looked around at the crowd of people in the center. All her relatives were there and many people she'd seen at church on Sunday. The table was decorated beautifully with fresh flowers, candles, and colorful appetizers. Everything from sauteed pecans to stuffed red snapper had been prepared. Everyone brought a dish or something to complement the meal. After all the work she'd done earlier, Natalie couldn't wait to start feasting.

After Wanda's welcome, it was time to light the candles and pour the libation. Everyone sat at one long table that spanned the length of the center. Wanda sat at the head of the table, surrounded by numerous children. The crowd stood for the lighting ceremony. Richard lit the first candle, with Wanda's help. Then all the other candles but one were lit by the remaining children.

Miss Liz picked up the Unity cup and poured the libation. Natalie looked in her direction, but she was actually looking at the man sitting next to her. Rod sat beside his great-aunt sipping from his cup in observance of the libation. As he put the cup down, he smiled at Natalie.

She tried not to look at him, or think about him. But now that she'd accepted his invitation to the dance, she couldn't keep her eyes off him. She wondered what the night would be like. Every time she was in his company she had a good time. Tonight shouldn't be any different, she told herself, except tonight they'd be dressed for the occasion. She couldn't wait to put on her new dress.

Her cousin Marvin picked up his program and read the introductory remarks. He acknowledged the seven principles of Kwanzaa, and gave a definition of each. Natalie picked up her program and read everything in an attempt to keep her eyes off Rod. Marvin recognized the guest and elders at the table. Natalie thought he did his job very well. She'd been told that the sixth day of Kwanzaa was hosted by the children. Wanda's children had been practicing a song for the ceremony all week.

She wondered if Rod would be speaking today. When she looked up at him, she noticed him looking down the table and shaking his head. Her eyes followed his until she saw Deborah smiling and giving him the eye. *That girl's crazy.* Here they were at a table full of people cerebrating, and Deborah had found a way to flirt with Rod. When she looked back at Rod, he smiled at her then lowered his head. She'd have to have a talk with her cousin. The girl was embarrassing herself.

Natalie sat beside her aunt looking at the food spread before them hardly being able to contain herself. She wanted to reach out and grab something to eat. After working all morning, and only having breakfast, she was starved. However, she couldn't eat too much. She didn't want her stomach sticking out in her form-fitting dress tonight. All she needed was a little something to stop the hunger pangs.

After several toasts were performed to recognize certain elders, it was time for the children to perform. The church piano player was there to play for the children. Grachel stood up front and sang louder than all the other children. Pauline grabbed Natalie's hand laughing.

"My God, that girl's just like her mother. She can't sing and she wants everybody to know it."

"But she's so cute." Natalie felt like a proud parent watching her little cousin out sing all the other children. The day had all the makings of a family reunion, Natalie thought. She had that same nostalgic feeling she'd had during her father's family reunion a year ago.

When all the ceremonies were over it was finally time to eat. Natalie filled her plate with a little fish, red beans and rice, and a sampling of fruits. She skipped dessert since she was going out later that night. Finally, she sat down next to her aunt to eat.

"Is that all you're eating?" Pauline asked.

"Yes. I don't want to fill up too much."

"Why not?"

"I'm going to the New Year's dance tonight with Rod."

"I know." Pauline smiled at her niece, pleased.

"Why am I not surprised about that?" Like Angela said, news travels fast in small towns.

"I'm just glad you have somewhere to go. I hate to see all the young people going out, and you sitting at home watching television."

"Yeah, well, you don't have to worry about that now. I've got a date." A date! Had she actually said that? Here she was going out on a date, when a man had been the last thing she wanted to be bothered with only weeks ago.

"Good evening ladies, enjoying yourself?" Rod sat across the table from Natalie and Pauline.

"Rod, honey, it's nice to see you. You've finished eating already?"

"Yes, ma'am. I was pretty hungry; it didn't take me long to finish off my plate."

"Where is Miss Liz?" Pauline looked around. "I need to talk to her."

"She's sitting over by the kitchen."

"Well, I need to talk to her a minute. Excuse me you two."

"Aunt Polly you're not even finished eating," Natalie pointed out.

"Oh, yes I am. I always put too much food on my plate. But, I'll take this in the kitchen to wrap up my leftovers. You know how I get hungry late at night." She picked up her plate and walked off. "Now where is that Liz?"

Natalie shook her head. "She's something else."

Before either of them could say anything else, Deborah took a seat next to Rod.

"Hi, Rod, I've been trying to catch up with you all night. Hi, Natalie." She gave a quick wave toward Natalie.

Natalie tried her best not to laugh as she spoke and continued eating. "Hi, Deborah."

"Hello Deborah, what can I do for you?" Rod let out a sigh and looked at the young girl.

"Oh, don't ask me that. At least, not in here." She leaned forward displaying her cleavage. Her sweater appeared to be about two sizes too small.

"Deborah, stop it. Don't you have any self-respect?" Natalie chastised. She couldn't help herself. Somebody had to tell this girl about herself. As good looking and fully developed as she was, some men would take advantage of her.

"What did I do?" She sat back in her chair and raised both hands palms out. "I just came by to ask Rod something."

Rod tried not looking down at her breasts, but it was impossible. This young girl was too much. She had the body of a fully-developed thirty-year-old woman. He'd spent the last six months avoiding her. Every chance she got she seemed to be pressing something up against him. She was lucky he wasn't like some of the men in this town. He could resist her no matter how great the temptation.

"What did you want to ask me?" He had to treat her like the child that she was.

"Are you going to the New Year's dance tonight?"

"Yes, I am."

"You'll save a dance for me, won't you? A slow one."

Rod thought Natalie would explode. She'd pushed her plate away and eyed her cousin like she wanted to wring her neck. The whole thing was funny to him, but he noticed she didn't share his opinion.

He turned and leaned his elbow on the table to face Deborah. "I will if my date doesn't mind."

"Your date?" She turned up her lip, looking surprised.

"Yes."

Deborah pushed away from the table and stood up. "Well, I'm sure your date won't mind. So, I'll see you later tonight." She walked away without saying another word.

"That girl's unbelievable." He shook his head watching her switch away.

"Isn't she though."

"I wanted to tell her you were my date, but she didn't give me a chance."

"Oh, she'll find out soon enough. Maybe that will get her off your back. Or maybe she'll meet a nice boy at the dance."

"Natalie, she's met all the nice boys in the county. I don't think she wants a nice boy. Deborah's looking for a man. But it won't be this man. I can handle her."

Rod checked his watch. He was ready to leave and get dressed for the dance. He couldn't wait to go out with Natalie tonight. What a way to start the new year. A date with a beautiful woman who turned him on.

"What time is it?" she asked.

"Eight thirty. What time are you leaving?"

"I'm not sure, whenever Aunt Polly gets ready. What time are you picking me up?"

"Well." He looked at his watch again. "The dance starts at nine o'clock. Let's say I pick you up around nine forty-five; we'll be there at ten. How's that sound?"

"That sounds good."

With the swirl of people mingling about in the room Rod didn't notice anyone but Natalie. He sat there talking to her for a few more minutes, not wanting to leave her company. Every time he made her laugh and smile he felt good. Tonight they would have a great time; he knew it.

Natalie ran around the bedroom feeling like a sixteen-year-old on her first date. From the minute they walked into the house she had one hour to get ready. Her aunt had left to pick up a friend before church. She must have looked out the window three times before he arrived. Finally, the door bell rang.

She slipped on her shoes and stood before the cheval mirror one more time before answering the door. Her long black dress hugged her body without the stomach bulge. She breathed a sigh of relief then went to answer the door.

"Well, well, don't you look all spiffy tonight." Rod grinned at her shaking his head. There was definite approval in his gaze.

"Spiffy! I hope I look a little better than that," she teased him.

"Oh, I'm sorry. Mama, you look so fine." He stroked his chin and cocked his head like a character in a hip-hop video.

Natalie gave him a quick punch in the arm. "You know what I mean." After he walked in, she closed the front door behind him.

"I'm just kidding. You look absolutely beautiful. You city girls sure do clean up good." This time he ducked out of the way before she swung at him.

"You look very handsome yourself." Delicious was more like it, she thought. No baseball cap, tight jeans, or cowboy boots tonight. Tonight he had on a taupe and brown striped suit, complete with tie and pocket handkerchief. He definitely didn't buy that suit in Hopkinsville; it looked too expensive.

"Thanks. Hey, spin around and let me see that dress."

Natalie did a little spin for him. She knew he wanted to check out how the open back laced up. When she turned to face him again he bit his bottom lip and winked at her.

"Perfection."

"Well thank you."

"Where's Pauline?"

"She went by Mrs. Clark's before midnight service at church. Let me get my coat, and we can leave."

Once inside the Armory, Natalie saw women dressed in just about everything. Just as they walked inside she saw a woman in jeans, and wondered if her slinky black dress wasn't overkill. It definitely wasn't too much for Rod; he couldn't take his eyes off her. Silver and white streamers hung from the ceiling. Balloons were everywhere. A net full of balloons hung securely over the dance floor. Party favors trimmed every table.

Every head turned as they walked across the floor. Natalie recognized a few faces from the shop. Almost everyone spoke to Rod, and a few spoke to her as well. She thought about what Angela said about this being such a small town. There was no telling what stories would be circulated after tonight. Eventually, she saw a few more women come in dressed for the occasion, which made her feel a little better.

After a drink, Rod was ready to dance. He wasn't Fred Astaire, and Natalie wasn't Ginger Rogers, but they burned up the floor despite that. Then a slow song came on, and Rod held her close to him. She didn't know if she could take it. The spicy scent of his cologne and the warmth of his body totally relaxed her and titillated her at the same time.

"That's my favorite song," he said, as he sang "Spend the Night" by The Isley Brothers softly into her ear.

The night was turning out so romantic to Natalie. He caressed her back and held her close to him.

Their bodies met and moved to the rhythm of the soft music. She closed her eyes and let herself be carried away. They could have been the only two people in the room as far as she was concerned. Being there in his arms felt marvelous.

"Hey, man, don't hold her so tight, you'll break her."

Natalie opened her eyes and saw a young man standing behind Rod. They could have been twins. Rod loosened his embrace and turned around to hug the young man.

"Natalie, I want you to meet my little brother . . ."

"Little! I'm his younger brother, Brandon."

She shook his hand and noticed Brandon had Rod's eyes and smile. They had the same full lips and full eyebrows as their father in the picture he'd shown her. Two very handsome men. They left the dance floor and returned to the table. Brandon and his girlfriend had arrived in town right before the dance. Moments later, his girlfriend made her way to the table and Brandon introduced her. They made a really cute couple. Natalie loved her long auburn hair and how it matched her dress.

Natalie noticed how well the two brothers got along. They appeared to be best friends. They talked non-stop and relished each other's company. Minutes later, Brandon and his date stood to leave.

"Natalie, it was nice to meet you. I'm glad you got Rod away from the house. The old boy doesn't get out much these days."

"It was more like he got me out. But, we're having a great time. It was nice to meet you, also."

"Cool, we'll catch you guys later. I see a few people I'd like to introduce Mia to." He patted Rod on the back and walked toward a group that had gathered across the room.

"He seems like a nice guy," Natalie said, as she watched them walk across the floor. She also noticed how crowded the room had gotten. Everyone in town must have come in after they did.

"He is a nice guy. I'm really proud of him. My parents would have been, too." He looked across the room.

The sadness in his eyes hurt Natalie. Rod was such a nice, decent, and honest man. He was the man she'd been looking for when she ran into Kevin. When he turned and looked at her, she sensed he knew what she was thinking. He winked at her and reached across the table for her hand.

"I'm a nice guy, too," he said, as he kissed the palm of her hand.

"I know, and I'm having a wonderful time tonight."

More might have come from the conversation, but suddenly people started coming from everywhere to their table. All the men wanted Rod to introduce them to Natalie. He did, but held her hand possessively, as if they were in love. When everyone left he turned and said, "What do you say we get out of here?"

"And go where?" she asked.

"I know where there's an after-party. Come on, it's getting a little too crowded in here."

It wasn't twelve o'clock yet, but she didn't mind. As they walked across the floor, she wondered what type of after-party they had in such a small town. Rod excused himself and ran into the kitchen for a minute. He walked out with a paper bag in his hand.

When Rod made a turn onto Route 1, she knew what type of after-party he had in mind. He turned into his driveway, killed the engine and smiled at her.

"Believe me, this party will be better than the one we just left."

He walked around to help her out of the car, and held her hand as they walked up the stairs and into the house. She didn't mind at all. She thought his maneuver was so cute; it made her feel like his girl. He didn't like all the attention they were getting at the party; he wanted her all to himself.

In the den, he turned on a lamp with a soft light, and took her coat. Before leaving the room he grabbed the remote and turned on the stereo. Soft music filled the air.

"Can I get you anything?" he asked.

"No, I'm fine."

He left to hang her coat up and returned with a bottle of champagne and two champagne flutes.

"I hope you don't mind me wanting you all to myself tonight?" he asked, as he walked into the room closing the distance between them.

"No, not at all." She wanted to be with him, but was still a little afraid. Did she really want to get involved again? Not with the wrong man, but Rod was the right man.

He set the champagne and glasses on the den table and turned to her. "Then may I have this dance?"

"Yes you may." She blushed and smiled at him.

He pulled her into his arms and they slow danced on his makeshift dance floor.

"Now this is the type of party I like. Just you and me. I don't want to share you with anyone else."

"So why didn't you just invite me out here for a party?"

"Would you have come?" He held her at arms length and looked down into her eyes.

"I don't know, maybe not."

He stood there gazing into her eyes. The music played softly in the background. She wanted him to kiss her, then pick her up and carry her into his bedroom, just like in the movies.

"You're so beautiful," he whispered in her ear. "Nat, I want you so bad."

Nat! He's already using my nickname. I've known this man for such a short time, but I want him. Before she could respond he pressed his lips over hers. She felt the heat from his tongue, and her knees gave way. He held on to her until she steadied herself.

"Rod, I know this is crazy, but I need you."

"There's nothing crazy about it. I'm here for you, baby. I'll always be here for you. Just don't leave me, because I need you to be here with me."

Natalie looked up into those big, beautiful eyes, speechless. He was a wonderful man. The man of her dreams. But could she be happy in Hopkinsville? On the other hand, did she have any reason to stay in Atlanta?

He pulled her back into his arms and kissed her again. This time his kiss was one of intense hunger. He wanted her as much as she wanted him. They stood there in the middle of the room, ready to rip each other's clothes off. He pulled back, and looked down into her eyes.

"Promise me you'll think about it?"

She couldn't say no. "I promise." Almost breathless she managed to get the words out. She threw her arms around his neck as he lifted her into his arms. It felt as if they floated down the hall and into his bedroom. Once inside, he turned her around to untie her dress. Her body tensed from memories of her earlier fears. He sensed it, because he turned her around to face him.

He kissed her neck and shoulders as he helped her out of the dress. "Relax, Natalie. I'll never hurt you." He kissed the top of her forehead and the tip of her nose.

"I know you won't." She reached up and helped him unbutton his shirt. Once his chest was exposed, she ran her hand across his hairy chest. That was one of her biggest turn-ons, a hairy chest. He moaned and grabbed her hand moving it down to his pants. She helped him out of his pants.

They discarded everything in a pile on the floor. He took her hand and led her to the bed. The slightest touch from him made her body shiver.

"Oh, Nat, you're so beautiful." His voice was heavy with emotion as he lowered himself to the bed. He pulled her close between his legs and caressed her breast.

For such a big man with huge hands, his touch was so gentle. His kisses were like feathers exploring every inch of her body. Natalie wanted to be nowhere more than she wanted to be here with him at this very moment. Rod brushed his lips past her breast and down her stomach. He stopped at her navel and licked.

Natalie wanted to pull her hair out from the roots; his touch was driving her insane. He raised his head and pulled her down on top of him. They rolled around and tangled themselves up in the covers, lost in the moment of desire for one another. At the feel of his hands gently sliding between her legs, Natalie spread them eagerly. She wanted him inside of her, filling her with his love. She needed him.

Rod's breathing grew heavier as he rolled on top of her and slowly entered her. They moved to a slow rhythm and together picked up the pace. Natalie wrapped her legs and arms around his body and closed her eyes, as they rocked into a peaceful space. She gave her body to him as he gave every ounce of himself to her.

Later, she lay beside him feeling happy, giddy, even silly. No man had ever made her feel the way Rod had. She wanted to burst she felt so good inside. She questioned herself, *Is this what love feels like? If so, if feels so good.*

Suddenly, Rod raised up and looked at the clock on his night stand. "What time is it?" He threw back the covers and jumped out of bed.

Natalie sat up wondering what the hell was going on. "Rod, what is it?"

"Look at the time!" He grabbed his robe and left the room.

Natalie turned to look at the clock, it was five minutes till twelve. A few seconds later Rod walked back into the room. He had the bottle of champagne in one hand and the glasses in the other.

"I almost forgot about the champagne." He held the bottle up smiling at her as he walked across the room.

Natalie sat up in bed pulling the covers up over her chest. The chill in the air gave her goose bumps. Rod sat on the edge of the bed next to her. He placed the bottle and glasses on the night stand and reached for the remote control.

"Now we can catch Dick Clark." After turning the television on he took a bottle opener out of his robe pocket and laid it on the table. Climbing out of his robe, he eased in bed next to Natalie.

"Are you cold?" He put his arm around her.

"Only my shoulders, it's a little chilly in here."

"Then let me warm you up."

He pulled the covers up around her, then wrapped her in his arms, running his hands up and down her arms and shoulders. Her body began to warm to his touch.

"Hold on, baby, we've got to toast in the new year." He grabbed the two champagne flutes and gave them to Natalie. "Hold these for me."

"Okay." She held the flutes and watched him open the bottle of champagne. If someone had told her she'd be spending her New Year's Eve in bed with a handsome man, she wouldn't have believed it. Here she was in bed about to share a New Year's toast with a man she'd met ten days ago, but she felt as if she'd known him forever.

He filled their glasses and turned up the volume for the countdown. They held their glasses up and stared into each others eyes. "Four, three, two, one, Happy New Year!"

He cupped her cheek in his hand as they shared a special kiss. Then they drank their champagne. Natalie sipped from her glass, not really being a champagne lover.

"Nat, I've got something serious to ask you." Rod refilled his glass and turned to look down at her. His eyes had a sincere look in them.

Suddenly she felt scared. "Yes," she whispered.

"Do you think you could give me and Hopkinsville a chance? I'd really like to get to know you better. I think we're good together, and I don't want to lose you."

"Rod, I want to get to know you better, too," she answered with an uncertain smile. Then she asked herself, *What am I returning to Atlanta for anyway?* This time she answered herself—nothing. She didn't have any family there, only a job she hated and a man she was afraid of.

"Rod, I don't want to rush into anything, so can we take it slow?"

He bent down and gave her a soft kiss on the forehead. "I understand. We can take it as slow as you want, as long as I don't lose you in the process."

"You won't. We've shared a New Year's toast and kiss, don't you know how special that is?"

The next morning Natalie awoke slowly and looked around the room. Where was she? This wasn't her aunt's guest room with the flowery wallpaper. She rolled over and saw Rod laying next to her. Yes, now she remembered!

My God, what will Aunt Polly think? she asked herself. *She's probably worried to death about me.*

Rod stretched and rolled over looking into Natalie's eyes. "Good morning."

"Good morning." She smiled at him, feeling completely satisfied for the first time in a long time.

"You know I hadn't planned on staying the night."

"I wondered about that when the phone rang around three this morning. Wanda wanted to make sure you were here."

"She wanted to make sure I was here!"

"Yeah, so I told her to relax. I'd bring you home some time today." He grinned at Natalie.

"Oh, yeah, so now I have to walk into the house in the gown I wore last night."

"Yes. But, that won't be the only thing you'll be wearing."

"What do you mean?"

"You'll also be wearing that beautiful warm glow you woke up with this morning."

"Thanks to you." She blushed and kissed him.

Rod reached out and pulled Natalie into his arms. She forgot about being anywhere this morning other than where she was—out on Route 1.

Eight

"Habari gani?"

"Imani," everyone responded.

Tonight was the last night of Kwanzaa. They were observing *Imani*—the seventh principle of Kwanzaa, which stands for faith. Wanda stood before the small crowd of people gathered in her living room and read the observance.

"To believe with all our heart in our people, our parents, our teachers, our leaders, and the righteousness and victory of our struggle. To care for each other and control our destiny." Wanda motioned for Arthur to join her in front of the fireplace. She handed him the unity cup as he proceeded with the libation.

Tonight Natalie's aunt Polly lit the last red candle. Wanda's family relit all the other candles.

Natalie sat on the couch with her shopping bag before her hardly able to contain herself. She wanted all the ceremonies to be over so she could hand out her gifts. In the ten days she'd been in Hopkinsville, she'd learned a lot about Kwanzaa. She had used several of the principles studied throughout the week to come up with her *Zawadi* (gifts).

Pauline closed the ceremony by remembering their ancestors. She talked about relatives Natalie knew nothing about. Since her mother left Hopkinsville as a teenager, they hadn't visited much. Natalie didn't know much about her grandparents, but was learning some on this trip.

When time came to exchange *Zawadi,* the fun began.

"Aunt Natalie, I made this for you." Grachel handed Natalie a piece of construction paper with a drawing on it.

Natalie held up the very colorful painting the child had made herself. "Grachel, this is beautiful, did you make this?"

She nodded her head. "Uh, huh, all by myself. You know what it is?"

"Well, let's see."

"It's a lady." She pointed at the figure in the middle of the picture.

"Oh, I see. Yes, and she's beautiful."

"She's a black queen, Mama said."

"Grachel this is the best gift." Natalie set the picture on the couch and reached into her shopping bag. "And I've got a little something for you." She pulled a video tape out of her bag. "Now your Mommie told me you didn't have this one."

Grachel took the tape and looked at the cover.

"It's *Jirimpimbira: An African Folk Tale.* You can have your Mommie play it for you tonight."

"Thank you, Aunt Natalie, I don't have a whole lot of video tapes." She leaned forward and kissed Natalie on the cheek. "Mommie, Mommie, look what I got." Off she ran to find Wanda.

Natalie reached in her bag for her aunt's gift. She had searched and searched for the perfect gift for her. Pauline had given Natalie these two weeks that she'd never forget. Her life changed over this vacation. She found Pauline in the den helping Richard tie up his shoes.

"Aunt Polly, I've got something for you." She handed her a book, *In The Spirit,* by Susan Taylor. "I know you already have everything by Maya Angelou but I didn't see this one on your shelf."

Pauline set Richard down and took the book. She stood to hug Natalie. "Oh, honey, thank you very much."

"It's a very inspirational book. I've got a copy of it at home."

"Natalie, this is from me and Arthur." Wanda handed Natalie a rather large box.

Natalie set the box on the table. "Man, what could this be." She began opening the box.

The doorbell rang and Arthur opened the door. The women in the kitchen could hear him talking to someone.

Natalie pulled a *Kinara* out of the box. Her eyes widened in surprise.

"Now you can start celebrating Kwanzaa yourself. You've learned a lot these seven days. And I can tell you enjoyed it."

All Natalie could do was hug her cousin. "Wanda this is a great gift. I am going to celebrate Kwanzaa next year. And every year from here on out. Let me go get yours, it's in my bag."

When Natalie walked into the living room she found Arthur and Rod sitting on the couch talking. Her heart skipped a beat. She hadn't planned on seeing him so soon in the day, but she was glad to see him. She'd been thankful Wanda or her aunt hadn't teased her about staying all night at his house. But, now she could be assured they'd bring it up.

Both men looked up when she walked into the

room. Rod smiled and stood up when she approached.

"Hi."

"Hello, I didn't expect to see you so soon."

"I wanted to bring my *Zawadi* gifts by. I meant to be here sooner, but Aunt Liz needed me this morning."

Arthur made an excuse and left the room to let them talk. Rod pulled Natalie into his arms and kissed her. They stood there kissing until Wanda walked in clearing her throat.

"Are we trying to repeat last night?" she whispered.

Natalie pulled away from Rod and started laughing.

"Hi, Wanda." Rod still had his arm around Natalie.

"Hi, Rod."

"Wanda, here let me give you the gift I have for you and Arthur." Natalie walked over to her bag and pulled out their gift. She walked over and handed it to Wanda. Arthur walked back into the room.

"What's that?" he asked.

"It's Natalie's gift to us." Wanda looked at the box while Natalie went to sit on the couch with Rod.

"It's a game. 'Journey to the Motherland.' Natalie, where did you find this?" Wanda and Arthur opened the box and looked at the game.

"I saw it in a magazine, so I called and had it overnighted here. I knew you'd like it."

"It's a board game of African-American trivia. I didn't even know they made things like that," Arthur said. "You know this will be good for the kids to learn on also." He looked up at Natalie shaking his head.

"Well, I guess we can say you learned what Kwanzaa means this holiday season."

"I did. And I enjoyed myself tremendously." She turned her head to Rod when she said that.

Wanda and Arthur left the room to show Pauline their gift.

"Well, Kwanzaa's officially over today." Rod scooted closer to Natalie on the couch.

"Yeah, but you know you're supposed to observe these principles every day. I read how you can incorporate the seven principles into your everyday life."

"But how can a single person celebrate Kwanzaa? It's not the same as when you have family members around."

"I know the books say you can, but I agree it's not the same. Wanda gave me a *Kinara*, so I can start celebrating Kwanzaa in Atlanta."

Rod slouched down on the couch. "Don't remind me about your going back to Atlanta. I don't want to think about it right now."

Natalie leaned her head against his shoulder and thought for a moment. She didn't want to go back to Atlanta either. She'd fallen in love with Rod and wanted to spend more time with him, not leave him. What were the chances of him coming to Atlanta to see her, or her returning to Hopkinsville anytime soon? Besides, she didn't want a long-distance relationship. For one, she wasn't a believer in them.

"I'm going to miss you. But I'll do my best to make it down in a couple of weeks. That is, if you want me to."

Natalie raised up looking at Rod in surprise. "You'll come to Atlanta to visit me?"

"Of course I will."

"But, I thought you hated Atlanta."

"I don't hate it. I've never been there. What I hate is that the last woman I dated deserted me for Atlanta. After one visit to her cousin's in Atlanta, she wanted to be a city girl so bad. She wanted to spend life in the fast lane. All the nightclubs and concerts Atlanta had to offer enticed her. Hopkinsville can't compete with that."

"It shouldn't have to compete. I like it just the way it is. If you want, I can try to come back sometime soon."

"Like how soon?"

"I don't know, maybe next month."

"Next month!" Rod leaned forward resting his elbows on his knees. "Natalie that's a long time without seeing you. I don't like long-distance relationships, but I don't want to lose you. We need to be spending more time together, not less."

She wrapped her arms around his arm and leaned on his shoulder again. "I know."

"Are you still leaving today?"

"I'm going to leave around six in the morning. I don't like to drive once it gets dark."

"Then I get to spend the evening with you?"

"If you want to."

"I do. I know you need to say goodbye to your family and all, but can I pick you up around six? We can just sit and talk."

"Okay, I'll be ready."

Natalie spent the rest of the morning packing and saying goodbye to her family. Grachel cried as she left Wanda's house. She thanked Wanda and Arthur for everything they'd given her in the last two weeks.

Pauline fixed Natalie a big dinner and they sat down to talk before Rod showed up.

"So I see you've quit treating him like he has the plague."

"Aunt Polly I never treated him like that. I was just scared he'd turn out like Kevin. But, like you said, all men aren't alike. Once I realized that and opened my mind to a few things I saw him differently."

"You learned a lot during Kwanzaa didn't you?"

"Yes, I did. And you know when I get back to Atlanta I'm going to take a close look at my life. I need to change a few things. First of all I'm going to examine my purpose in life. I never realized before that I don't have any direction. I've just been living from day to day."

"Honey, everybody needs goals, or a plan in life."

"Well before I thought Kevin and I would get married one day and I'd settle with being a housewife. But, you know, that's not what I want to do. When I get home I'm going to make some definite choices in my life. A family is important to me. My family is so spread apart, it's hard for us to unite the way we should."

"You're not thinking about moving to Minneapolis are you?"

"Are you kidding, I couldn't stand the cold. I know Mama handles it, but not me. However, I am going to focus on my family more. Maybe next year I can get all of us together to celebrate Kwanzaa."

"Now that sounds good."

The doorbell rang and Natalie quickly finished her food while Pauline went to let Rod in.

He took Natalie for dessert and coffee. They spent the next couple of hours talking about how much they'd miss each other, and how long it would be before they met again. Rod expressed his concern for her returning and having to deal with Kevin. He wanted her to call the police if Kevin showed up at her apartment.

Because she had to get up early the next morning, he reluctantly took her back to her aunt's house. They sat in the car for several more minutes, not wanting to leave one another.

"Natalie, call me the minute you get in town. After you call your aunt, of course. And don't forget, if Kevin shows up . . ."

"I know, call the police. Rod, I have no intention of letting him into my house, trust me."

"I know you won't. I'm just so afraid for you that's all. I wish I could go back with you."

A few minutes later, Natalie pulled herself away from him and walked into the house. She stood in the doorway and watched as his truck moved slowly down the street.

Natalie returned to Atlanta and the stress of her job. Every time she picked up the phone she prayed it would be Rod. A couple of times her prayers came true. He called everyday. At night they talked on the phone for hours. She missed him terribly.

Kevin came by, but she pretended she wasn't at home and didn't answer the door. She called the police to report someone lurking around her apartment. Kevin was still outside when the cops showed up. Two weeks later, she hadn't heard a peep from him.

At night when Natalie went to bed she dreamed of Rod. They had one wonderful night together. One very special night. She'd told her girlfriends about him and they all wanted to meet him. He had plans to come to Atlanta at the end of the month, but she didn't think she could wait that long.

After a terrible day at work, Natalie walked into her apartment and slammed the door. She'd had about all she could take. She kicked off her shoes, flopped down on the couch and picked up the phone.

"Hello."

"Natalie?"

"Yeah, it's me."

"What's wrong, baby, you don't sound so good." Rod detected a slight quiver in her voice.

"Remember when you asked me about giving Hopkinsville and you a chance?" *Here goes,* she said to herself.

"Yes."

"Well, I'm ready."

Rod exhaled. "What do you mean, you're ready?"

"I want to be with you. Can you come get me?"

"For how long?"

"For good."

"Baby, I'm as good as there. These have been the hardest three weeks of my life. I need you. We need each other."

Natalie wanted to cry she was so happy. "During my vacation I learned that I need a lot of things. I need my family. I need to take control of my life, and live it as I want to. I also need to do more for others. But most of all, I need you."

Six months later Natalie had her grand opening of Imani's, her specialty clothing boutique in the heart of Hopkinsville's antique district. Rod took her out to celebrate the occasion, and pulled a small blue velvet box from his jacket pocket during dessert.

They were engaged, and Natalie was truly happy

with her new life. She had a job she enjoyed, lived in a town she loved, and had the man she'd been looking for all her life.

WHISPER TO ME

Carmen Green

Chapter One

"Daddy, did you look at my new list to Santa? I faxed it to your office this morning before I left for school."

Slightly perturbed at her father's preoccupation with his tie, seven-year-old Anika Hamilton stopped lolling in the center of his four-poster bed, propped up on her knees next to her twin, and fixed him with a penetrating stare.

When he didn't immediately respond, she exchanged an anxious glance with her sister.

"Did you get mine too?" piped Medina, in a nearly identical voice.

Cedric Hamilton glanced through the tri-paneled wall mirror from his dressing room, his gaze coming to rest on his two favorite women. The resemblance to their mother began and ended with their cinnamon coloring and brown eyes.

They bore the signature genes of the Hamilton ancestors with jet black hair and dark, half-inch-long lashes.

Dimples like his graced their satiny cheeks, while their intelligent eyes stared back at him with feigned innocence.

He couldn't resist the smile that tugged at the

corners of his mouth. Ah, he thought, the gang-up-on-Dad approach.

Familiar with that technique of persuasion, he stalled, adjusting his tilted bow tie. When they began to fidget, he still delayed answering, taking his time to select and slip into polished dress shoes. He glanced slyly at the girls, feeling their unspoken frustration.

Cedric pulled at the sleeves of the starched white tuxedo shirt and crossed thick navy carpet to the armoire outside of the dressing room.

"As a matter of fact," he said, hearing them inhale, "I did receive something." He wiggled his eyebrows mysteriously.

They embraced and giggled and rolled on the bed.

Cedric smiled, wishing he could be so free. But ever since his wife's death, securing their future had been his primary concern. The smile slowly faded from his wide mouth. Things were good now, he constantly had to remind himself. He could breathe without fear they'd end up on the streets where he'd come from.

Contemplating throwing off the stiff white shirt and crooked bow tie, Cedric started for the button at his collar, then stopped. Duty bellowed like a horn on a foggy night.

The benefit auction was his baby. He had to be there.

Resigning himself to his evening's fate, he gave the crooked tie a final pat and pressed the mahogany armoire door. It swung open easily.

Tenderly, he pulled a worn gray velvet box from the drawer. Lenora had given it to him nine years ago. Thinking of his wife, Cedric lifted his eyes heavenward. He knew she was watching over them, protecting the family she'd been snatched away from.

The lid creaked as he tilted it up, and he became aware that the girls' giggles had ceased. They now stood beside him.

"Are those the cuff bl-, things Mom gave to you on your wedding day, Daddy?" Medina asked.

Cedric nodded, lifting the black and gold studs from the box. In order to keep their mother alive, he'd shared every memory with them. Except the most intimate. Those were safely tucked in a corner in his heart. Lately though, those memories had begun to grow fuzzy, distant.

Inquisitive eyes stared up at him. He finally answered.

"Links. Say it, Medina." Gingerly, he laid them in her palm as she rolled her tongue around in her mouth.

"Bw-bwinks," she stuttered, proud of her effort.

Cedric closed one eye, scratched his head, and gave her a nod of encouragement. "Close, and yes, they are the exact ones. Who's going to help me put them on?"

"I will," the girls replied in unison.

Cedric sat on the edge of the raised bed, waiting as they jumped from the hand-made footstool to sit beside him. His gaze slid from the stool to the dark mahogany furniture his wife had commissioned for them from her own designs.

It bespoke both their personalities in strength and firmness. Yet the hand-carved designs etched into the drawers and base were unique, complex. Looking at them reminded him of the love they'd shared.

Lately though, loneliness he'd felt only as a child had begun to creep in and steal his rare, private moments of peace. Those haunting childhood memories had ceased once he'd found love the first time. He believed he'd never be alone again.

Cedric stroked his chin, then dragged his hand down the front of his shirt, making sure it was straight. He wondered if he would ever find love a second time around.

Mentally, he pushed the thoughts away. So far no woman had been special enough to fit into his complicated world.

The demands of family and job were first and foremost, and that would never change. It wasn't likely he would find love again.

Cedric sighed, shrugging. Would be nice, though.

"Stay still, Daddy," Anika ordered.

"Sorry."

His gaze traveled over their bent heads, down their long braided hair. He lifted his shoulders and was fixed with a serious glare from Medina.

"Quit shrugging. I'm aw-most done." He held his breath when Medina's tongue jutted out as she concentrated on fastening the link.

"Lllll, links," he said, urging her to echo his pronunciation. Instead, Medina smiled adorably at him, dimples denting her cheek.

"You said it perfect. Very good, Daddy."

She bent over his wrist, her fingers intent on their mission, and he felt suitably put in his place. His mother's soft-spoken warning of pushing Medina too hard rang in his head. Difficult as it was for him, he tried to go easy on her. But he'd found out the hard way, life wasn't kind to those with weaknesses.

Anika's little hands pushed the air from his cheeks, making him turn toward her.

"Daddy, do you think Santa can bring all my presents on one sleigh and still fit everybody else's? My list is kind of long." She released his face and rested her hands on his shoulders.

"Wh-what?" Caught off guard, Cedric drew back, unsure he'd heard correctly.

"I think he should have one sleigh just for me," Anika said reasonably.

"Me too," Medina added.

Anika rolled her eyes in her head. "Okay," she said reluctantly. "He could probably attach a small one to mine and put your stuff on back."

Cedric stared at her, stunned.

"Daddy," Anika went on, "Santa might have to make two trips to the North Pole because he won't be able to carry our things and everybody else's too."

Anika held two fingers under his nose, forcing his eyes to cross as he looked down at them. "I need two life-size Barbie's, so they can be twins just like us. Two pairs of rollerblades, three pairs of gold earrings. I saw this carousel when I was in the mall with Grandma and it wasn't that expensive. It had a two, six, zero, zero, dot, zero, zero. Can you get that for me? It's not really a toy, so I don't think Santa will get it."

"Twenty-six hundred dollars," Medina offered as she straightened his cuff, giving his arm a final pat.

"I need . . ."

"Stop!" His tone commanded silence.

"But . . ."

"Enough, Anika!" Cedric held up his hands to ward off the completion of a list he feared would go on forever.

Cedric paced in front of them, wondering if these two gift-hungry children were his. He wagged his finger at them.

"Santa is not, I repeat, is *not* going to drive one

sleigh just for your gifts. Have you two forgotten the real meaning of Christmas?" When they shook their heads, a small margin of relief flooded him.

"No, sir. It's Jesus' birthday," Medina said solemnly.

Cedric breathed a sigh of relief, grateful at least one of his reasonable children had returned.

"That's right. It's also the season to give." His voice softened, and he lifted their chins so he could look into their identical brown eyes. "Not just receive."

"Yes, sir," they echoed, resignation weighing down their tone.

A quick glance at his watch indicated the late hour. Hurrying to the dresser, he pocketed his wallet, keys, and a few stray coins. "We need to talk, girls. Unfortunately, I have to get going. We'll have to do it tomorrow at breakfast."

"Are you going to make us bw-ueberry pancakes?" Medina clasped her hands together, a pleading look in her eyes.

More blackmail. Cedric did a mental check of pancake ingredients, then nodded. "I'll stop and pick up some blueberries before I come home."

He glanced at Anika. Her chin was thrust upward and her eyes gleamed with determination.

"Daddy, we give away dresses and toys all the time. Isn't that right, Medina? And sometimes you give away money to those kids. I know it's just a couple dollars, but won't that count for us too?"

Cedric executed a slow turn toward his eldest child by two hours and thought he might see a spoiled debutante in her place. The couple of dollars she referred to was a fifty-thousand-dollar college scholarship he gave every year in his wife's name to a graduating high school senior.

"Anika Michele!" His voice rang with warning. Cedric stopped. Blowing up at her wasn't the answer. Her words went deep, farther than she could ever know.

"I said we would talk in the morning. Go tell Grandma Elaine I'm leaving. You too, Medina."

When the girls quietly closed the door to his room, Cedric shrugged into his single-breasted, athletic cut tuxedo jacket. One last look in the gold-rimmed, tri-paneled mirror revealed more than he expected.

For the first time in many years, he wasn't pleased with what he saw.

Chapter Two

"Iman, you aren't going to win the painting. Come on, I'm ready to go."

Iman Parrish linked arms with her sister, Aliyah, and dragged her into the crowd that filled the turn-of-the-century home.

"Don't leave yet, okay? I'm going to win." *If you believe, then you can achieve,* Iman told herself repeatedly.

"No, you're not. Have you forgotten this auction is to raise money?" Her sister looked at her with that "duh" expression on her face. "People are here to spend money for a good cause, not bargain. Your bid was so low, I could have bid against you and won."

Iman looked around at the guests. So what if the city's most prominent and wealthy were present? So what if most had enough money to make her bank account look like bread crumbs? So what? Nobody wanted a painting by an unknown child painter but her.

She stared at the painting and was grateful no one lingered near the table. It was perfect. And, she reasoned, it wasn't often she wanted something so bad.

Iman withdrew her arm from Aliyah's. "None of

these people want it because the little boy isn't famous. Oh, shoot." Iman grabbed her sister's arm again. "Look at *him.*"

They eyed a tall, dark-complexioned man as he moved close to study the picture of children playing.

From behind, it was obvious his clothes were tailored and expensive. She eased to the left to see him from the side. His generous smile wasn't entirely lost on her. Her belly clenched uncharacteristically.

Everything about him spelled "I'm rich."

Rich enough to out-bid her.

To her dismay he stepped closer for a better look.

Iman's stomach jumped.

She had to stop him from bidding on her painting. Iman circled the table, approaching him head on. His dark eyes gleamed with appreciation. Her stomach plummeted. She'd seen that confident look before in other patron's eyes.

She'd felt it too—just before she'd placed her bid.

"He's picking up the pen," she whispered anxiously to her sister for no reason. The noise in the room was at conversational level.

"Told you," Aliyah knowingly replied. She tugged Iman's arm. "Come on. You lost."

Iman stared at the canvas her young friend had painted, longing for it. "I can't give up, Li. I promised Harold if he completed Kwanzaa class, I would buy one of his paintings. I want this one." She turned back to the man with the broad shoulders and long legs and smacked her lips into a determined line.

"He doesn't really want it. What would a good-looking man like that want with a picture of children?"

"Why don't you ask him why he wants it and explain why you have to have it?" Aliyah huffed impatiently.

"No."

"If that doesn't work, cry."

Iman drew in a breath of exasperation at her sister's suggestion.

"Bad joke." Aliyah shrugged, throwing up her hands. "Why don't you go say hi? Make pleasant conversation, use your feminine wiles, and he'll be putty in your hand."

Iman knew her sister was joking now. But she also recognized the devilish twist to Aliyah's brows and cringed. The matchmaker in her was rearing its ugly head.

She couldn't help considering the idea for a moment. The dark gentleman was something. Tall and broad across the shoulders, in a way she'd always found appealing in a man, his black hair cut close to his scalp, and the smoothness of his clean shaven face made her hand itch to caress it. He studied the painting with one hand in his pocket, the other hanging at his side, an aura of casual intensity surrounding him.

Iman felt the overwhelming sensation of wanting to take her place by his side. She stepped back, shocked.

He had probably come with someone. Probably not looking for company. Probably unavailable.

"Nah," she said, as offhand as possible. "He's not my type."

Aliyah's expression echoed her disbelief, but she kept quiet. Instead she pushed Iman ahead.

"Let's see if we can sneak a peek at Mr. Handsome's bid. Maybe you can beat it."

People filled the space between them, halting

their progress. "Shoot," Iman exhaled in frustration when the lights began to flash.

"May I have everyone's attention?"

Reluctantly, she and Aliyah turned toward the aristocratic voice of the hostess.

"My name is Imogene Osborne, and I am the director here at Stone Manor. I'd like to thank each and every one of you for coming this evening to support the fight for a cure for children afflicted with the AIDS virus.

"We all know there is an answer but we need resources to find it. Benefits like this help bring us one step closer to saving a child's life." Iman applauded while sneaking another look at the table. Her gaze was drawn away from the painting to the man beside it. He acknowledged her with a nod of his head. Iman bared her teeth in a semblance of a smile and returned her attention to Imogene, who had clasped her hands together gesturing with her index fingers pointed.

"Thank you for being so generous in your bids. It's for a good cause. While final bids are taken and the tallying completed, those of you with red tickets please convene in the west room to begin your tour of the house. Those with black, the east room, and those with green, remain here. Please respect the barriers protecting the rooms, and stay on the brown carpet. You will be notified after the tours are underway if you have won any of our auctioned items. Your tours will begin momentarily. Thank you for your support."

Applause rippled through the crowd and Iman turned back to the table. Her heart pounded. The collecting attendant picked up the book.

"Wait!" Pushing past a large woman in a red sequined dress and over the long wing-tipped shoe of her companion, Iman stumbled before she stood between the man and the attendant. A measure of satisfaction curled through her when Mr. Handsome, who'd been leaving the table turned and frowned. "Wait." She held up her hand to stop the attendant. "I want to place another bid."

"I'm sorry, ma'am. The bidding is closed." The attendant's sorrowful smile only made her want to plead. He moved to the next table leaving her to stare at his back. Aliyah walked up beside her.

"Did you catch him?"

"Yes. He said the bidding was closed."

Iman turned back to the man. "I was trying to catch the attendant," she offered, unable to hide her disappointment.

"I noticed." He stuck out his hand and she looked at long, strong fingers. "Cedric Hamilton. And you are?"

Her sister nudged her arm.

"Iman Parrish. Please excuse my manners," she said, grasping his hand. His warm touch made her shiver to the tips of her glittery shoes. She looked up and was captivated by caramel brown eyes, but she couldn't hold back her wistful tone. "I really wanted that painting."

His name rang a bell of familiarity and Iman searched his face until she realized how she knew him. Cedric Hamilton was on the board of directors of Stone Manor. He was one of the main reasons why she was there.

An elbow shoved into her side made her look at her sister. "Sorry. This is my older sister, Aliyah Easterbrook. Cedric Hamilton."

"Do you have to tell everyone I'm your *older* sister?"

Iman ignored the testiness in Aliyah's voice. The

handsome Cedric was having a strange effect on her. He extracted his hand from hers to take her sister's. Their shake was brief.

"Nice to meet you," she heard her sister say. "Hope to see you again. Goodnight."

Iman snapped out of the spell. "Wait Li, where are you going?"

"Jerome will be back from Jacksonville tonight, so I thought I would slip into something more revealing and be home waiting."

Iman frowned at her sister's brazen announcement and gave her a disapproving look. "Li." Her face heated in embarrassment and she knew her nose was beginning to glow a faint red.

Cedric's laugh tickled her spine. "He's a very lucky man. I hope to see you again, too." When Iman turned a stunned expression to him, both he and Aliyah burst out laughing.

"Not like that." He touched Iman's arm, leaving a warm spot before sliding his hand into his pocket. "I meant socially . . . with her husband."

"I knew what you meant." Aliyah winked, encouraging Iman toward Cedric with a nod of her head.

Iman waited for her sister to stop grinning like a fool. "Aliyah, I'm not ready to go yet. Why don't you wait for me? You drove, remember?"

"Yes, I remember. Catch a cab, all right? I'm ready to go home. Good luck with the painting." She kissed Iman's cheek, then turned to Cedric and shook his hand.

"Goodnight, Cedric. Call me tomorrow, Iman."

Iman watched Aliyah's cream dress swish around her legs as she walked into the crowd that was headed toward the west room. Aliyah raised her hand to wave and Iman did too, wishing her sister had stayed. At least with Aliyah there, she would have an opportunity to control her roiling emotions. The intensity of her physical attraction to Cedric startled her.

Iman turned back to him and looked up. The blend of shadows and firelight cast from behind him gave him a familiar yet larger than life presence.

"She's quite a lady. Is she always like that?"

In the warm light from the fireplace, his smooth, dark skin looked as delectable as Godiva chocolate. She fought the overwhelming urge to press her lips softly along the side of his face. Iman didn't know she had a thing for sideburns until she noticed Cedric's.

His questioning gaze broke her reverie.

"Always. Nothing Aliyah says surprises me any more," she answered quickly hoping her Rudolph nose wouldn't betray her. "Should you be getting back to your date?"

"I *am* my date this evening."

"Oh," Iman said. *Yes!* she thought. "And by day?" Talk about brazen. Aliyah must be rubbing off on her.

He regarded her with a long, penetrating stare. "I don't usually date myself. I'm single."

"Really?" she asked, watching the movements of his lips, wondering how they would feel touching her skin.

He nodded.

"How . . ." Their gazes caught and held. "How nice."

"I think so."

Iman pivoted on her high heels trying to get her bearings. She wasn't quite sure how to handle the explosion of desire that burst within her. She focused on the guests who entered the room using them as an easy distraction.

The lights dimmed. Unable to stop herself, Iman looked at Cedric. Something flickered to life within the dark brown depths of his eyes. It reached into her and warmed her making the backs of her thighs tingle and her knees wobbly under her gray and white evening dress.

He moved close and his jacket scraped her fingers. Intimacy was more than she'd bargained for.

His husky voice whispered close to her cheek. "Have you toured Stone Manor before?"

"No, I haven't had the pleasure yet." Iman inhaled his cologne, the faint bouquet of wine on his breath and felt lightheaded. She wanted to rest her cheek on his shoulder.

But her shoes were smart. They stayed rooted in place. His hand touched the small of her back and veered them away from the crowd to a door marked *Private.*

"Let me give you the grand tour. I'm an excellent guide." Iman found it difficult to say no. She nodded.

He opened the door allowing her to step through first. The hallway was long, narrow, and dark. Iman turned back in time to see Cedric fumble with something in his hands.

Apprehension snaked through her and she berated her hasty decision to follow him. Board of directors or not, she didn't know him. She took a step back.

"I think I should go back."

Cedric took her hand and placed a long object in it. He pushed a button. Light spilled to the floor. Iman stared down. *A flashlight.* Luckily the darkness shielded her tell tale nose and her guilty thoughts.

He pointed to the end of the hallway. "This is where the tour should actually begin. At the front door. Who ever heard of starting something in the middle?" His large hand closed around hers as he led her into the darkness, the round white circle their only guide. "There's nothing to be afraid of," he said softly. "I'll hold your hand the whole way."

As he led her from room to room, Iman listened intently to the history of the house and its occupants. She was most impressed with Cedric's knowledge of the antique European furnishings, and the unique sculpturing carved into the foundation of each room by black craftsmen. He knew every detail, even down to the year the silk damask wallpaper was hung in the dining room.

"Every room has a balcony but this one was designed to overlook downtown Atlanta." His fingers threaded through hers, his voice soft. "Isn't it beautiful?"

"Spectacular." Lights twinkled in the darkness and from this far away, the city noise eluded them, allowing them to witness its quiet splendor undisturbed. Iman loved the powerful feeling that she and Cedric were on a private island. "It's so secluded. So private."

"Like an island made for two." He looked down at her. "I feel that each time I come here."

It pleased her that his thoughts ran along the same line as hers. The mood shifted as they drew closer against a cool wind. Involuntarily, she shivered as much from the cold as from the budding emotions that sprang within her tonight.

"How long did the son live here after his father and stepmother's death?"

"Another forty years. Mitchell owned several businesses, and followed in his father's footsteps in philanthropy. He's one of my role models."

"How so?"

Cedric walked to the other side of the wooden balcony. His shoulders were stiff and he jabbed his hands into his pocket. He seemed troubled as he gazed into the cloudless sky.

"I want to teach my children those kinds of values. Mitchell learned from his father to never let adversity stop his dreams. His father was a slave, then opened a barber business in Atlanta and became a very wealthy man." His voice was awed. "Can you believe that?"

"It amazes me what people can overcome when they set their minds on a goal." Iman walked toward him.

"My girls are my pride and joy, but they're the most spoiled little people I've ever had the pleasure of meeting. I think their goal is to own the local toy store at seven years of age."

"Seven?" She shook her head, surprise making her eyebrows raise. "A precocious age. They must be a handful raising them alone."

"I'm fortunate to have both sets of grandparents to help whenever I need it. They help in the spoiling too, though. The girls love it."

This time Iman smiled. "Girls are made for spoiling. Don't be too hard on them."

He shook his head, his forehead creasing with thought. "No, they're worse than spoiled, and tonight for the first time, I feel the way I'm raising them may be a mistake." He finally looked at her. "Do you have children?"

"Not yet. One day."

Another breeze blew, this time making them step back with its chilling force. Iman shivered again.

"I wasn't thinking. Come back inside. You must be freezing." Guiding her by her elbow, he led her through the door and unfastened his jacket. "Put this on until you warm up."

"Thank you." She wrapped the coal black jacket around her shoulders, his body heat warming her. "I really should be going soon."

"What about the painting?" This time his eyes danced when he smiled.

Iman rolled her eyes. "You're trying to be funny, aren't you?" Cedric led the way back to the main area of the manor, a huge grin on his face. He left the flashlight in its original spot. "I'm sure my five-hundred dollar bid was slammed the moment you picked up the pen. Take care of it. A good friend of mine painted it."

Iman reluctantly slid out of his coat, handing it back to him. Their scents mingled enticingly, and the loss of its weight made her feel fragile.

He failed at looking wounded. "You make me feel guilty for wanting the painting." Iman knew he was joking. He didn't look guilty. He looked edible.

The centers of his eyes were dark pools and Iman felt herself absorbed by the black depths. She wanted to caress the masculine lines on his face, feel the sandy texture of his jaw against her palm, rest her head on his strong, broad shoulder. Instead, she had to look up several inches from her above average height to focus on his slightly crooked bow tie, Cedric's only outward imperfection.

Then their gazes locked. The house was now quiet, having been vacated by the other guests. Waiters quietly cleaned around them.

"I don't mean to make you feel bad. It's for a good cause." Iman stopped Cedric's fingers from drawing lazy circles on her arm. "Maybe if you win, you'll let me see it sometime. Right now, I need to get a taxi. It was an unexpected pleasure to meet you, Mr. Hamilton."

Iman squeezed his hand and hurried away afraid if she stayed any longer, she would embarrass herself by stepping into an embrace he would break. She retrieved her cape, spoke to Imogene for a moment, then looked over her shoulder before she called a cab.

No Cedric.

It was probably just as well. This Cinderella feeling had to be a warning. He probably *was* too good to be true.

Chapter Three

The outside of Stone Manor provided its namesake. Stacked stone walls installed in the early 1920s bordered the ground level of the house. Erosion made it necessary to relandscape the property, but the magnificent house had survived the years well. There remained the old southern style that made the house an unofficial historical monument in downtown Atlanta.

Iman descended the stairs into the parking lot and checked for her cab. A car rolled to a stop in front of her.

"May I play a humble second to a yellow cab?"

Iman shifted on cold toes, bent down, and stared at Cedric in the silver luxury car. The last car in the driveway pulled around them and Imogene Osborne waved good-night. There were no yellow cabs in sight. Heat wafted from the open window beckoning her. She wanted to get in, but held back.

"I should probably wait."

"I don't want to leave you out here. It's your choice."

A brisk breeze swept up her cape, the imitation fur collar doing nothing to protect her neck and head from the assaulting wind. She decided quickly. "If you insist."

Iman pulled the door handle and as elegantly as her stiff legs would allow, slid in. "I live near Piedmont Park. Were you really going to leave?"

His dimpled smile warmed her in places that hadn't felt heat in a long time. He turned the steering wheel and soon they were traveling down Martin Luther King Drive. "I saw your cab leave a long time ago while you were talking to Imogene. I was pretty sure I could convince you."

Iman nodded, remembering their brief chat. She fastened her seat belt and settled back in the luxurious leather.

"You didn't forget your purse did you?"

Iman couldn't resist teasing. "Imogene told me you won my picture, now you want my money?"

"I wasn't asking because I want your money." He chuckled. "You're very funny. It's been a while since I've found anything to laugh about." He pumped the brakes as they turned the corner. Iman enjoyed the rumble of his laughter and his eyes twinkled when he smiled.

"I didn't really think you were asking me for money."

"I'm glad to hear that. I asked out of habit. My girls are seven, and if we leave the house without their purses . . ." His brows furrowed in a pained expression. "There's hell to pay."

"You know all that tissue kept in those purses is very important," she teased. "What are their names?"

"Anika and Medina. Quite a combination."

"First grade, right?"

He regarded her from the corner of his eye. "Lucky guess."

Iman shook her head. "Experience. I worked with

a group of seven-year-olds last summer in a reading program. I have a way with them."

He laughed. "You do, do you? My girls can change any person's mind about kids with their antics." He laughed to himself. "They're my life."

Iman studied him for a moment as they drove in silence. He seemed to have erected a barrier around himself with his pronouncement. A single father raising his daughters alone was something she didn't see very often, but if he handled them with the same smooth control he used to maneuver the car, they were probably just spoiled, little daddy's girls.

She thought of the close relationship she'd had with her own father until his death several years ago. Being a daddy's girl was very special.

"I think they've spoiled you. You wear fatherhood well."

He blinked several times, surprised. "Thank you." Iman knew she'd caught him off guard with the compliment, but parents were rarely patted on the back for a job well done.

As the car slowed then stopped at the red light, Iman noticed women hovering over sidewalk grates for warmth.

White smoke fogged them, obscuring their faces, but it was obvious they would spend the cold November night on the street. Cedric leaned over to watch as a short person slipped out of a box. It horrified Iman to discover it was a young girl.

Iman couldn't drag her eyes away from the sight of the two homeless people, until she heard Cedric speaking on the phone. He gave the women's location and description and instructed the person to make sure they had a warm bed for the night if they wanted it.

She released a pent up breath, and allowed the relief of Cedric's actions to wash over her. How she viewed him grew disproportionately to his average male size.

A hero, she thought, his chivalrous attitude touching her more than she thought possible. They pulled away from a green light and the image of an old and young woman fitting themselves into the box were left behind.

"What a life," Cedric murmured.

"Because of you, at least they won't freeze." Iman turned to look out the back window as the women grew smaller the farther away they drove. Eventually they disappeared, but the memory would forever be embedded in her mind.

She was a little taken aback at the harshness of his voice when he spoke. "There's nothing like being cold and not being able to do a damn thing about it."

The seat belt pulled across her chest and Iman adjusted it to a more comfortable position.

"Ever been cold?" His voice held more challenge than curiosity.

Controlled pain tightened the skin around his mouth. She sensed an underlying current of anger. It had something to do with the women they'd just seen. Iman reached out to comfort him. She answered cautiously, unsure of where it would lead. "I've been plenty cold. I grew up in Buffalo, New York."

He grimaced and patted her hand, as if to dismiss her response. "You were lucky. That was voluntary."

Iman remained quiet for a tense moment then asked, "Do you want to talk about it?"

"No." Cedric shut her out. She resisted the urge to try to soothe his troubles away. Iman withdrew her hand and watched the lights of cars passing on the other side of the street.

"I need to stop at the store before I take you home. Do you mind?"

"That's fine," she whispered.

Cedric turned the steering wheel and they entered the near deserted interstate. Fewer cars passed the further they drove. The store had to be an out of the way place because there wasn't much open at this late hour, in this direction, she thought.

Iman trusted the instincts that told her she was in good hands. Cedric Hamilton was known and well respected in the community. Besides, Imogene had spoken so highly of him tonight, the discussion had piqued her interest.

Iman settled back against the seat and let the smooth motion of the car calm her questions.

Finally, Cedric glanced at her, then returned his gaze to the road ahead of them. His voice was more relaxed when he spoke.

"How do you think the auction went tonight? We planned it with the hopes of raising money for AIDS research, but we also wanted to bring the needs of Stone Manor to the public's attention."

"Considering I lost my painting, I'm sure *somebody,*" she exaggerated, "left happy."

"You can come see that painting any time your heart desires." His fingers linked with hers and squeezed lightly. Tiny jets of sensation shot through her arm.

"Anyway, I thought it was a huge success. I was honored to meet the governor and the mayor. Even the police chief showed up. Imogene and the board really pulled out the stops on this. I know you're on the board of directors. How close is Stone Manor to being accepted as a historical site?"

His eyes narrowed thoughtfully. "The chairman of the historical society was there as well as several of the members. The board hopes to know something soon."

"Do you think tonight's event raised enough interest?" Iman asked. Stone Manor was too important to Atlanta history to be destroyed for lack of funds.

"Definitely." His voice rang with confidence. Cedric disengaged his hand from hers. As he wrestled with his tie, Iman watched. He looked immensely pleased with himself when he tossed it over his shoulder onto the back seat.

"Better?"

"Much." He grinned. "You want to—"

"No, thanks. I think I'll keep all my pieces on."

Their silence lengthened and Iman's thoughts gravitated back to the man beside her.

Cedric's work to save Stone Manor had brought him to her attention many months ago. Widely respected as a shrewd and powerful businessman, his fundraising abilities had saved the old home from the wrecker's ball.

Iman had been informed by chatty Imogene Osborne over lunch two weeks before that Cedric sat on the board of directors of several prestigious companies. She'd also reported that while Cedric Hamilton was a successful businessman, his personal life was a bit of a mystery.

At the time, Iman had listened with polite indifference. Now, she had a strong need to know. She cast a sidelong gaze at her riding partner and enjoyed what she saw. His warm eyes and gorgeous lashes made her think of relaxing in a smooth Caribbean pool. His reassuring touch and easy manner also didn't jive with Imogene's veiled assessment.

There was nothing mysterious about the way she felt about Cedric. Her attraction was bold. And though she hadn't known him long, his work had been one of the reasons she'd accepted the offer to teach a class about Kwanzaa at the manor. Something clicked in her mind. Iman turned to look at him.

"I really admire the work you did last year to open Robinson Community Center. I'd heard about the private investors not coming through with the necessary funds. Aliyah and I wouldn't be teaching there now if you hadn't stepped in and raised the money."

He smiled appreciatively. "You were a natural choice because of your teaching experience." His voice was velvet soft. "Of course, had I known what I know now, there wouldn't have been any competition."

"And what do you know? I hope my qualifications set me above the other candidates."

He leaned toward her. In the faint light from the dash board she saw the outline of his face and the firm set of his jaw. "There's no question about that. We had many offers to teach, but once Imogene reported to the board that she'd taken your class and how it changed her life, you were in." Iman felt relieved and proud.

While Imogene was chatty and a bit of a gossip, she and many of the board members had worked hard this past month to pass along the principles of Kwanzaa at Robinson Community Center.

Kwanzaa was meant to bring families and communities together to celebrate the "fruits" of their labor and to set new goals and make plans for the next year. Cedric had been an instrumental part of that successful team of people who made it all come together. She wondered if he knew what a great effect his deeds had had.

"There are a few more reasons," he said.

Her stomach fluttered when his lips curled in a seductive smile. Somehow she didn't think her master's degree had been what tipped the scales.

"What are they?"

"We have the same taste in art, you're beautiful, single, and have a nose that glows. You were a shoo-in."

Iman touched the tip of her nose. Heat rushed to her cheeks. Soon she would look just like Rudolph.

She laughed. "So you've rounded out your resumé with comedian. I think somebody should keep his day job."

He hooted, laughing. "I think somebody should be nice to me, especially if said individual wants to see that painting ever again."

"I'm crushed you'd hold that over my head."

"I have to keep some leverage, don't I?"

"Tell me about your work at Dix."

"I'll tell you only on the condition that you tell me about Kwanzaa first. The other reason we decided to utilize Stone Manor's facilities for the classes was because of the overwhelming interest in the celebration. Refresh my memory. It sounds like something my daughters need."

Iman always enjoyed sharing the story of Kwanzaa's beginning.

"Dr. Maulana Karenga first celebrated the holiday in 1966. His intention was to give African-American people an opportunity to learn about their history and customs. Many of us fall into the commercialism trap that surrounds Christmas. We spend money we don't have and buy things we don't really need. Kwanzaa isn't like that."

"How is it different?" He frowned. "It's on the tail end of Christmas."

"It's based on the concept of a harvest festival that was traditionally practiced throughout Africa. It brings communities, friends, and family together to celebrate the 'fruits' of their labor and to give thanks to the Creator for their blessings. As a collective group, you evaluate your achievements and set goals for the year ahead."

He considered this a moment. "I've heard there are rules you follow during that week."

Iman shook her head. "Not rules. Principles, and it's not just that week. It's a lifelong commitment. We start on the twenty-sixth with *Umoja*. It means unity. *Kujichagulia,* self-determination. *Ujima,* collective work and responsibility. *Ujamaa,* cooperative economics. *Nia,* purpose. *Kuumba,* creativity, and *Imani* means faith. When you have all those factors working in harmony in your life, you're physically, morally, and spiritually able to harvest success."

"It seems as if those principles are practiced by people everyday anyway."

"They are to certain degrees. Kwanzaa is about incorporating all those principles into one celebration and governing your life by them."

"Do you have a favorite part of the celebration?"

Without hesitation she answered, *"Kutoa majina."*

"What's kootooa—?"

Iman enunciated the words. "Koo-Tee-ah ma-JEEN-ah. It's the calling and remembering of ancestors and heroes. I always remember what a fighter my father was. He was a fireman. My dad was a hard working, but gentle man. He was my hero." Cedric took her hand seeming to sense her vulnerability.

Iman blinked back the moisture that gathered in the corner of her eyes. It had been a long time since she'd felt emotional about her father passing. She held onto Cedric's hand and tried to catch a glimpse of the highway sign as they headed off the exit. The car wound up and around seeming to go in an endless spiral. Dense bare branches tangled on the side of the road, visible only in brief glances. She glanced at the dash clock, surprised to discover they'd been riding over two hours.

Iman looked out the window at the restaurant that stood at the top of the mountain.

"Pardon my French, but where in the blazes are we?"

Cedric answered solemnly. "Lookout Mountain, Tennessee."

Chapter Four

"Do you do this often?" Iman asked after returning from the ladies' room and taking the seat beside him. A fresh application of red lipstick coated her lips, and he drew his gaze away from them to meet hers.

Cedric felt himself relax for the first time since they'd entered the restaurant. Her teasing smile lightened the load on his mind. "I promise"—he held up his hand in a Boy Scout's honor salute—"I've never done this before. You're the first woman I've ever brought to Tennessee for a date."

"I'm thrilled at the honor." Her voice grew husky and her eyes shimmered seductively.

Over entrees of fried chicken, loaded potato skins, and fried cheese sticks, Cedric took the opportunity to study Iman. Short, carefully styled curls, accented her smooth nut brown complexion. The dark warmth of her eyes was addicting, making him feel calm, at ease. Cedric resisted snuggling against the delicate curve of her slender neck and inhaling deeply of her. He just wanted to relax and enjoy her company.

She munched heartily on the chicken leg, oblivious to his visual examination. She finished and laid the bone on the extra plate. After she wiped her mouth with the cloth napkin she looked at him.

"You're not worried about your arteries, are you?"

Cedric waved his hand in a sometimes expression. "I like fried chicken. I know what doctors say about cholesterol. But the best chicken in Tennessee is served"—he poked the table with his finger—"right here."

"You didn't have to bring me to Tennessee to get fried chicken. My kitchen would have done nicely."

"Seriously?" His expression bordered on disbelief. "Don't tease me, Iman. I don't get good fried chicken everywhere, so you'd better be prepared for a visit if you're serious."

"I am. Call first," she teased. "I don't do 'to go' orders."

"What's your number?" He was pleased when she rattled off the numbers and started in on her meal again.

She didn't eat much fried food, Cedric assessed. Her figure was too nice and shapely in all the right places. He was relieved she hadn't slapped him for damn near kidnapping her and bringing her to Tennessee.

Hideaway Mountain Restaurant was one of his favorite places and without consciously thinking about it, he'd wanted to share one of his private places with her.

His gaze glided over her figure hugging gray dress. She was quite beautiful. *Would she like my kids?*

Where had that thought come from? Cedric hurried to retrieve his clattering fork. The waiter rushed to replace it and scooted quietly away.

"Is something wrong with my dress?"

"Not at all," he said appreciatively. "I like your dress just fine," he said, scrambling for a graceful way out. "It's just that I would think you would be dressed more traditionally. More . . ." he hesitated, not wanting to offend her.

She gave him a knowing look. "More African?"

"Well, yes. I suppose that's what I mean. I have to confess, I don't know much about the traditions." She wiped her mouth on her napkin again. Cedric couldn't explain his sense of regret at the gesture.

"I do dress traditionally on occasion. But that has nothing to do with Kwanzaa directly. I dress in traditional African clothes because I feel good in them. I think they accentuate the inner beauty of the person wearing them." She laid her fork on the table and looked him over in a way that set his pulse racing double-time.

"In fact, this evening, I imagined you wearing the traditional clothing." She eyed him from head to toe. "You looked quite handsome."

"Were you checking me out?"

Iman looked away, controlling a grin that revealed even white teeth. Her long earrings hit against her jaw. "No, I wasn't."

"You're lying," he said and shoved a forkful of spicy rice in his mouth to hide a teasing smile.

"Not."

"I can tell, Iman."

"Who are you, Santa? You can tell whether I've been naughty or nice?"

Cedric groaned, crossing his index fingers in front of her. "Bad word. Tonight my daughter, Anika, asked me if Santa is going to make two trips to the North Pole because the first sleigh full of presents will be hers. She faxed me an updated list this morning. She's sure she's getting that many."

"Is she?"

Her serious tone caught his attention. Cedric sat

back in his chair. He rarely spoke of his girls. His mother and step-father, and Lenora's parents called him overprotective, but he didn't care. The girls were so important to him that in the past he'd refused to share them.

Iman covered his hand. "Don't get quiet on me. I'm just asking if she has any reason to believe she's getting less than she thinks." Cedric looked down at her hand. It was soft and supporting in a way that if he weren't careful would have him spilling his guts.

He answered honestly. "No, she doesn't."

Iman resumed eating. "So, what are you going to do about it?"

"What?"

"Her theory that Santa will return to the North Pole after stopping at your place. Millions of children around the world will be disappointed if Santa gets too tired and doesn't get to deliver their presents."

Cedric felt a bubble of laughter build in his chest. He grinned sheepishly, leaned his head back and groaned. "That's crazy, isn't it? What am I going to do?"

"Can her mom talk to her?"

"Only to her spirit. My wife is dead."

"I'm sorry." Her gaze dropped to her plate. Cedric wiped his mouth and sipped his imported beer. "It happened during their birth. She began to hemorrhage, and the doctor couldn't stop it. She died two hours after Medina was born."

"I'm sorry," she said. An odd expression crossed her face. He wondered if she felt sorry for them. Cedric hurried to quell any such thoughts.

"Thank you. We've overcome it."

She smiled tenderly and his heart expanded. Cedric glanced at his watch, the late hour making him wish for once he could add more hours to the day. He signaled for the check and paid the bill. Iman said nothing when he left a large tip but Cedric noticed her eyes widen.

They hurried to the car against the chill and with relief got inside. Its comfort enveloped them as they drove back toward Atlanta. "Where do you live again?" he asked.

Her smoky laughter tickled his ears and he couldn't help reciprocating with his own chuckle.

"Near Piedmont Park. I'll direct you once we get close."

He nodded. "This may sound like a silly question, but do you believe in Santa at all?"

"No," Iman said quietly. "I believe in Christmas. I celebrate the religious aspects of the holiday rather than the commercial." She grew thoughtful. "But if I had children, Santa would visit our home. Aliyah and I used to have so much fun watching the snow fall in Buffalo hoping we would catch a glimpse of ol' Saint Nick. It was a wonderful time in our lives. My children deserve that thrill."

Cedric remained quiet. He'd never had a tree. Santa never visited the leaky, one-room apartment he'd shared with his mother. He hadn't had a reason to believe. Not as a child. Only through his girls was he able to recapture those lost moments.

"Now that I've talked your ear off about what I do, tell me about your plans for the future at Dix."

Cedric launched into a discussion on his dreams of finding medicines that would aid in the irradication of diseases like sickle cell anemia, diabetes, and AIDS. He was surprised at how easy Iman was to talk to, but soon they were admiring the twinkling lights that draped bare branches throughout her neighborhood. Cedric stopped in the driveway she indicated. He left the engine running, not wanting her to go inside. He realized the evening had been the best adult fun he'd had in a long time.

Over the gray fur collar of her cape, she turned to look at him. His chest tightened.

"Iman I—"

"Take my card." They spoke in unison.

"I don't—"

"Oh. You don't want it?" She fidgeted with the card, then dropped it. It fluttered to the floor.

"No—" Cedric shook his head. He bent to retrieve it, but she stopped him.

"I understand. I just thought . . . well . . ." Her brows furrowed and when she met his gaze, Cedric saw a flash of determination.

Iman held up her hands. "Cedric, I hardly ever give advice on raising children. But I've worked with kids and I know that Kwanzaa teaches them responsibility, they learn to love and care for things, and they also learn how to earn them. Let me help you," she said softly.

He sank into her gaze. "Yes—"

Cedric stroked her bottom lip with his thumb. To his delight it quivered and she lightly caught it between her teeth before letting go. Maybe he could let her know how much he wanted to see her again with his touch since his voice was failing him. His hand dropped to his side.

"I try to make class fun for them." She dampened her lips and went on. "You said yes, didn't you?" she whispered.

The shaking sigh of her whisper drove him wild inside. "I said yes."

Iman opened the door, the lights brightening the

dark interior. "I'm sorry. You have to stop me sometimes. I can go on and on."

"Really," he said, a smile tugging at his mouth as he leaned closer. "I hadn't noticed."

Cedric lay in bed, head resting against his palms. He had been this way for over an hour since dropping Iman at home and picking up the blueberries for breakfast. Yet sleep hadn't come. The last few moments in the car with Iman replayed in his mind.

For an instant, he had been a tongue-tied kid again, and had blown his opportunity to ask her for another date.

Quickly, he flipped on the bedside light and hurried into his dressing room. Inside his tuxedo jacket pocket, Cedric found what he sought. Taking her business card back to bed with him, he crawled under the covers and stared at it.

Iman Y. Parrish. The scripted lettering looked whimsical and made him think of what a good sense of humor she had. Though easily embarrassed, she was charming.

At the bottom of the card were both her home and work numbers. He stared at them until they were etched in his memory. So there was hope for his last minute loss of speech capabilities. At least he could call her.

When he'd leaned close before she'd gotten out of the car, instinct told him she was going to let him kiss her good night.

Only her lips never touched his.

Cedric resisted kicking himself. Some kind of businessman he'd turned out to be. His job involved controlled predictions, near perfect assessments, and precision. There was no margin for error. But those learned techniques had eluded him this evening.

In the darkness of the car, Iman had lifted his hand, maneuvered it over and around hers several times, then let it go. She was out of the car and into the house before he could react.

He hadn't caught on until it was too late. He hadn't even walked her to the door. Now, of course, he knew what she'd been doing.

She'd given him a soul shake.

"Can I pour the blueberries in now?"

Plastic high heels clomped against the floor as Anika headed toward them holding the cup of blueberries over her head. Cedric reached behind Medina to steady Anika's arm as she slid between them.

"Pour them in," he instructed, then let her arm go. He glanced toward her feet. "Must you wear those now?"

Keeping a watchful eye on Medina, who held the hand mixer precariously over the mixing bowl, he took hold of Anika's arm again and helped her to the chair. "Medina." His voice raised with warning.

"Yes?" they both answered.

"Be careful."

Cedric took one look around the kitchen and made a mental note to get an extra special Christmas gift for his housekeeper, Joan. How she did it everyday, he would never know. From top to bottom, the kitchen was a mess. He dreaded cleaning it.

Medina took his moment of reflection to raise the mixer. Pancake batter spewed everywhere.

"Stop!" he barked.

The order came too late. Startled by his voice, Medina lost her balance and slipped backward. The mixer flew across the counter spitting batter as it twirled.

Cedric bit back a curse, grabbed the handle, and pulled. "Sit down. Right now!"

The cord snapped from the wall and the kitchen fell into a stony silence. Cedric held the counter for support, counting to ten, then back to zero. The girls stared at him with worried expressions. Medina's chin quivered and her mouth bowed.

"I'm sorry," he started, hoping to head off the inevitable. "I didn't mean to yell."

Cedric cringed when Medina let a loud wail rip anyway.

"You screamed at me!" Sliding on heels that matched her sister's, Medina stomped to the kitchen door. He wondered for an instant if she would storm out, something he absolutely forbade.

"May I be excused?" she asked tearfully.

Cedric decided they both needed a moment to cool down. "Yes, go ahead."

Anika crossed her arms over her chest in a way that reminded him of himself when he was lecturing them.

"You should say you're sorry."

Cedric bit his tongue as he listened to his seven-year-old offer him advice. He looked at her inquisitively. *Why is everything always Dad's fault?* He braced his sticky hands on the counter. "I already apologized, Anika. But your sister is stubborn. She'll be back."

"You always say stubborn is good. Is it bad now?"

The sticky mixture on his hands made him want to eat his words. "No. It's just that you have to listen to learn. You girls have only been here for seven years. You don't know everything. I've been here thirty-two years, and I don't know everything."

Wisdom-filled eyes stared at him. "You know a lot, Daddy. Otherwise you couldn't have passed to the tenth grade." Anika patted him on the back and then stuck her finger in the mix. She licked it off while he wiped at the drying goo on the counter.

"Thank you, sweetie. That makes me feel better." He rubbed her back in return. "Do me a favor and go get your sister, please."

Cedric cooked as many pancakes as batter would allow while alone in the kitchen. When they returned, they wore their fuzzy bear slippers and had brushed their hair. The gesture was meant to appease him and it did. He hugged them both and waited while they quietly got their placemats and set the table.

"Daddy? It's okay if you lose your temper and yeyeww, and make me cry sometimes."

Cedric had a fleeting flash of the future when the girls would have boyfriends and eventually husbands. He didn't want them to think any type of verbal abuse was all right. Silently, he damned his behavior.

Thick maple syrup oozed down the pancakes and onto the plate before he turned the bottle upright. He brought the plates to the table and sat down.

"Medina, it's not okay to yell and make you cry. I'm sorry."

"I forgive you, Daddy." Cedric felt worse when her forgiving gaze rested on him. Children were so innocent. So pure. She actually felt sorry for him for yelling at her.

There had been a lot of yelling when he was a child, but nothing was worse than the silence that remained once his father had left for good. He pushed that memory from his mind. It didn't matter now. No one could turn back the hands of time.

They said grace and began eating.

Iman's declaration of having a way with children

flew into his mind. He immediately remembered his decision about Kwanzaa. Cedric decided to broach the subject while they were eating.

"Girls, I thought it would be fun for us to learn about a celebration called Kwanzaa. It's *Kiswahili,* meaning 'first fruits.' "

"Why?" Anika asked between bites.

Cedric smoothed more thick syrup over his pancakes before he answered. "Because it teaches you about African-American culture and traditions." Iman's voice seemed to come from the air as it reminded him of the rich celebration he'd never explored.

"There are seven principles of the"—Cedric searched his mind for the word Iman had used last night—*"Nguzo Saba.* I can't explain it all, but I think we should give it a try."

Both girls shrugged, looking unconvinced.

"Where are we going to learn it? Television?" Anika's voice was hopeful.

Cedric cringed. That was his weakness, especially old black and white movies. He shook his head to her question. "I met someone, a woman named Ms. Parrish." Cedric enjoyed the way her name tripped off his tongue. "She teaches the class. She's a very nice lady."

The girls started snickering. "Daddy, you have this goofy wook on your face. Is she your girw-friend?"

Caught off guard at the question, he stuffed his mouth full of pancakes. His jaws worked and he tried to stop smiling. "She's not my girlfriend. She's just a very nice lady. So, what do you think?"

The girls consulted each other and Medina nodded, while Anika regarded him suspiciously.

"We still get our presents from Santa?"

"Yes. One has nothing to do with the other. But

I'm going to warn you, Santa doesn't take kindly to greedy children. And I know for a fact that any act of selfishness will not be rewarded. I haven't mailed your lists yet, but I think if you cut them down to four items, Santa will be pleased."

Dumbfounded, they stared open mouthed at him. He chewed thoughtfully then wiped his mouth. "Maybe three items."

"No, four!" they practically sang. "May we be excused?"

Before he could properly answer, they dashed from the kitchen leaving a puff of flour in their wake.

Cedric smiled and withdrew Iman's card from his pocket. Suddenly kitchen duty didn't seem so bad after all.

Chapter Five

"What did you do again?"

Iman sipped from an ancient tea cup as Aliyah paced in front of her. Shaking her head, she lowered the cup and bent low over her old Singer sewing machine, completing the edging on the *mkeke* mat. The phone rang and her gaze snapped to it. She held her breath, hoping, but not wanting to get her hopes up. They deflated when Aliyah lowered the receiver and continued her tirade.

"Why couldn't you just ask him to take you out again, Iman? Have I taught you nothing about dating men?"

"I gave him my card. Well, almost," she muttered, remembering her fumbled attempt. "Anyway, that's how it's done these days. You've been out of the dating scene too long," Iman informed her sister knowingly. "People give each other cards and hope the other will call."

"Did he give you his?"

Iman bent her head over the machine, her foot leveling the presser foot. Fabric spilled from the back of the machine. "No."

"See? He was probably wondering what planet you were from," Aliyah scoffed. "He was probably wondering if you had dated anyone over eighteen recently. Only kids play games like that. Back in our day—"

"The man asked the woman out," Iman finished for her. She defended herself. "He must not have wanted me to have it because he didn't offer it."

"Well after you gave him the soul shake, can you blame him?" Aliyah pounded her chest and gave her the Black Power fist. Iman burst out laughing.

"You're a fool. Don't we have another order you can prepare while you advise me on the finer points of dating in the nineties? For which I might add you have no experience since you've been married this entire decade."

Aliyah gave her a sisterly kiss on the cheek and mussed her already destroyed hairdo.

"I just hoped you would get married before the next millennium."

"You're sooo funny."

"Tell me really, was he nice?"

"He didn't scratch his butt once." Iman straightened at her sister's warning glance. She didn't want to tell Aliyah she hadn't slept a wink all night. Correction, she reminded herself. All morning. And it was broad daylight before she'd even closed her eyes. Once she had, every gesture and facial expression, every shrug, and even the timber of his laughter replayed itself over and over in her mind.

"He was more than nice. Li, I've never met a more attentive man. He really listened. Usually, I yawn and sigh in that order when I'm out on a date because I'm bored to death listening to my date drone on and on about himself. Cedric wasn't like that. He asked about me and listened to my answers. Honey child, I could get used to that." She shook herself from the cloud. "He's got to have faults. Nobody is that good and still single."

"It's possible. I hope he calls, Sugar Baby." They slipped easily back into the names they'd made up for each other so many years ago.

Iman lifted the *mkeke* mat from the machine and held it carefully flat. The cardboard box lying on another worktable was half full of items needed to have a Kwanzaa feast.

"Aliyah, make yourself useful and give me the *kinara.* I already have the candles packaged, but I'm missing some things." Her sister brought the wooden candle holder that would hold three red, one black, and three green candles.

"Let's go down the checklist." Aliyah glanced at the contents in the box. They positioned themselves assembly line style. "Do you have the *Mazao* fruits and vegetables, and the *mkeke* mat?"

"Got it." Iman nodded affirmatively.

"*Zawadi* gifts?"

Iman hurried to the shelves lining the back of the room and removed the forgotten examples of gifts. "Got it."

"Condoms?"

"What!"

"You should always be prepared," her sister said with a leering smile. "I'll drop some off this afternoon."

"I can handle my personal business, Aliyah. What's next on the list?"

"The phone," Aliyah said to the ringing interruption.

"Got it," Iman answered, relieved to change the subject. "Hello?"

"Iman Y. Parrish, please."

"This is—" She shivered in anticipation. She knew immediately who it was. After all, once she'd fallen asleep this morning, all she'd heard was his voice.

"This is Cedric Hamilton."

"Hi." Iman fanned herself with one of the "Addie" books her company suggested as a *Zawadi* gift. It had suddenly gotten hot in the office.

"What does the Y stand for?"

"Mmm?"

"The Y in your name."

"Yvette."

"Very nice." His voice deepened, and she swooned for Aliyah, who left the room with a huge grin on her face. "Does anyone ever call you that?"

"No. My sister calls me . . . Never mind."

"What?" he coaxed.

"I'm not telling," Iman vowed. Hearing Sugar Baby off *his* lips seemed too intimate. It was a natural defense, she assured herself. They'd only known each other for such a short time. But that didn't explain why her attraction felt absolutely right.

"Don't tell me," his voice echoed in her ear. "I like uncovering secrets." The challenge came through the phone lines, leaving her ear heated and tingly.

"Well," she teased to ease her discomfort, "this is one you'll never hear from me."

He laughed and the hope that she would be able to complete any more work flew out the window. There were orders to fill, but Iman knew she wouldn't be able to focus. His laugh and the sound of his voice through the receiver would dominate her thoughts.

"I called to apologize," he said.

Disappointment ebbed through her veins, slowing her thundering heart. "You forgot to tell me you're engaged to be married, right?"

"No, that's not it."

"You're a wanted man and the police are at your door?"

He chuckled. "No, to both parts."

Her heart rate returned to its former drum roll pace.

"Well then, what?"

"I meant to walk you to your door last night, but I was stunned by your—"

"Handshake," she finished for him. "It surprises people sometimes."

He cut off her nervous chattering. "I enjoyed your company and I want to see you again. Do you have plans for later today?"

Excitement rushed through her. "No. I don't have any specific plans. What did you have in mind?"

He chuckled deep in his throat. Iman's lower body warmed in response. She sat straight up in her chair.

"I thought we'd go skating. Dress casual and bring a change of clothes for dinner."

"Sounds like an adventure. I'll be ready. Cedric?"

"Yes?"

Iman blurted before she lost her nerve, "Thanks for calling. I'll see you later."

"Cedric, got a minute?"

"Sure, Ronald," Cedric said, while depositing the receiver into the cradle. He waved his vice president into his office. "Come on in. What's up?"

Ronald sat in the chair across from Cedric's before he answered.

"A representative from an organization called Retired Seniors of Georgia or RSG is requesting to see you. I've talked with the gentleman on several occasions, but I don't think what I've said is satisfactory anymore."

"What does he want?"

"He wants Dix to lower the prices on twelve medications that are predominantly used by the elderly. Here's the list."

Cedric's eyebrows quirked as he stared at the neatly typed medications. He whistled low. "Does he want the shirts off our backs too?"

Ronald shrugged. "Eventually we're going to have to see him. He's threatening to picket if he doesn't get a meeting. He's here right now."

Cedric stood and buttoned his jacket. "Ask him in. Might as well deal with this now." Ronald rose from the chair and walked to the door. "Any kinks I should know about in the Blythe deal?"

"No sir. Business as usual." Cedric nodded and the man left.

Patiently Cedric waited for Jack McClure, president of RSG, to stop speaking. The elderly man was soft spoken, but had the eyes of an eagle. He seemed to sense whenever Cedric wanted to interrupt and would neatly thwart his objection with a preplanned counter argument.

After fifteen more minutes of careful listening, Cedric tried to inconspicuously smooth frustration from his face. This was going on too long. "Mr. McClure," he cut in, "I understand your concerns, but from a business standpoint, I can't simply cut prices."

"Why? The cereal companies did it. You can do it."

"Yes, sir," Cedric said admiring the man's quickness. "But they're conglomerates. The levels in this company are far smaller, the profit margins are also. Really there is no comparison. I'm afraid Dix can't do what you're asking. Perhaps we can devise another program where seniors can go for blood pressure or diabetes checkups once a month."

The elderly man's smooth face broke into a smile. "Appeasing will only get us so far without the proper medications. But, we'll take it. And a decrease in the drug prices too." Jack extended his hand. He spoke before Cedric could object. "We may have lost round one, but Mr. Hamilton, old folks are like pesky relatives. Everybody knows one, got one or gonna be one. We'll meet again."

Cedric shook the man's hand and saw him out.

Iman massaged her rear and watched with jealous envy as Cedric rollerskated with great ease toward her. It seemed as though she'd spent more time on her bottom than on her skates.

"I used to be good at this," she grumbled when he dug in his stopper and halted by her side.

"You told me." Cedric's patience was neverending as he helped her up for the fifth time. "The next skate is couples only. That should stop you from running over those bothersome kids again."

"That's not funny." Yet, Iman couldn't help laughing. She swallowed a groan when she straightened from the hardwood floor and held onto Cedric's waist. Relieved to be standing, she let him guide her. He bracketed his arms around her on the carpeted waist-high wall, while watching the skating monitor clear children from the floor.

Her body moved before her brain could send out the stop order. She lifted her hand to his jaw, turned his face to her and kissed his lips.

For a suspended moment, Iman thought she'd made a mistake. "Oh, shoot," she murmured against Cedric's mouth.

The air was squeezed from her lungs. His arms

tightened around her waist until her skates left the floor.

Her hesitation evaporated with his words. "Don't move. This is right." His lips covered hers gently, persuading them to accept him. Iman opened without hesitation enjoying the silky feel of his tongue as it lit fires within her depths.

Suddenly she was floating, the strength of his chest never separating from hers. Iman wound her arms around his neck and broke the kiss, but not the bond that forged itself between them as they skated around the rink.

Skating had been a dream compared to horseback riding, Iman thought as she slid off the back of the powerful animal and walked as if it were still between her legs. Her aching bones was why it took Cedric nearly two weeks of daily dates and smooth talking to convince her to give riding a try.

The stable hand led the huge brown mare away to be rubbed down in the barn.

Iman sighed, glad to see the horse go.

She groaned uncomfortably. Her body was paying for every ounce of pleasure she had derived this afternoon.

She glanced back at Cedric, who was dismounting. Fluid grace, she thought with a tinge of jealousy. She had all but fallen off the back of her horse.

Cedric stood beside his black mare offering it carrots and worshipful pats. His face was unmarred by strain as he played with the animal. He looked at home on the ranch. Iman rather liked it too. She dragged her hands over her wind blown face and shivered. They'd started early that morning, but now the temperature had begun to drop.

"Cedric, I'm freezing."

He left the horse in the care of another stable hand and squeezed her shoulder, dropping his hand to her waist.

"You're always cold," he said gently.

Iman let her hand rest on his and enjoyed the leisurely stroll back to the house and the secure feeling his solid chest provided. The unexpected invitation to spend the weekend with his family gave her a special feeling deep inside.

Iman gazed up at him and reveled in the wave of tenderness that washed over her. That Cinderella, swept off her feet feeling claimed her again. Iman walked on more slowly. She had to admit Cedric got points for originality. She swung her arm around his back and hooked it into his belt loop.

He tightened his arm around her waist and looked down at her, warmth radiating from his eyes. "Sore?" he asked.

"Nah." Iman tried to cover her wince of pain with a smile. "These muscles are in great shape." They stopped and he looked down at her abnormally wide stance, and laughed.

"I can tell."

They resumed walking.

The girls and Elaine, Cedric's mother, greeted them at the porch. Anika jumped in front of Iman causing her to step back. Her body protested furiously.

"Miss Iman, did you like the horses?"

Iman tried to smile, but her face hurt from the cold air. Initially, she had trouble telling the girls apart, but she'd learned that Medina had a slight lisp, and the more she got to know them, it became easier to tell them apart.

She answered Anika's question. "Loved them." Iman reached for the porch railing and groaned.

"Help her, girls," Elaine said, taking pity on her.

Iman smiled her thanks at Cedric's mom and accepted the girls' shoulders to rest her arms on.

"Elaine, you're a wonderful woman." Iman dragged herself through the screened porch door and into the large Afrocentric decorated great room. She immediately plopped down on one of the overstuffed sofas and laid her head back.

"Son, you had a call from Ronald Eubanks. He said there's going to be a huff on the news. Something about a deal you made going through. He said turn it on at five o'clock. Channel eleven."

Iman lifted her head and turned to Cedric who stood just inside the door. He looked so handsome in his cowboy attire. Faded denim pants hugged his body in all the right places. The red flannel shirt, covering a black turtle neck, was drawn taut across his broad shoulders and flat stomach. As sore as her arms were, Iman lifted them to reach for Cedric, but under strenuous protest, lowered them.

She prided herself for not acting on her wicked thoughts. He'd been the perfect gentleman, holding her hand, kissing her cheek, even draping his arms around her waist occasionally. Their relationship was progressing but there were times she saw a raw hunger in him. It matched hers. She wondered how long it would be before they acted on it.

Their days and nights had been filled with family fun. Cedric never conducted business when they were together.

Now, stress lines marked his forehead. Iman silently cursed Ronald Eubanks for bothering him.

Cedric glanced at his watch then at her. He strode into the room.

"Why don't you soak in a hot bath with some Epsom salts? After that, I promise you some private time."

Distractedly, he glanced at the desk he kept in a corner of the great room. "I need to find out what's going on."

"Sounds fine to me."

He offered her a hand up, and to her embarrassment, her bones cracked. The girls giggled.

"Be nice," he scolded them lovingly. Cedric walked her to the stairs and swatted her bottom gently before he walked off hand-in-hand with the girls.

Iman climbed into the hot water and soothing bath salts and sunk into the luxurious heat. Her rear still tingled where Cedric had playfully touched her.

She soaked until the water cooled then toweled herself, her muscles no longer protesting so stringently. Cedric was a patient man. He had allowed their relationship to grow steadily, and now it seemed he was placing it in her hands.

She stared at her reflection in the mirror and the comfortable navy sweat suit she'd just put on. Iman looked into her own eyes and knew she was ready. She wanted the relationship to move to another level.

What that was though, was unclear.

The clock chimed five times and she walked on stiff legs back to the great room. She sat across from Cedric who had also showered and changed.

The newscaster's voice captured their attention. Iman gasped sharply when a none too flattering picture of Cedric flashed across the screen. It was made to resemble a mug shot.

"Another corporate hit man has struck. Cedric Hamilton

of Dix Pharmaceuticals is a living Scrooge in the eyes of many Blythe Pharmaceutical employees. One hundred people got their pink slips today as they entered the building for work. Mr. Hamilton was reported to be vacationing with his family at his company's Helen, Georgia, ranch and was unavailable for comment."

Iman felt terrible for Cedric as they watched the newscaster interview an ex-employee. The woman called him insensitive, boorish, and claimed his heart was dead.

Iman barely heard the rest of the report as the girls' bickering interrupted the announcers words.

Cedric's mother asked, "Did you do the right thing, son?"

"I did what I had to do. It's business, Mom."

"I know, honey," she said loyally. "Come on," she said to the twins. "Let's go fix dinner."

Iman tried to forget the grimness of the announcer's voice, but couldn't. It permeated the air, thick as smoke, leaving her to wonder about the man she wanted to get to know better. Cedric worked hard, she told herself. Certainly he had a good reason to let so many people go—particularly right before the holidays.

Silence surrounded them. Cedric swiped his head with his hands and brought them down over his face. Tension radiated from him. "It's business."

The curt words bored into her as did his gaze, seeming to beg her to understand. He stretched out his hand to help her up. "Come on," he said roughly. "We're leaving. I need to be alone with you."

Iman waited while he held her coat. She shrugged into her short wool coat and winced only once as she wrapped his scarf around her neck.

"Shouldn't we tell your mother where we're going?"

Cedric gently took Iman's hand. Sounds of his mother and daughters discussing dinner filtered into the room.

"We'll be back," he called. He couldn't know how his words made her tingle.

In the fall, Helen, Georgia was a place vibrant with color and blooms. Now, it was asleep, preparing for the spring buds to restore it to its eclectic luster.

The bare brown branches seemed to float by as they drove unhurriedly through the quiet town, neither sharing their thoughts.

Cedric turned on the radio of the ranch's pick up truck, flipped around the dial, then turned it off again.

"Corporate hit man! Ridiculous," he muttered. "They didn't bother to mention that one hundred other employees still have their jobs."

"Why right before Christmas? Surely you can understand how the employees must feel." When he continued to scowl, Iman spoke in a measured, careful tone. "Would it have hurt the company to wait until after the new year?"

Cedric turned off the main highway onto a dirt path. It stretched endlessly ahead. Iman slid her arms out of her coat and stored it behind the seat.

"Is it ever a good time to lose your job?" He drummed his thumbs against the steering wheel as the truck continued to roll over the hard, bumpy road. "Should I have let those parents buy gifts they couldn't afford? I guess you think it would have been better to do it after the new year, after everyone had gone into debt buying things they don't need."

He came to a stop in the clearing and Cedric

eased the gear shift into park, letting the truck idle. He turned to look at her and his eyes sparkled with smoldering anger.

"Would it have been better to keep everybody on and in six months when I couldn't meet payroll, lay everybody off?"

Iman shook her head wanting to ease his frustration. This wasn't how she'd hoped to spend their first moments alone.

"No. You have to do what's best for everyone. I realize I work far from the corporate world, but I'm guessing that the timing could have been handled differently."

Iman stroked his stubbled cheek to soften the directness of her words. When he closed his eyes, she bathed him with her touch. She drew her index finger lightly over his forehead, down his nose and around to his cheek.

He looked so tired.

Cedric's chest filled then sank as he exhaled. "I tried to keep the people who would best help both companies. We offered early retirement, and severance pay. Those that stayed, took a risk." He finally looked at her. "There wasn't much more we could do."

"Don't think about it now," she whispered. "Where is that happy man who rode his horse today like a champion?"

He captured her hand in his. "You're so beautiful."

Iman felt the familiar flush rush through her cheeks. Cedric leaned over to kiss her nose. His arms were around her. His mouth settled roughly against hers demanding a response. Iman's banked desire unleashed and met his fevered passion, but she yelped in surprise when Cedric brought her to him.

"Seat belt," she muttered. His fingers grappled with the release, freeing her. He pulled her until she straddled his lap.

Iman groaned as much from the ache of her sore muscles, as she did from the pleasure of feeling the thick bulge of desire curving from Cedric's pants and pressing into her. He drank of her mouth, the trail of kisses on her neck burning silent promises into her flesh.

Iman sighed against his lips when he gently kneaded her thighs. He lessened the pressure to a caress.

"Still sore from skating?"

"And horseback riding," she breathed heavily.

He whispered in her ear, "Lean on me." Moving his hands up her thighs, he trailed a path to her back. Iman rested her cheek on his shoulder, her lips a breath away from his neck.

She closed her eyes languishing in his touch.

His callused hands massaged the sore tissues, eliciting a contented moan from her. His fingers slid down her sides, then around her back to the waist of the sweat pants. He took hold of her bottom, kneading it into complacency. It felt so good.

Cedric then dragged the sweatshirt over her head. He unfastened her bra and it fell away making her gasp at the exposure. Their gazes met briefly, before he decided which of the twin peaks to taste first. Iman arched toward Cedric's mouth when his eager tongue lapped at the right. He came up for air to nuzzle at her chin. "You're beautiful, *and* you taste good."

Iman chanced a look at Cedric's tongue when he went back to stroking her erect nipple. "Mmm" was all she could manage when he claimed the other one.

Masterfully, he tasted her until she dissolved into a helpless, quivering mass on his lap. His mouth sapped her energy. All she could do was let him fulfill her desire.

She fumbled with the buckle of his belt trying to loosen the metal clasp.

Cedric held her and leaned forward to give her easier access as she slid the leather from the loops then dropped it to the floor. His flannel shirt was tucked inside his jeans, and Iman struggled to free it while he drove her crazy with his mouth.

She finally got the shirt half up his chest.

She sought the button at the waist of his jeans, then hesitated, her fingers tangling in his dark hair.

I'm going to do this in a truck?

Cedric blew on her nipple and it hardened into a tight nub.

She sighed. *Possibly.*

"Don't stop now," he urged seductively.

His gaze sought hers in the darkness and he pressed his erection into her softness. His hand stroked her once through the fabric and a shudder rippled through her. He passed his fingers over her desire again and her head fell back as she shook with anticipation.

"Having second thoughts?" he asked, but continued the rhythmic pattern. Her head dropped to his chest. She couldn't think straight under the tender assault.

"Yes." His thumb pressed the space where her opening was and she shook some more. "No, sweet mercy. No, I'm not." He stroked her there again. Iman caught his face between her hands and offered him her breast.

He obliged, much to her delight.

"It's up to you, Iman," he murmured, his mouth full.

Iman doubted that as his lips closed over her breast again and he shook his hand. Arrows of heat and desire tore through her. She couldn't deny him.

"I want you now," she said weakly.

Iman urgently helped him peel her sweatpants from her body. She tugged at his jeans, but her hands shook so, she let him work the zipper and drag the jeans over his hips. Their lips met again as he guided her above him.

The phone in the truck rang. Iman jumped at the intruding sound. Holding her close, Cedric reached around her and picked it up.

"Hamilton here." Iman felt him change immediately. He patted her rear. She stayed still.

His voice demanded an answer. "Was any equipment damaged?" His gaze flicked to her and he murmured out the corner of his mouth, *"It's business."*

Iman leaned to the right when he more firmly patted her side. Reality dawned on her. He wanted her off his lap!

"Did they arrest anybody?"

Iman kept her anger under control as she raised herself and moved off his lap. He never looked at her while he pulled his pants over his bottom and carefully tucked himself in.

Iman drew on her clothes, anger blocking her pain.

"Johnson from research was there too? Not surprised." He added, a grim tone to his voice, "I'll be back in the morning. No," he hesitated, looking at her for the first time. "I'm in to something tonight. See you in the morning."

You're in to something all right. Iman crossed her arms over her chest and sat as far against the passenger door as possible.

She waited until he hung up. "Everything that woman said about you is true. You're insensitive *and* boorish." Iman looked down at his waist, then up at him. As sweetly as she could manage she said, "You need me to zip those for you?"

Chapter Six

Two weeks of Kwanzaa class made a believer out of him. Anika and Medina had changed. They no longer talked only of Christmas lists and toys. Now their animated discussions were about all the new friends they'd made and *Zawadi* gifts.

Anika had even surprised him by asking if she could have five dollars from her savings account to buy books for Medina.

But what touched him deeper, was the close relationship they'd developed with Iman.

Cedric's gaze swung to her as she kneeled in front of the class, rehearsing dance movements with the dancers who would perform in a week at the *Karamu*.

He inhaled deeply, remembering.

So many wasted days had passed since their night in the truck. Cedric tried hard to forget his abhorrent behavior.

Iman had refused all of his apologetic overtures. Every gift he'd sent, had been returned. She'd only kept one thing. A card he'd finally written late last Friday night, while sitting alone at home.

It had been the first time he realized that he didn't have to be alone because there was somebody special in his life. Someone he enjoyed and who for some reason, liked him.

Those feelings were what had carried him to his desk and what had spilled onto the paper. Cedric grew warm thinking about his heartfelt apology. He hoped Iman would give them another chance.

Slightly off key singing drew his attention back to the children and Iman. The children sang the first principle harmoniously, but the second was a tongue twister. Several of them mumbled, and Iman nodded encouragingly singing louder.

"*Umoja,* unity. *Kujichagulia,* self-determination." They survived the five remaining principles, then Iman applauded them for their effort.

He waited until after the final call of "*Haban gani! Umoja!*" before making his way toward the throng surrounding Iman. His girls pulled Iman toward him.

"Daddy," Anika said, "Miss Iman said she would come over our house and work on our speeches with us, didn't you, Miss Iman?"

Cedric faced Iman. He wanted to apologize and make her understand how sorry he was. He wanted to pull her into his arms. To touch her intimately the same way the soft African material hugged her body, and to relive their near-union. To make the end of their evening together something beautiful, as beautiful as Iman deserved.

She held the girls' hands and looked away from him to Medina.

"Yes, sweetheart. I said I would help you. We can do it at my house, or stay here, I suppose."

He touched her. Her gaze snapped up. "You can come to our house, tomorrow."

Aliyah approached, halting Iman's response.

"Iman, Ada is asking for you." She pointed to the

other side of the room. "I'll keep Cedric and the girls company while you see what she wants."

Cedric felt Iman's impatience. She dropped the girls' hands. "We've got to talk," she said decisively to him.

"I'll wait here for you."

She nodded as she started away.

Aliyah stepped beside him to give his girls room to run around. "Long time no see."

Medina tagged Anika, who then turned to chase her. He didn't bother to stop them. They could have somersaulted over his head and he wouldn't have said a word. Iman was coming to his house, tomorrow. Thoughts of her telling him to get out of her life forever plagued him. He pushed them away. It was too sobering.

He turned to Aliyah. "How have you been Aliyah?"

"I'm always fine, Cedric." Her feline grin made him shake his head. Her humor was infectious.

The weight on his shoulder lessened.

"So, when are you going to ask Iman out again?"

His eyebrows shot up. Had Iman told her about their weekend? He grew slightly uncomfortable. "We're handling it," he said avoiding a direct answer. Something occurred to him. "What's her nickname?"

"Sugar Baby. Why?"

It was his turn to smile. "Just wanted to know."

Aliyah's thirteen and fifteen-year-old daughters fussed over Anika and Medina, giving him time to watch Iman and the older woman named Ada.

His gaze was riveted to her as Iman hugged the older woman. Iman broke the embrace when the woman's body began to wrack with a hacking cough. There wasn't much to her slight frame but a colorful head wrap. And the frailty of her bony hands and wrists was obvious.

Cedric stepped forward to offer assistance, as Iman held her gently around the waist, a look of concern on her face. But the coughing spell ended and another woman assisted Ada into her coat. The threadbare wool, thinned with age, wasn't much protection from the cold winter air.

Cedric was taken aback when Iman unwrapped the scarf that covered her own head and draped the woman's neck. Her generosity humbled him.

It was too cold to be without a hat or scarf, yet Iman gave without regard for herself. Her actions reflected how deep her beliefs lay. Iman had a way about her that attracted people.

Cedric was surprised at the strength of his attraction.

It was far more serious than he realized as he watched her from beneath hooded lids. He thought of her all the time, could describe her in his sleep, how she smelled and tasted. Everybody loved her. *I could love her too.*

The idea startled and provoked him.

His heart thundered against his ribs. *Not me,* he decided over his body's raging response. Too soon.

Iman returned with her bags of books and her purse in hand and silently gave them to him. They stood before each other in a face off.

"Daddy? Daddy?" Anika tugged on his hand to get his attention. "Can we go outside with Miss Aliyah?"

"Please?" she and Medina begged in unison. Cedric glanced from Aliyah, to his girls, then to Iman. He needed to talk to Iman alone.

"I think I'm outnumbered. Behave," he said more sternly than he'd planned. Anxiety always made his voice harsh when he didn't really mean it to be. He softened it. "Behave, girls." They ignored the warning, and ran toward the door.

"Wait. Anika, Medina," Iman called, snatching their coats off a nearby chair and shaking them. "Coats, hats, scarves, and gloves." She kneeled down waving them back. "I can't have my best speech readers sick, can I?" She bundled the girls up and tied their hoods tight.

When they resembled something out of an arctic clothing catalog, she patted their heads and let them go. They waddled off, barely able to move.

Cedric waited as she attended to each child who came within her reach, repeating the task until every child was bundled up.

He felt oddly out of place as it was he who usually attended to his girls. Yet a big part of him enjoyed watching her take care of the children.

Finally, they were alone in the room.

"You've been avoiding me," he stated without preamble.

"I know I have. I needed time."

Greedily he drank in the sight of her. Cedric shifted the bags in his hands to a chair.

"I've been trying to apologize for two weeks. It was my fault." When she didn't disagree, he smiled. "Why wouldn't you let me apologize face-to-face? Why did you return all my gifts?"

She looked up at him. "Because they weren't from your heart. Your card told me how you really felt." She rubbed her neck. "I forgave you days ago."

His brows knit in confusion. "Then why didn't you call me?"

"Because." She turned, but his hand on her arm stopped her. Her nose started to glow. "I had some things to sort out." The tip reddened. "I've been thinking about you." She looked at him, then away, "And me."

Her voice dropped, just above a whisper. "Sometimes you look so tired, I think you're going to tumble off these horrible metal chairs. But you still come to class, girls in tow." The flush spread to her cheeks. "I know it's hard, but you do it anyway. You're a devoted father." Her hand stroked her neck where the red had begun to travel like hot lava.

Cedric yearned to bury his face in the heat.

"I wasn't sure how to tell you . . ."

His insides clenched nervously. "Tell me?"

Iman fidgeted with her hands; her lips trembled. He reached out his finger to stop them.

"I don't know why I feel this way. When you're business, you're *all* business." He grimaced. "But I know that's only a part of who you really are. You were a sweetheart to those homeless ladies." She pointed to his chest. "I know there's a heart in there. So here goes."

Cedric got lost in the beauty of her gaze. He desperately wanted to tell her everything was going to be all right.

A nervous smile parted her lips.

His heart thundered when her voice dropped to a whisper. He strained to hear. "A part of me is falling in love with you."

Cedric pulled Iman to him, and pressed his lips to her matted curls. He wanted to share his warmth with her, to let her feel the beat of his heart. It felt as if someone swiped at the world and set it spinning on its axis. Her words set his whole body afire. Everything was going to be all right.

Cedric lifted her chin saying, "I think we should celebrate that good news." He lowered his head, their breath mingling. Her lips parted in expectation . . .

"Uh-hm. Mr. Hamilton?" the janitor interrupted.

"This better be good," Cedric's voice rang with irritation.

"I'm locking up, sir. Should I give you another few minutes?" Cedric took one last look at Iman's wonderful mouth and swore under his breath. He wanted to taste her so bad he could feel desire to the marrow of his bones.

Her breath quickened when he inched her closer to him. Because of her revelation, his heart hadn't stopped singing.

"It's getting kind of late. And Mrs. Winston will want me home soon . . ." The janitor's voice trailed off.

Cedric spoke loudly, while still maintaining eye contact with Iman. "No, we're coming now, Mr. Winston."

Iman backed out of his grasp and got her coat.

"I'll be at the door waiting," the older man called.

Cedric didn't hear him. He was too intent on Iman. He stopped just behind her. "Thank you for telling me."

She nodded and buttoned her coat. Black curls stopped at the collar of her bare neck. He unwrapped his long gray scarf from his neck and covered hers with it.

"I hoped you would join me tonight for a special date," he said, drawing her back against his chest. He felt a deep sigh leave her body.

She turned and a light burned in the soft depths of her eyes. "Where did you have in mind?"

"The mall," he said casually.

Surprise made her mouth O. "The mall? And Aliyah thought you were too mature for me. I think we're about equal." Her teasing lessened the tension that bubbled between them.

"I have to pick out some things for the girls, and I need a woman's opinion." He added in an offhand manner, "No one can say you're not opinionated."

Iman pretended to pinch him. "I hope you're not implying that I'm not a woman."

"You're all the woman I need. How about it?" They walked out the door and checked on the girls. Aliyah stood watching over the brood.

"What about the girls?"

"My mother and step-father would love to watch them. How's seven o'clock?"

Medina raced by, bumping Iman as she went. Her apology was lost as Iman struggled to regain her balance. Their breath mingled into mist as Cedric firmly gripped her waist, steadying her.

"Thanks." She stepped away. "Okay. Seven is good."

Anika tugged on his coat, looking up. "Daddy, it's cold. Can we go home now?"

He tore his gaze from Iman's to look at his daughter. "Yes, baby. Go tell your sister it's time to leave." Medina appeared at that moment and took her father's other hand.

"Good bye, Anika. Good bye, Medina. *Harambee.*" The girls looked at Iman quizzically. "It's a Swahili greeting," she told them. "It means, let's work together."

Cedric waited until she was safely in her car. A slow grin, like the slow heat rippling through him, curled his lips. He read her lips as she drove slowly past them.

"I'll see you later."

Chapter Seven

Iman glanced through the rows of clothes at Neiman Marcus and cringed at the prices.

"Great! They'll like these." Cedric picked up two dresses and checked the tags. "Do you see two size eights? Only in different colors?"

The fluffy dresses made Iman think of a bed of whipped cream. Not right for two active seven-year-olds.

"Cedric." She looped her arm through his and steered him away from the billowing ruffles. "Don't you think the girls would like something more, how do I say this," she considered out loud, "more playful?"

He stared at her. For a moment she thought he was angry. Then his face fell. "They hate when I shop for them. I like ruffles and fluffy stuff. It reminds me of when they were babies. But since they're big first-graders they don't like my style." He sounded hurt. "They beg my fifty-two-year-old mother to shop for them."

Iman held in her smile at his crestfallen look. He obviously took this issue to heart. She steered him toward a place she knew was a hit with Aliyah's girls.

Music pumped as they entered the store and Cedric visibly cringed at the attire on the mannequins inside the window.

"Come on, Dad," she said, hoping to lessen his reluctance. "Don't take yourself so seriously. Let's look for one outfit each. If they don't like them, you can bring them back."

"Kids don't like this stuff." He flicked distastefully over the baggy jeans and hooded shirts. "It's all too big."

"Kids do like this stuff," Iman countered. Her eyes drifted to the denim that covered his muscular thighs and bottom. He looked good in a suit and polished shoes, and great in a pair of jeans and shirt. Cedric needed to loosen up. He was definitely too upper crust.

"Just look at one outfit," she said convincingly. "You *asked* for my help, remember?" That seemed to straighten him up a bit as his lips pursed into a smirk.

Telling him her true feelings hadn't been so bad, Iman reflected, trying to keep things positive. Although, he hadn't responded the way she'd hoped. The fact that he didn't share her feelings stung, but the words were out. Too late to take them back.

"May I help you?" A young woman who looked about twelve bounced to Cedric's side. Iman held his arm so he wouldn't flee the store.

"No thanks, ma'am," Iman said around a giggle. "We're just looking."

"Okay. Let me know if you need anything." Happily she skipped away. Cedric stared at her with a disbelieving look on his face.

"Doesn't Georgia have child labor laws?"

"She's old enough. My, my, for such a young dapper dude, you sure have old fogy taste."

"Oh. Is that right?"

Iman offered token resistance but let herself be guided to him. When she was close enough, he slid his hand under her coat, and tickled.

Iman jumped, laughing. "Stop. People are looking. Cedric!" Giggling, she grabbed for the rack and in the process knocked clothes all over the floor.

"Now look what you made me do." She glanced around guiltily, enjoying herself immensely. Cedric's expression remained innocent. "I'll get you for this," she whispered.

"Is there a problem over here?" the young clerk demanded.

"I'll take each of those in a size eight, please," Cedric said casually, before moving away. Iman stared in amazement as the young woman's frown turned into a smile.

"Just a minute." Iman peered at the girl's name tag. "Sissy." She walked over to Cedric. "There's at least ten dresses down there. Are you sure?"

"Definitely."

He pointed to the clothes. "I want all of those." Iman tried to hide her shock. He took her hand leading her toward a rack of expensive jackets. "Come help me pick out two of these."

Two stores and an hour and a half later, Iman sat under a mountain of packages, barely able to move. She stared blankly across the mall at a television that telecast a follow up report on corporate hit men. Cedric's picture filled a corner of the nineteen-inch screen. His photograph flashed away. The newscaster began talking about the phone company president.

Each time she'd seen a report on company closings, Iman visualized she and Cedric locked in an intimate embrace in the truck. But the dream would be shattered when he would say, *"It's business."* Iman

An important message from the ARABESQUE Editor

Dear Arabesque Reader,

Because you've chosen to read one of our Arabesque romance novels, we'd like to say "thank you"! And, as a special way to thank you, we've selected four more of the books you love so well to send you for FREE!

Please enjoy them with our compliments, and thank you for continuing to enjoy Arabesque...the soul of romance.

Karen Thomas
Senior Editor,
Arabesque Romance Novels

Check out our website at
www.arabesquebooks.com

THE EDITOR'S "THANK YOU" GIFT INCLUDES:

- 4 books absolutely FREE (plus $1.50 for shipping and handling)
- A FREE newsletter, *Arabesque Romance News*, filled with author interviews, book previews, special offers, and more!
- No risks or obligations. You're free to cancel whenever you wish... with no questions asked.

BOOK CERTIFICATE

Yes! Please send me 4 FREE Arabesque novels (plus $1.50 for shipping & handling). I understand I am under no obligation to purchase any books, as explained on the back of this card.

Name ____________________

Address ____________________ Apt. ______

City ______________ State ______ Zip ______

Telephone (   ) ____________________

Signature ____________________

Offer limited to one per household and not valid to current subscribers. All orders subject to approval. Terms, offer, & price subject to change. Offer valid only in the U.S.

Thank you!

ANHL1A

Accepting the four introductory books for FREE (plus $1.50 to offset the cost of shipping & handling) places you under no obligation to buy anything. You may keep the books and return the shipping statement marked "cancelled". If you do not cancel, about a month later we will send 4 additional Arabesque novels, and you will be billed the preferred subscriber's price of just $4.00 per title. That's $16.00 for all 4 books for a savings of 33% off the cover price (Plus $1.50 for shipping and handling). You may cancel at any time, but if you choose to continue, every month we'll send you 4 more books, which you may either purchase at the preferred discount price. . . or return to us and cancel your subscription.

wondered if he could survive without business. The answer in her heart left her cold.

"Hello, Iman? Are you asleep with your eyes open?"

Her stomach felt weak. "Mmm? What did you say? I was drifting."

"Do you like these?" He held up some earrings carved in the shape of the Black Madonna. Iman took them in her hand and was surprised at how heavy the beautiful pieces were. She raised them high and her eyes widened at the price tag.

Carefully she chose her words. "They're beautiful. But for two little girls, you might, perhaps, maybe you could go with something less . . ."

"They're too big, right?" His thumb caressed the earrings. "I thought so, too."

He turned to the salesman. "I'll take these and two pair of the smaller ones identical to these." This time her mouth gaped. The final bill was staggering.

"Are we ready?" Iman asked once the order had been packaged.

"Just about. I need to make one more stop." They walked to the valet parking attendant who took the packages and stored them away. Cedric took her hand and steered her back inside the mall. "I thought we could get something to eat, then make the last stop. Did you have any other plans?"

Her stomach growled in response. "Not really. I'm so hungry a box of rocks sounds appetizing." She fell in step beside him.

"Why didn't you say something before? We could have eaten hours ago." He stopped and turned fully to her. "Just tell me what you need, and it's yours."

"I didn't want to end up at the top of Lookout Mountain again."

He laughed and pressed his lips to the back of her fingers, chills chasing her doubts away.

The dimmed restaurant was crowded with other late-night shoppers but was festively decorated. Red and white stockings adorned the waitresses' heads, and holiday streamers hung from the ceilings. Holly-laced tablecloths covered the tables while red candles provided romantic light.

Quickly they were shown to a semi-circle booth, and a waiter appeared to take their coats. Before they could slide in, the waitress stopped them.

"Now that you're comfortable, you know what to do."

For the first time, they both noticed the mistletoe arched over the entrance. Neither moved.

"The only people who get away without kissing are sisters and brothers. Are you two related?"

Iman's eyes were fixed to Cedric's lips. She shook her head almost imperceptibly.

"Then do it. I'll bring complimentary glasses of champagne in the meantime. I'll know if you don't kiss her," the waitress said to Cedric. "The bartender will make everybody boo you." She left them alone.

Images of hot fervent kisses filled her head. Involuntarily, she licked her lips.

"Shall we?"

Iman nodded. Cedric stepped forward and their lips met awkwardly. Her nose and his meshed together, then slid up, then down, until the fit became perfect.

Absolutely, blissfully, perfect.

His mouth tenderly touched hers, giving just enough satisfaction for the moment, but leaving sensual promises in its wake. He smiled against her lips before he broke away, leaving her body crying for more.

The bell clanged and people applauded, enjoying their embarrassment.

"That was unreal," Iman muttered as she slid inside the booth. He sat beside her and surprised her by placing another proprietary kiss on her cheek.

The champagne arrived and they took a moment to order.

Iman sipped from her glass and hoped her feelings were from hunger. No matter his blind side about business, being in his arms made her want to commit herself forever. Iman felt as if she had just dived off a very high cliff into darkness. She focused when he repeated the question.

"Is Ada related to you?"

"Not really. We've kind of adopted each other. She's been a member of the Kwanzaa Association for a long time. Every fall, Ada heads up a fundraiser so members of the association can teach Kwanzaa classes at local schools and community centers.

"Recently, she's had a bad cough. The medicine her doctor prescribed is sixty-seven dollars a bottle! She just can't afford it. I called the pharmacist today, and they suggested I call around to get a better price, then they would match it. Can you believe that?" Iman shook her head, disgusted. "Bartering medicine prices. What are these drug companies thinking of?"

"The bottom line." He grimaced. "We have to stay in business."

"I wasn't making an indictment against your company," Iman said quickly. "I just can't help feeling the elderly are taken advantage of, when it becomes their job as the patient to find the best price."

He shrugged off her apology. "Unfortunately, competition in this field is fierce. You can have a drug that works well, but the company down the street has a generic brand. Every company has to fight to stay one step ahead. That's why they make you call around for pricing. Nobody is willing to lower their price and lose profits. I tried to explain this very thing to Jack McClure, president of Retired Seniors of Georgia recently. What he's asking is impossible."

"What does he want?"

"Dix to do the unthinkable. Lower the prices of twelve medications." He shook his head. "Can't be done. No amount of petitions or pickets can change the current situation. It's business."

"Well, business sucks," Iman said distastefully.

Cedric laughed. "That's one way of putting it. Look at it this way. Nobody is sitting around with a room full of dusty dollars. Every drug company reinvests the money in new drugs to find new cures. We're still trying to help people. Despite"—he gave her a candid look—"situations like Ada's."

"I don't think she'll be able to do the farewell for *Kuumba*. She suggested we find an eloquent, dynamic speaker who will wow the crowd. She suggested you."

"No." Cedric shook his head adamantly.

Iman went on as if he hadn't spoken. "I thought of asking one of the brothers, but when Ada brought up your name, I agreed; you're the perfect choice." She eyed him speculatively. Cedric began to suspect he was a specimen under a microscope, being studied by a mad scientist.

"I'll think about it," he said warming slightly. "Ada reminds me a lot of my own mother." Cedric stopped short, a black abyss gaping open before he could finish the sentence. He faced the dark hole, contemplating what lay on the other side. The urge to share his tragedies and triumphs with Iman was overpowering.

He waited for the feeling to pass as the waiter placed their food on the table and sprinkled grated cheese over his spaghetti.

Only it didn't go away. The closer Iman sat to him, the more her wonderfully female scent snaked into his senses, the more he wanted to bare himself before her and confess all his secrets.

"In what way?" The hollow musical strands of her voice reached inside him and unlocked his private room.

"My mother was sickly. Jobs weren't sympathetic to her illnesses, so just as soon as she got a job she'd lose it for absenteeism. It wasn't easy for us, but we made it."

"How did you live? That must have been very hard."

"Let's just say I have a working knowledge of how to fold a box just right to block the wind."

"The two women on the street . . ." she whispered.

Her expression was sad, stunned. She barely managed to utter the words. "I'm so sorry."

Cedric couldn't seem to stop himself once he got started. "Not long after that I got a job, and ever since I earned my first paycheck, I never looked back." He closed his hand and realized he'd linked it with hers. "It felt like gold bouillon."

She studied him. Her voice rose barely above a whisper. "You know that's not going to happen to you ever again, right?"

He breathed easier, drawn to the trust radiating from her dark eyes.

"Logically," he managed around an uncharacteristic croak. "But you never forget."

She slid close and placed her hand beneath his arm urging him toward her. Heat spread through him when his arms grazed her breast.

Her lips touched his ear. She whispered, "The girls are safe. It's never going to happen to them."

Involuntarily, he jerked, his body shaking once before he regained control of himself. She had found his biggest fear and confronted it.

Iman brightened an otherwise bleak place with her unqualified trust in him. Cedric grasped hold of her belief and let it rage through his blood. He tried to relax, but his stomach did violent somersaults. Her hands hadn't left his arm. He finally gazed into her eyes.

"How did you know?"

"Honey, you bought the girls ten dresses today." Her gaze softened on his. "Have they worn all the others in their closets?"

"No, but—" Cedric started to respond but she cut him off.

"It's natural to want to protect them, and you have. From what I can see, they're very well cared for. It's time to stop worrying, Cedric."

"I don't worry."

"Ah, well." She nodded. "But you can go too far in certain instances. If you want to improve their value system, let them follow their daddy's example." She patted his hand and gentled it into a caress. Love filled her eyes. "You turned out just fine. They will too."

She let him go, and resumed eating.

The enveloping darkness that once surrounded him faded, leaving him glowing in her wisdom. He twirled his fork in his hand for a moment.

Iman was a very smart lady.

Cedric's thoughts turned to the upcoming Christmas holiday. He couldn't imagine a day without her. The past weeks proved that.

"Iman, do you have any plans for Christmas?"

"Christmas afternoon I always spend with Aliyah. My famous holiday goose is a hit despite what Aliyah says." She smiled at him. "Why?"

"I want you to spend some time with me and the girls. I want you to share Christmas with us."

Her eyes shined. "I would love to. 'Course, I'm hoping for a white Christmas."

"Why?" Cedric asked incredulous at the thought of not being able to go to work if snow fell.

"I guess my fondest holiday memory is the winter of seventy-seven. We were snowed in for days. I don't know how much fun it was for my mother and father, but Aliyah and I had a ball."

"Sounds like Anika and Medina," he said dryly. "They enjoy fanning the smoke detector when I burn something in the kitchen."

She shot him a wry look. "Kids are supposed to have fun. During that snowstorm, we must have played *Chutes and Ladders, Monopoly,* and *Candy Land* at least fifty times each."

The memories made her giggle. Cedric loved the light in her eyes. He wished he could have been there.

"The fourth day of the storm, my dad ran from the room yelling at the top of his lungs that he would fling himself in front of a snow plow before he played another board game. My mom suggested he tell us stories."

Her tone grew wistful. "Once he started, there was no stopping him. He told us all about his grandmother and grandfather. Then somehow we got on the subject of Kwanzaa. It wasn't as well known as it is now. But from those tales, I felt a connection."

"Tell me some," Cedric encouraged. He rested his head against the high back of the booth and folded his arms. Her voice was soft and melodious as she recounted the tale of a young African warrior who was brought across the ocean to America.

Some of the fables were funny, others were serious, but he was sure of one thing. Iman was indeed the best story teller he'd ever heard. Her voice truly entranced him.

"You should tell stories all the time," he said when she finished. "You're very good at it. Was this fable passed down from your father's grandparents?"

Iman nodded, her eyes still glowing, but she had grown sad. "Yes. I miss my father's interpretation, but I've added my own twists and style. To keep them alive, I tell my nieces and someday, when I have children, I'll tell them. I plan to tell a few at this year's celebration."

The waiter brought the check. Iman slipped into her coat, by-passing the mistletoe.

Cedric couldn't put into words how he looked forward to their goodnight kiss. He paid the bill and they started walking. "How are the plans for the celebration shaping up?"

Iman draped her head and neck with his long, gray cashmere scarf. He'd always considered the scarf efficient, useful. Now it was pretty because it protected the silky curls on Iman's head. Cedric shook his head in wonder.

"It's going to be the best celebration yet. A New York dance troupe has confirmed. We also have local dance groups performing, a drum selection, a karate demonstration. The children have planned some surprises."

"That's what Medina was talking about?"

"Yep. Oh, and our farewell speaker is going to dazzle us with his eloquence."

Cedric handed the valet attendant his ticket and glanced wryly at Iman. "Don't count on it."

She whispered, "You're going to be great." The valet stopped the car in front of them.

He raised his eyebrows inquisitively. "Why do you do that?"

Her lids lowered and a shy smile danced around her mouth. "What?"

He said, "Whisper?"

"Because then you can hear."

Cedric stopped. She was right. She had his undivided attention.

It took twenty minutes for the men to decide how to pack the car with all the bags. Iman watched, careful not to offer advice as they loaded the trunk. Cedric's jacket hung open as he wrestled with a bag full of ornaments. Memories of being in his arms floated back to her as she paced the sidewalk to stay warm.

No wonder he was successful, she mused. He focused to a fault on whatever he was doing at the time.

"We'll be done in a minute," he said over his shoulder, just before he unloaded the car and started over.

Iman shook her head.

She focused on his hands as he piled in one bag at a time. Those hands were always gentle with the girls, quick to clap or praise them with fatherly love whenever they were near him.

Cedric turned a box sideways and cupped his

hands to his mouth to heat them before grabbing another bag.

Those same hands had carefully draped her in gray cashmere when she was freezing outside Stone Manor earlier tonight. And he had strummed her intimately and made her keen with pleasure.

She followed the hands to the face of the man she had fallen in love with. It was more than a part of her that loved him, as she'd told him. Somehow, her heart had grown committed to him somewhere over the last few weeks.

Iman felt strangely light.

Cedric's bottom stuck out of the car. He uncurled to his full height and looked at the bags at his feet, then at her.

"We've almost got it. Not too cold are you?"

"I'm okay; do you need any help?"

"No." He glanced at the valet, who looked annoyed. "We can handle it."

Iman waited fifteen more minutes then couldn't take another cold breeze attacking her ankles. "I'll hold those two on my lap," she offered when Cedric started to unload the car again.

"I'm glad you offered. That guy looked like he wanted my blood." Cedric started the car and heat bathed her cold feet.

Iman half turned in her seat and looked at the full back seat and then at Cedric who drove carefully away from the store and onto the highway.

"Where are you going to hide all this stuff?"

"I hadn't thought of that. The girls are at my mother's but they know every hiding place in my house. They go through there like gift-sniffing dogs."

"I did the same thing. We had a crawl space in

our house and my parents hid our gifts there until I left for college."

"I can drop them by my office, then Monday, while they're at school, I'll sneak the gifts into the house. Of course that doesn't help about wrapping them. But I can do that the night before."

Iman smirked. "You smart guys sure know how to complicate things."

"What? I thought that was a very well thought out plan. Okay smarty," he challenged. "You come up with something better."

"You can bring them to my house and wrap them there. Then when Christmas Eve arrives, pick them up. The girls can search the Hamilton home to their little hearts' content, they won't find a thing. I'll even help wrap. Easy, huh?" Iman fought to hide her grin of satisfaction.

"I was going to suggest that as plan B," Cedric said, pasting on his best poker face.

"Yeah, sure you were."

"Really. It was on the tip of my tongue."

"Uh, huh. Sore loser." Iman savored the thrill of victory. He started a slow grin. "I was just going to say that."

"Your nose is growing, Pinocchio."

They bantered lightly all the way to Iman's driveway.

Chapter Eight

Iman showed Cedric to the second floor bedroom where he stored the gifts. A worktable cluttered with *Kente* fabric and materials for *mkeke* mats covered one wall, while books spilled from shelves opposite it. The floor space was wide open until bags and boxes, colored wrapping paper, and clothes filled the hardwood. They backed out of the room, gawking.

"That's insane." Cedric appeared stunned. His usual cool eluded him. "I can't believe we did this much shopping in one day."

Iman led him downstairs to the kitchen where she had coffee brewing. "That was you," she threw over her shoulder, her delicate fingers gliding over the black glazed counter tops. "I'm an innocent shopping bystander."

He spooned one sugar into his cup and sat at the glass-topped table for four in the cozy kitchen.

Cedric's presence in her home made Iman nervous. She straightened the pictures of her nieces that hung on the wall by the sink and wiped the stainless counter with her hand. She wiped her hand on her jeans.

"Are you nervous about me being here?" Cedric asked quietly.

Iman washed and dried her hands, stalling. Finally she answered, "It's silly, but I am. I shouldn't be," she rushed on, her voice higher. "I mean, we just made up, I told you how I felt . . ." Iman stopped abruptly and covered her face with her hands. "I'm making a complete fool of myself."

"No you're not. I cornered the market on that the night in the truck."

Iman sat beside him. "I missed you," he said.

She looked at him. The words were plainly spoken, but had the impact of a one-two punch.

"I missed you, too."

He tugged her into his lap and she went willingly.

"I want to make love to you. No phones, no interruptions. No truck." He nipped at her ear lobe.

The promise in his voice turned her insides to mush. A yearning beyond conscious emotion seized her.

Iman brushed the soft curls that swirled on her head, her gaze on the floor. The checkerboard pattern of the tile blurred under her penetrating gaze.

She'd forgiven Cedric, but she hadn't forgotten how hurt she'd been.

"We should take it slow." Iman had difficulty talking, with her ear in his mouth. His lips released her. "Cedric, this feels too much like we're teenagers. Like we're being careless. It feels too right," she whispered hoarsely.

She looked into his eyes, and found understanding. "I never used to believe in love at first sight. I never thought I would tell a man I loved him before he told me." She rushed on. "I'm not trying to pressure you."

"You're not," he reassured. "We'll take it slow." He gathered her closer to him, as sexual awareness swirled between them. His hand moved possessively up her side and around her back. His voice was uncharacteristically ragged.

"I'll wait until I can't stand it anymore. Until the sound of your voice makes me so hard I'll just about explode at my desk at work. Then I'll come looking for you, Iman."

"I'm in trouble," she murmured once she looked into his eyes.

"You sure are." He kissed her tenderly.

Cedric was a patient, deliberate man. He wouldn't have to wait too long, the way she felt.

Iman was first to break away. "I can come over tomorrow about four-thirty to help Medina. If you need some help with your speech, I'd be glad to give you some books."

"I'll take all the help I can get. I'd better get going before I break my promise to wait."

Rising from his lap was difficult. Iman wanted to stay locked in his embrace, letting desire take them where logic had no place.

But she'd made the rules. Cedric steadied her on her feet. Iman retrieved his coat from over the arm of the chair. "I had a good time."

He pulled a new scarf from his coat pocket, brushing her breast as he looped it around her neck drawing her near.

"I had a good time too."

His lips descended on hers for a fiery reminder. Their good-bye kiss lasted another five minutes.

"I . . . I meant shopping."

A flush colored her cheeks when she came up for air.

"I didn't." Cedric's arms draped possessively around her back and they stayed close enjoying the feel of the other. She rested her head against his chest listening to the quickened beat of his heart. It matched her own.

He tilted up her chin. "Good night Iman Yvette Parrish. My Sugar Baby." He kissed her brilliant nose and walked out the door. Iman walked on watery legs back to the sofa and collapsed.

Chapter Nine

"Say it again, Medina. Take your time. Start here." Cedric handed her the paper and waited for her to start. He drew a frustrated hand over his hair as he listened to Medina recite her speech for the tenth time in two hours.

"Kwanzaa is a time to draw people into your homes and ask them to ce-webrate"—she cringed but kept reading—"with you. Fami-wy and friends—Daddy I can't do it."

Cedric folded his hands in his lap and exhaled. "Stop saying you can't." He rubbed his temples, his nerves frayed. "You have to try harder. Practice the 'll' sound. Don't start crying. Why are you crying?"

"I'm tired and thirsty," she said rebelliously.

"You can get a drink, but we have to go over this again."

"I don't want to," she wailed, tears dripping off her chin. "Miss Iman's nice to me when she helps me. You're yeww-ing again and you promised to stop." She let the paper slip from her hands. "I don't want to do this anymore."

His patience snapped. "Well too bad. You made a commitment and you have to keep it. Iman's been coming over here all week to help you and in a few days, she's going to need you to do this speech. You're not backing out!"

Cedric heard the doorbell, but ignored it. He paced his study and watched his daughter.

"Daddy, it's too hard. I don't want to do it anymore. I quit."

"You can't quit!"

"Hello."

Cedric hadn't realized he'd raised his voice until he heard Iman's low familiar tone from the door. He cleared his throat and glowered at Medina who raised her chin stubbornly.

"Medina, can I talk to your daddy alone for a minute?"

The little girl nodded, then took off like a shot.

"You're coming back," he yelled from the door. Medina's bedroom door banged shut.

"I swear, Iman, why don't kids come with a manual? They give them to you and then don't tell you how to raise them." He stalked past her. "She says she's not going to do her speech." Cedric collapsed into the high-back leather chair behind his desk.

Iman entered the room and laid three bags beside the sofa on the floor. "Why do you always have so much stuff?" he asked with irritation.

"These are books I thought might help you with your speech on *Kuumba*. Don't attack me because you're being unreasonable about Medina."

He scoffed. "Unreasonable? She has to learn the same way everybody else does that if she makes a commitment to something, she has to keep it." He shook his head and waved his hand carelessly. "I won't have any of this fickle maybe I will, maybe I won't."

"I thought she was happy with her speech. Why

did she change her mind?" Iman loosened the sash on her coat and sat down.

He glowered at her. "Because she has a speech impediment. She can't pronounce some of her letters correctly and she's shy about it. Practice," he announced. "She needs to practice."

"Cedric, I'm not going to tell you how to raise your children," she said softly.

"Sure you are," he cut in sarcastically.

Iman ignored him and continued. "But it seems to me that another way to handle someone like this is with positive suggestions. Give her positive encouragement. Tell her things like, you can do it, I believe in you, you did great." Her warm smile captivated him. She was whispering again.

Cedric felt himself falling.

"Iman," he warned.

"I believe in you, you're going to be great." She grinned sweetly. How he loved her mouth. Cedric shook his head.

"How come you think you know me so well?" Her smile widened victoriously. Cedric was hopelessly lost.

"I know you want Medina to believe in herself. That's why you work so hard to help her. But you get frustrated when she doesn't try as hard as you think she should."

He shrugged, agreeing. "I try not to be so intense with her."

"I know, I heard you. The housekeeper let me in. I listened awhile before I came in here. I know you want the best for her." Her voice was soft. "Try to take it easy on her. She's just seven."

"How come you know so much about children? You don't have any." Hurt and anger played across her face and he stopped short. "Sorry, that was unfair."

"I may not have children, but I've worked with them for years. And as you've said, they don't come with a manual. Any fool could do it."

His lips quirked. "I guess I deserved that. But if I have to give my speech, so does she, damn it." Cedric sighed raggedly. "What are you laughing at?"

Red looked so good on Iman. She slipped the wool coat from her shoulders and threw it on the couch. A brilliant red silk shirt was tucked into nicely fitting jeans with a complementing vest hanging open in the front. Long earrings dangled from her ears and she wore a thin gold chain around her neck.

"She's doing it, damn it," she mimicked his deep voice. "Cedric, do you think your terrorist tactics helped? Positive thinking gets positive results."

He shook his head mimicking her silently and waved off her assessment. Cedric could see where this was going and he didn't like it one bit. Somehow he knew he was going to be wrong. He dragged his gaze away from her matte red lips and stared out the side window.

"I'm not the one that's wrong here. I agree my tactics may need some work." He scowled. "Medina made a commitment and she's going to keep it." He needed to change the subject. His body ached for Iman. "Come here."

Iman stayed where she was. She arched an eyebrow at him. "Ask nicely."

"Come here, damn it," he said, smiling. He was winning. He could feel it.

"Come here damn it, please," Iman tossed back.

Cedric pushed his chair from his desk and

planted both feet firmly on the floor. "Come here damn it, please, Iman, and take care of your man."

Iman took her time closing and locking the door to his study before she came to him. She placed her knee between his legs on the chair and rested her hands on his shoulders. "That's much, much better."

She tasted exactly as he remembered only better, Cedric thought fuzzily. He slid his tongue over her lower lip, then sucked on the fullness. Her mouth eased opened in invitation and her breath rushed out. He sampled the velvet warmth, losing himself to her flavor.

"The girls," she murmured, when his hands stole beneath her vest and found the buttons of her shirt. He wrestled the silk shirt from the waist of her pants bunching it beneath her breasts. The vest fell to the floor.

Cedric dropped his head and sucked on her indented belly button. Iman gasped and writhed when he licked up her rib cage. Her fresh scent deepened into a powerful aphrodisiac as her temperature rose.

"Daddy? Can we come in?"

They both jumped off the chair. Iman fumbled with her blouse shoving it hastily into her jeans, bumping into the desk as she headed for the couch.

"Just a minute," Cedric called. "Iman," he whispered, waving her back. He tucked the flap of her shirt into the front of her pants, helped her into her vest, then grasped her face between his hands. He kissed her soundly. "I just wanted to make sure this wasn't a dream or a conspiracy against me for wanting you so much." His bulging pants relayed his desire.

"It's for real," she agreed, pressing herself lightly into him. "Open the door before they think we're up to something." Cedric got to the door and turned the handle but didn't open it. "I'm definitely up *for* something." Her nose brightened and a moment of silence hung between them.

"I . . ." The words stuck to his tongue, and Cedric didn't force them. He just couldn't say what lay on his heart. Iman smoothed her hair and looked questioningly at him. "Cedric, do I look okay?" She fussed with her shirt and vest, then smoothed her jeans. She was gorgeous.

"You look fine."

He flipped the latch and turned the handle on the door.

The girls burst in and headed straight for Iman. Both spoke at once. "Hi, Miss Iman."

"Hi, Anika. Hi, Medina." Iman inclined her head in their direction. "Let's leave your daddy to his work and go practice our speeches." They crowded out the door, leaving him alone.

Cedric stood in the doorway helplessly aroused with no outlet readily available. He watched Iman disappear around the corner with the girls and resigned himself to work. If only he could manage to concentrate.

He worked on his speech for *Kuumba* and leafed through the books Iman had in her bags. He quickly completed the thinner books, saving the thicker ones for later.

The sound of giggling filtered into his office through the half closed door.

He laid his pen down, and contemplated joining them. The legal pad he'd been writing on held only a partially completed speech. With *Kuumba* only days away, there was little time to waste.

Cedric shook his head and tried to concentrate.

But the sound of Iman playing with the girls and

their joyous laughter was too distracting. It didn't help his body recover either. He still wanted her.

Cedric picked up the warbling phone on his way to the kitchen. "Hello?"

"Cedric, it's Mother. Are you lifting weights? You sound out of breath."

Cedric refused to look past his waist again. It wouldn't do any good. "Something like that," he said dryly. "What's up Mom? Everything okay?"

"Of course it is," his sprightly mother replied. She claimed good health now, but he still worried about her.

"I'm just asking. How's Richard?"

"Richard's gone hunting with his son. Don't know what you could kill in the middle of winter but I said go. I called because I want my grand-bunnies to come over and spend the weekend with me. If you don't mind."

"Yes! Mom you saved my life." Cedric responded before he could think twice. The pulse in his lower region thundered in anticipation. Relief was just around the corner.

His mother laughed. "You must have plans. Got a hot date with Iman?"

"I plan to make one. Thanks Mom," he said before hanging up.

Cedric passed the picture he'd bought at the auction. The one Iman loved so much. It depicted children playing, their carefree spirit leaping off the canvas.

The first night he'd seen it, it had touched a lonely space inside him. He'd wished he could have been one of those children. Then he'd met Iman and he hadn't been lonely since.

The picture belonged to her. She'd seen it for

what it was and she'd found something in him. It was her spirit that held the strings of his heart.

Cedric picked up the painting and headed for the basement, where he wrapped it carefully, then stored it in the trunk of his car. He'd surprise her with it later.

He headed up the stairs to the girls' room. The door was ajar and he peeked through. Iman lay on her stomach on the floor, with Anika on her right and Medina on her left.

"My dad is very smart. He graduated to the tenth grade," Anika said importantly.

Iman shook her head. "He went to college, didn't he?"

Cedric held his breath. For some reason, uneasiness crept through him.

"No. He went to work. He has extra skin on his hands 'cause he had to work so hard." Medina crinkled her nose. "Sometimes he peels it."

"Then we put lotion on it," they said together.

"Your daddy is a very good man." Iman's husky voice made his heart swell. "We'd better get back to work. Medina, I don't want you to worry about your L's. You did perfect tonight. Absolutely, positively perfect."

"For rea-wl?" Hope surged in Medina's voice. She looked at Iman as if she'd hung the moon.

"For real," Iman reassured.

Cedric's heart swelled more than he thought it could.

"Anika," Iman went on. "Nobody told me you could sing. I think I have another job for you." Both girls giggled.

"Don't ask Daddy to sing. He sounds just like a rhinoceros." Anika giggled.

Cedric started to push the door open.

"Miss Iman, are you married?" He stopped and waited.

"Not yet."

"Are you going to marry our daddy?" Medina asked.

Iman sat back on her knees away from the girls. They followed her up and sat beside her with their legs crossed. She seemed to be studying the cranberry colored carpet intently. Cedric held his breath.

"He hasn't asked."

"If he did, would you?"

She laughed. "You two sure are inquisitive." She stood and reached for their hands pulling them up. "Let's just say that if he brings it up one day, I'd think about it. How do you feel about that?"

"Good," they responded unanimously.

"Really? Why?"

Cedric pressed his head against the door while they considered her question. It occurred to him they might be unhappy. His chest tightened, not knowing. Finally Anika spoke.

"Everybody in our class has a mother. We just want to have one, too. Daddy needs a wife so he doesn't have to be by himself all the time."

"I see," Iman said. "Well I'm sure things will work out for him."

Cedric knocked on the door. He wiped mist from his eyes before he walked in. "How's everything going?"

"Fine," they all responded. Cedric looked at Iman. She stared at the floor for a long time before meeting his gaze, briefly.

"Grandma wants you to come spend the weekend with her." Cedric pretended to shake from the girls squeals of happiness. "Since that's a yes, we'd better get some things together. But you have to practice your speeches while you're there." He walked to the mirrored wall closet and slid the panel open.

"Daddy, can Miss Iman help us?"

"Well . . ."

"I don't mind," she said coming to stand beside him.

Cedric touched her arm. "I'll be waiting downstairs." He walked from the room, closing the door behind him.

Chapter Ten

Iman stared at Cedric's long legs, which were stretched out in front of him. She'd come to know his favorite reading position as he crowded the corner of the couch with his lean frame, giving the book on his lap his undivided attention.

They had come to her house after dropping off the girls and he had assumed that position an hour ago working fervently on his speech.

Troubling thoughts assailed her. He was in her house, her life, but he hadn't said a word about her confession of love. What if he didn't feel the same way? Had she made a complete and utter fool of herself? Iman silently berated herself.

She tried to imagine herself without Cedric and the girls, but couldn't. Their reason for seeing each other so often would soon be gone.

What would happen to them?

Iman lowered the book from her lap and strolled to the window unobtrusively so as not to disturb him. The clear, cold, starlit sky held no fireworks, no exploding bombs, no blazes of light that scorched "Love" in neon lights in the stars.

But they were bright. Luminous as if she'd never seen them before. Some formed a smile, while others danced.

Iman shook herself. Who'd ever heard of dancing stars?

"The stars are beautiful tonight," she remarked. Surely, if he looked, he would see what she saw.

Absently he glanced over his shoulder and nodded.

"Mmm."

Discontent swirled through her.

Iman settled back in the armchair to watch the man she couldn't imagine being without and wondered why he didn't see the same damn dancing stars she did.

Earlier in his study, she'd thought he might say he loved her. Instead, he'd opened the door for the girls and the opportunity vanished.

He loved her, she could feel it. But would he ever say it?

"I'm going upstairs to wrap presents," she announced, hoping he would stop her. Her hopes were dashed when he only nodded.

Iman took the wooden steps slowly. She gathered wrapping paper, clothes, boxes, and bows and dragged them to her room where she got comfortable on her queen size bed.

Methodically she cut, wrapped, and taped. Bows and ornaments in brilliant reds, greens, blues, and purples lay strewn on the bed and she peeled the backs off several, matching the perfect bow to each color paper.

Iman tossed the others in a growing pile of discarded wrapping paper which covered the top corner of her bed. A flash of guilt coursed through her at her wastefulness.

Her thoughts wandered to the woman from Cedric's company on the television screen. Iman knew it wouldn't help, but she folded several of the larger pieces to use later.

"Need anything?"

The door to her room was wide open and Cedric leaned one shoulder against the frame. Although his stance was casual, tension radiated from him. It made desire coil inside her like a hot spring.

His smoldering gaze caressed her bare leg that dangled over the side of the bed. Slowly it moved up and over the colorful caftan that gathered at her thighs.

She watched his tongue caress his lower lip.

Iman began to perspire.

His gaze lingered at her breasts, then locked with hers letting her know it wasn't Christmas presents he was talking about. Her concerns slipped away under the heat of his gaze. "I need you."

He started into the room. Iman slid both legs off the bed, her knees slightly apart.

She closed her eyes when his strong fingers tunneled through her hair, forcing her head back.

The long zipper on the back of her caftan made a cutting noise in the silence, broken only by the sounds of their heavy breathing. The caftan pooled around her waist.

His hands guided her up and the *kente* print dress dropped around her ankles. Strong fingers slid under the straps of her bra and peeled them down her arms. His forehead touched hers and his mouth was slightly open.

Their lips met and the tip of his tongue tantalized her.

Iman reached around and unhooked the back of her bra. It dropped between them, deep brown nipples peeking over the lavender lace.

"You want me?" she asked seductively against his

mouth. His thigh nudged hers and his hand slid boldly up between her legs. Her panties were no match for his probing fingers.

Iman cried out, rising on her toes, wanting more.

He held her still and sampled her wetness. With the slowness of a predator stalking its prey, his fingers drew a moist path through her dark patch of hair, stopping long enough to make her left breast ache, then mercifully ending at her lips.

Cedric tilted her chin up and stroked her other breast lazily. "Do *you* want me?"

Iman nodded yes, mute.

He suckled and licked the rest of the clothes from her skin. It was maddening, his loving was so good.

"I don't want to be naked by myself." Iman reached for Cedric, but he stepped out of her arms. She couldn't control her shivers of anticipation as he performed a slow striptease for her. Iman crawled to the center of her bed and waited.

This was what she'd dreamed about. Yearned for. Desired so much. Him. With her. Inside her. Taking her places she hadn't been in a long, long time. Iman silently thanked Aliyah's forethought as she handed him the little foil packet. Her heartbeat quickened when Cedric kissed her his thanks. She didn't know what she would do if they had to stop.

Wrapping paper protested under her back as he lay her down and loved her with such tenderness her eyes dripped tears from the splendid ecstasy.

Afterward he stroked her until the tears subsided and the pleasure began again. This time when the back of her thighs met the front of his, it was with an intensity surpassed only by their coupling of moments ago.

Iman lay on top of Cedric, her arms resting on his broad shoulders, her head against his chest. He held her still as he peeled another Christmas bow from her bottom.

"Ouch, what was that?"

"Christmas bows. Be still." She jerked when he disengaged the last bow from her skin.

"No," he groaned. "Don't be still. I like when you do that." His large hands rotated her hips against him.

"I tingle," she murmured.

"Is that *all?*" He slowed the movements and looked down at their bodies pressed together.

Iman grabbed the bow from the scattered covers. "I meant my rear tingles from where you pulled this darn thing."

He took it from her hands and pressed it on the tip of her breast. Iman slapped playfully at Cedric's arms when he swiftly flipped her onto her back and loomed over her.

"Hey, how are you going to make sure that doesn't hurt when you take it off?" He lowered his head. "Oh, good, yes," she sighed a moment later when he used his tongue to remove it.

Chapter Eleven

Cedric reclined against the wooden head board and watched Iman sleep. She was beautiful in all her naked glory. Her skin was a soft brown, even in coloring from her head to her feet. Except her nipples. The tips were as dark in hue as his skin. And tasted better than any delicacy he'd ever sampled.

He'd had a chance to taste every inch of her over the last three hours. His body stirred at the memories of their passion. She loved him. *She loved him.*

The next move was his. But what did Iman want out of life? Did she want to be a wife, an instant mother?

Those thoughts plagued him as he silently slid out of the bed and into his jeans. Her house was southern, comfortable in a way he'd experienced only later in his life. It hadn't been until he was grown and on his way to wealth that he'd been invited into nice homes.

Life was strange. Iman seemed happy with her life in a way few people were. She loved what she did.

He couldn't say the same thing. A long time ago, Dix had been a golden opportunity, a means to an end.

It didn't hold the same meaning anymore. The takeover of Blythe Pharmaceuticals bothered him more than he cared to admit. He couldn't get the faces of the people out of his head.

Company morale remained low and for the first time, his personal life was good. He wanted everybody to be as happy as he. Damn it.

Cedric hurried to the car and got Iman's painting from the trunk. At least he could do one thing right. He hung it in the spot she'd indicated the first time he'd come to her house and then went to the refrigerator. Something in his life had to change.

He provided a stable home and had secured a solid future for Anika and Medina. Not bad for a man with a tenth-grade education. So what was missing? Would having someone to come home to cure his restlessness?

"Are you trying to cool off America with that door open?"

Cedric closed the refrigerator door and leaned against it. "Just thinking." A long, white lace robe sheathed Iman. The darkest parts of her were still visible. He could feel himself growing and tightening beneath his half closed jeans. His gaze raked her. "Is that thing supposed to do something?"

She struck a pose, then slid her hand down from her waist to her thigh where she parted the thin material.

"It's supposed to titillate, tantalize, and tease the mind, body, and spirit." She walked forward slowly. "Is it working?"

He kissed her nose. "I'm completely under your spell."

Iman rose on her toes and kissed his mouth. "I know it's the middle of the night, but I want something to eat. Are you hungry?"

"Only for you."

Iman opened the silverware drawer, pulled out a

spatula and swatted at him with it. "Back. I was talking about frying some chicken."

"Chicken is good, too. What do you want me to do?"

She handed him some potatoes. "Peel."

Iman had the chicken in the frying pan in no time.

Cedric dropped peeled and cubed potatoes into a pot of water on the stove, while Iman pulled two beers from the refrigerator and set them on the table.

When everything was bubbling appropriately, they sat at the kitchen table with their drinks.

Iman studied Cedric. He seemed so relaxed with his naked chest and bare feet.

The discussion with the girls that afternoon gave her a better understanding of him. She now realized he was so intense because of the immense responsibility he'd had from a young age. The knowledge that he'd only been educated to the tenth grade stunned her. His recent problems with the two companies merging came to the forefront of her mind.

"Have things settled down with your new employees?"

He shrugged. "Some are resentful their friends got let go. Others are grateful they still have jobs. Others are worried I'll fire them next month. Overall, it's been a cautious undertaking." Iman sensed something more, something he wasn't saying.

"Would you do it again?"

"Yes." He looked into her eyes. "It's not personal. It's business."

Iman shivered at his tone. "I know. But you must understand how they feel."

"What am I supposed to do? If it weren't my company it would be somebody else. I didn't let forty thousand people go like one of the Bell companies. I didn't pull something like that. It was one hundred people. Let's drop the subject."

He got up and stalked to the stove. The grease popped as he turned the chicken, then he slipped the metal cover over the snapping oil. It sizzled, then settled back into its regular bubbling level.

Too restless to sit, he leaned his shoulder against the refrigerator and crossed his arms.

"When did you discover teaching was right for you?"

Iman watched him closely. Cedric didn't like talking about himself. Whenever he was uncomfortable, he changed the subject. He'd done it before. She decided not to call him on it and answered.

"I've known since I was six years old. What about you? Will you always run Dix?" Iman felt driven to know the "It's business" part of Cedric. For an inexplicable reason, it mattered.

He put the cooked chicken on plates and dished out the potato salad. "I don't know." His answer shocked her. They began eating. His potato salad tasted delicious.

"Have you ever considered doing something else?" she asked.

"No. I never have." Iman looked up from her plate at him. There was a finality to his voice that made her sad. He was bound to something she got the impression he didn't like. Iman felt sorry for people who didn't like their jobs. She loved hers so.

The overwhelming urge to cuddle with Cedric filled her. Silently, she eased onto his lap and wrapped her arms around him.

It took a long time before she felt his arms move. Then his body curved and molded to hers. Their strength bonding.

"Let's go back to bed," he murmured against her hair.

"I'll race you." The seductiveness of his touch made her anxious to repeat their earlier pleasure and to forget the world.

Cedric swept her up into his arms. "We both win, we have all night."

"Ada, it's Iman. Where are you?"

Slightly out of breath from climbing three flights of stairs to Ada's apartment, Iman dropped her key on the table close to the door and stepped back.

Ada's apartment always overwhelmed her when she first entered. Having called the same place home for over fifteen years, Ada had long ago filled up every corner with its capacity of decorations.

Now everything went up. Iman always had the sneaking feeling that something was going to fall off the wall and land on her head.

She heard Ada's answering cough and hurried to the bedroom. Her frail body was dwarfed beneath a mountain of ancient hand stitched quilts. The vaporizer hummed a steady cloud of steam, while crumpled tissues littered the floor.

"Iman," she wheezed. "Chile, what you doing here? We don't have much time before *Umoja.* You got everythin' taken care of?"

Iman took off her coat and dropped it at the foot of Ada's bed. Despite the woman's weakened state, the room was tidy. Iman threw the stray tissues in the can. She touched Ada's forehead, sucking her teeth at the dampness.

"Everything's fine. I came looking for you. I called you yesterday but nobody answered."

"I had a doctor's appointment at two o'clock. He

gave me a new medicine, but I took the last of it last night."

"Why didn't you call me? I would have taken you." Iman caressed Ada's hand while she talked. She couldn't bear to think of her in the cold winter air by herself. Ada gave her hand a strong squeeze.

"I knew you were at the manor decorating and practicing for the *Karamu.* That doctor must be crazy to think I'm going to spend sixty-seven dollars for a bottle of medicine.

"Don't worry about me, chile. I mixed up something myself."

Medicine bottles, a cup with dark goo in it, and a half-melted candle cluttered the bedside table. Iman wrinkled her nose when she picked up the foul smelling cup and took a whiff of the concoction.

"Honey, what is this?"

She drew her nose back sharply from the pungent odor.

"It was good enough for you crumb snatchers," Ada said sharply. She coughed long and hard. "Only thing is, I didn't have enough eye of newt to finish it."

Iman laughed softly. That was Ada's way of putting her in her place. She was proud of her Haitian heritage and scoffed at conventional methods of healing. Only, the medicine she needed today was very conventional and very expensive.

Iman made her some tea and held her head so she could sip it. "Do you have any more sample bottles of medicine from the doctor?"

"No. He only gave me one."

Ada raised up on her elbows when Iman stood.

"Don't go rousting the pharmacist, Iman. They told me how you showed out last month trying to get that other medicine for me at a discount. They're giving me the best they can. It's my own fault I'm like this."

Iman held her through another coughing fit. "No, it's not. It's the drug companies' fault for overpricing these medicines. And I intend to do something about it."

Ada's eyes followed her movements. "Chile, I smoked cigarettes for fifty-five years. These old lungs belong only to me. I made them this way."

Iman straightened Ada's covers, raising her chin stubbornly. "You would be well if you could afford the medicine."

Iman gently patted Ada's shoulder. She followed the phone cord to Ada's rotary phone.

"I'm calling Aliyah to come sit with you while I go pay our friendly pharmacist a visit. The last time I was there, he said the drug company was right here in Atlanta. I'll need this." Iman grabbed the bottle from the table and shoved it in her coat pocket. She braced the phone under her chin twirling the dial. "Don't you worry, I'll take care of everything."

"Oh, goodness," Ada groaned. "Have mercy on them."

Chapter Twelve

Iman stalked into the lobby of the Dix Pharmaceutical Company, Inc. Before she left, Ada had almost passed out from the coughing fit that shook her frail body. But like always, she refused to go to the hospital.

Iman was desperate and she knew of only one person who could help her. The ride up to the fourth floor of the washed stone structure gave her a chance to formulate her scattered thoughts. She squared her shoulders and stood tall. She would present her argument in a logical, reasonable way, and he would see reason.

The doors breezed open. Iman stepped into the lobby and walked the few steps to the receptionist desk.

"Cedric Hamilton, please."

The tiny receptionist flicked down the mouthpiece of her headphone and looked at her.

"Do you have an appointment?"

"No, but he'll see me."

The woman gave her a polite smile. "Mr. Hamilton is a very busy man. He operates on an appointment basis only."

Iman impatiently nodded her head. "He'll see me. I'm his—" She stopped. They hadn't defined their relationship with labels. She'd said she loved him, he'd said thank you.

"His girlfriend," Iman managed.

"Just a minute, ma'am." The woman hurried away and slipped into a room down the hall. Iman clenched and opened her fists. She reassured herself that things would be fine.

The door opened and Cedric stepped out. He approached her in long strides. Immense relief flooded her once her hands were within his.

"What's the matter?" His concern made her weak. Everything was going to be all right.

"It's Ada." He wrapped his arm around her shoulder.

"Did she . . . die?"

She hurried to reassure him. "No, she isn't dead."

"Then what is it?"

Iman looked into the eyes of the man she loved. In his arms she had found pleasure beyond her wildest dreams. Now she felt support. She knew why she loved him. Words spilled from her mouth.

"Ada needs our help. Cedric, your company manufactures the medicine her doctor prescribed to make her better. You have to lower the price so she can afford it." Iman retrieved the bottle from her coat pocket and pressed it into his hands.

The pencil the receptionist's had been writing with snapped.

Cedric took her by the hand. "Come into my office." He guided her down the hall and closed the door behind them. The expensively decorated office was a blur as Iman turned to face him.

"Cedric, did you hear me? Ada needs your help."

"I can't do what you're asking."

"Why?" She searched his features for a clue.

Cedric pushed himself away from the door and walked around his desk.

"Iman, drug prices can't arbitrarily be lowered. That's not how business is done. There are two hundred people that work for this company. Those people have families that depend on them. They count on me to make sure they get paychecks. If we're not profitable, then people lose jobs."

A steel trap seemed to be closing over her. Iman fought for air. "Cedric, this is Ada we're talking about. She's not some nameless, faceless person from RSG. She's my friend." Her voice quivered, but she continued to meet his level gaze. "Be reasonable." The words were more personal than she intended. Iman waited, hoping he would transform before her eyes.

His expression remained one of pained tolerance. "I'm being reasonable, and it seems as though I'm the only one who's doing so. What you're asking is ludicrous."

Fire rushed through her. Her voice came raggedly in impotent anger. "I know the medicine from that little bottle doesn't cost sixty-seven dollars to make. For goodness sake, senior citizens are the predominant market for this drug." She flung her arm out. "Most of them are on fixed incomes. How are they supposed to afford it?"

He settled behind his desk in the high-back leather chair, unfazed by her outburst. Iman's hope began to unravel.

"Most of the people who use this medicine have some kind of insurance or another. There's only a small number that actually pay market price."

She braced her hands on his desk. "Then what do the Ada's of the world do?"

His steepled fingers flew open. "It's not for everybody. Iman, this is business—"

Iman held up her hand. She resisted screaming at Cedric's tolerant look. "If you say that to me one more time, I swear, I'll scream."

Her throat constricted, but she forced herself to go on. "You know, that's your problem. You're so wound up in *business* you can't see your own face. Cedric, you've forgotten what poverty is like because you're hiding behind expensive suits and useless dresses for the girls." His eyebrows shot up, but he remained silent. Iman went on.

"You've reached a comfort zone that many don't ever see. You're too *rich.*" Iman shuddered distastefully.

His voice was as sharp as jagged glass. "I worked my butt off to get where I am today, and I won't just give it away on a whim. I give back to this community the way I know how. I do care. Lowering the price of a medication is not the answer. Why can't Ada get on one of the social programs?"

"She's afraid she'll be deported. She's not a United States citizen." Iman's eyes watered. She made her final plea. "Cedric, please. I've never asked you for anything before. For Ada." *For me,* she said silently.

"Lowering the price of the medication isn't the answer." His voice rang with finality.

Iman firmly placed her purse strap on her shoulder. "My bottle, please." She extended her hand; she couldn't look at him.

"What are you going to do?"

"I'm going to take care of Ada myself."

"You mean buy the medicine yourself."

She looked at him. "Yes."

Miles separated them.

All Cedric cared about was his precious bottom line. She should have known. It was business. Shame washed over her. The last time he'd said that to her should have served as enough of a warning.

Iman focused on the reddish-brown bottle in his hands and waited for him to give it to her. She wanted to leave before her tears started to flow.

Cedric placed the bottle on the desk between them. Iman slowly took it and dropped it in her purse. She walked to the door.

"Are you going over there now?"

She nodded. Breezy indifference failed her. Her voice wavered. "I'll be busy over the next few days."

"Let me come with you."

"No. I don't need—" Iman struggled with the words that pushed at her throat. "You've done enough."

"Will w-we—" he stammered. "Will I see you later?"

"No." She met his bewildered gaze. She deliberately whispered. "Good-bye."

Iman disappeared through the door.

Chapter Thirteen

"Mr. Hamilton, may I have a word with you, please?" Cedric looked up from the computer screen surprised to find he wasn't alone. Most of the skeleton staff of employees had already left for the day. Considering it was the day before Christmas Eve.

Debra Gray, his receptionist, waited expectantly in the doorway. "What is it, Debra? I thought everyone was gone."

"I was leaving about an hour ago, but a delivery arrived. It's waiting for you in the conference room."

He rose from the desk, annoyed. "If it's a normal delivery, why didn't it go through receiving? I don't have to sign for every little package that comes into this office."

Cedric followed the silent woman to the conference room, further aggravated that she didn't defend her actions.

Ever since his showdown with Iman earlier that day, he'd been spoiling for a fight. He stepped through the door into darkness.

"What in the hell's going on here?" The overhead lights flickered and illuminated the room.

Cedric's jaw went slack. At least one hundred

brightly wrapped Christmas packages spilled from the table onto the chairs. When that space ran out, the gifts covered the floor of the conference room.

All of Anika and Medina's Christmas gifts from Iman's house were wrapped and ready to be delivered.

Debra stood silently behind him. He finally spoke.

"When did she come back?"

"She left about five minutes ago. She said not to disturb you. You were busy . . ." The rest of the sentence died on her lips.

"She said I was busy doing what?"

"Fleecing the elderly."

Cedric pushed a gift to the floor and sat in a conference room chair. A bow and ornament stuck to his pant leg, and he pulled it off.

The brilliant purple glass ball distorted his facial expression. His head was wide, making the grim set to his mouth seem monstrous.

Probably how I looked to Iman and Jack McClure when I said no.

"Thank you, Debra."

The door closed quietly.

He caressed the thin glass. It was perfect in shape, pleasing to the eye. That was the main reason he'd chosen it. Cedric looked around the room.

Everything mirrored the same controlled perfection. Books stood upright as if monitored by a military general. His office, always impeccably neat and orderly. The staff at Dix, efficient and highly qualified. And it was all his.

On the surface, everything looked great. He'd even tried to have perfect children. Guilt over his behavior toward Medina assaulted him. Indeed, he had used tyrannical tactics to make her into the person he wanted her to be.

But the finely woven fabric of his suit couldn't hide his true identity. That poor, cold child from his past still lived inside.

Once a skinny kid, he'd been fattened, polished by strangers. People who stood to gain nothing personally. But they loved him enough to instill in him the values of hard work and achievement which later fostered his success. Those were the values he wanted to pass to his children.

Cedric rose from the chair and packed the gifts in his car.

Back in the office, the printer surged to life after he hit the command and signed off the computer. He stared at the numbers that declared Dix's hefty profits on all twelve medications, Ada's being one of them.

Cedric lowered himself into his chair. What had he become? Too rich, as Iman claimed? So far above others he no longer cared for their suffering?

A man of too much ability and means, but lacking the one thing money couldn't buy.

Where was his heart?

I can do this, echoed in his head. The pronouncement shook him to the core where his deepest fears lay. His past replayed through his mind like photos from a single framed camera. Highlights of the worst times flashed. Bitter cold, nonstop hunger pains that eventually ebbed into dull flatness. Hopelessness. Fear. He shut his eyes immersing himself in all he used to despair.

Then there was Lenora. Michael Dix. His beautiful children. His mother on her wedding day. Iman.

Iman. His love, his life.

I can do this. Cedric looked in the Rolodex and punched buttons on the phone. "Jack, Cedric Hamilton, sorry to bother you at home. I've decided to lower the prices on the medications on your list."

Cedric smiled when the man's buoyant laughter echoed through the phone.

"A Monday morning meeting sounds good. Goodnight, Jack."

Cedric grabbed his coat and drove slowly, making decisions that would change his life forever. He prayed Iman would want to share the future with him.

Cedric checked the doors as he locked up the house for the night. The girls were asleep, his house still twinkled with white lights, and the Christmas goose was a few pounds lighter than when it had arrived with his mother and stepfather hours ago.

But Cedric was alone.

Iman hadn't wanted to see him. She'd declined to spend Christmas with him. She'd taken time to call and speak to the girls, wishing them a happy day, but when he'd gotten the phone when they were done, he'd met a dial tone.

Today, unlike less than a week ago, there was no giggling. No anticipation growing inside him, like the last time she'd been there.

He was alone, and he hated it. Convincing her to share her life with him might not happen. Cedric shook off the depressing thoughts as he stacked the unopened presents under the tree. The girls had been so ungrateful. They'd only wanted two things, and when they found them, refused to open any more.

He shook his head.

"Daddy?" Cedric stood from his crouched position. He approached Anika and placed his hand on her forehead.

"Hey, there. You feeling okay?"

"I feel good. Medina went back to sleep so I came to talk to you about our plan." He sat down on the couch and drew her on his lap. "What kind of great plan could pull you from your bed in the middle of the night?"

She pointed to the tree. "We want to give our Christmas presents away."

Cedric drew back, stunned. Realization surged through his veins. When he found his voice it was emotion filled. He stroked her long braid. "Why?"

"Because we got a lot. More than other kids." Her solemn gaze met his. "We won't do it if you're going to get mad."

Cedric shook his head recognizing how they'd all changed. His voice filled with pride. "I'm very proud of you and your sister for making such a grown-up decision." He scooted her off his lap and held her hand as he guided her to the stairs. "You know, your old man could take some lessons from you girls. You're very smart." He tucked her in and kissed her forehead.

"You're very smart, too. I love you, Daddy." Anika snuggled next to her Addie doll and drifted off, unaware of the love glistening in her father's eyes.

Chapter Fourteen

Kuumba was upon them.

Cedric ran his hand nervously over his head and knocked off his *kofi*. Hastily he put it back on and dropped his hand to his side. He rolled his head on his shoulders and shrugged to loosen himself.

"Daddy, you're going to be great. Re-wax." Medina squeezed his hand, her eyes dancing merrily. Cedric knew he was acting uncharacteristically nervous, but tonight was important.

"I'm okay, sweetie." He kneeled down, a rush of paternal love filling him. Medina was a smart girl. And he told her so.

"Medina, I'm very proud of you. It doesn't matter how you do today, I just want you to know that I love you and . . ." Cedric stopped when her name was called to join her class.

"I love you, Medina."

She kissed his cheek in an exuberant rush and hugged him with a quickness that almost had him on his bottom. She walked away then turned and said, "I love you too, Daddy."

Cedric barely controlled the tears that sprang to his eyes. She'd said it. The perfect L.

He turned his attention to the capacity crowd that filled the basement of Stone Manor. Just over a month ago, he'd come to the magnificent house alone, and incomplete.

Through his studies of Kwanzaa, he'd learned more about himself and the course his life would continue on.

Yet, there was one part missing.

Iman.

He'd spotted her earlier with Ada, who looked healthier and happier from taking her medication properly. He'd visited her several times during the week and had been pleasantly surprised by her snappy humor and straightforward opinion on his and Iman's relationship. He held on to her confidence that everything would work out. Several members of RSG were present also which made him feel even better about his decision.

Cedric turned his attention to the program. Impromptu dancers from the audience dazzled the crowd during the drum-playing segment much to everyone's delight.

Then a libation was poured to deceased ancestors. Cedric wished he could hold Iman's hand. He knew she was thinking of her father.

Then all the children congregated in front of the stage for the lighting of the candles. Medina and Anika read their speeches and everyone applauded loudly giving the youngsters a standing ovation for their effort.

Iman hugged each child, exclaiming how proud she was of them. She told stories, just as she'd promised, captivating the crowd with her voice. She was a hit.

Cedric gave the New York dance troupe and karate demonstration only half his attention. His focus was on Iman and their future together as a family.

The Negro National Anthem music started, and

the crowd rose and sang, then a local dance group concluded the evening with uplifting African dances.

Cedric took a deep breath. He'd researched *Kuumba* and labored over his speech for days. It was perfect. He was ready. Finally, it was time.

He walked on-stage and shoved the speech in his pocket. The applause died down and he called, "*Habari Gani!*"

The crowd echoed its response.

Cedric stood before the audience in full African attire looking very kingly in gold, the color of prosperity and royalty.

"Tonight my charge was to be eloquent and moving. But I stand before you humble in my responsibility." He gazed out over the crowd and found Iman.

"When I was first asked to present the farewell, I said no. I thought, what do I have to say that's good enough to take our families into the next year? Then a little voice said to me, 'You're going to be great. I believe in you.' The funny thing is, the other day, I began to believe it too."

Cedric's voice reached inside her and stopped Iman's pacing. "I'll tell you what I've learned through Kwanzaa."

He folded his hands on the podium and looked out over the crowd. "Opening yourself up and stepping outside your comfort zone are the scariest things a person can do, because outside represents the unknown. It's where fear hides, doubt reigns.

"I used to believe that until recently. Someone I love challenged me to do my collective work and responsibility toward my fellow man. At the time, I didn't know what she meant."

Several people nodded. Others shook their heads.

Iman stared, amazed. She couldn't believe Cedric was telling everybody their story.

He continued. "I felt I had served my purpose, done what I was supposed to do. Given all I could give." He shook his head. "I didn't know how much more needs to be done until I was faced with losing something . . . someone special." He looked into the audience and seemed to address each of them personally.

"Don't be like me and put worldly goods before things that really matter like imagination, trust, and most of all faith and love. My challenge to you is to utilize your talents, knowledge, and beliefs to help improve the lives of those around you. The rewards will come back to you one hundred times over."

Through blurred eyes, Iman watched Cedric straighten and catch himself being eloquent and moving. He'd relaxed as he'd spoken and moved away from the microphone, his confidence captivating the capacity crowd.

He stood behind the podium again.

"Most important of all, listen to the voice that whispers. It's probably telling you something you can't afford to miss. Thank you."

People applauded around her. Cedric left the podium and headed to the back of the stage. Iman tried to reach him, but it was time for the feast.

She didn't see him again until the entire festival was over and only a few straggler's remained. Elaine had long since taken Anika and Medina home with her, leaving them free to talk undisturbed.

Cedric stacked the last of the chairs, while Mr. Winston and other brothers completed the clean up.

"You two go ahead and leave, we've got the rest," Mr. Winston said.

Iman hesitantly dragged on her coat. She wrapped Cedric's scarf around her head and waited while he pulled his coat on. She turned to face him. "Thank you for the picture. I didn't get to say it before. You didn't have to."

He stood beside her, staring intently into her soul. He reached for her bags, speaking softly. "It was your *Zawadi* gift from me."

They walked down the long hallway which led outside.

"Want to take a ride?" he asked.

Anticipation surged within her. Her mouth quirked. "Sure."

This time she paid attention when they entered interstate seventy-five heading to Tennessee.

"I have a lot to say to you." Cedric drummed his thumbs on the steering wheel nervously. "Iman, I'm sorry about Ada. I know how important she is to you and I never wanted to hurt you or her. It's just that, well, when you asked me to lower the price of the medicine, I took it as a personal attack. I know how irrational that sounds, but, I couldn't get past the thought that my family would suffer the way I had."

He looked at her briefly before returning his attention to the road. His voice was soft. "Dix has been my life for a long time. I got my start there, and it's provided a stable future for my family. A part of me didn't want to disturb what's gotten me where I am today."

Iman broke in. "I was being unreasonable. I had no right to challenge your livelihood. It's just that I don't want to lose Ada. And I took my fear out on you."

"You didn't; you opened my eyes. I love you for that. I realized lowering the prices isn't going to hurt anyone. In fact, so many people will benefit, maybe other pharmaceutical companies will do the same. Even if they don't, I know I did the right thing. However, there is a question about our future."

Cedric guided the car to the side of the road and stopped. He turned toward her.

"What about it?"

He took her hands in his. "I love you. And I hope you still love me enough to give us a chance. I want us to start a life, together."

"I want that too. Do you really love me?" she whispered.

He gathered her in his arms, and touched her softly with his lips. Happy butterflies danced in Iman's stomach.

"Very much. I want a future with you," he whispered, "forever," then nibbled her ear and neck.

"Forever?" she asked breathlessly. "As in today and the rest of our lives? As your . . ."

"As my wife. Do you have a problem with that?" His deep voice rumbled close to her ear.

"Not at all." Her heart soared. His kisses were tender as they moved against her lips, marking his territory, leaving unspoken promises.

Iman responded with all the love inside her. She caressed his face with her fingertips. "How much farther to Lookout Mountain, Tennessee?"

"Thirty minutes. Why?" Cedric took her hand, love radiating from him.

"Because I can't wait for us to start our future where we began our lives together."

HARVEST THE FRUITS

Margie Walker

Selinae noticed she was not the only runner taking advantage of the spring-like evening. Enticed by the pleasant weather, several joggers traversed the trail that twisted over the sloping landscape high above MacGregor Bayou. Though it was now dusk, it had been sunny and bright all day. Not atypical in Houston, even in late December.

As if unaffected by the change in seasons, oaks, pines, and magnolia trees stood tall and proud in well-tended grounds around grand, two-story homes strategically located on either side of the bayou in a predominantly African American neighborhood. Decorations featuring Santas, snowmen, and reindeers graced practically every yard.

A professional-looking runner passed Selinae easily and continued across the Scott Street light. Selinae smirked as she watched him go. She turned up the paved sidewalk, crossing to the other side of the bayou on the return run to her original destination, MacGregor Park. She had no idea the distance she had come, and she was beginning to regret that she had ever set out. She hated running. It hadn't always been that way.

But she didn't have anything else to do, she reasoned to herself and wasn't up to being in the company of others. And in the privacy of her own house, there was too much temptation to wallow in despair. She had to get out.

Her sense of alienation and loss was always amplified during the holidays, a time when suicides were high. In that regard, she was not alone. The day after Christmas was always a letdown, even to the happiest of people.

But the day before, Christmas Day, had been no joyous occasion, either, she remembered.

"Forget it," Selinae said, the command instantly carried away on the wind.

With the back of her hand, she wiped at the sweat dripping from her forehead, then rubbed her hand dry on her pants. Pumping her arms in sync with the moderate tempo she'd set, her mind jogged back in time.

At the start of the year, one of her resolutions had been to bridge the gap between herself and her parents. Olive branch gestures made during the year were to culminate in a Christmas truce. Her brothers and their families planned to come in from out of town. She was going to spend the whole day celebrating the holiday with her family. It would have been a first in many, many years.

While there had been no major blow-up with her father, she almost wished there had been. It would have been better than the facade of cheer and grudging politeness that permeated the affair. She left shortly after the elaborate dinner her mother and sister-in-laws had prepared.

But not soon enough, she remembered. Not before her mother caught Selinae staring at her father, bouncing his chubby eight-month-old grandson on his knees. His face was as animated as the baby's; it was hard to tell which one of them was enjoying the moment the most.

Selinae hadn't needed a mirror to see her expression. She was certain it fully conveyed her lachrymose spirits. She was on the precipice of dredging up even more painful memories.

"It's time you put your bitterness aside," her mother had whispered in her ear.

Mission unaccomplished, Selinae thought. Whoever said time healed all wounds apparently never knew the depths of pain her indiscretion had wrought. It defied forgiveness.

Since she couldn't have the latter, she'd better work harder on forgetting and building herself a new emotional life, she told herself. The cycle of guilt, regret, and despair had been with her for too long.

Yet, letting go was hard.

Suddenly, Selinae picked up her run in an all-out sprint. Almost there, she told her legs, which were burning at the calves from the effort. *Almost there.*

Finally, she reached the corner of Calhoun and North MacGregor. She ran in place, waiting for the light to change before crossing the street.

When the oncoming traffic stopped, she sprinted across the street and over the grassy landscape of the park. With only yards left to go, she set her sights on her car, a black convertible Mustang. It was the only car parked in the lot across from the fenced-in swimming pool, which was closed for the winter.

Nearing the lot, she slowed to a walk, drawing deep breaths of oxygen into her lungs. Glad the run was finally over, she planned a nice, long bubble bath for when she got home.

No more than twenty feet from her car, she spotted several young men walking toward her from the opposite direction. They were coming from the basketball court. She paid them no particular attention, fiddling for her keys in the small pocket of her jogging pants. They reached the car at about the same time she did.

"This your car?"

The key now clutched in her hand, Selinae looked up. She counted heads, noting quickly that there were five of them. They were sweaty looking, but nowhere near as exhausted as she was.

On the surface, the question was innocent enough. But a sidelong gaze revealed one of the gangly youths eyeing her car covetously, rubbing a proprietary hand across the hood. Selinae immediately felt threatened. A shiver ran down her spine; it had nothing to do with her body temperature.

Her gaze split between the adorer of her car and the speaker. A slender, tough-looking youngster of about thirteen, he was the smallest and the shortest in the group. He returned her curious look with practiced cockiness. She assumed he was the leader by his stance and the menacing smile curled on his lips.

Trepidation replaced exhaustion. She thought about turning around and running in the opposite direction. Reasoning that she probably couldn't outrun them, she decided to hold her ground.

"It's my car, yes," she replied at last.

"Nice," he said.

She wanted to hurry and open the door, but was hesitant to approach them. Realizing she was convicting them in her thoughts, she felt a twinge of guilt. Innocent until proven guilty, she reminded herself. These were kids, after all, and they had done nothing criminal . . . yet.

"How 'bout giving us a ride?"

His tone posed more of a challenge than a request, and it caught Selinae by surprise. She shifted uneasily, not sure how to answer. Despite their youth, these young boys were potentially dangerous to her health.

"Not today."

She tried for a friendly, firm tone; instead, her voice sounded scared. Holding the key defensively before her, she casually took a step toward the door. She could feel her legs shaking.

"But we tired," the youngster declared, stepping into her path.

Though she could look down into his face, standing so close he seemed taller; his boldness defied his size. The other boys closed in around them, and a hard fist of fear clenched in the pit of her stomach. She railed herself silently for not running when she'd had the chance.

Street lamps automatically popped on around the park. Selinae looked, but saw no one in the area to call to for help.

Sterling saw them as he crossed the street on his way to the hillside jogging trail above the bayou. A female—he couldn't tell much about her from this distance—surrounded by a gang of youth.

Returning from a three-day out-of-town trip, he was feeling pretty tired, but it was too early to call it a night. He intended to run a couple of miles, then return home for a big meal, a beer, and bed.

It may be nothing, Sterling told himself. And then again, he'd feel awful if tomorrow's headlines informed him that a woman had been assaulted right across the street from his front door.

It wouldn't hurt to check it out, he decided, cutting across the yard toward the side-street parking lot.

The circle of young men was closing in on her. He saw the woman's head, a mass of soft black curls, moving from side to side, and knew she was searching for a way out. Sizing up the situation, he recognized it as one he'd seen the world over in his photographic jaunts. A gang of youth emboldened by their power in numbers, looking to take out their frustrations.

Standing at about five-six or five-seven, the woman towered over the lead bully by a good three or four inches. She could have stood a chance against them had there been only one, but together, they were like Michael Crichton's velociraptors. She didn't have a prayer if they all decided to strike.

He wished he had Hannibal with him to even up the odds in case the situation turned violent. His ninety-pound Rottweiler could teach them a lesson or two about terror and fear. But there would only be the two of them if things got ugly. Hopefully, it wouldn't come to that. He felt his adrenaline level rising, and hoped they weren't packing.

Sterling slowed his gait and settled on an approach strategy. The woman had assumed a "last stand" position as she poised to defend herself.

An attractive woman of about thirty, maybe younger, she had a quiet oval face, dark and delicate. She had a small mouth with full, pursed lips. Her chin jutted out bravely. Her deep brown complexion glistened with perspiration.

As Sterling approached, she looked up, over the head of her aggressors and into his face. Sterling stopped in his tracks. She was beautiful. Her most remarkable feature was her eyes. A light brown flecked with gold, they were bejeweled amber buttons. He wished for a moment that he had his camera with him, but then, he remembered his purpose.

Excitement mounted within him. He felt dually motivated. An aggressive band of youths to be reckoned with; a chocolate darling, he suddenly dubbed her, in distress.

So intent in their terror-tactics, the youths neither saw nor heard him walk up on them from the front of the car. When one standing on the outskirts of the circle noticed his presence, it was too late.

Sterling broke their circle, as if oblivious to their ill intent, and sauntered straight to the woman. "Hi, babe. I see you beat me back."

He lowered his head to kiss her cheek as he took her hand in his. It was ice cold with the same fear that blazed in her big, doe-shaped eyes. Conscious they were under the watchful gazes of the human velociraptors, he gave her a reassuring smile, a look that implored her to play along, before turning his attention to the group's young leader, who stared at him with a decidedly displeased look.

Selinae stared, speechless. He'd addressed her in an unmistakably intimate tone, pecked her cheek like a lover, then stood at her side like a protective warrior. Her heart was hammering in her chest, but now it wasn't fear she was feeling.

She was mesmerized by the stranger with the dark, liquid voice. He moved with the languid grace of a cheetah. He had a light brown complexion and deep-set eyes whose color she couldn't discern in the light. He wasn't very tall, a few inches shy of six feet. In a blue and white body shirt and running shorts that revealed muscular everything, she only saw a black knight in shining bronze armor.

"You can gloat if you want to," he said, prompting her.

She met his eyes, caught and received their message. It brought her wits sharply together. "I told you I was faster," she replied sweetly, taking up the game.

"That you did," he said, winking at her.

Then he turned to the youngsters. They had already backed up a step. Noticing the curiosity and disappointment on their faces, Selinae realized she had nearly forgotten all about them.

"Yo, little brothers, what's up?" the knight said.

"This yo' woman, man?" the leader asked, folding an arm across his chest, a fist under his chin.

"That's my woman," he said, with proud ownership in his tone.

Selinae could feel the giveaway heat rush to her face as a torrent of warmth coursed though her.

"Man, you let a woman beat you?" another of the youths asked.

"Sometimes they do that," her knight replied, reaching for her hand again.

Not only was she grateful for his timely appearance, Selinae was happy to let him take charge. She basked in the sudden turn of events and her elevation to a stature of importance, blithely ignoring the voice that told her it was only a temporary game.

"I wouldn't let no woman beat me," one said.

The leader, Selinae noticed, appeared skeptical. "Well, if she yo' woman, how come yawl coming from two different directions?"

Selinae couldn't think of an answer. She sought the eyes of her knight, her mouth open. She watched his eyes rake her with a possessive look before he lifted her hand, still balled in a fist, to his mouth, and kissed it. A jolt of desire forced her to look down at her feet which suddenly seemed suspended two feet off the ground.

"It's our way of giving each other space," he replied. "Couples have to do that sometimes to keep the relationship from getting boring." As he angled his body to unlock the car door, he said, "Now, if you gents will excuse us, we're going home for a long shower and dinner." He opened the door and helped Selinae into the driver's seat. "You might want to do the same. Be careful going home."

"Why don't you give us a ride?" the young leader asked. Selinae saw that he was not convinced by her and her knight's performance.

"Sorry," the knight replied with no apology in his voice as he walked around to the passenger side of the car. Opening the door, he said over the top of the car, "Ask your own woman to give you a ride."

Once he was in, Selinae locked the doors.

"Looks like we're going to have to leave together to convince our little friend," he said.

Having escaped the immediate danger, Selinae stopped to think. She was now in a locked car with a stranger. What if her situation had merely gone from bad to worse? Her hands trembled as she put the key in the ignition.

"My name is Sterling Washington," he said. "You don't have to be afraid of me. I'm not going to hurt you."

Selinae didn't trust herself to speak. She nodded, eyed the lingering youths, then backed out of the lot.

"That could've been a bad situation," he said. "I know how you must feel. I've been there, too. I live right across the street on Calhoun. You can drop me off and be on your way."

"They're still hanging around," she said, looking out her side mirror. Still slightly shaken—she didn't know which encounter was affecting her more—she could barely lift her voice above a whisper.

"Drive up North MacGregor, down to Cullen, and turn left, then circle back up," he instructed. "They should be gone by then."

"Thank you," Selinae said as she drove off. "I mean, for stopping. Most people wouldn't." Good, she thought, strength was returning to her voice.

"You're welcome," he replied.

"My name is Selinae Rogers," she said.

"Selinae Rogers," he repeated, as if testing the name on his tongue. "I don't think I've met a Selinae before."

"I'm glad you decided to meet one today," she said with a hint of relief in her voice. Then she was silent again. She wasn't out of the woods yet, she reminded herself.

In the lingering quiet, Selinae felt herself growing calmer, her hands steady on the steering wheel and her eyes on the street. Questions about her handsome passenger began to surface in her head, but she asked none of them. Sterling's voice finally broke the silence.

"So, how did you happen to run into the homies?"

"They ran into me," she replied. "When I first saw them, I was just finishing a run I wished I hadn't started, so I wasn't paying them too much attention. That was my first mistake. Then when I reached the car and the little guy asked for a ride, I thought about all the things I should have done."

"You can never prepare for those situations," he said. "You just make do and hope for the best."

He'd spoken as if it were his philosophy of life, she thought, and somehow it gave her a peaceful feeling.

"Kids aren't what they used to be," he said.

"That's true," she said with a hint of sad fatalism in her voice. Neither are families, she added to herself.

The fading light outside and darkness creeping into the car afforded Selinae a moment to chance a stealthy glance at the handsome profile of her passenger. His slim, powerful build filled the bucket seat. Though dressed for running, it was clear he hadn't even started.

"Sorry about interrupting your workout."

"That's all right," he said. "I really wasn't up to it, anyway. I was just doing something to get out of the house for a while. Do you run often?"

"No," she said with a laugh. "I needed to get out of the house, too." She turned back onto Calhoun and slowed the car to a crawl.

"It's the next one," he said, pointing toward a newly paved driveway.

Following his directions, she pulled up to the front of a closed double-car garage. It was connected to a recently constructed two-story contemporary home. Work was still being done to the yard, where small mounds of dirt had been dumped.

She put the car in park and let it idle. "Thanks again, Sterling Washington," she said, feeling suddenly shy. They had come to the end of their journey, and she felt reluctant to part.

"You're more than welcome, Selinae Rogers," he said, his hand on the door handle. "Take care of yourself." He started to open it, then changed his mind. "Hey, look, if you don't have anything planned, why don't you come in and have a drink or something?"

"I wouldn't want to impose on your generosity any more than I have already," she said halfheartedly. Even though she wasn't eager to return to her empty house and morose thoughts, which had sent her away in the first place, she was still guarded where he was concerned.

"It's no imposition at all," he replied. "Come on. You're still safe. I don't turn into a vampire until midnight."

He flashed a broad grin at her that made her stomach flip. It was so tempting, she seriously thought about accepting his invitation. But in her silent debate, caution and common sense ruled.

"No, I don't think so," she said. "Besides, I need to go home and shower."

"Selinae, I know we didn't meet under ideal circumstances." He spoke slowly, feeling his way. "But the truth is, I'd like to see you again. That is, if you're not already involved."

"I'm not involved," she replied, too quickly, perhaps.

"Okay, that's one down," he said with a smile. "Since I'm on a roll, I might as well keep going. If I give you my number, will you call me?"

"Yes," she replied, again without hesitation, then wondered what it was about this man that made her want to take risks she normally wouldn't consider.

"When?"

"When what?"

"When can I expect to hear from you?" he asked. "I don't want to jump every time the phone rings. Can you give me some idea when you might call?"

"You're persistent, aren't you?" she asked, though she was more than a little flattered by his interest.

"Aggressive," he quipped. "A trait expected of men, I'm told."

He was too good to be true, Selinae thought. First appearing out of nowhere to rescue her, then pursuing her as if any woman couldn't be his for the asking. Selinae suddenly became suspicious. "How do I know you don't have a wife waiting for you inside?" she asked, nodding toward the house.

"If I had a wife, she would be out that front door by now demanding to know what happened. Then she'd invite you in and insist you stay until you truly felt safe. But there is no wife, inside or any place else. I'm the one that has to insist you stay. And you are safe with me," he emphasized. "You'll just have to take my word on it."

"Where on earth did you come from?" she asked laughingly, when she really wanted to ask, *Where have you been all my life?* "I didn't think a man like you would have to work so hard for a date."

"I don't know what you mean by a man like me," he replied, "but I believe that if you want something, you have to work hard for it. I don't have any problem with hard work. So," he said, brushing his hands together, "when are you going to call me?"

She stared at the clock in the dashboard. It was 6:05. Hours before she could reasonably expect sleep to claim her; that meant hours of thinking and rethinking the things she wanted to forget. It was time to look to the future, she reminded herself.

Selinae gazed directly at Sterling. Yes, there was humor glinting in his eyes, but there was also something else. She was hard pressed to define it, but the look infused her with new hope. She was anxious to see, to know the color of his eyes in a clear light.

"Right after I clean up," she replied. "Want to go celebrate Kwanzaa with me?" She spoke fast, as if fearing she'd change her mind and rescind the invitation. He stared at her in surprise, and she laughed, simply because it felt good to do so. "You *do* know what Kwanzaa is, don't you?"

"What time shall I be ready?"

Despite all the books on the wall-to-wall bookshelf behind him—two full shelves devoted to photography—not a one was on Kwanzaa.

While the study was complete, it appeared his library wasn't, Sterling mused. He was sitting in a soft, black leather chair behind a massive cherry desk in the bluish-gray-walled room, a copy of *Our Texas* clutched in his hands. He was reading an article on Kwanzaa.

The study and the kitchen were the only rooms downstairs he'd had time to completely decorate. It was only three months ago that the house had been ready for its owner to take up residence.

Since then, he hadn't been home for more than two weeks at a time. He didn't complain about the long absences because they meant he was working. Since going off on his own as a freelance photographer, he was happy to get as many assignments as he could.

In truth, he was tired of being on the go, but resigned to it, especially if the position he was pursuing with a local paper didn't come through. At thirty-six, he wanted more than the satisfaction he'd enjoyed from his career. He wanted a home. Not a big empty house, but a place that teemed with warmth and welcome and love.

And he wanted it in Houston, the city of his birth, he mused, a faraway look alight in his eyes. With his thoughts embracing the image of Selinae Rogers, he stared unseeingly across the room, a dreamy expression on his face.

Shaking his head to clear her image from his mind, he forced his attention back to the article. It wasn't easy, but finally he was able to concentrate on his reading.

Shutting his eyes tight, Sterling tried to visualize the words he'd just read.

"Matunde ya Kwanzaa means first fruits," he quoted from memory. "The seven principles are called *nguzo saba. Umoja* means unity. Uh, what's that next one? Come on, you can see it," he cajoled himself. *"Ku . . . kuji . . ."* he strained, biting down on his bottom lip.

"Ahh," he muttered with disgust, opening his eyes to look down at the words. *"Kujichagulia* means self-determination."

He dropped the magazine on the desk before him and leaned over it, poring over the information as if preparing for a test. He hadn't studied this hard since high school, when Mr. Churchwell, his physics teacher, had told him that if he didn't pass the final, he wouldn't graduate.

The instant Selinae had driven off, he'd rushed inside to look for information about Kwanzaa. He'd heard of it, had even read about it. But that was a long time ago, and his memory was stale. What he remembered wasn't much.

He knew it grew out of the 1960s movement and was designed to be more than a symbolic gesture to instill blacks in America with a sense of pride, self-worth, and values that they could call their own. But as far as the rituals and practices were concerned, he was ignorant, having never celebrated the holiday.

Lucky for him, the magazine had done an article on Kwanzaa celebrations across Texas. Now if only he could digest everything—he looked up at the elegant gold-rimmed clock on the wall—within the next thirty minutes, he should be reasonably informed.

He wanted to impress Selinae with his knowledge about something she apparently cared about. She'd promised to pick him up at 6:45; the celebration began at 7. It was going to be held at the Harambee Community Center, only a short ride away.

Sidetracked by the reminders of her eminent return, he thought about the short ride they had shared from the park to his house. He knew she had been still shaken by her encounter with the young hoods and sensibly afraid of him. She must have wondered whether she'd jumped out of the fire and into the frying pan, he thought.

He didn't believe she was the talkative type, even when at ease. Rather, he guessed she had a fiercely protective way about her. She hadn't parted with her phone number, though she had his.

Still, he wondered, what had changed her mind about him? Curiosity or attraction?

He wasn't entirely oblivious to the effect he had on women. Some women, anyway, he amended. He had long years of practice, honing his charm. It served him well in his profession, but he wasn't so foolish as to think that charm alone made him highly sought after by the opposite sex.

If he picked up that attitude from a woman, he

wasn't interested in getting to know her past her name. His one-night-stand years were over.

He didn't get that impression from Selinae. There was something he instinctively liked about her and how it made him feel, like a promise of something wonderful about to happen. He was both curious about and attracted to the woman with the beautiful name.

"Selinae," he said, an unconscious smile stealing across his face.

The very first time he locked gazes with her, he'd seen a fire in her eyes that hinted at a woman of unlimited passions. Recalling how she'd been prepared to defend herself in what would have been a futile effort, he was impressed by her courage.

Still, there was something else about her, he mused. He couldn't define it, the sensibility he felt emanating from her. Maybe she'd let him photograph her and he could capture and study that elusive quality that shone in her eyes.

The first night of Kwanzaa always drew a big crowd. The parking lots surrounding the Harambee Community Center in the predominantly black Third Ward community were filled to capacity.

Cars lined Almeda Street three and four blocks in either direction. Sterling and Selinae joined a throng of other arrivals, heading toward the Center four blocks away.

Though Sterling did most of the talking, joy bubbled in her voice when she spoke and shone in her eyes, as bright as the stars twinkling overhead in the clear, black night.

She wasn't ready to concede Sterling had anything to do with this blissful happiness that made her feel fully alive. She couldn't stop looking at him as if expecting horns to sprout from his head and fangs to protrude from his firm mouth.

"You know, Kwanzaa is celebrated practically all over Africa, even though it was founded here," Sterling said. "The names are different, and they're agricultural in nature, but they're still harvest celebrations. I read someplace that even the ancient Egyptians had a first-fruits celebration."

Selinae was familiar with his recitation because she had written several stories about Kwanzaa over the years. But she wasn't going to interrupt a lesson from Sterling. She just liked hearing him talk. His voice was so mesmeric, she would just have happily listened to him recite the alphabet.

He had been entertaining and attentive from the time she picked him up. She felt herself being drawn to him with every passing second in his presence. No man had ever spoiled her with such eager attention before. If she weren't careful, it could go to her head.

"I don't know if they celebrate for seven days, though," he said, as if puzzled by the thought. "I wonder how he came up with seven."

The "he" to whom Sterling referred was Dr. Maulana Karenga, the creator of Kwanzaa, Selinae knew. Even though the seven-day African American holiday had been celebrated since 1966 in the United States, all the angles had not been covered in news and feature articles about the holiday. But it was generally known that the celebration ran from December 26 to January 1 of the new year, and that one of the Seven Principles was honored each day.

"As I understand it," Selinae replied plainly, "the number seven has a cultural and spiritual significance in African culture. Dr. Karenga wanted to develop an Afrocentric value system in which to rebuild the black community. The *Nguzo Saba,* or Seven Principles," she said, looking up at him, "are geared toward that end, of highlighting the importance of community over the individual."

He flashed her a shamed-face little grin. "I must have been boring you to death," he said almost apologetically. "You already know all this stuff."

"Not at all," she replied. "Besides, I wouldn't want to be guilty of gloating twice in the same day. It's not good for your image with the homies." She smiled.

"Well, I guess I'm going to have to redeem myself," he replied with challenge in his voice. "Do you know the Seven Principles by heart?" he asked, then emphasized, "In Swahili?"

"I warn you," she said, "I'm up on *matunda ya Kwanzaa. Matunda* means fruits and *ya Kwanzaa* means first."

"Aw, she reverts to the old stalling tactic," Sterling teased. "That was not the question, Ms. Rogers."

She smacked her lips at him in jest. "Want to make a small wager?" she asked.

"I wouldn't want to let the brothers down," he replied with bravura. "Count me in."

"What's to be my prize?" she asked saucily.

"Hmm," he muttered, as if in deep thought. "If"—a finger pointing heaven-bound—"you can name the Seven Principles . . ."

Cutting him off, she interjected, *"Nguzo Saba."*

"Same thing," he quipped. *"If* you can name them all in Swahili, dinner is my treat for a week."

"I hope you're a good cook," she said.

"Start naming," he chortled.

"Umoja; Unity," she said, counting them off on her fingers as she spoke. *"Kujichagulia;* Self-

determination. *Ujima;* Collective work and responsibility. *Ujamaa;* Cooperative economics. *Nia;* Purpose. *Kuumba;* Creativity. *Imani;* Faith." Looking up at him smugly, she asked, "When do I collect my first meal?"

Just feet from the door to the entrance of the center, the inside light and a chorus of drums spilled out onto the sidewalk. Sterling pulled Selinae aside to let others pass, then looked at her, his bottom lip folded in his smiling mouth.

His eyes were the color of root beer, she now knew. The look he sent her implied she could very likely be on the menu. The thought sent a barely imperceptible shiver through her.

"Anytime you want it," he replied quietly.

Selinae couldn't find her voice; his was resonating in her ear and creating havoc with her senses. He shouldn't be allowed to speak in public. That voice belonged in the bedroom, she thought, unable to stop herself from imagining the two of them in her own. Shaking the wayward thought from her head, she let him usher her into the lobby of the center.

"You'll have to be my teacher tonight," he said, lowering his head to her ear. "This is my first Kwanzaa."

Casting a sidelong, suspicious glance up at him, Selinae didn't know whether or not to believe him.

Without even looking at her, he said, "I read a lot."

His disclosure was so insignificant, Selinae thought, she didn't know why she felt as if he'd shared a long-held secret with her. As she struggled to quell her skittering pulses, she wondered where were those horns.

The gathering in the lobby of the Center resembled a high school or family reunion. She could always count on seeing people whom she hadn't seen in a long time. While a chant of *"Harambee"* reverberated from the adjoining room, Selinae stopped to speak to longtime friends and associates.

Hearing the phrase, *"Habari gani?"* and a roaring reply of *"Umoja,"* she excused herself. "We've missed the opening," she explained to Sterling, leading the way.

They reached the entrance, which was the back of a room that had once been the showroom of a furniture store. As big as a high school gym, it was capable of seating hundreds, with standing room for hundreds more. Tonight, every square inch of it was packed.

"Wow," Sterling exclaimed softly.

"We give thanks to the Creator for bringing us together in *Umoja,* for we are the most valuable fruit of the nation," the speaker was saying. "On this first night of Kwanzaa, we commemorate our ancestors who have brought us this far. We recommit ourselves to the dreams we have and the actions we must take to uplift our families, our communities, our nation. Unity!" he cried extollingly.

"Unity!" the crowd echoed.

"Umoja!" he refrained.

Under the two-worded chant, *"Umoja!* Unity!", echoing through the room, Sterling and Selinae looked for two seats. Finding none, they searched for a spot alongside the wall where several others had already assembled near the stage. Room was made for them to snuggle in a tight space, with Selinae standing in front of Sterling.

As the speaker lit a black candle in the center of the candle holder, Sterling recalled his reading. According to the article, wine or grape juice was poured into the unity cup, then the liberation statement was made. It was followed by the lighting of the candle to represent the principle that was being celebrated. Because the black candle represented African Americans in unity, as well as the first principle of the seven that were recognized, it was always lit first.

They wouldn't be late tomorrow night, he declared to himself, placing his hands on Selinae's slender shoulders. He felt the muscles in her shoulders rise and tense under the tempered weight of his hands. Then they settled under the light pressure, and he too, relaxed, realizing just how anxious he'd been about their date, afraid he'd scare her away with his eagerness.

When she'd arrived at his door in her red African-styled outfit, a subtle and intriguing fragrance surrounding her, he wanted to take her in his arms and just hold her. She'd been wise to decline an invitation inside. But the prohibition against touching only fueled his desire. He felt a response as age-old as the sea threatening to rise in him.

It was best not to think about that right now, he counseled himself, forcing his attentions elsewhere.

Impressed by the ceremony, Sterling swelled with pride. The colors matched those of an island carnival. Even though it was a serious occasion, an aura of festive reverence permeated the room.

His photographer's eyes scanned the room, focusing on the faces of the people. A joyous anticipation shone in their features. He imagined the expressions were the same Sojourner Truth saw when she successfully guided enslaved Africans into freedom.

Some were garbed in African attire; others dressed as casually as if they were going to a movie. It was like attending a church with a come-as-you-are policy, he thought.

Down center of the platform stage, a *kente* cloth displaying the symbolic colors of liberation—black, red, and green—was draped over the sides of a table. Atop it were items he recognized, but he couldn't recall all their Swahili names or remember their significance. But even without that information, Sterling could see that Kwanzaa was no different from any other holiday, in that symbols were part of the ritual.

The speaker sat down to applause and the emcee, whom he recognized as a local news anchor, introduced a performance by a percussion ensemble of young boys. As the instruments were set up, he bent to ask Selinae a question.

"Is the *kente* cloth merely for decoration, or does it have symbolic significance to the celebration?" he whispered.

"The selection of *kente* is decorative," Selinae replied softly, angling her body to look up into his face, "but the cloth is traditional. It's called the *bendera ya taifa,* which means 'national flag.' I'm sure you recognize the colors."

"Yes," he replied, "black for the people, red for the struggle, and green for the future. I believe Marcus Garvey had something to do with it." Selinae nodded in the affirmative. "What's that straw mat?" he asked, noticing a woven floor covering, atop of which were several fresh ears of corn and a large basket of fruit.

"It's called the *mkeke,*" she replied. "And the corn and fruit represent the crops, called *mazao.* You'll also notice those wrapped boxes. They represent the gifts, called *zawadi.*"

"I remember that," he said. "And that big brass cup is the unity cup, right?"

"Yes," she replied. "It's the *kikombe cha umoja.* You

already know about the *kinara* and the *mishumaa saba,*" she said.

"Yes," he nodded. Hearing the names, he recalled that the *kinara,* or candle holder, was the symbol of ancestry. It contained seven holes for each of the seven candles, three red and three green ones on either side of a black one. The candles symbolized the *nguzo saba.*

The young percussion ensemble began to play, effectively ending Selinae and Sterling's conversation. The program continued with entertainers interspersed between speakers. They all expounded on the values of Kwanzaa and encouraged living the *nguzo saba* beyond the seven-day holiday.

Nearing the program's end, a hush settled over the room. The emcee held an extinguisher over the still burning black candle.

"Umoja," she said reverently, and the word was repeated in that same reverent tone by the audience. She put out the light.

Selinae turned to look up into his face, peace shadowing her expression. "Happy Kwanzaa," she said softly.

He was humbled by the experience, but never more so than by the woman who'd introduced him to this warm gathering. He felt enjoined to her in the spirit of *Umoja.*

A diverse selection of Christmas music played by the college radio station flowed continuously from the tall floor speakers in the sun-bright orange room. The KTSU announcer deftly segued from Charles Lloyd's "Merry Christmas Baby" into the mastery of John Coltrane blowing the tenor in a rendition of "My Favorite Things."

Selinae became aware of the music for the first time since she'd sat down to work. She pressed the save key on her keyboard, and as the computer safely stored her document, she took a sip of lukewarm coffee and glanced at the polished wood, Africa-shaped clock on the wall. It read 10:55.

She was in her home office, formerly the master bedroom in an old A-frame house. She'd purchased it five years ago when she was a reporter with one of the local dailies. It wasn't wholly hers yet; she shared ownership with the mortgage company.

Setting her cup down, she double-checked the printer for paper, pressed the print command, then settled back in her chair. The printer quietly went about its work.

With the exception of the computer workstation, stereo entertainment center, and a few art items, the furnishings were Salvation Army and garage sale purchases. The teacher's desk, twin bookshelves, daybed, and army-green file cabinets had been either refinished, recovered, or simply washed and cleaned. The thin beige carpet covering the floor had come with the house.

The room was streetside, perpendicular to the living room separated by a hallway. The four windows, two each on the front and side walls, were covered by the same heavy black-and-white fabric featuring African animals as the comforter on the bed and seat cushion in the wooden armchair.

Normally an early riser, she had slept late this morning, but had gotten more work done in a few hours than she had in weeks. It was amazing what a little sleep could do, she thought, picking up a sheet of paper that the printer spit onto the holding tray.

"You can call it what you want," she smiled to herself with a chuckle, replacing the page.

Sitting back with her feet on the edge of her chair and mug in her hands, the image of Sterling Washington appeared full blown in her mind. A blush of pleasure rose to her cheeks, and she felt a tingling sensation in the pit of her stomach.

As their evening wound to a close, he had seemed as reluctant as she to part, she recalled. She hadn't trusted herself to go inside his house, though he'd invited her. Instead, they had sat talking in her car, parked in his driveway.

Sitting a bucket-seat away from each other had altered her definition of a romantic setting. It could be anywhere, requiring only one ingredient—a sexually attracted couple.

While outside, the temperature dropped several degrees, inside the car, the atmosphere had teemed with the electric sparks of their mutual attraction. She had been hungering for his touch from the time they left the center.

And even before that, she told herself. In fact, she felt her passion on a low boil even now, just thinking about him. She knew what would have happened had they gone inside the house.

But the boldness that propelled her to ask him to Kwanzaa vanished in spite of her desires. She was paralyzed by a caution that carried with it endless arguments against fulfilling the desires running wild and rampart in her. It was too soon, she thought. She really didn't know him, nor he, her. He might think her too forward, and she feared being labeled a tease, or any of the names she'd been called before by someone she least expected.

Besides, she reflected, slow and methodical,

rather than brash and brazen were more in keeping with her nature.

When they finally called it a night and he went inside, she had driven home with the heavy ache of an insatiable hunger. After a warm shower, she fell into bed. Sterling was the last waking thought before sleep claimed her.

Swallowing a sip of coffee, she stared absently at the computer screen and began to wonder what Sterling was doing now.

A loud shot erupted outside her window. Startled, Selinae jumped, spilling coffee on her work clothes, a purple blousey top and black lycra pants. When silence rather than screams and chaos followed, she realized it was merely a car backfiring. She drew a deep calming breath, but the minor incident evoked her memory of the perilous situation she'd gotten herself into the day before.

"God takes care of babies and fools," she mumbled in the mug as she took a sip of coffee.

She'd put her life in danger at the hands of a gang of teenagers who were out to prove their manhood, she recalled. She never had to contemplate suicide again. All she had to do was make herself visible and some nut would be happy to oblige, she mused sarcastically.

"I'll never do that again," she said, setting the cup on the desk. Sterling Washington, her black Adonis, might not happen along again, she thought.

With her head cocked to the side, her expression smiling and thoughtful, she supplanted the name Horus in her thoughts. Horus, the Avenger. It was more appropriate, she decided, and an appreciative sigh that began in her chest seeped past her lips.

It had been a while since a man had noticed her. Or maybe it was the other way around. One thing was for certain, she'd never felt such an exhilarating response to any man as she did for Sterling Washington.

Feeling herself getting carried away, Selinae cleared her throat and busied herself collecting the sheets from the printer tray. Nothing had changed the arguments for caution, she reminded herself.

Besides, Sterling Washington was as dangerous to her as the young thugs that had surrounded her had been. If, she told herself with emphasis, she couldn't control her response to him.

Maybe she was making a big deal out of nothing, she mused, inserting the typed pages into file folders. One date does not a future make, she told herself.

But then again, she thought, holding the stack of folders, to be on the safe side, maybe she'd better reconsider collecting any of the meals she'd won and forget him altogether.

The doorbell rang, interrupting her silent debate. Wondering who was calling on her, she lay the folders on the corner of the desk and rose to traipse down the hall on her way to the front door in the living room.

"Who is it?" she asked before looking through the peephole.

"It's us, Sel."

Only one person in the world called her Sel, and that was her baby brother, Anthony, whose own name had been shortened to Tony. Confirming her visitors' identities through the peephole, she saw her brothers Tony and Oscar, Jr., and her nephew, Andrew.

They were the last people she expected to call on her. Infrequent visitors to Houston, when they did come home, their parents hardly let them out of their sight.

Opening the door, she asked, "What brings you guys this way?"

Tony, carrying Andrew, Oscar Jr.'s son, walked in and promptly deposited the baby into her arms. "We figured you weren't working today, so we thought we'd drop by," he replied.

"Hi, lil sis," Oscar said as he walked inside, a blue and white baby bag hanging from one shoulder, a gift bag in his other hand.

"Have a seat," she offered, dropping onto the couch, the baby propped on her knee.

Instead of sitting down, however, Tony meandered about the room, looking at and touching items of interest. Nosy, Selinae thought. Oscar, Jr. was more subtle in his perusal. She freed them both to be openly inquisitive with a nod of her head. With the baby in her lap, she examined her brothers as they examined her home.

Tony had a slim build like Selinae and their mother. Oscar, Jr. was a big, muscular man becoming heavy in the middle, though he, like Tony, had inherited their mother's caramel complexion. Their grandmother used to say their parents had practiced on Selinae and Oscar, Jr. before getting it right when they had Tony, she recalled. He was good looking and knew it. But luckily, he'd grown out of his teenage conceit.

Oscar Jr. was the complete opposite. Staid and steady, he had always been old-acting and old-thinking. When he spoke, he sounded as if he'd rehearsed his words in front of a mirror. A labor attorney with a prominent law firm, the temperament suited his profession well.

"I like what you've done to the place," Tony said

from the door separating the kitchen from the dining room.

"I like it, too," Oscar, Jr. echoed.

From where Selinae sat, she could see clearly into the dining room, as far as Oscar had ventured. The room featured a glass-topped wood table with matching high-back chairs and a china cabinet. The room led into the kitchen, the door of which was open as well.

"It's rather appealing," he added, retracing his steps to the living room.

Selinae couldn't tell whether or not he was sincere. Not that she cared. The room revealed an Afrocentric-minded owner. It was decorated to satisfy her recognition of and appreciation for her two cultures—on a budget.

A waist-high wooden bust featuring big eyes and thick lips stood on the polished hardwood floor in the space between the couch and love seat, which was upholstered in a gray, black, and peach African-print fabric. A hanbel rug of Moroccan origin lay under the wood and glass coffee table, decorated with porcelain-sculptured animal figurines. Colorful paintings and prints depicting black lifestyles adorned the white walls. There was plenty of greenery from plants both potted and hanging.

"Mama said it looked like a jungle," Tony said, dropping onto the couch next to her. "But I like it."

"No tree," Oscar, Jr. observed, raising a questionable brow at her.

"Yeah, you don't have a Christmas tree," Tony echoed.

"No," she replied, laughing inside. They *would* notice that, she thought, but not the symbols of Kwanzaa she'd neglected to put out for the same reason she hadn't gotten a tree. Sterling would notice, she thought, *if* she gave him a chance. With a fond light of memory in her eyes, she decided to put up the *kinara* and *mishumaa* later.

The baby began to squirm in Selinae's lap. "I guess visitation time is up," she said, handing the child to Oscar, Jr.

"Come here, Daddy's big boy," Oscar, Jr. said. He settled on the love seat, Andrew in his arms.

"We tried to reach you yesterday, but you weren't home," Tony said. "You forgot to leave your answering machine on."

No, she didn't forget, Selinae thought. She'd deliberately turned it off and muted the phone bell so she wouldn't have to hear it ring, though she hadn't expected to hear from her family.

"And, you forgot your gift at the house the other day," Oscar, Jr. said, glancing around him. "What did I do with that bag?"

Selinae looked puzzled. "I got everything."

"Here it is," Tony replied, reaching over the side of the couch for the bag. He dropped it in Selinae's lap.

"Well, Mama told us to drop it off if we stopped by," Oscar, Jr. said.

Peering into the bag, Selinae recognized the gift immediately. It was a cashmere sweater, pretty, pink, and expensive. "Your dad picked it out," she recalled her mother boasting proudly, and a spark of hope sprang in her chest. But it was extinguished quickly. A glance at her father's expression had revealed the truth. Her mother had lied.

"Can I get you guys something?" she asked as she got to her feet, gripping the thin straps of the bag.

"I'll take coffee, if it's not too old," Tony replied.

"You're in luck," she replied. Walking off, she

dropped the bag on the dining room table, intending to give the gift to someone who needed it. Continuing toward the kitchen, she called back to her brothers. "Where are Darlene and Andrea? Why didn't they come with you?" she asked disappearing behind the kitchen door.

"The wives went shopping with Mama," Tony replied, his voice carrying the distance.

"Tony!" Selinae heard Oscar, Jr. whisper in disgust as she reached to get a cup down from a cabinet overhead.

"What?" Tony replied innocently.

Then hot whispered muttering penetrated the walls to her ears.

"Selinae didn't want to go shopping," she heard Tony reply defensively.

"Keep your voice down!" Oscar, Jr. commanded, his harsh whisper carrying back to her.

Left out again, Selinae thought. Her brothers' wives saw her mother more than she did. As determined as she was not to let the exclusion bother her, she couldn't help but feel hurt as she filled a cup with coffee from the coffee maker.

Tony was right—she had plenty to do at home, rather than blowing her budget, spending money on things she didn't need. But that wasn't the point. She wasn't even given the opportunity to refuse. Who knows? It's possible she would have joined them if asked. She didn't have to buy anything.

She dropped a tablespoon of sugar in the cup, then stirred it before returning to the living room, her feelings masked from review under a blank expression. Oscar, Jr. wore a peeved frown, while indifference shone on Tony's face as he accepted the mug from her.

"Thank you," he said.

Oscar, Jr. put the baby down. The boy immediately began crawling around, heading straight for the coffee table.

"What's on your agenda for the day?" she asked.

"Nothing much," Tony replied. "Still belong to the gym?"

"No, I let my membership go," she replied.

"Too bad," Tony shrugged. To Oscar, Jr. he said, "We can probably find a pickup game at the park."

"What are you going to do about Andrew?" she asked, grabbing for the toddler's hand as he tried to eat a porcelain elephant. Oscar, Jr. reached him first, handed the figurine to Selinae, then settled back on the love seat with Andrew in his lap. The baby started to whine.

"Tony, look in the bag and get me a bottle, will you?" Oscar, Jr. instructed.

"You haven't spent any time with your nephew," Tony said, rifling through the baby bag. He pulled out a bottle, then tossed it across the room to Oscar, who stuck the nipple in his son's mouth. "We figured you'd like to baby-sit."

Selinae burst out laughing. Andrew stopped feeding to turn his head toward her, a curious look on his face. "I should have known this was not a social call," she said.

"You're about as tactful as a cactus," Oscar, Jr. chided his brother.

"I'm just doing my part to help move things along," Tony said. Oscar, Jr. snarled at him. "All right, all right," he said. Setting his mug on the coffee table, he sidled up next to Selinae and draped his arms around her shoulders. "My dearest, most favorite sister in the whole world—"

"I'm your *only* sister," she interrupted. "And no,

I'm not going to baby-sit while you two run off and have fun."

"Come on, big sis," Tony cajoled, smothering her with kisses.

"Get away from me," she replied, laughing.

"Come on, little man," Oscar, Jr. said, joining them on the couch. He held Andrew close to Selinae. "Wouldn't you like to spend some time with your auntie?"

Tony playfully wrestled her to the floor, and Oscar, Jr. set the baby in her arms. They were all laughing uncontrollably.

Gosh, it felt good being with her brothers like this, Selinae thought. They hadn't laughed together in so long, she'd almost forgotten what it was like.

Finally, laughed out and exhausted, Selinae sat on the floor, her back against the couch, her nephew in her lap. She rubbed foreheads with the baby and giggled as he blew spit bubbles in a sign of glee.

"So, how you been doing?" Oscar, Jr. asked, his tone suddenly serious.

"Good," she replied.

"How's your career coming along?"

"Fine," she replied, a hint of wariness in her tone. "Why do you ask?"

"Can't we make a polite inquiry without falling under suspicion?" Tony replied. "We hardly get a chance to talk to you. You're always so busy, looking for a story."

"Before you got famous, you used to let us know when you had a piece published," Oscar, Jr. said. "I just happened to pick up a copy of *Ebony* this past summer and saw your name on an article."

He was exaggerating; she wasn't famous. When acceptance of her work was scarce, she recalled, they'd never really seemed interested. They'd make subtle hints that she'd made a mistake quitting her newspaper job. After several offers to help her find an eight-to-five job, she stopped talking about her work to them.

"What have you been working on?"

"*American Visions* bought the piece I did on the Creoles in Houston's Frenchtown. It'll come out in the upcoming spring issue," she said. "And I'm working on a documentary script for a production of it by the local PBS station. All the details haven't been worked out yet, so it's still tentative."

"Good," Oscar, Jr. said. "I'm glad to hear things are going so well."

In the ensuing silence, Selinae occupied herself playing patty-cake with her nephew. She didn't notice the somber looks her brothers exchanged over her head.

"You know," Oscar, Jr. said, as if feeling his way, "the folks are getting older. As much as they'd like us to believe they can do everything they used to, the truth is they're slowing down."

Staring at him curiously, Selinae felt her insides begin to quiver. She'd always thought her parents were healthy and would be around for many years to come. Her mother was fifty-two, worked out regularly, counted fat and calories constantly and looked 20 years younger for her efforts. Her father was another story, but he was still relatively young at fifty-five. Maybe Oscar, Jr. and Tony knew something she didn't know. It seemed they had a motive for visiting more profound than baby-sitting after all.

"The house is getting to be too much for them," he continued. "They're talking about selling it and moving into a retirement complex."

Selinae began to relax; she had been thinking the worst, that some deadly ailment had claimed her parents' bodies. "That seems like a good decision for them," she said matter-of-factly. "More coffee, Tony?" she asked, passing Andrew to his father.

"No, I'm fine, thanks," Tony replied.

"It would be a shame for them to sell that house after all the work they put into it," Oscar, Jr. said.

"Yeah," Tony added, "it sure would be. Not to mention what moving is going to do to their income."

"Why are you telling me all this?" Selinae asked, glaring from one brother to the other.

"Well, it doesn't make sense for the three of you to live in the same town, maintaining two separate households, when if you—"

Selinae cut Oscar, Jr. off. "Hold it right there," she said tersely.

"Just listen a second, Sel," Tony said.

"Stop," she said, holding up both hands. "I don't know what your motivation is for even bringing up the matter, and I don't want to know. But save your arguments for willing ears."

"But Sell," Tony countered.

"If you want a baby-sitter for them," she said in a chilly voice, "hire a nurse. If you like that house so much, buy it. If you're that concerned about their income, let them move in with you. But keep me out of your plans. I have no intention whatsoever of moving in with them," she vowed stringently. "Not that they'd go for it anyway."

"We talked to Mama about it," Tony said. "In fact, she was the one to bring it up."

"Well, as you mentioned, she's getting older. It's making her delusional. You saw us together the other night. Nothing's changed in fifteen years."

Feeling embittered emotions rising, Selinae reined in her temper and clamped her mouth shut. It was useless getting angry with her brothers, she reasoned. They were not the root of the problem.

"Now, Selinae, don't go getting all upset," Oscar, Jr. said.

"What brought this on?" she asked, curiosity overriding her declaration of disinterest. She noticed that both of her brothers lowered their gazes, guilt and shame clouding their faces. "It can't be that bad," she said, forcing humor to her voice in order to draw laughter from them.

"The old man pulled out the will last night," Tony said somberly.

A tense silence filled the room. Selinae looked questioningly from one brother to the other.

"He cut you out of it," Tony said at last.

Selinae just then realized she had been holding her breath. With her brother's statement, she let it out in a rush. Her father hadn't merely cut her from a piece of paper she could care less about, she thought, his gesture symbolized cutting her out of the family. She never would have believed that his disappointment in her was so great as to lead to disclaiming her existence.

"Well," she said. She didn't know what else to say. She shrugged her shoulders and took another deep breath. She felt numb. "Why am I not surprised?" she said with rhetorical, calm indifference.

"Selinae," Oscar, Jr. said ruefully, "that's why we thought if we could get you together in the same space, you'd be able to work this thing out. I think you'll agree, it's gone on too long."

"I do agree, Oscar," she replied, dropping wearily onto the couch, "but we're not your clients. You can't intermediate for parties who are not willing to sit at the same table. It was quite evident at dinner the other night that we can't."

"We just thought we'd put some sort of solution on the table," Tony said. "Christmas dinner was a bust," he said with a disgusted snort. "The two of you snarling across the table at each other."

"We never said a word to each other," she corrected.

"You didn't have to. You shot enough daggers at each other to qualify," he said with dry sarcasm. "I was starting to feel like a soldier in Custer's army."

"I'm sorry about that," she said.

"That's not good enough," Tony exclaimed contentiously. "We're supposed to be a family. You and Dad are forgetting that. What do you think this is doing to Mama? What about us?" he demanded.

Before today, she hadn't given much thought to the effect the rift with her father was having on Oscar, Jr. and Tony. But now it seemed clear that they had been more than mere witnesses to her shaming. She had destroyed their childhood, taken it from them the night they were forced to watch her humiliation.

So engrossed in her own sense of victimization, she couldn't comfort them, and they had been too young to know how to comfort her. Then, for a long time, neither of them could bear to look the other in the eye.

As she looked at her baby brother, abject defeat in his posture, she wished that she could give him what he wanted. But too much time had passed in refusal and denial. It was just too late.

"Selinae," Oscar, Jr. said, "Tony's right. It's not fair for us to be caught in the middle like this."

"I've done my part," she said quietly, taking them both in her gaze. "I'm tired of beating my head against a wall. I'm not going to do it anymore. I'm getting on with my life."

She felt a strange sense of resignation come over her. Her sadness was tinged with relief. It was as if saying the words aloud somehow made it easier to accept the truth of what she had known deep down inside all along.

"You can't give up," Oscar, Jr. said desperately.

"I'm through," she said softly, with finality.

"But Selinae—" Oscar, Jr. protested.

With a finger at her lips, she shushed him. Taking both of her brothers in her sights, she looked at them with a half-smile of knowing on her face. "Tell Mama you tried," she said.

She was eager to escape before the build-up of tears in her eyes fell and intensified her brothers' discomfort. Though they never said it, she was the cause of the rift that tore their family apart, she thought, feeling the burdensome weight of blame. They would never let her forget it.

She walked out, ducking down the hall to her bedroom at the back of the house. Leaning against the bedroom door, she let the tears fall freely down her face.

Meandering about the room, she picked up a store bought frame with a picture of a girl smiling up into a man's face. The girl, long-legged and long-haired, wore a track club uniform and was holding out two gold medals that hung from red, white, and blue ribbons around her neck. The man was touching them, pride beaming in his expression.

Selinae nearly choked on a bitter sob as she set the picture facedown on the dresser. She tried to stop the flow of tears, pressing her fingers under her eyes. But they kept coming. They were tears of mourning. For a family, for a young girl's soul.

"Selinae! Selinae! Are you all right?"

With a jerk of her head, Selinae snapped to attention at the sound of the distinctive voice echoing down the hallway. She would recognize it anywhere, regardless of the tone. Sterling's voice. She felt a lurch of excitement within her.

"Selinae!"

Frantically, she wiped the tears from her eyes, using the back and front of her hands. What was he doing here? she wondered, opening the door to hurry down the hall. She wasn't in the mood for company. She even wished her brothers would leave.

Rounding the hallway corner into the living room, she froze, startled and confused by the picture that greeted her. Tony and Oscar, Jr. stood side by side like a couple of defensive tackles, while Sterling looked poised to rush.

A loud noise drowned out the thudding of her heart. Andrew was slamming a porcelain animal on the coffee table. She went around her brothers to rescue the tiny giraffe from the baby's clutches.

"What's going on?" she asked, picking up Andrew, who started to cry.

"Are you all right?" Sterling asked.

Her gaze met his and locked. Filled with a sudden longing, her breath suspended in her throat as he approached her, but he hadn't gotten very far when both her brothers stepped in his path.

"We told this guy you weren't seeing anybody," Oscar, Jr. said.

In that instant, Oscar looked and sounded just like their father, Selinae thought, her head snapping as she stared at him as if for the first time. She could almost see a red aura of hostility encircling him.

"Yeah, we told him to come back another time, but he refused to leave," Tony said, parroting Oscar,

Jr. in tone and demeanor. "Common courtesy dictates that you call before showing up at somebody's house, anyway," he said to Sterling.

Selinae's eyes narrowed in annoyance. Where did they get off, trying to run her life?

"How do you know that he *didn't* call?" she replied, her tone challenging. She returned her brothers' shocked gazes as she placed Andrew in Oscar, Jr.'s arms.

"W-Well," Oscar, Jr. stammered lamely, "we were having a family meeting."

"The meeting was over," she said.

"Selinae," Tony said in a patronizing tone.

Selinae stuck out her chin. "I said it was over," she repeated tightly.

The instant Selinae walked into the room, Sterling felt a curious swooping pull at his innards. Except for a nod in passing, her attention was focused fiercely on the two men who tried to prevent him from seeing her. She looked like a warrior queen, ready for battle. It was a definite turn on.

He hadn't noticed the family resemblance between Selinae and the two men until she walked into the room. Had either one of the men offered an explanation of their presence in her home before, he thought, slightly miffed, he would have turned around and left. Instead, they had acted like rogues, causing him to fear for Selinae's safety.

But no introduction seemed forthcoming, and he wasn't about to press the issue. Selinae must have her reasons, he thought. Witnessing a war of gazes—two sulky pairs versus her steely one—he felt suddenly uncomfortable.

"Well, we'll just get our things together and leave

you to your company," said the bigger of the two men.

"That's a good idea," she replied.

Sterling noticed her tone had thawed somewhat, though she didn't give up any ground. He couldn't take his eyes off her as her brothers made fast work of leaving. From the periphery of his gaze, he saw them scampering about, righting items the baby had upended or rushing off to dispose of a soiled diaper.

With his eyes riveted on her face, he noticed a slight puffiness just beneath the long elegant black lashes encircling her beautifully white eyes. She'd been crying.

His emotions split between anger and arousal. He wanted to wring her brothers' necks and take her in his arms and comfort her.

But he didn't move, other than clench and unclench his hands at his sides, immobilized by her impenetrable expression. Only her posture revealed her mood. She said nothing to him; nor did she look his way. He felt safe from her wrath. For now.

She was standing by the wooden head statue, arms folded across her middle like a belt, cinching her top to reveal firm, full breasts and a small waist. One long fine leg crossed over the other in black pants that fit her fine hips and shapely thighs like a second skin. She was the picture of regal assurance.

She hadn't called as she'd promised, and fearing losing her, Sterling had come to force the issue. He was driven by something about her that connected to a sensual, persuasive feeling within him. He didn't know whether it was real, imagined, or plain lust, but he had no intention of dropping it until he knew for sure.

He didn't have her consent, but hoped he would

be able to talk her into going with him. There were three cameras in his car, fully loaded with both black-and-white and color film. One was for her to use.

He wanted them to share a fun outing, taking pictures. No private places, but public, in a crowd of people, so she'd feel safe in his company. It was a safety measure for himself, as well, he mused, wishing her brothers would hurry.

"Maybe we can get together again tomorrow?"

The brother with the baby spoke. Standing at the door with the infant in one arm and a diaper bag in the other, he'd gone from big bad bully to meek, mild lamb, Sterling thought.

"Call first," she said. "And thanks for stopping by." She smiled at them, and flicked the baby's cheek affectionately with her thumb.

He nodded meekly, then turned and walked off. The other brother leaned to kiss her on the cheek. He, too, had become docile.

"Bye, Sel," he said. "Sorry if we overreacted, okay?"

"Okay," she said with forgiveness in her tone.

Locking the door, Selinae's hand lingered on the knob. She lowered her head and wondered what she was going to say to Sterling. She had enough changes in her life to contend with, she mused. Severing one relationship was about all she could handle at a time.

She decided to thank him again for his timely appearance, then send him on his way. Pivoting, her lips parted to speak, she came to a sudden stop. She stood riveted, facing him. Her voice failed her.

She couldn't say what it was that affected her so,

but coherent thoughts scattered like a crowd dispersing under the threat of gunfire. Maybe it was the pose he'd struck, as if he'd staked a claim on some significant discovery. Or, it could have been the fit of the burgundy knit shirt and freshly starched jeans he wore, refreshing her memory of his lean, sinewy body. Or just maybe it was the look in his eyes, piercing dark brown nuggets that were full of unspoken promises. Whatever it was quickened her pulse.

"Habari gani," he said.

Selinae shuddered inwardly as his deep, dolce voice, like a sweet rondo passage on a harp, went through her. She noted his Swahili greeting, the English translation of "what's the word?" She swallowed the lump in her throat before she replied with the traditional response. *"Kujichagulia."*

They fell silent. The atmosphere took on a dreamlike quality, hypnotic, lulling. Then Sterling moved toward Selinae, closing the short distance between them.

"You've been crying," he said, reaching out a hand to touch her.

"Yes," she said quietly, finding she couldn't lie to him. "But I'm okay now," she said against the hand that rested on her cheek.

With the warmth of his hand on the side of her face, she felt a yearning that was puzzling in its depth. Her heart was pounding; she didn't know how she steadied herself; her legs felt as if they had turned to jelly. He took her hands and pulled her against the wall of his chest. She leaned into him and rested her weight against his strength.

"You should have called me," he said, stroking her back tenderly.

"There was no need," she whispered raggedly.

But the need was within her and building. The heat that started on her face stole down her body. She breathed in his warmth, reveled in the faint smell of his skin, and when he tilted up her chin, she didn't resist. Everything that had happened to her that morning suddenly seemed unimportant, and she succumbed to his kiss. His mouth was firm, his kiss persuasive in a way that reminded her of his voice. Draping her arms around his waist, she kissed him back.

When he finally pulled away, her lips tingled from his brandishing, and she was breathless and dazed with wonder. She placed her hands on him for support and took hard, short breaths, noticing his breathing was as arrhythmic as hers, skipping across his chest as he drew new air into his lungs.

"Have you had breakfast?" he asked, then looked at his watch. "Maybe we better make that lunch."

Selinae's head was still spinning; it took her a while to catch up with this speedy change of direction he'd tossed at her. "Uh, no. Uh, what time is it?"

"Eleven-forty-five," he replied. "Why don't you change and we'll run out for a bite, then—"

"Wait a minute," she said with nervous laughter in her voice, hands over her bosom, "slow down." Her breathing still hadn't returned to normal.

"Uh-uh," he said, shaking his head from side to side, "we're getting out of here as fast as we can."

Propping her hands on her hips, she stared at him in defiance and disbelief. She didn't need a keeper to replace the two she'd just kicked out, she thought.

Sterling arched a brow, fixed her with a knowing look. "Otherwise, we won't leave at all," he explained patiently. "And while that's not a bad idea," he said, his gaze roving over her seductively, "I have a feeling you'd regret it in a couple of hours."

Selinae flushed, realizing there was more than a grain of truth in his caustic words. Her resolve to send him away had flown out the window in his arms. A few more minutes cloaked in the warm blanket of desire and they would have been right where her body wanted to go, she thought disconcertedly. With the fight for her independence deflated, she nodded her head in agreement.

"Now hurry," he said.

Wordlessly, Selinae backed from the room and vanished down the hallway.

Despite the chill in the air, a warm sun brought out families looking for an inexpensive, fun outing within the Hermann Park complex. From their hillside view, Sterling and Selinae could see people spilling out of cars, heading toward the Burke Baker Planetarium.

They were sitting on a blanket spread over the low-cut rye grass that maintained its greenery even during the winter months. Selinae was eating a chicken leg, while Sterling was adjusting the ASA on one of his cameras.

They didn't stop to lunch upon leaving her house four hours ago. Sterling had started babbling excitedly about wanting to capture the halcyon spirit that he saw on the faces of the people who attended Kwanzaa the previous night. She had agreed to postpone lunch. At the time she was more than willing to become involved in an activity that would take her mind off her hunger. She got caught up in his enthusiasm, having felt a similar emotion numerous times when she was working on a story that was as exciting as it was challenging.

He'd looked for it in several places—the Galleria, a couple of museums, and finally, the nearby zoo. Though he'd taken dozens of pictures, he wasn't hopeful. An hour ago, he called it quits for the day, and they stopped to fill up the picnic basket he'd brought.

Stealing a glance at his arresting profile, an unconscious smile settled across her expression and a warm feeling of tenderness spread through her. Her first impressions of him held true in their second meeting, she mused. He was a take-charge man, fearless of the consequences, whatever they might be.

His home and his urbane manner spoke of a man who enjoyed a comfortable life. Yet, today he seemed like a man on a serendipitous mission. One of his missions seemed to be rescuing her, she thought, folding the chicken bone in a napkin to toss in the designated trash bag in the basket.

A burst of youthful laughter caught her attention. She looked in the direction from where the sound originated and spotted three young children playing tag with a man and woman, most likely their parents, as home base. A family, she thought, feeling a little happy, a little sad, a little envious.

"A penny for your thoughts," Sterling said.

Selinae looked at him abruptly, and his root beer eyes held her still. She was amazed by the tender gleam in their depths. She had to remind herself to breathe.

"I haven't had a lazy day like this in a while," she said, a smile spreading slowly across her face. For the first time in a long time, she felt a surge of the teenage exuberance that had made her popular in school among students and teachers alike. The cause of her happiness was literally right in front of her, though she couldn't believe that one man could so quickly change her entire world. Well, almost her entire world. "Thank you," she said.

"You're more than welcome," he replied. "Tomorrow I want to get an earlier start. Now that I know what I have to do to get you out of the house in a hurry." His look traveled the length of her body.

Selinae blushed, and Sterling's rich laughter filled the air.

"I'm sorry," he said, capturing one of her hands between his. "I didn't mean to tease you."

Her hand tingled in his touch. She smiled. "Yes, you did." She pouted, feigning hurt feelings as she pulled her hand from his.

Suddenly, he sat back on his legs and trained the camera on her. "I want to take your picture."

"No," she protested, turning her head away from the camera's lens. "I don't photograph well."

"Believe me," he said with confident assurance, "it had nothing to do with you; it was the photographer. He didn't know what he was doing."

Shaking her head, she affirmed, "No. Please, don't."

With a slight tilt of his head and an admiring look in his eyes, Sterling said, "You're beautiful . . . you know that."

Selinae studied him back, his words lingering in the air between them.

"I'll put it away if you insist," he said.

"Let me think about it," she replied after a while.

Sterling set the camera next to the others, then lay on the blanket facing the sun. A flock of white winged birds sailed across the clear windy skies.

"Tell me about your family," he said.

She started to say "I don't have one," but knew that reply would only result in questions that would be even more difficult to answer. "It's a pretty typical, dysfunctional family," she said, trying to keep her tone light.

"Your brothers seemed quite protective," he replied.

"Presumptuous," she corrected. "Actually, they came to do a patch job, so to speak."

"Ah," he said. "Who have you upset, your mama or your daddy?"

"My dad," she replied. "But that's nothing new. This time, he cut me out of his will."

"He'll get over it," Sterling replied, adjusting his hands beneath his head.

"He hasn't gotten over it in fifteen years," she said.

Sterling whistled. "Sometimes our expectations of the people we love are just too darn high," he said.

"Sounds like you know a lot about it," she replied.

"Firsthand," he replied. "Only, in my case, I was the one with the unrealistic expectations. It took me a while to get over it, but I did." He sat up and rested his elbows on his bent knees, staring absently across the park.

"What happened, if you don't mind my asking?"

"Oh, my mother did something that was unforgivable. At least, when I was nineteen, it was unforgivable. It involved a man, not my father. My father had been dead for quite some time. I was in my first year at Texas Southern University. I was a photography major, but awed by Dr. John Biggers, the art professor. I decided I wanted my photographs to resemble his art."

"I love his work," she said. "It's so soulful."

"I know what you mean," he said wistfully. "That's what I want to do with the camera, create images that go beyond the merely visual." He fell quiet for a moment, then cleared his throat. "Anyway, all during high school I was going about my business, not paying attention to practical matters. You know, the usual self-absorbed teenage mentality. We weren't rich. When my father died, my mother didn't know how to do anything except clean other people's houses, so that's what she did. I hated it, but we had to survive. She had worked about four years for this family when they hired her to manage one of their rental properties. By that time, I had started college. She got to live in one of the apartments rent-free. But there were other benefits, too," he said pensively. "She got a car, we had food on the table all the time, I got new clothes. We seemed to have money. I never thought anything about it, particularly when she gave me cash for tuition and books. I never questioned where our newfound wealth came from. Then one day . . . It was during the Thanksgiving break. I finished my exams and went home. He was there. I was crushed. My mama was sleeping with the boss's son. We argued and that's when I learned where the money for my education was coming from. I dropped out of school, left home, wanting no part of her. I left the city and went to Chicago. It took me a while to figure out I was punishing myself."

"What's 'a while'?" she asked.

"A little over five years," he replied softly.

As Sterling related his tale, Selinae had feared she was enthralled by a man who was just like her father. Hearing him admit his capacity to forgive, among other things, infused her with a wonderful sense of relief. She noticed his thoughts taking a turn, censoring memories as he continued.

"I was a stubborn young punk," he said derisively. "I had to learn the hard way. I was determined not to sell out professionally. I wanted to be an *artiste,*" he said, raising his hand and pinching his fingertips together. "But having to make a choice between a roof over my head and food on the table made for a painful, but valuable lesson. In the final analysis, I opted for eating and paying the bills."

"Is she still with that man?"

"Yes," Sterling said, glancing at her with a smile. "The social climate changed enough for them to come out of the closet. They got married six years ago."

"And how do you feel about that now?"

"I'm jealous," he replied. "Not of him," he added hastily, "but of what they have together. I've never seen her so happy before. I want what she has. And I regret the time I've wasted, now that I know it never had to be that way."

"I guess we each come into our own when we're ready," she said musingly.

"Yeah," he said. "What about you? Are you ready?"

With the night of *Kujichagulia* fading, Selinae reveled in her good feelings and likewise, in the man whose arms were guiding her so assuredly and gracefully across the dancefloor. The music, the wine, and the gaiety surrounding them made her feel light-headed and giddy, as if all were right with the world.

It was in her world, Selinae mused, her head resting against Sterling's strong shoulder.

After leaving the park, they returned to her home with plans of attending the evening's Kwanzaa celebration to be followed by dinner out. An invitation, which was really a command from her aunt Rae, to a house party, came unexpectedly. Presented with an opportunity to extend their time together, they added it to their list of things to do.

They arrived at a home bursting with a holiday-spirited crowd. Young children were scampering back and forth, replenishing plates of food, while teenagers manned the small living room, ranking on each other playfully. The bravura challenges of bid whist and domino players could be heard occasionally drifting down the open stairs to compete with the festive din of the conversationalists crowding the dining room and kitchen. None of it intruded on the mood set in the family room of the thirty-something generation.

Under low ceiling lights, several couples danced, wedded to the music and each other. Even before Sterling and Selinae walked in, the mood had been established, and it extended to embrace them in its romantic arms.

Rachelle Ferrell's "Waiting" was drawing to a close. Selinae softly hummed the tune. It was one of several old songs that had been taped for tonight's occasion, and it was one of her favorites.

With the phrase "patiently waiting" echoing in her head, her thoughts turned melancholy. She felt the refrain applied to her. It was what she had been doing, waiting patiently for her father to come around and accept her, shortcomings and all.

The song segued into another oldie, "I Try," interpreted by Will Downing.

Selinae felt the pressure of Sterling's arms tighten gently around her waist. Held so close to him, she wondered why she was ruining her evening with unpleasant memories. Particularly when new ones, happier ones, were even then being made.

She concentrated on savoring the moment, the music, the man next to her. They swayed, easy and slow, in tempo with the tender ballad, enraptured by its melody.

Selinae felt herself pulled even closer, Sterling's essence surrounding her, overwhelming her senses. Pressing his chin against the side of her head, his hands explored the hollows of her back, touching her with tender strokes that transmitted a sensual message up and down her spine. Her head lost the battle of restraint to her traitorous body. She snuggled into his all-male, all bracing nearness.

From the very beginning, an undeniable magnetism had existed between them, she thought. Even as she tried to deny it, then rationalize it away by giving it another name, it refused uprooting. And he, like a farmer tending his prize crop, never failed to water the seeds of attraction.

At the song's end, they sauntered to one of the love seats pushed against the wall in the room. Other couples sat along the curtain of the brick fireplace, while others remained on the floor as the next song, a jazz instrumental, started up.

Feeling betrayed by her own thoughts, Selinae fanned herself with her hand. She couldn't look Sterling in the eye, wondering if he had felt the swell of her breasts, still tingling against the fabric of her dress.

"Want something to drink?" she asked.

"No, thank you," he said. "I just want to sit here awhile and catch my breath." He took her hand in his.

"Haven't gone dancing in a while," she teased. "You're out of shape."

"The dancing part is true, but my being out of breath is mostly your fault," he said.

"If you don't stop talking to me like that, we won't be planting that garden you wanted to get started on tomorrow," she said.

With a gentle, teasing laugh, Sterling pulled her closer and his breath tickled her ear, sending a tingle down her spine.

"Am I finally getting to meet the real Selinae?" he asked. "Or is the wine going to her head?"

Something had gone to her head, Selinae mused, but she didn't believe the wine deserved the credit. Shaking her head, she chuckled softly. "You're making me say crazy things."

"Good," he replied, "then that makes us even."

A mischievous look glinted in his eyes, an easy smile playing around the corners of his mouth as he raised her hand to his lips and planted a kiss on her palm.

"Sterling," she breathed as a shudder passed through her.

"What?" he drawled innocently. "I merely asked a simple question. Which you have yet to answer."

"You ask too many questions for a photographer," she quipped, knowing he meant the question he asked earlier that day. "Asking questions is *my* job." She poked a finger to her chest.

"Then ask away," he replied, crossing his legs at the knee.

All of her questions were self-directed, she thought, now forced to come up with some innocuous inquiry. "What's your middle name?"

"Neal," he replied. "Yours?"

"I'm asking the questions here," she said laughingly.

With a strange, faintly eager look flashing in his eyes, he replied, "Tit for tat, lady. I'll accept nothing short of sharing."

Selinae could tell by the tone in his mellow baritone voice, it was a point he would not concede, no arguments, no compromises. She felt on the precipice of exotic ground, afraid of taking that step forward and afraid not to. She swallowed the lump in her throat. "Antoinette."

"Selinae Antoinette Rogers." Sterling savored the name on his tongue as if it were a fine delicacy. "Okay, what's next?"

Selinae wrinkled up her face in quick pondering. He was a man who knew his mind, she thought, while she could barely think past the desire smoldering in her. "No more questions," she replied at last.

"What?" he asked, somewhat amazed. "There's nothing else you want to know about me?"

"See how easy I am to please?" she asked, then realized the implications behind the innocent question.

"No you're not, lady," he replied, shaking his head from side to side. "You're complicated, and you scare the dickens out of me."

If he were scared, Selinae mused, she wondered where she fell on the Richter scale. She had a feeling the day of reckoning was fast approaching and could only hope she had answers by then. "Why don't you grow horns or something," she moaned.

"Why don't you just admit you want me as much as I want you?" he retorted.

At his brash declaration, her eyes blinked rapidly in stunned succession before they settled on his face to study him silently. He studied her back; the look in his eyes contained a sensuous flame.

"I know what you've been thinking," he said. "Is he only interested in getting me into bed? Does he want a short fling or a long-term relationship? Can I trust him not to hurt me?" He looked at her pensively, then glanced down at her hand in his possession. "I can give you an answer to each and every one, but I can't answer for you." He looked up straight in her eyes; his were masked by some indefinable emotion.

It seemed everything Sterling said made sense, Selinae thought; everything he did was right. She didn't know if she could cope with his perfection, fearing she couldn't live up to it. She swallowed hard before she spoke.

"I find it hard to believe that you're afraid of anything," she replied in a barely audible voice.

"I'm afraid of making a mistake with you," he said. "I'd like nothing better than to take you to my bed and love you senseless. But I know you're not sure about me and I don't know how long I can wait for you to get all the answers you need. I'd like to think my patience is unlimited, but my . . ." He fell silent, a sheepish half-grin on his face, before continuing. "Well, I'm not so sure anymore." With a somewhat self-derisive chuckle he held up her hand. "See? I can't even sit here without touching you. I've been wanting to do it all day, but I held back because you held back. I asked you earlier today whether you were ready. What I should have asked was . . . are you willing to take a chance on me?"

By the time they returned to her home, Selinae

felt as if her emotions and thoughts were in dreamland. All evening Sterling had lulled her with his sagacious rhetoric and mellifluous voice, breaking down barriers of confusion and draining away her doubts.

Now she stood in her living room as he had commanded while he conducted a safety precaution search of her home.

If those horns haven't come out yet, she told herself, *they never will.* She had been searching for an excuse to say no to any combination of questions in her head, while every bone, cell, and nerve strand in her body said yes. Jubilantly and definitively so. He had answered all her unasked questions, and it was as he'd stated: The rest was up to her.

She supposed her skepticism was much like that of the millions of African Americans when first introduced to Kwanzaa. They questioned its value and relevance. Now, that same million and more embraced the celebration annually. They had been asked to take a chance, and in doing so, found something that was essentially part of them—a missing link they couldn't do without. The parallel stuck in her mind.

"Everything checks out okay," Sterling said.

Selinae tracked his approach from the dining room with her inflamed heart in her eyes. She felt it beating in time to the echo in her head. *Take a chance. Take a chance. Take a chance.*

Stopping inches from Selinae, Sterling saw the confusion and desire in her amber eyes, a hint of vulnerability in their jeweled depths. He returned her gaze with his photographer's eyes, assessing the conflicting emotions he read in them.

It was no joke that he was afraid . . . afraid of losing her even before he could make her his. She was such an enigma to him. Never had he met a woman who radiated such warmth, yet guarded her life so vigilantly.

She seemed to respect his privacy almost too much, he mused. He found that irregular behavior for a journalist. He wondered if her lack of curiosity about him was self-protective. Although it presented an exciting challenge to the courtship, their lack of knowledge about each other made their relationship like walking through a mine field. He'd done that once before and swore he'd never do it again, he recalled, but his attraction to her had made a liar out of him. It was strong, had been from the beginning, and continued to grow more powerful by the second in her company.

Then again, there were instances when reminders of the first time he saw her at the park seemed like an ancient memory. He felt as though he'd known her for a long time. Her calming influence made him feel like he was home. He'd begun to suspect that his preconceived notion about settling down was somewhat outdated. A physical structure wasn't needed, he told himself, a physical sensation was. And one was swelling right then in the center of his groin.

Taking her hands in his, he said, *"Habari gani?"*

"Ujima," she replied softly.

He saw the breath tremble in her bosom and felt an uncanny urgency erupt in his gut. He wanted to protect her from the demon troubling her soul . . . to win her trust in him . . . to make her want him as much as he wanted her. He lowered his head to kiss her temple and waited. She stared up at him with a sweet expectant smile curled on her soft lips, pure desire now settled in her beautiful eyes, on her arresting face.

As if in slow motion, his head lowered to kiss her

eye, on to the slightly rounded tip of her nose, then to her cheek. Guided by age-old instincts, his mouth wandered to the moist hollow of her throat, lingering there to enjoy the enticing fragrance of her skin. He could hear his own breathing roar in his ears, a tidal wave crashing against the walls of his chest.

A tiny mewl seeped past her lips, a tantalizing invitation for more, and he captured her mouth in a kiss full of passion and need.

In the bright lights of the living room, under the blessed symbols of Kwanzaa on the coffee table, he made love to her mouth, spoke to her soul with his lips, both gentle and demanding on hers. With their arms draped around each other, their bodies pressed together in arousal, their tongues sought each other out. In the inner recesses of wanting mouths, a libation was offered, paying homage to the communion of man and woman, the building ground of family.

Sterling tore his mouth from Selinae's and stilled her wanton, wandering hands, holding them behind her back as he rested his forehead against hers. Seeking his breath, he said with an uncharacteristic falter in his voice, "Selinae . . . if we don't stop now, I'll—"

It was as far as he got, for she silenced him. In one fluid motion, she took his restraining hands and placed them around her waist. She stood on tiptoes, lifting her head as her lips brushed his. The whisper-light contact slew his thoughts of retreat. Lowering the white flag, he surrendered to her irresistible pull and reveled in the punishing sweetness of her kiss.

Touching became an art form. Neither body suffered a second's want for it as hands and fingers, driven by the urgency of mounting excitement, went to work. The purple, white, and yellow headwrap she wore fell first. The black, high-neck collared shirt next. Shoes made a trail to the bedroom.

Under the soft light of the bedside lamp, Selinae and Sterling paused to feast hungry gazes on each other. He was all honey and firm from his sculpted strong face, lightly pecked by a warm sun, down to his wide-shouldered, well-toned body. She was sienna and slim with firm, high-perched breasts and a tiny waist that widened into agilely rounded hips.

"You're beautiful," she said almost reverently.

"I've never known the meaning of the word before now," he replied, trailing a hand from the side of her face down to her breast, the tip dark and pebble-hard. He felt the tremulous breath she exhaled and sucked it into his lungs.

Selinae moved to her bed and waited for him to join her there. He did so without hesitation, stretching his strong body atop her soft one. Like a crofter, he began cultivating her aroused senses anew. She was an arable entity, her body and mind a fertile pasture to his sensuous tilling.

Her skin tingled when he touched her, and everywhere he touched her brought a gasp of wonder from her throat, traveling all the way up from her center. Twisting under his weight, arching her body as if to immerse her essence with his, she reaped as good as she sowed, and it was the best tending he had ever experienced. Her hands were magic tools, and he felt like a sapling under her ministrations.

She let him kiss her greedily and satisfied her own needy appetite from his lips. Then he moved, leaving her mouth burning with fire as his lips seared a path down her neck, her shoulders, and the satin plane of warm flesh beyond.

The old house came alive with Selinae and Sterling's harvesting, as if it had been waiting for such vibrancy to return to it ever since its past owners had left. Up until now, it had gone unfulfilled by its new mistress. Up until now . . .

When Sterling moved into Selinae, he gasped at the tightness of her sacred center. He attempted to restrain his thrusts, but her body insisted on the full strength of him, coiling tightly around his hardness. The breath rushed from him again in a wild gasp of pleasure.

He had to fight off the dizzying current racing through him as he followed her lead, matched her seductive overtures into him stroke for stroke. With each possession, she arched up to receive him, propelling him to return for more. Their bodies made music and danced to it, as awe and passion-inspired sighs and groans filled the air.

Sighing praises to his name, Selinae felt herself infused with liquid fire. A fleeting thought, a wish for this ecstasy-ache to last forever, descended all too soon. Gasping in sweet agony, she shattered into a million glowing stars and her soul climbed to a heavenly place. Sterling joined her there shortly, his voice a rough moan of erotic surrender as he filled her with his love.

"Selinae," he said in a prayer-like whisper as his lips captured hers in a kiss that caressed her spirit. Then, windless, exhausted, divinely satiated, he collapsed atop her to hear her low, ecstatic laughter in his ear. With his head buried in her neck, he said in a muffled voice, *"Habari gani."*

"Kwanzaa yenu iwe na heri," she replied. With her arms wrapped loosely around him, she placed a gentle kiss on the side of his head and sighed with supreme contentment.

Too tired to move anything but his mouth, he said, "Translation, please."

"May y'alls Kwanzaa be with happiness," she said, and smiled.

Later, in the dark of the room, silent tears of joy slid down Selinae's face. With Sterling's sleeping form beside her, she could not stop pondering what had happened to her. She felt suffused with reverent sensations, a mixture of wonder, fear, and love.

The passion they'd shared, the reality and depth of it, was shocking. She couldn't help wondering if the way her body responded to him was a fluke as she glanced at Sterling, enraptured.

She also wondered what was next. Recalling his confident assertions, she knew he had an answer, but could he have anticipated one whose question had yet to be born?

Looming pervasively was the all-embracing affection she felt, the one that put rhyme before reason, feeling before thought, the one named love. Yes, love, she thought, even as she pondered how it was possible, or when it had happened, or whether she was confusing it with sex.

Yet, she knew deep down inside that no other word could describe what she felt. It was the most honest emotion she'd had in a long time, and she felt guilty for soiling it with questions and ruminations.

It had been too long, she mused. Much, much too long. Not since David, her very first lover, had she been able to complete the act of making love. They had both been young. Quite a bit of bumbling and fumbling had taken place. Though it hadn't been a totally unpleasant experience, it could never compare with her dreams and now with her indisputable proof of how utterly fulfilling sex could be with the right person.

A second attempt with a different partner while in college never progressed to consummation, she recalled somewhat sadly. Verbally abusive taunts from her past had crowded her memory and stolen the moment. She had cried so hard, the poor young man she was with had been too startled to get angry with her.

A small cry escaped her throat unexpectedly, and Sterling was immediately awake. He saw her wet eyes, the tracks of tears on her face, and sat up to pull her into his arms.

"Ah, Selinae," he crooned gently. "Tell me," he pleaded.

Shaking her head, Selinae dried her eyes with her hands. "It's nothing." She let out a small laugh. "I'm just being silly, that's all."

"No, that's not all," he said with concern. "Damn. I knew it. I knew this would happen."

"No, no," she said, shushing him, her hand covering his mouth. "It's not what you think. I'm not sorry, and I have no regrets. It was the most wonderful thing that ever happened to me."

He kissed her on the temple before he spoke. "I detect a 'but' in that confession," he said. "It's been a long time for you, hasn't it?"

She smiled against his warm flesh. "A very long time."

"While it wouldn't have made any difference had it not been," he said, "I'm glad." He felt her smile widen. "Yes, I got some of the homies in me, too," he said, laughing at himself with her. Suddenly silent, he lay his head on hers. "Please . . . tell me what you're thinking."

Selinae sighed. Where to begin, how much to tell? Was she ready for disclosure, could he handle the truth? Her memory dipped into the past, dangerous territory.

"Selinae," he prodded gently, squeezing her body.

She pushed herself up, propping a pillow at her back and pulling the covers up to her chest. She drew a deep breath before she spoke. "I got pregnant when I was fifteen." She stared sidelong at Sterling, assessing his reaction. His face remained blank. "You're not . . ." she began, then fell silent, picking absently at the spread.

"What?" he asked. "Shocked? Disappointed? No, baby," he said, shaking his head. "We all have histories, Selinae. What happened? Did the boy desert you to the wolves?"

She detected a hint of anger in his voice when he said this last. "No," she said, a small smile tilting up the corners of her mouth. "He was very supportive and ready to assume his responsibility."

"Okay," Sterling said. "What happened?"

"We thought we were in love," she said, her thoughts filtering back to happy times. "He was a junior, vice-president of the student government, star basketball guard, honor roll. You know, the perfect guy."

"The kind daddies like to see their little girls date," Sterling said.

"His name was David," she said, then drew a tremulous sigh. "He wanted to be with me when I told my parents, but I wasn't so sure about their reaction. I had believed we were the kind of family where we could always go to each other, but this was different. My mother and I were never really close, but I knew my daddy would be disappointed. I knew what his expectations were for me. I had had a lot of success up to then as a runner. Our track team had made it to the nationals that year, and I had placed first in two events. There was a lot at stake, college scholarships, maybe even the Olympics. My father loved to go to the meets. He loved to help me train. He had everything set in his mind about how it was going to be. I knew the pregnancy would change things between us, but I had no idea how much. I thought it would be better if I told them alone. David let me have my way on this and my way turned out to be all wrong."

She shook her head slowly from side to side. "Never in all my life could I have dreamed a worse nightmare. My father went ballistic." She swallowed the lump that had lodged in her throat. "I didn't recognize him," she said in a soft, barely audible voice. "He was . . . a monster. It wasn't my daddy. It wasn't my daddy. It was some stranger . . . shouting and screaming, calling me horrible names, threatening violence. I almost believe he would have killed me if there had been no one there to intervene. My mother was screaming for him to calm down. My brothers were crying and trying to pull him away from me. Everything was loud and chaotic . . . all the crying and shouting, Daddy's angry threats. I tried to get away. He stopped me just as I reached that first step. I don't think it was deliberate. He just didn't realize his strength. His hand was on my arm and . . . I fell. All the way down to the bottom." She exhaled slowly, as if the action itself caused her pain.

Sterling suppressed his shock and dismay, envisioning the scene. A deep anger rose in him; he wanted to lash out, wanted to turn the violence she'd been subjected to back on her tormentor.

She held herself under tight control, her expression vacant, almost as if she were talking about someone else. She told her story like a journalist, he thought, matter-of-factly, a straight reporting of events. He gently touched her cheek.

She continued. "My mama called Aunt Rae and Uncle Lou, who rushed over to the house. My daddy was throwing my clothes down over the banister, yelling at me to get out. They took me home with them. Later that night, they rushed me to the hospital. There was so much blood. So much blood. I lost the baby."

Tears fell in earnest, blinding her eyes and choking off her voice. Sterling pulled her into his arms and crushed her to him. "It's all right," he whispered as he stroked her back gently. "It's all right now."

"I didn't see him again until I was released from the hospital. He didn't come to see me. My mama took me home, but it was over between us, my daddy and me," she said, sniffing, wiping her running nose. "We didn't speak to each other for months. We were like two zombies. Then one day, he told me to get my shoes, but I wouldn't. I couldn't run for him anymore," she said, looking up at Sterling, as if pleading for him to understand.

"He'd lost respect for me as his daughter. And when I refused to run, he had no use for me at all. He told me to get out. I moved in with my aunt and uncle." She sought the warmth and comfort of Sterling's nearness, wrapping her arms around his waist, laying her head on his chest.

"I'm sorry. So sorry," he said over and over as he continued to hold her, trying to stroke the pain from her body.

"I thought I was special to him because I was his firstborn and only daughter," she said in a young girl's voice, then self-derision marred her tone. "I used to think that, you know? But what it boiled down to was that I was his star runner. The one who was going to get him to the Olympics." She snorted bitterly. "Now you know all my dirty little secrets," she said lightly. "I'm the rotten seed in the Rogers' family. And all you can do with a rotten seed is throw it away."

"Stop that," he commanded, his anger slipping into his tone.

"This Christmas was the first time we've spent more than thirty minutes together in the same place," she said as if speaking to herself. "But there's nothing there anymore. If there ever was any truth in our relationship, it's been dead a long time. I just never wanted to admit it. Now I can," she said in an emotionless tone.

Sterling didn't believe her for a minute. He took the declaration for what it was—a form of denial, a painkiller to deaden the deep wound.

This woman, his woman, he thought, was much too caring and sensitive. She felt too deeply. After all, it was her warm and enchanting nature that had attracted him to her in the first place.

While it was good for him, the trait worked against her as far as her family was concerned. He'd seen glimpses of her vulnerability, recalling the confrontation he'd witnessed with her brothers, although she'd tried to hide it under a strong, impassive facade.

Still, he thought, never in a million years would he have guessed the shadows on her soul had been cast by her father. He'd like to beat the hell out of Mr. Rogers, but he knew Selinae would rush to the bastard's side like a mother hen in a second.

Recalling his lament of ever getting next to her,

he had no complaints about her response to him in bed, he thought. He recognized the oblation of her flesh to him and was all the more determined to cherish it like the priceless gift it was. She was more woman than he expected, more than he could have ever hoped for. But he wanted all of her: *both in and out of bed.*

And he thought he had all the answers, he chided himself. But he had no answer for this. At least, not one Selinae would entertain.

Even as he feared he was no match for her enemy, he knew words of comfort alone were not enough for his woman. He was going to have to show her she no longer had to suffer in silence.

It was going to be a painstaking lesson, he thought, knowing that family fights were far more harmful than a gang of homies. The scars ran deeper; the healing took longer.

Wondering whether he was up to the task, Sterling prayed for the guidance and strength from the Creator.

Selinae finally drifted off. Sterling contented himself with just holding her in his arms until he too joined her in the liberating state of dreams.

But bright and early the next morning, reality came calling once again with the ringing of the doorbell. The sound roused them both out of sleep. Both hoped it would subside; neither wanted to leave the haven of the other's warmth.

"Maybe they'll go away," Sterling said, pulling her closer to him. He nuzzled the side of her neck, crushing her to him. "Hmm," he sighed at length. "I could get used to waking up next to you."

Feeling the stirring of desire awakening in her,

she arched her body into his. "I know what you mean," she said. He drew a sensuous moan from her throat as his mouth devoured the softness of hers.

The ringing of the doorbell persisted.

Lifting his mouth from hers reluctantly, he asked, "Want me to send them away?"

"It's probably my brothers, who will positively drop dead at my front door if you answer," she quipped laughingly.

"I'm not afraid of your brothers, Selinae," he said in a plain, serious voice.

Selinae stared into his face; a savage inner fire glowed in his chocolate eyes, bold lights of confidence and determination in their depths. The look strengthened her resolve to take a chance, shored up her still distant goal of liberation. Wanting to feel only the protective weight of his arms around her, she said softly, "Then go . . . send them away and come back to me."

"Where's Selinae?"

The question, more like a demand, hung in the air as if supported by an invisible string of thread. Sterling merely stared in stunned amazement at the two women at the door.

The speaker was bedecked in a teal designer suit that complimented her slender frame and caramel complexion to perfection. Long, thick black hair fell in luscious curls around her shoulders; her makeup was expertly applied. The features of her oval face were delicately carved, but her expression was austere, her manner haughty. Sterling realized at once that he was facing a mother's wrath.

His heart began to pound like a kettledrum in

his chest. What a state he was in—shoeless, shirtless, clothes discarded the previous night folded over his arm; his plan to shock Selinae's brothers had ridiculously backfired. With an insipid smile spreading across his face, he opened his mouth to speak.

"Where's my daughter, young man?"

"I told you we should have called first," her companion chided.

Sterling flashed a weak smile at Mrs. Rogers's companion, Selinae's aunt Rae, whom he'd met the night before. Finding his voice, he said, "Good morning. Won't you come in? I'll get Selinae for you."

Aunt Rae winked at Sterling as she trailed Cora Rogers into the living room.

After locking the door, Sterling was eager to escape. Reaching the hallway door, he bumped into Selinae. He flashed her an "uh-oh" grimace. She gave him a seductive smile and patted him on the arm, then winked in response to his mildly scolding look that told her to behave.

Walking around Sterling into the living room, Selinae tightened the belt of the robe she'd put on. "Good morning, Mama, Aunt Rae. What are you two doing up so early?"

"It's almost eleven," Cora Rogers replied, staring pointedly at Selinae before turning her gaze on Sterling.

Pointing a thumb at the woman by her side, Aunt Rae said, "I couldn't stop her from coming, so I figured I might as well come along. Good morning, Sterling." She flashed him a broad, winking grin.

"Good morning, Rae," Sterling replied. Absently, he rubbed the side of his neck. He hadn't been this nervous since his first date in high school.

Pulling Sterling alongside her, Selinae said, "Sterling, I'd like you to meet my mother, Cora Rogers. Mama, this is Sterling Washington."

"Sterling," Cora said flatly.

"How do you do, Mrs. Rogers?" Sterling replied. Regaining his wits, he extended a hand to her, his most charming smile intact. "It's a pleasure to meet you."

Unimpressed, Cora shook his hand weakly as if afraid of catching something.

"Uh, why don't I put on a pot of coffee," he said, backing from the room, clutching the armload of clothes.

"That's a good idea," Aunt Rae said as she situated herself on the couch.

"I keep the coffee in—" Selinae started.

"I'll find it," Sterling said, cutting her off as he vanished behind the kitchen door.

Silence reigned until Sterling was no longer visible, then conversation levels dropped to a soft decibel.

"When your brothers told me you kicked them out—" Cora began in an incensed whisper.

"How are you doing, Mama?" Selinae said, kissing her mother on the cheek. "You look wonderful, as usual."

For a second, Cora was flabbergasted. "I'm fine, Selinae. How are you?" Before Selinae could answer, Cora pointed toward the kitchen. "I suppose that's evident."

"I want details," Aunt Rae said, clapping her hands together in a sign of eager excitement. She smiled at Selinae with anticipation, undaunted by the glower on her sister's face.

"Will you behave yourself, Rae?" her sister snapped. "Selinae, what do you know about this man?" she asked, setting her expensive handbag on the coffee table.

Pulling up her caftan and resting her leg on the couch, Aunt Rae replied in a bored tone, "I thought we'd covered that ground."

"I don't want to hear any more of your nonsense," Cora returned, then faced Selinae headlong, her arms folded across her bosom.

It never ceased to amaze her that her mother, Cora Shaw-Rogers, and her aunt, Rae Marie Shaw-Willis, were of the same blood. Aunt Rae was a practical, earthy woman who embraced life heartily and without fear. She was usually robed in African attire. Her mother, on the other hand, clung to some outdated etiquette code that had never applied to black women in the first place. Though she was stronger than she looked, she lived the stereotype of the genteel Southern woman. They had been at odds from the moment Selinae graced this earth. A tomboy, she had always been daddy's girl. At least, until . . .

"Selinae," Cora said impatiently. "Are you going to answer me?"

Sliding onto the love seat, Selinae crossed her legs at the knee, careful to close the folds of her robe. "It's always good to see you, Mama, but I'm curious as to what precipitated this visit. Does your husband know you're here?"

"That's your father you're talking about," she scolded harshly, "and I don't need anybody's permission to visit my daughter."

"She never said or implied that you did," Aunt Rae said, coming to her niece's defense.

"Selinae," her mother said, her eyes trained on her daughter, "what do you know about this man? Your brothers said you didn't even introduce them yesterday, and last night at Rae's house you barely said a word to them."

Selinae smiled to herself. She and Sterling were leaving the party as her brothers had driven up, she recalled. She had called out a greeting and then continued on her way. She didn't want another interrogation, not when she had been having such a blissful evening.

"You just met him, Mama," Selinae said. "His name is Sterling Neal Washington."

"That's a name that means absolutely nothing to me," her mother said.

"I already told you, he's got a good income, he's single and he doesn't have any venereal diseases," Aunt Rae interjected, finishing with an impatient tsk.

Selinae hid a smile behind her hand. Sterling was going to get an earful today, she thought.

"Rae Marie Shaw-Willis, shame on you," Cora chided, outraged. "And how do you know that, anyway?"

"I asked," Aunt Rae replied. "I get all the pertinent information up front," she boasted proudly. "What more do you want to know?"

"I sure don't want to know any more from you. Selinae, you never mentioned this man when you came over for dinner the other night."

"The subject never came up," Selinae replied. She didn't dare tell her mother *when* she'd met Sterling. Not after he had answered the door in such a state. "We've been seeing quite a bit of each other. He's a photographer. Maybe you've seen his work."

"Who does he work for?"

"The question is who *doesn't* he work for," she replied. "He's taken pictures for the *Smithsonian, National Geographic,* and lots of other publications, as well as for individuals and corporations. He's from Houston, attended TSU, just recently moved into a new house right across the street from MacGregor Park." Watching the interested gleam come to her mother's eyes, she knew she'd put Sterling's assets in the proper order.

"Well, that's a blessing," Cora said with a hearty sigh of relief. "At least he's not a bum." She sat on the opposite end of the couch from her sister, closest to Selinae.

"I've never dated bums," Selinae replied softly.

"You know what I mean," her mother said, waving her hand dismissively. "Is it serious between the two of you?"

"I'm not sure I understand your question," Selinae replied, stalling.

"Yes, you do," Cora said. "I didn't raise no dummies."

"If you're so sure about that, then why are you here?" Selinae replied, giving her mother a sidelong glance. She had a sinking feeling the visit was going to duplicate the one she'd had with her brothers the day before.

"We're concerned about you," Cora replied. "There's no need to be flippant. Maybe he'd like to come with you New Year's Eve. We're all going to church together. In fact, that's one of the reasons I came by. I want to take you shopping."

"It's too late," Selinae said under her breath.

"What was that?" Cora demanded.

"I said Sterling and I have other plans for New Year's Eve," Selinae replied.

"What's more important than spending time with your family?" Cora shot back at her.

"You want a list?" Selinae said, losing patience.

"What's that supposed to mean?" Cora asked.

"You know damn well—" Selinae started, then caught herself.

Wagging a finger at Selinae, Cora said, "Listen, young lady, I'm your mother. You don't use that kind of language in my presence."

"I'm sorry," Selinae said, suddenly contrite. "You're right, of course, but that still doesn't change anything. I'm sure Tony and Oscar junior told you how I feel. I don't feel up to repeating myself."

"Two wrongs don't make a right, Selinae," Cora said. "I thought you were mature enough to realize that."

"Oh right, make *me* the villain here," she snapped. "I guess I do have to repeat myself and I promise this is the last time I'm going to say it. I've had enough," she stressed emphatically. "I'm not going through it anymore with your husband. My hoop-jumping days are over."

"So what does that mean, that you've cut all of us out of your life? You disavow us as a family. Is that it?" Cora inquired hotly, her voice rising.

Was that what she had done . . . mentally severed ties with her family? Selinae asked herself, her bottom lip folded in her mouth. She answered with a shake of her head. No, she thought, she didn't believe that. She wasn't that vindictive. She was merely determined to pull the pieces of her life together the only way she knew how. Running home again at the promise of mending the bond that had long ago been severed was destructive to her. She couldn't let herself be fooled again, to hope where there was no hope.

"Selinae . . . ?"

She looked up to see Sterling completely dressed, smiling down at her, and felt renewed strength. This was the direction she wanted to move in. Toward life. Toward love.

"Where should I set this?" he asked, indicating the wooden serving tray with service for four in his hands.

Sterling had hoped that some vigorous yard work would help him pass the time. The euphoria he'd felt after having charmed Mrs. Rogers had worn off. Now he was playing a solitary guessing game of "she's coming, she's not coming" with himself as he tilled a square plot of land in his backyard under the bored gaze of his dog.

The garden was in the far back left-hand corner of the spacious yard. It faced his neighbor's, separated by a fence that was covered with clinging vines. A roll of chicken wire and empty bags of compost and fertilizer lay on the ground nearby.

His fat puppy Hannibal was stretched out on the patio floor near a kidney-shaped pool in the center of the yard. The pool held dead leaves and streaks of dirt instead of water.

It was early evening, between five and six. The air smelled clean and fresh, with a faint odor of pecan wood burning in a nearby fireplace. The weather was clear but nippy; the air current was rising with the promise of a winter's cold.

Sterling felt only frustration as he worked up a sweat.

Wondering how long it could possibly take to buy a dress, he squatted to untangle a piece of plastic debris from the moist black dirt imbedded in the iron spikes of the tiller. He tossed it aside and remained squatting, absently massaging a handful of soil, resting his head along the wooden handle of the tiller.

She should be here with me, he thought fiercely.

He'd made a mistake, he chided himself. He shouldn't have encouraged Selinae to go off with her mother and aunt. He should have insisted on keeping to their plans of starting the garden together, he told himself, gripping the handle of the tiller.

He ran the risk of not seeing her again, he thought fearfully, vigorously mixing the soil in the bed. Or of her losing her newfound faith in him at the hands of her family.

Sterling stilled. Leaning against the tiller handle, the memory of the previous night closed around him, blacked out the present and filled him with a keen yearning. With the indelible sensations of one night in her loving arms running freely through him, Sterling felt confirmed in what he'd up till then only suspected. He could strike out lust, he decided; what he felt was no temporary diversion. Selinae set his heart into motion. He'd only been surviving before he met her.

He was fragile as far as Selinae was concerned, he thought uneasily. She could easily scorch him.

He wiped his sweaty palms on his pants and resumed his task. There wasn't a thing he could do about his present situation except try not to think about it, he told himself, and yet his thoughts continued to drift back to the obstacles between them.

The distance between her and her father could conceivably work to his advantage, he mused with a slight sense of relief. But for all her dainty, ultrafeminine ways, Cora Rogers he pegged as a viper.

That left him in a precarious situation. He didn't know if Selinae's trust in him was up to the test if it came down to a contest of wills between him and her family.

He couldn't recall ever being so afraid of losing anything in all his life. And even *that* had been on the line before, he mused, recalling the week he'd spent in Johannesburg photographing the first elections open to black South Africans.

Just then, he heard what he thought was a car engine shutting down out front. His suspicions were confirmed by Hannibal. The short-haired, black and tan dog lifted his big head, his snub nose pointed alertly. Tossing the handle of the tiller aside, Sterling hurried into the house, Hannibal on his heels. He ran through the kitchen, bypassing the family room, and down the short corridor to the foyer, his heart racing ahead of him. Reaching the door, he drew a deep, calming breath, but was too impatient to compose himself further. He opened the door with a flourish.

"Did I come at a bad time?"

The dog wagged its tail jubilantly, while animation fled from Sterling's expression. He managed a slight smile as he looked into a face that was a female version of his, the features softer, smaller, and older. "No Mama," he said, "come on in." He tried not to sound too disappointed.

"Hi, baby," she said, patting Hannibal. To Sterling, she said, "I got some stuff in the car." Backing from the door, with Hannibal running playfully around her legs, she said, "Come help me."

Dutifully, Sterling followed her to the luxury blue car, trying to summon some enthusiasm. His mother pulled out a large roasting pan from the backseat and put it in his hands, then grabbed two large bags. The smells wafting from the containers didn't go unnoticed.

"Boudain?" he asked with a slightly raised brow, a grin starting to spread across his face.

"And lemon meringue pie and praline cheesecake," she replied. "All your favorites."

Suddenly suspicious as to the nature of her visit, he asked, "Mama, where's Guy?"

"Oh, he went to see about his sister," his mother replied, heading back to the house. Hannibal led the way.

Reaching the door, Sterling hesitated. What if Selinae came by and saw his mother's car parked outside? If she thought he was entertaining another woman, she would surely drive off without coming in.

"Mama, let me put your car in the garage," he said, setting the pan on the floor inside the foyer.

"I'm not going to be here that long," she replied.

"Mama, just give me the keys," he instructed, his hand held out to her.

Moments later, with his mother's car safely tucked in the garage and the door pulled down, Sterling strolled into the kitchen. His mother had already laid out a plate of food on the bar counter and was putting more away in the refrigerator. He saw Hannibal sneaking out the back door, his massive jaws clinging to a long boudain sausage.

"Mama, he shouldn't be eating that," Sterling scolded mildly.

"It ain't gonna kill him," his mother replied.

Sitting at the bar on the kitchen side, he picked up one long sausage and took a big bite. "When he starts complaining about his dog food, I'll send him to your house," he said, chewing.

"I put some smoked turkey, dirty rice, and cornbread dressing in the box," she said. "Your grandma sent you some étouffée. It's in the freezer." She grimaced as she turned around to face him. "You could have washed your hands. I at least taught you that much."

"Tastes better this way," he said with a mouthful.

She merely shook her head. He smiled, continuing to eat with his fingers. His Mama wasn't an educated woman—she had never graduated from high school—but she was smarter than a lot of people he knew. A dark-skinned Creole woman, bronze complexioned like he was, she retained her Louisiana accent even though she'd been in Houston for nearly forty years. Neither fat nor muscular, she had a hefty bosom and ample hips. Hair that fell to her waist was peppered with gray strands at the temple. It was customarily plaited and twisted into a ball at the back of her head. Though she could cuss and fuss with the best of them when in a temper, it had been her warm, caring nature and good cooking that had attracted Guy Ladd to his mama.

Staring across at her profile, Sterling felt a certain tension in the air. His mother looked worried, he suddenly noticed. Immediately, he grew concerned.

She trained her large, expressive brown eyes on him; a smile faltered on her wide lips. Sterling stopped chewing. He gulped down the chunk of food in his mouth, wondering if she and Guy had had a fight. Licking his fingers clean, he got up to go to her.

"Mama, what's the matter? Are you and Guy getting along okay?"

"We're getting along fine," she said.

"Then what's wrong?"

She walked away from him, into the family room. He followed, watching as she scanned the contents of the room: four large packing boxes, a floor lamp, and a red beanbag chair.

"When are you going to fix up this place? Ain't nowhere for a person to sit," she fussed, propping her hands on her hips.

She spun around and bumped into Sterling. He put his hands on her shoulders and stared down into her face with a stern look. "Patricia Thibodeaux-Ladd, talk."

"You just like your father," she said huffily. "Think you know everything . . . always trying to drag stuff out of people. That's why ain't no woman here now. You probably scare them off."

"I'm too old to bait, Mama," he said, a hint of a smile in his expression.

"Ain't nothing to talk about," she scoffed. "I told you ain't nothing wrong."

"I don't believe you," he said, holding her still when she tried to squirm out of his gentle possession. "Here," he said, leading her to a stool at the counter, "sit down right here and tell me what's going on."

She obeyed, situating herself comfortably on the high stool. She set her hands primly in her lap, but couldn't keep them still. "I guess I might as well get over it, huh?" She looked up at him, biting down on her lip. "I'm pregnant," she said, a bittersweet expression on her face.

"Pregnant," Sterling whispered absently. A sudden panic that had nothing to do with his mother's announcement assailed him. Selinae's image filled his wide-eyed, faraway gaze.

"I'm not that old," his mother said. "I was sixteen when I had you. I am older than the average mother, but the doctor said I'm in good health and he don't anticipate any problems."

He barely heard her, his mind elsewhere. Selinae! He hadn't used anything to protect Selinae, Sterling thought with a shiver of vivid recollection. And with everything he knew about her previous encounter . . . ! He clutched the sides of his head and bit off a curse.

"I knew you'd be upset," Patricia said, resigned.

Sterling felt split in two as he took in his mother's woebegone expression. "No, Mama," he said, eager to make her understand. "I'm not upset with you." With a hollow chuckle, he said, "Hell, it's none of my business." He gave her a broad grin and kissed her on the cheek. "Congratulations. I think it's great news. How does Guy feel about it?"

"Guy can't contain himself," she replied laughingly, wiping at her misty eyes. "Are you sure you not mad at me? I mean, you still my baby, you know." She smiled at him shyly.

"Mama, I'm thirty-six years old," he said, laughing at her. "I'll still be your baby if you want, but I'm a little old to be jealous, don't you think?"

"You're right. You need to be having your own babies," she scolded teasingly. "If you had been supplying me with grandbabies . . ."

"Oh no, you can't blame this one on me, old lady," he replied, draping his arms around her in an affectionate hug.

"I'm not old," she retorted.

"No, you're not," he said. "I'm really glad for you and Guy."

"Now, where's that woman?"

"What woman?" he asked.

"The one you were expecting when you opened the door to me," she said, grinning at him slyly.

Sterling felt his face grow warm with embarrassment. When the doorbell rang his blush doubled in intensity. "I'll be right back," he said with a quick snap of his shoulders as he hurried from the room.

Nearing the door, he braced himself and schooled his expression. Filled with anticipation, he opened the door.

Selinae was staring up at him with an admiring gleam in her gaze, a hint of erotic memories in her bright eyes. Though she was chicly dressed in a black and white mesh wool blazer with a single button over a white blouse, starched jeans hugging her fine hips, and black boots, he saw her naked, her slender brown body glowing with desire and passion.

A thrill of excitement coursed through him. He thought he'd explode with joy at seeing her.

"I was afraid you wouldn't come back," he said, his eyes raking her possessively.

"Don't make me do that again," she replied, crossing the threshold to step into his waiting arms.

As she draped them around his waist, he heard the thud of her handbag and all-weather coat as they hit the floor. He laughed; it was partly nervousness, but mostly just because it felt good to do so as he crushed her to him.

"Was it that bad?" he asked, his lips on her hair.

"No. Not at all, really," she replied, her head resting against his shoulder. "Tiring. It was different. I don't know. I—"

She stopped talking suddenly, perhaps fearing she'd disclose more than she intended to. Sterling wasn't sure how to interpret her mood, wanted to question her about the time she'd spent with her mother, but Cora Rogers didn't seem too important right now. Selinae was here in his arms, and all his dread vanished.

"I missed you," he said, kissing the side of her face.

"I missed you, too," she replied. She looked up

at him and tweaked her nose. "You obviously started without me."

He threw back his head and let loose a peal of laughter, then squeezed her to him for a quick hug. "I need a shower, I know."

"Is it big enough for the both of us?" she asked.

"Sterling . . . ?"

Selinae's head jerked up and she backed out of Sterling's embrace, staring at the woman approaching them from the back of the house.

"I think I'll run along and let you entertain your company," Patricia said.

Looping an arm around Selinae's waist, Sterling spun around to face his mother. "You just couldn't wait for me to bring her back to meet you, could you?" he said with a teasing grin.

"I heard the mention of a shower and figured I'd make tracks," Patricia said. "I didn't expect you to be standing in the door."

"Well, it's all right, Mama, and you don't have to leave," he said. "Meet Selinae Rogers. Selinae, this is my mother, Patricia Ladd."

"I'm so glad to meet you, child," Patricia said, taking Selinae's hands between hers.

"It's nice meeting you, too, Mrs. Ladd," Selinae replied shyly.

Noticing the blush on her face, Sterling smiled down at her with a conspiratorial look in his eyes. "It's been sort of a mothers' day, hasn't it?" he said.

As eager as she had been to get back to him, Selinae didn't mind sharing Sterling with his mother. She was introduced to Hannibal, who enjoyed her attention and stayed at her side during a tour of the house, and then when they all adjourned to the kitchen.

"You hungry, child?" Patricia asked. "I brought some good old turkey and dressing and—"

"Mama," Sterling interrupted, "Selinae doesn't eat meat."

"Oh, you one of them vegetarians, huh?" Patricia said. "What about shrimp? You eat shrimp?"

"Does she ever," Sterling said. "I took her out to dinner the other night, and she ate a whole plate all by herself."

"That's not true," Selinae said. She feigned an outraged look at him, then slapped him on the shoulder playfully.

"Ouch," he said, rubbing the spot.

Without further instructions, Patricia set out to prepare a feast. Within minutes, the counter was laden with plates of food and dessert, and a bowl of étouffée for Selinae.

"Give me that back," Sterling said, chasing Hannibal, who was clutching a large turkey drumstick Patricia had given him. Hannibal scooted out the back door, his jaws firmly around his meal. "Mama, I've told you already about giving my puppy table food," Sterling said.

"It ain't—"

Sterling cut her off. "I know, it ain't gonna kill him," he said in the familiar Louisiana accent, sitting on the stool next to Selinae. "Are you going to eat some of this, too?" he asked Patricia, indicating a plate laden with food—turkey, dressing, two large slices of two different pies—on the counter before him.

"No, that's yours," she replied, taking a bite of her own slice of pie.

"Goodness, Mama, you must think I'm a growing

boy," he replied, shaking his head as he picked up his fork.

"Eat what you can and put the rest back," she advised reasonably.

"It would have been a lot simpler if you hadn't warmed up so much," he said.

"Selinae, is he always fussing about something around you, too?" Patricia asked.

"Let's just say," Selinae replied diplomatically, "he has something to say about everything."

"That's him. Always been that way," Patricia said. "That's why I was so happy when he got his first camera. He stopped talking when he got behind it."

"I'm thirsty," Sterling said, rising. "How about you? I got Diet Coke."

"That'll be fine," Selinae replied.

"I'll get it," Patricia said.

"No, you sit down," Sterling commanded, sauntering to the refrigerator. He popped the tops of three cans of soda, then filled three glasses and passed them around.

"Is that hot enough for you, Selinae?" Patricia asked, indicating the bowl of shrimp stew.

"It's incredible, Mrs. Ladd, thanks," Selinae said. "You're a wonderful cook."

"You gave her enough to feed a hundred people," Sterling grumbled good-naturedly as he forked a piece of pie.

"Don't talk with your mouth full," Patricia replied.

Selinae felt content to sit quietly eating, as the talk evolved to entertaining stories about Patricia's Creole relatives, who'd refused to embrace the twentieth century. Occasionally, Patricia would slip into her patois and Sterling would admonish her to speak English.

"I don't want Selinae to think we're talking about her," he explained.

Selinae felt cherished. Sterling gave completely of himself to both of them. He was respectful and wonderfully patient with his mother, and attentive to her. With each passing second of this day, she mused, she had a new blessing to count.

Witnessing the loving exchange between Sterling and Patricia, Selinae thought about her own relationship with her mother. She was still somewhat surprised by the conversation they had had that day. Aunt Rae, for the most part, had been a silent buffer. She had come to act as referee. As it turned out, she wasn't needed in that role.

Her mother had surprised her by not talking further about Sterling. That was not to say he hadn't been in her thoughts, Selinae mused, a smile spreading across her face. She had a feeling that the outraged performance Cora Rogers had put on at her house was just for show, an act for Sterling's benefit.

They had gone to Cora Rogers' favorite shopping center, the Galleria Mall, she recalled, taking a sip of her drink. Though she had no intentions of letting her mother buy her anything, she indulged her by trying on some of the high-priced, designer clothes her mother picked out. Modeling an elegant knit pantsuit, bespeckled with hand-sewn pearls, she knew the outfit looked gorgeous on her. It didn't take too much encouragement from her mother and Aunt Rae for her to buy it. It was going to set her budget back for six months, but it would be appreciated, she thought, stealing a glance at Sterling.

Switching his attention from his mother to her, he caught her staring at him, and tenderly his eyes melted into hers. She felt an electric current travel the length of her spine as an unspoken communication passed between them.

"I'm sorry, Mama, what did you say?" Sterling asked after a moment.

Freed from his enraptured gaze, Selinae wetted her suddenly parched throat by taking a drink. As Patricia Ladd launched into another tale, Selinae couldn't help believing that her feelings for Sterling had opened up a new world to her, as her thoughts returned to her mother.

After spending two hours in the ritzy store, they'd strolled through the mall, window-shopping. With her box clutched in her hand, she was afraid to look at another item for fear she would cave in to a call-to-purchase.

They stopped at a café overlooking the mall skating rink for coffee and dessert. The better part of their time together was spent there, absently watching the skaters and talking.

No, she amended silently, they did more than talk. They *communicated.* Though her mother had given her quite an earful, one thing in particular stayed with her.

"The reason you and your father used to get along so well was because you're so much alike," Cora had said. "Then when you became a woman, an independent thinker, he simply couldn't take that his little girl was growing up and away from him. He thought he could be everything for you. Despite repeated warnings," she added, laughing softly before a pensive silence fell across the table.

She had noticed Aunt Rae take her mother's hand as if to pass her strength into her. Another surprise. She had no idea the two sisters were so close.

"That's why," Cora had continued softly, a tenuous smile wavering on her lips, "he was so hurt when you got pregnant. To him, it meant you had cut him out of your life. He simply couldn't handle what he perceived as your rejection of his love."

"But I tried since then to show him that wasn't true," Selinae protested, unable to keep the hurt from her voice. "You know I tried."

"Yes, you did," her mother said, covering her hand affectionately.

She had snatched her hand away. It wasn't in offense at her mother's touch, Selinae mused, but because she feared the gesture would make her lose it. She hadn't wanted to cry.

"See, that's what I'm talking about," Cora had said. "You've always done that to me, Selinae. Your father is the same way. After all these years of marriage to him, there is still an area of his life that he won't share with me. As if he expects *me* to compound his hurt. I don't know what to do about you two anymore."

It had taken her a while, Selinae recalled, a second glance at the sad gaze in her mother's eyes to realize what her own pride had wrought. Without saying a word, she took her mother's hand between hers. The simple gesture seemed to alter their relationship, elevate it. At least her view of it. All these years she felt her mother had abandoned her when she'd needed her the most, when now she had to consider the possibility that she had been the one to push her mother away.

"It's getting late," Patricia was saying, bringing Selinae out of her reverie.

Embarrassed to have been caught woolgathering, Selinae smiled politely as she rose to walk around the bar to the kitchen. Sterling was helping his mother into her coat.

"It was nice meeting you, Mrs. Ladd," Selinae said.

"I hope I see you again," Patricia said. "If this boy of mine gives you a hard time, you just call me."

"And what you gonna do?" Sterling said playfully in a gruff voice.

"Go upside your head," Patricia replied, knuckling his temple.

"I'm going to have to hire a bodyguard to protect me from you two," Sterling said as he pulled Selinae next to him, his arm around her waist.

"It's been a good day," Patricia remarked as she led the way to the front door.

"Yes, it has," Sterling echoed, smiling down at Selinae.

After seeing Mrs. Ladd off, they returned to the bright warmth inside the house. Selinae felt a bottomless peace and satisfaction as they stood in the foyer. Sterling was looking at her with an entranced gaze, his hand still on the knob of the door.

"Stay with me tonight."

It was part question, part declaration. Selinae didn't hesitate in reply.

"My overnight case is in the backseat."

"I'll be right back," he said as he vanished into the cold night.

Finally, she thought, the spirit of the holidays had seeped into her soul. Wishing she could bottle it up for safekeeping year-round, she strolled into the study and clicked on the light. She had noticed earlier the *kinara* and *mishumaa saba* already set up on the coffee table and wanted to light the next candle. It was still the day of *Ujima,* the fourth day.

Had it really been only four days ago that Sterling had come into her life? she asked herself, amazed.

Sterling peeked into the room and caught her looking through the desk drawer.

"If you're looking for a light," he said, "it's in the bottom drawer. I'll run and get the wine."

When he returned shortly with a brass wine goblet, Selinae was already on her knees before the coffee table. He joined her, setting the goblet on the corner of the table.

"Can we amend this as we go along?" he asked, tugging at his shirt. "I'm still in dire need of a shower."

Selinae chuckled. "Me, too."

He grabbed her around the waist and growled into her neck playfully. She laughed before he stilled, staring at her with an intent look in his eyes. She felt at once tongue-tied and full of words as she caressed the sides of his face, her eyes bright.

"I've never felt this way before," she said in a soft voice. "It's a little scary, you know. We've only known each other a short time, but I feel as if I've known you forever."

Sterling took her hand in his and clasped it next to his mouth, his adoring gaze never leaving her face. "Thank you," he whispered in her palm before he kissed it and held it reverently next to his cheek. "You've given me so much, and the more you give, the more I want. I went crazy today without you. I don't think I'll ever get enough of you."

Selinae stared at him, almost unable to believe that he cared as deeply as she.

"My mother," he said in an affected voice, "came by to tell me she's pregnant."

Selinae's eyes widened. "Is that good?" she asked tentatively.

"Yes," he replied. "I believe Guy has always

wanted a child, but she's always refused. She was afraid to tell me," he said with a soft chuckle.

When one was happy, she wished happiness for the world. "Good for them," she said sincerely.

Sterling swallowed, then breathed in deeply.

"What's the matter?" she asked, alert to the sudden change in his expression, the unfamiliar hesitancy about him.

"I didn't do anything to protect you when we made love. I've been thinking about it ever since my Mama told me her news. I'm sorry, Selinae." His eyes narrowed with regret.

"I'm not," she said in a barely audible voice.

"What? What did you say?"

"I said I'm not sorry," she repeated in a stronger voice. "Admittedly, getting pregnant was the last thing on my mind for a while there," she said in a sensual, teasing way.

"Selinae, how can you say that? I mean, what if you're pregnant?"

Selinae shrugged dismissively.

"You can't possibly want to put yourself through that again," he said. "Things would go from bad to worse."

"Sterling, what are you talking about?"

"I'm talking about you and your father, that's what I'm talking about."

"I don't have a father," she said, a hint of annoyance in her voice. "And so what?" she asked, flicking a light over a candle. "This is my body. I do with it what I want, father or not."

Halting her, Sterling said in a stern voice, "Not in this." He took the lighter from her and flung it on the table.

Selinae sat back to stare at him wordlessly, her heart pounding, a puzzled frown on her face. She was momentarily transported back in time. She felt she was looking at a stranger, the same way she had felt about her father all those years ago . . . Sterling's expression made it obvious that she had made a mistake, she thought. *Again.*

Even as she prayed it wasn't true, she mused morosely that Sterling wasn't the man she thought he was. She felt his gaze on her, but she couldn't return his look, and fastened hers on the candles. Both sets, the three red ones on the left and the three green ones on the right blurred into the black candle in the center of the *kinara* under the threat of her stinging tears. She pinched the corners of her eyes with her fingers.

Spacing out the words evenly, she said in as strong a voice as she could muster, "Oh, you don't have a thing to worry about, Mr. Washington. If by chance I do get pregnant, I won't hold you responsible. I'll swear it on a stack of black bibles." Raising a hand as if taking an oath, she said, "I, Selinae Rogers, hereby promise not to—"

"Stop it!" he said, grabbing her hand from the air and holding it tight. "You're talking nonsense. You think I'd abandon my own child? How could you think so little of me?"

He forced her to look into his face, his dark eyes. They matched hers, showing the tortured dullness of disbelief.

"I don't even know why we're having this stupid argument," she said with frustrated contriteness. Drawing a deep breath, she picked up the lighter and lit one of the green candles. "There is no child."

She stared at the light, trying to make it take hold on the short cord protruding from the top of the candle. She found herself wishing desperately for the light to hold. But she hadn't left the fire on the wick long enough, and the flame was extinguished.

"Does the possibility exist?" Sterling asked.

Staring absently at the candle she had tried to light, Selinae reasoned that she had been presumptuous. She had felt one-hundred-percent positive that her disclosure would prove to Sterling that she really was ready for a commitment. She now saw that it took a long time for the fires of commitment to take hold. She placed the lighter back on the table, then sat back, her hands folded in her lap.

"Does it?" he demanded.

Selinae swallowed as she nodded her head affirmatively.

"You used me, didn't you?" he asked.

Her head jerked up to stare at him. "I *used* you? What is that supposed to mean?"

"You knew I couldn't resist you," he said. "You led me by the nose right to your bed, knowing all along the chance we were taking. And stupid me did all my thinking below the waist."

"That's right, blame me," Selinae spat out, getting to her feet. "You're no different from the rest of my family."

"You used me to get back at your father," he said, following her into the foyer.

Selinae spotted her overnight case on the bottom step and grabbed it. "Getting pregnant would be the perfect plot of revenge against him for cutting you out of his will," Sterling continued.

Opening the hall closet door, Selinae got her coat and purse.

"Well, let me tell you, it's juvenile, a teenage girl's twisted logic. Where are you going?" he demanded as she opened the front door.

"Someplace where I don't have to listen to *you,*" she tossed over her shoulder.

"That's right, run away," he retorted, following her outside. "I thought you didn't want to run anymore, that you'd hung up your running shoes."

As she got into her car, she said, "I'm walking, then. How's that?"

With tears rolling profusely from her eyes, Selinae argued both sides of their disagreement on her drive home.

Maybe she'd expected too much from him. He'd been so strong and secure within himself, she had failed to assign a very human trait to him. Fear.

She had spoken from the heart at the moment with no serious consideration as to what she was saying. Though it was true that she would love to have Sterling's child, she realized how selfish her thinking was, even immature. A child was a major responsibility. But she had felt so strongly about Sterling, so . . . right. Revenge against her father was the last thing on her mind.

Arriving home, Selinae changed her clothes, then ambled about the house. She went into her study and turned on the light. The red glow on the answering machine informed her of messages. She pressed the button, then waited as the tape rewound.

"This message is for Selinae Rogers." She stood alert, instantly recognizing the stentorian voice on the machine. Her father's voice. "If you want this box of medals and trophies, you better have someone pick them up. Otherwise, I'm throwing them out."

The machine clicked to a halt. In the dead silence, Selinae stood as if pinned to a wall. Fresh tears streamed down her face.

Moving with efficiency and purpose, Selinae began collecting the tools of her trade from the desk drawer in her study as the printer droned softly in the background.

Tape recorder. Pens. Notebook. Beeper. She put them all in a black leather bag that was on the floor, propped against the desk.

When the print job was completed, she set the bag on the desk, then removed the page from the tray. She scanned it thoroughly. Satisfied, she placed the sheet in a manila folder and laid it on the desk.

She reviewed the notes she'd scribbled when she got the call at seven that morning from Marcia Matthews, an old friend who was the managing editor of the *Houston Triumph,* a local black newspaper that came out bi-weekly, on Saturdays and Wednesdays.

It was the kind of story she no longer wrote, the kind that had contributed to her burnout as a crime-beat reporter. But because Marcia was a close friend and caught in a pinch—all of her reporters were either on vacation, sick with the flu, or on an out-of-town assignment—she agreed to cover it.

The paper was put to bed on Friday and Tuesday evenings. It was now after nine; she had until three today to pull all the pieces together.

Crime didn't take holidays, she mused, as she shut down her computer and printer. A teenage girl had disappeared from the Galleria skating rink. The incident had occurred the previous night, and the police had no leads. Though the father was not yet a suspect, the police investigator whom she'd interviewed over the phone was ruling nothing out.

It was not her job to pass judgment, Selinae reminded herself. Just report the facts. She was on her way to interview the father who'd reported the girl missing.

No photographer had been lined up, she noted, as she grabbed her bag and left the room, darkening it behind her. She hoped the family had a decent picture of the girl.

In the living room, she picked up her coat from the couch at the door. She wondered if she should feel guilty for the sense of purpose she felt. While the assignment was taking her mind off her own troubles, it came at the expense of someone else's misery.

After a night of tossing and turning in her bed, which seemed ominously big and empty, she decided the turmoil she felt over Sterling was just not worth it. She had enough conflict in her life and needed less of it, not more. She would get over him. It would just take a little time.

As she adjusted the coat over her knit pantsuit in saddle and white, his image flashed briefly through her mind. She held the folds of the coat in tightly clenched hands. The purposeful light in her eyes dimmed.

It was as she had feared, she thought: she'd imagined Sterling to be something he wasn't. He had been unable to distinguish her feelings for him from those for her family. He thought he knew what was best for her better than she herself did. He was indeed very much like her father. A disheartened sigh escaped her lips.

Reminding herself that she had a job to do, Selinae gathered her things, opened the door, and walked out into the cold, bright morning. The promise of winter had at long last come. It was a pretty day, with the sun perched high in the clear blue windy skies. Several kids were outside, bundled in coats and knit caps, giving their Christmas toys a workout. Selinae locked her front door and headed for her car, which was parked in the narrow driveway.

When the dark green Jeep Cherokee rolled to a stop on the street in front of her house, she came to an abrupt stop, her heartbeat accelerating. Sterling got out of the vehicle, and Selinae swallowed the lump that had suddenly lodged itself in her throat.

Feasting on him with her gaze, she felt her resolve crumble. He was dressed in a sleeveless sheepskin jacket over a gold plaid shirt tucked at his narrow waist into starched black jeans. Boots completed the ensemble.

The tentative, unsure quality of his movements surprised her. She guessed that he was trying to assess her reaction to his unexpected appearance. It was the most vulnerable she'd ever seen him, and it softened her hard-sought determination to put him out of her mind.

Then he seemed to change. With the customary grace of one who was in total control, he became imbued with purpose. Like a modern-day avenger, she thought, ready to take the weight of the world on his broad shoulders.

Nearing her, Sterling said, "Good morning."

Selinae attempted to banish her desire to embrace him. "Do you have your equipment with you?" she asked, fighting to keep her tone professional.

Caught off guard by the query, Sterling slowed his pace to a halt. Staring at her warily, his eyes were sharp and assessing. The glare from the sun caught the curious hue in their sassafras depths. He glanced over his shoulder at his vehicle, then back at her.

The impulsive question now out, Selinae wondered what she was doing, inviting the enemy into her camp. Trying to prevent the inevitable, she answered herself chidingly. It was much like the game she'd played with her family, allowing them to toy with her emotions, even knowing it was useless. When would she ever learn?

"It's in the truck," he said.

Committed, she couldn't back out. "I need a photographer for an assignment I'm on," she said.

"Your car or mine?" he asked without hesitation.

"I'll drive," she replied.

Backing away, he said, "Let me get my stuff."

It took several tries before she could get the key in the car door to unlock it. With a mixture of hope and dread creating havoc within her, she rationalized that she'd made a sound, professional decision. A photo of a distraught father, she told herself, would go a long way to creating a heightened interest in the story. After all, a young girl's life was at stake.

Within seconds, Sterling was tossing his camera bag in the backseat, then he opened the front passenger door and got in. Wordlessly, she backed out the drive and drove off for the Southpark residence in the southeast section of town.

"Mr. Simpson, I'm Selinae Rogers, the reporter from the *Triumph*, and this is Sterling Washington, a photographer," Selinae said, introducing them to the Simpson family, a father and two daughters, who opened the door to them.

"Yes, please come in," Mr. Simpson replied, ushering them inside. "This is my oldest daughter, Charlotte and my baby, Jackie," he said, pointing from one to the other daughter. With acknowledgments exchanged between them, he led the way to the back of the house.

The house was of the same one-story design as the others on the block, in a neighborhood that was borderline middle-class, Sterling noticed. Hardworking people struggling to make ends meet. But the sense of a close family permeated the neat, clean interior, with its furnishing outdated and worn. The smell of coffee and nicotine permeated the den, a homey, midsize room bursting with items collected over the years.

"Please have a seat," Mr. Simpson said, gesturing around the room.

While Selinae settled in a tattered floral-print armchair, Sterling unpacked his camera bag. The three Simpsons took the couch. Sterling checked the light against his portable light meter.

"May I open this?" he asked.

Receiving a wordless nod, he strolled across the room to the picture window on the east wall to open the curtains to the morning's bright sun. Again checking the meter against the extra natural light, he nodded, satisfied. He would have to push the film a little, but he could make the adjustments in his darkroom during the developing process, he told himself confidently.

As Selinae performed her reporter's preliminary introduction, Sterling double-checked the cameras, then stood unobtrusively at her back, with an uninhibited view of the family.

They were all of a berry-brown complexion, with the same piercing dark brown eyes and long, arched brows. He wondered with mild curiosity what the missing daughter looked like, as Selinae explained to the family why she used a tape recorder in addition to taking notes.

Recalling their cold, silent drive to the Simpson home, Sterling felt jealous of the warmth she extended them in her tone and manner. Still, he was impressed by her skill at putting the worried father at ease in his own house.

He had yet to figure out how to bridge the deliberate distance she put between them. Shortly after backing out the driveway, she gave him all the details of the incident surrounding the missing girl, Tierney Simpson, as well as the possible angles she might pursue and the kind of shot she was looking for to accompany the article. It was all done with professional detachment, reporter to photographer.

Then she was silent, he recalled. She never took her eyes off the road. Her demeanor was stiff and reserved, prohibiting conversation. In the silence that engulfed them, he felt unnerved by the change in her, the unfamiliar, stoic face she wore.

But whatever she was feeling, he reminded himself, the invitation to accompany her was his good fortune.

"Would either of you like a cup of coffee?" Mr. Simpson asked.

"None for me, thank you," Selinae replied, setting her tape recorder on the coffee table.

Sterling echoed her reply. With a camera hanging around his neck and another in his hands, he remained at the ready. As the eldest daughter went to fill her father's cup, he said, "I'm going to take a lot of pictures, and I'd like to get one of Tierney before we leave." To Selinae, he explained, "I'm going to shoot both black and white and color."

Selinae turned her gaze on him. "We already went over what I need," she said with a significant lifting of her brows.

He got the message; he could shoot whatever he wanted as long as she got the picture she requested. His jaws clenched tight in a sign of pique. It was an insulting comment.

He could ring her lovely neck, though it was buried under the collar of her knit top. Her outfit, though flattering to her complexion and figure, was like a suit of armor, he thought. Wondering if she covered up for herself or against him, a hint of amusement lit up his eyes. A brief memory of the ecstasy they found in each other's arms entered his mind.

"I know this is a painful time for you, Mr. Simpson," Selinae said in a soft, sympathetic voice, "but—"

"No, no, no, Ms. Rogers," Mr. Simpson replied. "I'll do whatever I have to do to get Tierney back."

The tone triggered Sterling's full attention to the job he had accepted. It was obvious that the fifty-something father had been up all night. His dark eyes were bloodshot. He was unshaven; his short beard was a stubble of knotty hairs on his troubled brown face. His big calloused hands shook as he accepted a cup of coffee from Charlotte, who rejoined the group, kneeling on the floor next to him. *Click.*

Mr. Simpson had been chain-smoking, he noticed. The ashtray on the coffee table, where the tape recorder was running, was full of butts. A crushed pack of cigarettes lay next to a newly opened one.

Rubbing his hands together nervously, Mr. Simpson said, "I don't know where to start."

"Wherever you want to," Selinae replied, her pen poised over the pad in her lap.

"Tierney likes to skate," Mr. Simpson began slowly, in a wavering voice. "She wanted to take up skating, but it's expensive, you know." He reached for the pack of cigarettes, then changed his mind. "She's on the school's track team. You ought to see her. Boy, can she eat up a track." He chuckled with a proud musing light twinkling in his dark eyes.

Sterling tried to read Selinae's reaction, but her expression was impenetrable; whatever she thought or felt did not show in her expression.

Damn! Sterling chided himself, he'd missed a shot.

"She tried to talk some of her friends into going with her, but she couldn't get anybody," Mr. Simpson continued. "I didn't want her to go alone, but Tierney . . . she's a determined one, that child. All of my girls are like that," he boasted proudly. "And every last one of them likes to do something different. Charlotte is into designing clothes, and my baby here"—he paused to squeeze Jackie's hand—"plays basketball. I like them to do things, you know, be involved in something constructive." He took a sip of coffee, then set the cup down and reached for the pack of cigarettes. Charlotte snatched the pack before he could reach it.

"You've been smoking like a train," she scolded mildly. "You're stinking up the place with these nasty old cigarettes."

Mr. Simpson chuckled halfheartedly. "They're always after me about these cigarettes. If Tierney was here, she woulda flushed them down the toilet. I waste more money buying cigarettes I don't get to smoke, you'd think I'd get the message." His eyes clouded, and his voice choked off. "I'm sorry."

"That's quite all right, Mr. Simpson," Selinae said soothingly. "Just take your time."

He sniffed, wiped at his teary eyes with his arms. *Click.*

"I dropped Tierney off at the rink around two yesterday," he said. "I was supposed to pick her up at five, but I was running late. I got together with some friends of mine to watch the game at a buddy's house. We got to drinking and talking . . . well, you know how that is."

He looked headlong at Selinae with guilt in his eyes, glassy with tears. *Click.*

"The time got away from me. I didn't leave his house until almost a quarter to six. I called the house to see if she had called, but wasn't nobody here."

As the sorrowful voice of Mr. Simpson droned on, Sterling caught his mind wandering. He wanted to distance himself from the Simpson family's plight.

Oh yeah, he sympathized with them, but for the most part he felt immune from the horrible ordeal they were suffering. He took comfort in the fact that it was not happening to him. The perception went against the very nature of Kwanzaa, he reminded himself. It meant he hadn't internalized the principles celebrated for seven days to be practiced yearlong, the sense of community it purported to instill in all African Americans to enhance appreciation for and recognition of the value each individual brought to the group.

But what if he were in Mr. Simpson's shoes? What if it were Selinae who was missing, who had been plucked right out of his life as if she never existed?

". . . but she wasn't where she told me to pick her up," Mr. Simpson was saying. "You know, by the movie theaters. I just knew she was going to fuss about my being late."

Disconcerted by the thought, Sterling recalled his fear of losing her in a battle between her parents. Now, staring at her lovely profile, he realized he could have lost her even more effectively all by himself.

". . . I went inside to look for her. I thought maybe she'd forgotten the time, too, and I'd find her out there on that ice, skating her little heart out . . ."

After she'd stormed out of his house, Sterling considered whether he'd overstepped his bounds. He believed initially that he had not just a duty, but a right to point out her immature thinking. Roaming about his house, alone and completely dissatisfied with himself, he was forced to reexamine his motives for the psychological diatribe he'd subjected her to. And he hadn't liked some of the answers he came up with on his own . . . without reminders of the anguish in her eyes that had haunted his sleep.

Dabbing at the tears filling his eyes, Mr. Simpson said, "I asked around, but nobody saw her. I didn't know what to do, what to think. I ran into one of the security guards and that's when we decided to call the police."

Sterling had debated calling her to confess his doubts, but decided against it. He convinced himself that once Selinae analyzed the situation, she would see that he was right. He'd held fast to that belief until now.

In blurting out his suspicion of her plot to exact revenge on her father, he'd overlooked a painful element of his own personality. He never had considered himself a coward, but this time he had been a victim of fear. His feelings for Selinae were so intense, subconsciously, he felt in grave danger of losing himself. To deal with his own fearful emotions, he'd turned his anxiety on her.

Unconsciously, Sterling lifted the camera gingerly between his hands and peered through the small aperture. Sitting serene and attentive, Selinae's alluring profile filled the viewfinder. His chocolate darling, he mused with a soft smile. *Click.*

She nodded her head, the pen held to the side of her mouth. *Click.* She scribbled away on her pad as the corners of her mouth tightened. The camera caught the agitation that flickered across her eyes. She was obviously disturbed by the story. *Click.*

Assailed by a flurry of disconnected thoughts, Sterling recalled the young toughs in the park, cloaked in macho myths of what constituted a man. Switching cameras, he photographed the tears flooding Mr. Simpson's eyes, and felt ashamed of himself. He knew better than the homies, he chided himself, but had behaved no better than they.

"If I'd been on time, instead of off somewhere drinking," Mr. Simpson exclaimed with grief and guilt, "this wouldna' happened. My Tierney would be home now. God, please take care of my baby," he cried, breaking down.

Click. Photographing the father's wretchedness, Sterling recalled fathoming himself as wise as Solomon on the subject of love. Experiencing it for the first time, however, he now knew his contentions were nothing more than intellectual sophistry.

"I'm sorry, Miss Rogers," Mr. Simpson said, rising. "Excuse me."

"Take your time, Mr. Simpson," Selinae said in a quivering voice.

Click. The camera captured Selinae touching the

corners of her eyes, as she pressed away droplets of tears.

He loved Selinae, he thought, lowering the camera. That was the truth, plain and simple. The acceptance of it was freeing. He felt a warm sensation, like a soft cloud floating through his body, a halo settling over the spot that was his heart. He wondered why he'd ever fought the feeling.

Selinae poured her third cup of coffee. With the fatigue of the previous day oozing from her every pore, she felt as sluggish now as when she awakened that morning. The Tierney Simpson piece had taken a lot out of her. She was an easy target for the despair that lay dormant in her, now that the story was behind her.

Steaming mug in her hand, she sauntered to her study and sat down feebly on the daybed. The phone rang as it had been doing ever since she got up an hour ago. It was what had awakened her in the first place, and she had yet to take a call personally.

"Selinae, this is Holly. I was reading my *Triumph* this morning and lo and behold, there's your name on a front-page story. I just wanted to say what a good job you did. Talk to you later, girlfriend."

Recording the message for later playback, the tape on the answering machine rolled to a stop. Just as it reset, the phone rang again.

"Selinae, this is your mother. I know you're probably not at home . . ."

Selinae chuckled sarcastically at the implication in her mother's voice, before sadness settled over her expression like a gray cloud. She wished against her better judgment that she *were* with Sterling, as her mother no doubt assumed.

". . . Anyway, we saw on the news last night about that missing girl and your brother went out and got a copy of the *Triumph* this morning. I read your article," she said, with pride in her voice. "I'm sure I don't have to tell you, but I found it quite moving. And the pictures taken by your Sterling Washington were absolutely wonderful. Call me when you get in."

"He's not my Sterling, Mama," Selinae whispered tormented.

As the machine clicked off to reset, silently, she conceded that she and Sterling did work well together. He was an attentive photographer, capturing the spirit of the quotes she'd selected to use. Even without the story, she would have been inspired by his photographs.

But of course, that was to be expected. She needn't read anything more into it than a harmonious professional rapport between them, she told herself. Marcia had been so impressed with the quality of the pictures that she decided to give the story more space and run all of the photos he'd submitted.

And to his magnanimous credit, damn him, he didn't charge the paper a dime, she recalled. He told Marcia to call it his "contribution to the community."

Just as she was convinced he wasn't the man she thought or had hoped he was, Selinae thought, he did something to highlight the error of her belief.

His largesse to the community, however, didn't extend to her, she thought, recalling his accusation. In a way he'd been right; she had used him. She'd been so determined to make changes in her life, she hadn't stopped to analyze her choice.

With the mug to her lips, she stared absently across the room. The object in her gaze was but a black space, a nondescript emptiness. It was her future looming over her. She knew what she had to do. With pain glittering in her eyes, she took a deep breath.

There were several story ideas already outlined and ready for her undivided attention. Work—researching, interviewing, writing—had never failed her. It would be her manna again.

The peal of the doorbell broke into her thoughts. Guessing the identity of the unexpected caller, she sat frozen as if the lack of movement would make her invisible. "Go away," she pleaded softly. "Please, just go away."

When the doorbell stopped, pounding followed. "Selinae, I know you're in there." It was Sterling, as she'd guessed. "Come on, Selinae, open up," he called out persistently.

She couldn't prolong the inevitable forever, she told herself. The sooner she got it over with, the sooner she could begin to heal.

Opening the door, her eyes took in his powerful presence, drank in the sensuality of his physique. Looking down at her with a light of desire illuminating his mellow brown eyes, she felt an eager tension emanating from him. Instantly and automatically, her traitorous body made a mockery of her vow—at the base of her throat a pulse beat and swelled as though her heart had risen from its usual place.

He wore a bulky navy sweater with geometric designs patched in leather across the front, blue slacks, and stylish boots. How was it that he seemed to grow more virile and infinitely more desirable each time she saw him?

"Habari gani," he said.

She debated replying . . . to the greeting that had become a ritual between them . . . to the intimate tone in his voice . . . to the look in his eyes bathing her in approval.

"Kuumba," she spoke at last.

He leaned toward her, and unconsciously she felt herself gravitating toward him. But at the last second she caught herself and pulled back. The kiss that would have touched her forehead instead grazed her eye.

Visibly undaunted, he crossed the threshold into the living room. "Can I get a cup of coffee?" he asked.

"Suit yourself."

Taking the cup from her hands, he said, "I'll warm yours up while I'm there."

As she turned to walk off, eager to escape the warmth of his expression, he pulled a rolled-up newspaper from his back pocket and slapped it in her hand. With a shuddering sigh, she watched him stride off to the kitchen.

She tried to muster a shred of anger at her vulnerability to him, but the hot emotion coursing through her was desire, plain and simple. Settling for self-disgust, she marched off to her study, the newspaper in her grip.

She spread the paper out on the desk and smoothed it flat with her hands, trying to calm the erratic beat of her heart. Staring down at the paper, she blinked several times to clear her eyes, and forced herself to focus.

The layout was impressive. The name TIERNEY SIMPSON appeared in bold black letters and graced the top of the color photo on the top fold of the newspaper. Below it were the words HAVE YOU SEEN HER?

Selinae reread the quote from Mr. Simpson she had chosen to set off in italics.

"I don't understand what's becoming of this society. Females are treated like expendable items, not the bearers of the future we claim to be so concerned about."

A three-column article followed the quote, with a sidebar of Tierney's physical description, as well as the photos taken of her room in which posters of famous black runners donned her walls. But it was the quote that stuck in Selinae's mind.

As before when Mr. Simpson had uttered the words, she felt envious of the love this father had for his daughters, his reverence for women in general. Absently drumming her fingers on the paper, she couldn't help thinking that her father felt just the opposite about her. Why was she so hard to love? she asked herself.

If her own father didn't love her, how could she believe that any other man would?

She'd made a big enough fool of herself once, she thought, recalling all the overtures she'd made to her father. She simply couldn't put herself through that again. It was too hard on the mind. Her heart simply couldn't take any more abuse from the people she cared about. Even the man she loved.

Suddenly, she felt Sterling's presence. The sexual magnetism he emitted telegraphed his entrance into the room before he spoke. Even the air around her took on a different feel.

"You see the article?" he asked conversationally, striding toward her with two cups of coffee.

"Yes," she said, accepting the mug from him.

Standing so close to him, she felt overpowered by his scent. It worked like an aphrodisiac on her senses, precipitating an unwelcome surge of excitement in her. He was so disturbing to her in every way, she feared succumbing to a perilous fate. She sauntered to the other side of the room and sat on the daybed, deliberately taking up the entire couch.

"We do good stuff together," he said, glancing proudly at the paper. He leaned with his hip on the desk, looking at her. "Just think what we could do with prep time. We'd be seriously in demand."

That day would never come, Selinae thought. She would see to it. But she held her tongue.

"What else are you working on?" he asked.

"Nothing," she lied, taking a sip of coffee.

She heard the frustrated sigh that escaped his throat, then looked up into his face. His brown eyes were a mixture of humble pleading and unquenchable warmth, and the combination sent her mind swimming through a haze of feelings and desires. She wondered for a fleeting wistful second whether her decision was too hasty, before reminding herself to stay on course, regardless of what he said or did. Regardless of the gaping hole widening in her heart.

"I'm so sorry about the other night," Sterling said, abject guilt in his expression and voice. "I was out of line. I can imagine what you thought of me, and every time I think about what a coward I was . . ." He fell silent, his expression grim. He drew a deep breath before he spoke again. "Will you forgive me?"

She stared at him, momentarily speechless in her surprise at his apology. She was finding him to be an ever-changing mystery; he was bigger than she thought. But no apology was needed, she mused, scooting closer to the back of the bed, quiet and withdrawn.

"How about we get out of here and see what kind of trouble we can get into?" he suggested hopefully.

"I don't think so," she replied.

"Well," he said, rubbing his hands together with relish, "we could get breakfast. Have you had breakfast? I haven't."

"No," she said, shaking her head from side to side. Forcing conviction into her voice, she said, "Nothing. We can't do anything together anymore."

Staring into his face, she watched the light extinguish from his eyes as his jaws clamped together, his expression questioning. Unable to hold his eyes, she lowered her gaze into her cup.

"Selinae, I don't get it. What's going on?"

"We're different, you and I," she said, her heart pumping against her rib cage.

He raised the mug to his lips as if to drink, then set it down carefully on the desk. "From where I sit, that's good."

"Don't be cute," she said sharply. "You know what I mean."

"All I hear, or think I hear, is you trying to tell me that it's over between us," he said. "When the truth points to just the opposite."

"I don't know what arrow you're looking at because I don't see it that way," she said. "It was nice, but it wasn't meant to be. I admit I'm at fault for letting things get out of hand, but there's no way to go back and undo what's been done."

"So let's pack it in right now and cut our losses, huh?" he said sarcastically, his arms folded across his chest. "Is that what you're saying?" His steady gaze bored into her.

Selinae winced slightly. "Yeah," she replied slowly. "That's it." With the cup raised to her lips, she said mirthlessly, "You have a way with words. Maybe you ought to consider adding writing to your career."

"Uh-huh," he muttered mockingly. "Well, try these words on, Ms. Rogers. In the short amount of time that I've known you, I know that I care for you more than any woman." He paused to clear his throat. "I—"

The phone rang, and he turned toward the intrusion with a grimace. It rang a second time. "Are you going to answer that?" he asked.

The answering machine clicked into action. Within seconds, a male voice resonated clearly through the connection. "Selinae, I heard about the story you wrote, so I guess that's why you didn't respond to my previous message. I'll keep your medals and trophies until tomorrow night. If you haven't collected the box by then, I'm taking it to the dump site first thing Monday morning."

Selinae felt as if she were starting to disappear from the world. As the haughty voice rang in her ears, her mind was blank. She absently noted the angry mask that was Sterling's expression, the fury glowing in his eyes.

"Selinae."

Reaching for her, his quiet voice of concern nudged her out of her musings, a consciousness of cessation, a strange emptiness.

"Get out," she said softly, her expression void of emotion.

"Selinae," he crooned, pulling her into his arms. She stiffened in his embrace. "Please, let me—"

"I said get out."

* * *

Sterling stood at the front door of a desirable address in an upper-middle-class, racially mixed neighborhood in Missouri City, a scant twenty-minute ride from Houston. The temperature had dropped significantly. It was freezing; the sun had hidden its face.

Warmed by his residual anger, Sterling was oblivious to the cold. He recalled leaving Selinae's, feeling helpless, without an idea of what to do. He only knew his feelings for her wouldn't allow him to sit on his hands and let her father destroy her with his cruelty.

She probably wouldn't appreciate his interference, he thought, but it was not in his nature to do nothing. Besides, he didn't have anything to lose. Selinae had kicked him out of her house; he would not be thrown out of her life, as well.

He was prepared to beg if he had to, to accept any terms she set, as long as she didn't let his one mistake keep them apart. He may be a fool, but he believed with all his heart that they belonged together. And that meant eliminating the obstacles between them. He pressed the doorbell again.

Finally, a big, insolent-looking black man whose once well-toned body had gone soft with age and lax diet, opened the door. Sterling recognized him instantly. He had Selinae's mesmeric eyes and smooth, rich complexion. There was no mistaking the two of them were father and daughter.

"Yes?" Mr. Rogers inquired, instinctively on guard.

"Mr. Rogers," Sterling said, "my name is Sterling Washington."

"Ah," Mr. Rogers replied, his face full of mocking. "The man who is sleeping with Selinae, who got my wife and sons all in a tizzy."

"No," Sterling corrected, "I'm the man who's going to *marry* Selinae." He was trembling with rage, but he suppressed it. He didn't know what this visit would accomplish; it might blow up in his face. But it couldn't make matters any worse.

"Well, Mr. Washington, I don't know why you've come to see me. If it's to ask my permission to marry her, let me tell you, you don't need it. I could not care less who she's sleeping with."

"I didn't come for your permission. I just want you to keep your wife and sons away from Selinae," Sterling said. He was pleased by the surprise that crossed Oscar Rogers's face. "They only upset her with what I can see for myself are nothing more than false promises of reuniting the two of you."

"There will be no reunion," he said sternly. "There's no one for me to reunite with."

"Good," Sterling replied, smiling coldly. "Now if you'll just give me Selinae's things and keep the rest of your family out of our lives, everything will be just dandy."

The center was buzzing with excitement; the program was well under way when Selinae arrived. Though she wasn't in the mood for the dual festivities, the celebration of *Kuumba* and the *karamu* that followed, she wanted to get her mind off Sterling. She came to glean enjoyment from the young, as part of this night's events was given over to the children.

The children's program was dedicated to Tierney Simpson. The missing girl's picture graced thousands of brightly colored flyers offering a reward for information leading to her return. Everyone who entered the center was asked by a young host or hostess to contribute to the fund.

With a flyer in her hand, Selinae made her way into the center of activity. A plethora of delightful aromas met her at the door. The room was packed, not an empty seat visible on first glance. The works of young artists, murals depicting the cultural life of Africans and African Americans were tacked high for viewing. Red, green, and black streamers hung from the ceiling. Tables laden with food in covered dishes were set up around the outer aisles; chairs were placed in a semicircle; the Kwanzaa setting occupied the center atop a large *mkeka.*

Selinae deposited her offering—several loaves of banana bread—in a colorful handwoven basket, then searched for a seat among the crowd. As a troupe of youngsters demonstrated various martial arts skills, she located a spot nestled between a couple of tables midroom.

Remembering the first night of Kwanzaa—Sterling literally at her side, pressing into her with all his warmth—Selinae felt a bittersweet regret. The tender emotions for him were still there, though slightly impaired by her decision to rid her life of him. All day she had pondered how to erase him from her memory when he had fit into her life with such frightening ease, and all day she had drawn blanks; no answers, only despair.

Applause jolted Selinae back to the present. The emcee, an experienced teenage celebrant of Kwanzaa, walked up to the microphone. He led the audience in another round of applause for the performers, then announced the next offering. A kindergarten-age group of youngsters from the Freedom School assembled on stage.

All were clad in African attire, the boys separated

from the girls. The adult leader stood off to the side of the platform stage to orchestrate their performance. A young girl stepped out from the choir of children to the lowered mike. She stood patiently poised, awaiting the cue from her teacher before she spoke.

Unconsciously, Selinae pressed her hand across her stomach. To have a child, a little girl like that, with Sterling. To be a family. She chided herself for the thought. She had to stop thinking about him.

"We are African Americans," the youngster began, loud and clear. "And proud females to boot; we were born into a legacy of greatness; of which no man dares dispute. We don't deny the grandeur of others; but hold our own in high regard; tonight we bring praises to our mothers; whose faith has brought us this far. The seeds of our knowledge are centuries old; and of course, all our stories have yet to be told. . . ."

The audience was awed, and the proud parents of the girl beamed as the precocious child delivered forth the words like a wise old woman. Selinae was similarly impressed and lost herself in the child's speech.

"Running through my veins is the wisdom of Cleopatra the Seventh; the courage of Nzingha; the truth of Sojourner; and the creativity of Maya Angelou. The Goddess Ma'at sits on my shoulders, balancing truth and justice in my soul, filled with my mother's love.

"I am proud to proclaim my past. I am prepared for the challenges of the present. I shall be ready to meet my future. After all, ain't I a woman like Cleopatra, Nzingha, Sojourner, Maya, and Georgia Townsend, my mama?"

Applause like a giant roar resounded through the

room. The young boys from the school took center stage next, but the young girl's words continued to ring in Selinae's ears. She wiped at the tears brimming in her eyes.

Many black women had overcome greater adversities than her own. She felt ashamed of herself for not following the examples of strength and courage and wisdom laid out before her so clearly. She had behaved as if she were a child, but without the benefit of the wisdom this special child spoke, she thought.

On the heels of the silent taunt was an equally damning one. If she indeed carried Sterling's baby, then she had already failed the test passed by many mothers before her.

Selinae didn't stay for the closing celebration. The seeds of thought planted in her mind by the children, she left before the *karamu* began, missing the *tamshi la tutao-nana,* the farewell statement given to close out the *karamu* and end the year. Her mind had yet to close out the present one.

A chorus of percussionists played a lively beat to accompany the festive gathering for the *karamu.* Even as his mind told him he'd never find Selinae in the crowd, Sterling forged ahead, gripping his camera next to his chest. With a sheen of purpose in his eyes, he scrutinized female faces, looking for a chocolate-coated, ethereal one with enchanting, sensitive eyes.

He spotted her once in the crowd, catching a mere glimpse of her before losing her again. She sported a new hairstyle; small curls of her dark hair were entwined with red and gold beads, forming a crown on her head. She looked like a goddess.

Cutting through a line, he made his apologies and

left the hub of activity to check the offices on the other side of the dividing wall. He even paid a girl a dollar to check the ladies' room. Still no Selinae. He returned to the main room, where the food lines had thinned while the myriad of sounds—voices, music, merrymaking—had increased.

He believed he'd captured the look he'd been searching for and could hardly wait to develop the rolls of film he had shot tonight. Particularly those of the children. Watching them perform, he felt as proud as their parents must have been. He couldn't help but wonder what it would be like to have a child with Selinae.

Oh, he knew it was irresponsible, but the night's celebration created a strange feeling in him. The children were so eager to embrace the harvests of life. So unafraid.

Sterling stopped to rub his lids, his eyes aching from his intense search. He'd give anything to have Selinae come to him. But that wasn't going to happen, he chided himself.

After making so many overtures to her father, she was not about to put herself in a position to be rejected again. Not unless she was absolutely certain of her welcome.

Uttering a heavy, weary sigh, Sterling wondered what it would take, how far he was willing to go to get the woman he loved.

But he already knew the answer. There were no limits where she was concerned. Making his way through a line to leave the center, he wondered what kind of father he would be.

On New Year's Eve, the sixth night of Kwanzaa, with no place to go, Selinae chided herself for sitting in the car, idling in the driveway of her home.

"Wasting gas," she mumbled.

The heater was blowing at full blast; its muffled sound competed with the announcer on the radio, playing a countdown of the top recordings of 1994.

Despite the lights shining brilliantly around her little house, it appeared big and ominous and sinister. She debated going inside, fearing the empty silence would haunt her.

There was a place she *could* go, she mused. Sterling's. Whether he would let her in was another matter. She had kicked him out, told him nothing he could say would change anything between them, she recalled. But now she questioned her decision to be rid of a man who made her feel whole.

In spite of the doubts and reservations she had, she wanted him. High-handed assumptions and all. After all, there could be no conditions on love.

The solution was simple, she told herself, her hand moving to the gear stick as if with a volition of its own. He lived nearby; she could be there within ten minutes. All she had to do was drive over, ring the doorbell, and see for herself how he truly felt. How he interpreted his claim of *caring for her more than any other woman.*

But her fear returned. Could she accept his answer if it weren't the one she wanted to hear?

Selinae felt bewildered all over again. But one thing was absolutely clear. She loved Sterling Washington. Love wasn't a cure-all for the aches and pains that had plagued her life, but it was the only truth in her world of shifting realities. She had but one two-part question to answer, she told herself.

Was she an inheritor of the legacy of strength, wisdom, and courage of her ancestors? If yes, then, was she prepared to risk harvesting the fruits of love?

Selinae backed out of the driveway and drove off.

Driving home on deserted streets, Sterling envied the revelers inside warm houses celebrating as the New Year rang in. He was exhausted and cold from sitting for hours parked in front of Selinae's home waiting for her to return.

Pondering where she could be, he guessed she was hiding from him. And from her family as well, no doubt. He was disgusted with all of them for creating an environment that had sent her running off to be alone. They were all guilty of imposing their wishes on her, never stopping to consider her feelings.

Good intentions, he mused sarcastically, braking at the red light.

From the traffic signal, he could see the flood-lights surrounding the exterior of his house. As the light turned green, he was filled with abhorrence about returning home. Sleep was out of the question. Maybe developing the pictures he'd shot tonight would help the time pass tolerably, he thought.

As he turned into his driveway, he did a double take, seeing Selinae's car in front of one of the closed garage doors. His heart began to beat as if a pack of wild horses were stampeding through his chest. He braked to a jolting stop and hopped out of his vehicle to run to her car.

Her head rested against the headrest, her eyes closed. Alarmed, he rapped on the window.

Selinae sat up with a jolt, her gaze disoriented as she looked out the window. He noticed her sag with relief in her seat, then he heard the locks pop up on the doors.

He opened hers and stared transfixed, as if she were sage words on a page to remember forever. She offered him a small, shy smile that sent shivers down his spine.

"It's freezing out here," he said at last. "Why don't you come inside?"

"Are you sure?"

Sterling was awed by her hesitancy, her voice as soft and tentative as the expression on her face. He had to curtail his eager excitement. *Don't blow it,* he cautioned himself.

"I went to your house."

"I wasn't there."

"I know. I left the *karamu* when I couldn't find you."

"You were there . . . at the celebration tonight?"

"Yes," he replied to the flicker of surprise in her eyes. "I spotted you once, but by the time I made my way through the crowd, you were gone."

He watched as her lids came over her eyes, noted the familiar serene persona she donned.

"I didn't stay for the *karamu.* I had too much thinking to do to celebrate."

The thoughtful quality in her voice and the reality of her presence bore witness to the truth, he thought, nodding with understanding. He wondered what finally had convinced her to come.

"I parked in front of your house and fell asleep behind the wheel, waiting for you to come home."

"I'm sorry," she said, her eyes leaving his face for the briefest of moments.

"Don't apologize. This is better," he said insistently. "I'm just glad you're here . . . safe . . . with me. You are staying, aren't you? I mean, at least for tonight. You don't have to, I just thought . . . Goodness," he said, laughing, "I'm babbling like an idiot."

"If that's what you want," she replied.

Sterling felt a shudder course through him. She had no idea how sensuous her voice sounded, the utter delight he felt hearing her promising words. So affected by her presence, he had to clear his voice before he spoke. "Yes. It's what I want more than anything."

"Then I'll stay . . . at least for tonight."

He was willing to accept any condition—one night or forever. He extended a hand to help her from the car. "Did you bring your case?"

"No," she said, pulling her coat around her tightly. "Just me."

Closing the car door, he took her hand in his and led the way inside the house. Hannibal greeted them at the door, barking noisily.

"It's just me, boy," Sterling said, clicking on the lights in the foyer. Hannibal's vigilance turned into happy yelps as he sought Selinae's attention for a rub behind the ears.

"Hi, boy; hi, Hannibal," she said accommodatingly.

"Let me take your coat."

With her coat and purse in his grip, Sterling stared at Selinae. He couldn't be jealous of a dog, he told himself, but he would much rather it were him that was the object of her affection.

"Go to your room," he commanded to Hannibal as he hung the coat and purse in the hall closet. The dog whimpered, displeased, but obeyed his master.

Selinae stood, her hands crossed loosely in front of her. Apprehension still lurked in her eyes. Coveting her with his gaze, his eyes roamed the length of her, the warmth of her shapely throat, the suggestion of nubile curves beneath the simple, long sleeved black dress with its dropped waist and pleated skirt, her ankles sheathed in black velvet boots. She looked like a young princess, exquisite and fragile, unaware of her powers over him. Feeling his pulse beat in his throat, he swallowed hard.

"Would you care for something to drink? Some food? Have you eaten?"

"No. Nothing, thank you," she replied.

She moved lightly but with enough sway to pull the skirt of her dress in alternative directions as she backed away and sauntered off to the study. He followed, and stood in the doorway to see her staring at the box on his desk. It overflowed with trophies, ribbons, and medals. He felt a moment's panic and rushed forward, an explanation tripping off his tongue.

"I, uh, went by your parents'. Well, I guess you can see that . . . uh, I thought maybe . . ." He couldn't decipher her look; she was so still, he feared her response.

"Turn off the lights."

Puzzled, he watched as she dropped to her knees in front of the coffee table and began lighting the *mishumaa.* After lighting the sixth candle, she looked up at him with a significant lifting of her brows.

Goaded into action, he turned off the overhead light and paused near the door, letting his eyes adjust to the new light. The candles flickered and danced in the dark, casting her in silhouette. She sat Indian-style on the floor, the skirt of her dress bunched primly around her legs.

He kneeled next to her and fixed his eyes straight

ahead at the candles, as she did. "There's so much I want to say to you."

"Then tell me; I'll listen," she replied softly.

"I know; you always do," he replied ruefully. "Maybe I should shut up and listen to you for a change." Imploring her with his gaze, he said, "Tell me, Selinae. Tell me what you want, what you need."

She raised her legs and clasped her hands around her ankles, her chin resting on her knees before she spoke. "It's not that easy," she began slowly, as if feeling her way. She stopped suddenly and smiled in exasperation. "It's why I prefer writing. I can get my point across better."

"Take your time," he said gently. "Get it right . . . the way you want it."

"I think I told you before that I'm not hard to please."

"Every time you give me a headline answer," he said, "I put words in your mouth."

"I have simple wants, simple needs," she continued softly, her eyes open, frank. "I want to be needed and I need to be wanted."

As her voice faded to a hush stillness, Sterling felt a cascade of warm sensations rush through his body. Even as he cautioned himself not to assume she expected those things from him, he couldn't suppress the sense of sublime appeasement he felt.

There. She'd said it . . . as plain and simple as she knew how. Watching Sterling's expression, she knew that the specifics weren't important. There was no mapping out love. One could not plan it like a crop, with dimensions and seasons. It grew, and those imbued with its powers flourished and died, leaving its legacy for others to consume. It was the natural course of life.

"I'd forgot some valuable lessons . . . fundamental to living, in fact," she continued. "Some came from observing other people's pains and victories; some I experienced firsthand. There are different kinds of love. The highest, the supreme kind, of course, is seldom attained by man . . . especially those of us who aren't attentive, or attuned to and respectful of self and nature." She lifted her shoulders in a sigh. "They are defined by the particular sender and object of affection . . . you know, brother-to-brother, sister-to-mother, daughter-to-father, woman-to-man."

Wondering if comprehension reached him, she lifted her gaze to his. He was still watching her with gentle eyes, patience and understanding. She continued.

"It's all love, the feeling between these partners . . . but it's different. Humans are greedy. We want it all and we want to control it. Then it's no longer love; it's something else. To limit or temper the depth of love is sacrilegious, regardless of the reason. But you and I both know it happens so much, we chalk it up to human shortcomings—if we bother to examine it at all. Nevertheless, it does not mean that we should stop striving to attain perfection or even disclaim the potential for love from another source just because one seems missing." She folded her bottom lip in her mouth, looking at him with a profoundly contrite expression. "It's what I did to you, and I'm sorry. I convinced myself that I couldn't accept your affection and was willing to throw it away, just because I didn't have my father's love. And that's not true. *I'm* bigger than that; my capacity to grow, to love and accept love is limited only by small-minded thinking." With a sheepish half-grin on her face, she said, "I like to think I'm a fairly intelligent person . . . most of the time."

"I love you," Sterling said.

Selinae felt doubts and fears flee her soul, replaced by a new sensation. A sense of rejuvenation coursed through her, gathering her emotions together in righteous harmony. She looked at Sterling with a smile that transformed her face into pure delight, her brilliant eyes lit from within. "No questions?" she asked softly.

Sterling shook his head from side to side. "I have all the answers I need or want," he replied, his voice simmering with emotion.

Reading his thoughts through his eyes, the sparkle of untethered desire in their depths, Selinae finally followed her heart. She wrapped her arms around his neck; his automatically curled around her waist.

They both it seemed, had been waiting for each other forever. The struggle they had gone through to reach the present only enhanced the pleasure they felt now. Tingling from the inside, she lifted her head to meet his mouth halfway. Their lips touched in a series of slow, revelatory kisses.

"Stay," he said, his lips touching hers like a whisper.

Quivering, she replied, "Forever."

"Yes. Forever," he echoed, and their mouths sealed in earnest for a lingering kiss that sent currents of desire through them both.

The kiss recovered stolen moments and restored memories that had been placed aside in order to build a stronger foundation of unity. His tongue delved past her lips, forging a special truth in the inner recesses of her mouth. She answered with a moan, accepting his tongue to define their partnership as equals. In passionate solidarity, both were consumed by the commitment inherent in the kiss, its sweetness and its depth.

It was late, or rather, very early in the new year, when the telephone rang in Sterling's sleep. Dreaming of passions spent, he smiled unconsciously, and tightened his possessive grip on the soft, warm body curled next to his.

The phone rang again, and he frowned; he mumbled unintelligibly. It was echoed by an equally muddled, female sound of protest.

The telephone rang a third time, rousing him awake. Clearing his throat, he reached for the phone on the bedside table.

"Hello," he said in a groggy voice, his lids still closed. "Yes, it is; who's calling?" Opening one eye, he peeked at Selinae, her head on his chest. "Yes, she's here, Mrs. Rogers. But she's asleep and I'm not going to wake her up. I'll have her call you at a reasonable hour," he said sourly. "Emergency? All right, what's the emergency? . . . Oh," he said, "in that case . . ." Pulling the base of the phone to the bed, he said, "Selinae, wake up, it's your mother."

"Tell her Happy New Year and I'll call her later," Selinae mumbled, otherwise not moving a muscle.

"It's about your dad," he said.

"What else is new?" she quipped, sleepy-voiced.

"He had a heart attack, babe," he said somberly, "he's in the hospital."

* * *

From high in the endless blue skies, the mild sun shone down on the fabulous array of colors in the stands and on the field of the high school stadium. It was the second Saturday in April; the first meet of the youth track and field season; the year, 2002. A picnic kind of day, it was perfect for the athletes: no wind, no hot sun.

The stands were packed with spectators; the center of the field was just as full with long jumpers, pole vaulters, discus throwers, and runners warming up. Coaches who were not allowed on the fields sat anxiously, hoping their young athletes would remember their training. Parents watched eagerly.

Sitting up high on the wooden bleachers amid a cluster of fans, Oscar, Senior felt perfectly content. He was acting on doctor's orders to eliminate stress in his life, and had adopted the axiom *what will be will be.* Having survived a major heart attack, he was just grateful to be around to witness this magnificent event. Like many others, he held a pair of binoculars in one hand, a stopwatch in the other.

The first heat of the primary girls race was about to start. Four teams of girls between the ages of six and eight spaced themselves one-hundred meters apart on the synthetic, all-weather track for the relay. Poised attentively, he raised the binoculars to focus on one runner in a navy and white uniform. His heart filled with pride and love.

Bronze-brown with liquid amber eyes, the young runner was already well-toned at six years and seven months old. Long dark braids were clasped together at the back of her head with a rubber band.

She was Imani, the new light in his old life. Her name meant faith, and thanks to the faith her mother Selinae, possessed, he had been granted the honor of knowing his granddaughter.

He glanced at Selinae, sitting beside him, hand in hand with Sterling. His beautiful daughter glowed from within and again his mended heart felt a pang as regret raced through him. He had hurt his daughter so much that no apology could properly absolve him. Oscar smiled as he remembered the depth of her forgiveness.

It had not been easy for Oscar Rogers, Senior to admit his faults to his daughter or himself. He had seen Selinae's struggle during their first shaky steps towards reconciliation. But her husband Sterling had much to do with her strength and healing, and he felt that he could never find the right words to give his thanks.

He looked at Imani again, her name the last feast day in the Kwanzaa celebration. The last day of the holiday had changed all their lives, he recalled. Being so close to death changed his view on life. Selinae had found the impetus to enter the family again, and even the missing girl Tierney Simpson was found, safe and unharmed. It was a new beginning for all.

The starter on the field raised his pistol in the air, and the runners took their starting positions: some stood upright, some crouched, and some assumed three-point stances like football players. The gun fired, and simultaneously Oscar, Senior pressed the starting button on the stopwatch. His gaze was riveted on the team's lead-off runner as she sped around the track, the blue aluminum baton a blur with the pumping motion of her arms.

Watching her run forward in full speed, his

thoughts sped back to over twenty years ago. He'd been a fool for many of them, he recalled. He'd been granted a reprieve by the Creator and Selinae to enjoy what was left of his life.

And if he didn't want to miss the rest of this race, he told himself, he'd better pay attention.

The tempo of his pulse picked up as the second runner handed off to the third, who kept running. Coming up the curve toward the final leg, he stood, a coach's prayer echoing in his mind. He stared enthralled and amazed at the poise of Imani. She didn't break a stride as she took the baton, heading for the finish line. He wanted to boast loudly, "That's my grandbaby."

"Good handoff," he exclaimed instead above the roaring din of cheers. His heart pounded in sync with her lightning-quick strides as her little feet in brand-new spikes ate up the track, leaving a trail of imaginary dust in her opponents' faces.

"Go, Imani, go!" he shouted, his encouragement louder than even his daughter's. "Move them arms . . . run, baby, run . . . that's it. All the way . . . all the way! That's my girl," he said.

Imani crossed the finish line first, and his hand jerked as he depressed the timing button on the watch. He didn't bother to look at the time; it wasn't important. The victory was in running a good race, he thought. He wouldn't have cared if she came in last.

"I almost missed this," he whispered tearfully, a proud smile on his lips.

"We'll make regionals this year for sure!" someone yelled amid the cheers erupting in the stands. A fellow parent seated three rows below called up to Oscar, Senior.

"Whadda ya say, Oscar . . . think you got a future Olympian on your hands?"

Oscar Senior smiled proudly. "Only if she wants it," he replied, pinching back the tears in his eyes.

SEVEN GUIDING PRINCIPLES OF KWANZAA

UMOJA

Umoja (ooh-MOE-jah) means unity, and it is the principle for the first day of Kwanzaa. Our families and communities need unity in order for them to be productive and to survive. On this day we pledge to strive for—and to maintain—unity in the family, the community, the nation that we have helped to build, and with our people.

KUJICHAGULIA

Kujichagulia (koo-gee-cha-goo-LEE-ah) means self-determination and is the second day of Kwanzaa. On this day we pledge to define ourselves, name ourselves, create for ourselves, and speak for ourselves, instead of being defined, named by, created for, and spoken for by others. On this day we design for ourselves a positive future and then vow to make that prophecy—that dream—a self-fulfilling one.

UJIMA

Ujima (ooh-GEE-mah) is the third day of Kwanzaa and means "collective work and responsibility". On this day we celebrate working together in the community to help others. For Ujima we pledge to rebuild our communities and help our people solve problems by working together.

UJAMAA

Ujamaa (OOH-jah mah) means cooperative economics and is the fourth day of Kwanzaa. On this day we pledge to develop our own businesses and support them. We strive to maintain shops, stores, and industries that contribute to the well-being of our community and drive out businesses (boycotts, etc.) that take from our communities and give nothing back.

NIA

Nia (NEE-ah) is the fifth day of Kwanzaa, and it means "purpose". On this day we pledge to build and develop our communities, schools, and families. We also pledge to provide a strong communal foundation from which our children can develop into strong and productive people.

KUUMBA

Kuumba (koo-OOM-bah) is the sixth day of Kwanzaa, and it means "creativity". On this day we pledge several things. We pledge to do whatever we can to make our communities and homes more beautiful and better than we found them. We also pledge to use our creative talents and energies to improve young minds and hearts.

IMANI

Imani (ee-MAH-nee) is the seventh and last day of Kwanzaa. Imani means faith. On this day, the beginning of the new year, we pledge to believe with all our hearts and minds in our people, our parents, our good and dedicated teachers and leaders, and in the greater good of the work we do with and for one another, for the community, and for the people.

KWANZAA RECIPES TO CELEBRATE THE SEASON

(suggested by Yanick Rice Lamb)

Sumptuous Sweet Potato Pie

This recipe is a favorite at family gatherings, and I don't dare step through the door without extras—especially around the Lambs. It includes extra spices and a dash of rum, depending on the crowd, to blend my Haitian and Southern roots.

2 pounds fresh sweet potatoes
1/2 stick butter or margarine
3/4 cup sugar
1/2 cup brown sugar
1 teaspoon cinnamon
1 teaspoon nutmeg
1/8 teaspoon allspice
dash of anise
3 eggs
3/4 cup low-fat evaporated milk
2 teaspoons vanilla extract
3 tablespoons rum, preferably Barbancourt Rhum from Haiti (optional)

Preheat oven to 375 degrees. Wash sweet potatoes and boil until tender. (Don't remove skin, otherwise they will absorb the water like sponges and become mushy.) While potatoes are still hot, carefully peel and place in a medium-size bowl with butter or margarine. Use a potato masher to soften the mixture. Stir in sugars and spices. Beat in eggs one at a time. Stir in milk, vanilla, and rum (if desired). Pour evenly into two pie shells (see recipe below). Bake on middle rack for 30 to 40 minutes, or until slightly browned and firm to the touch. Serve warm. Yield: 16 slices.

Double Pie Crust

2 cups flour
1 teaspoon salt
2/3 cup shortening
5 tablespoons ice water

Mix the flour and salt in a medium bowl. Using a pastry blender or two knives, cut the shortening into the flour until small lumps begin to form. Sprinkle in water, a tablespoon at a time as needed, mixing with a fork until mixture becomes dough. Divide dough in half, shape into two balls, and then flatten each into disks on a lightly floured surface. Roll out dough to 1/8-inch thickness, roughly 1-2 inches wider than inverted pie pan. Carefully fold into quarters, and unfold evenly in pie pan. Roll up overhanging dough, or trim a half-inch from rim of pan. Flute or crimp edges, if desired. (You can also trim dough evenly along edge of pan and use the tines of a fork to form depressions.) Bake as directed in pie recipe. Yield: two crusts

'Chelle's Crab Cakes

My sister, Michelle Rice, begs me to make these crab cakes for her birthday party each year. They disappear almost as soon as I put them on the table.

1 pound fresh crab meat, picked through
juice of half a lemon
salt or Old Bay seasoning to taste

freshly ground pepper to taste
1 tablespoon fresh parsley, chopped
1 medium onion, minced
1/2 teaspoon baking powder
1/4 teaspoon cayenne pepper, red pepper flakes, or hot sauce
1 egg, beaten
1 tablespoon Worcestershire sauce
1 tablespoon mayonnaise
1 teaspoon Dijon mustard (optional)
1 slice of soft bread, crumbled in food processor
1/2 cup bread crumbs
canola oil

In a medium-size bowl, break up crab meat and pick through for pieces of shell. Sprinkle with lemon juice, salt or Old Bay, and pepper. Mix in parsley, onion, baking powder, and cayenne, pepper flakes, or hot sauce. Add beaten egg, Worcestershire sauce, mayonnaise, and mustard, mixing well. Stir in crumbled slice of bread. Cover the surface of a plate with bread crumbs. Form crab mixture into patties, and coat with bread crumbs. In a large pan, fry patties in 1/4-inch layer of canola oil until each side is golden brown. Remove from pan, and place on paper towels to drain excess oil. Yield: two dozen patties.

Red Beans and Rice

2 cups red kidney beans
6 cups water, cold
1 large onion, chopped
1 green pepper, chopped
1/2 pound ham, cubed or 1/2 pound smoked sausage, sliced
2 cloves garlic, chopped
1 bay leaf

1/2 teaspoon salt
1/2 teaspoon pepper

Wash beans in cold water. Drain beans and put in covered pot with cold water. Add ham or sausage to pot. Bring to boil slowly. Add chopped onions, garlic, green pepper, bay leaf, salt and pepper. Simmer for 2 hours stirring occasionally until beans are soft. Mash some of the beans against the side of the pot to make a creamy sauce. Serve with rice. (Serves 6)

Jambalaya

1 pound smoked sausage, sliced
1/2 pound ham, diced
1 tablespoon oil
2 onions, chopped
1 green pepper, chopped
1/2 cup celery, chopped
1/2 cup green onions, chopped
1 can tomatoes (16 oz)
3 cups beef stock, chicken stock, or water
2 cloves garlic, chopped
1 bay leaf
1/4 teaspoon pepper
1/2 teaspoon salt
2 cups rice, uncooked
1 pound shrimp, peeled and deveined

Heat oil in skillet. Fry the sausage and ham. Add onion, green pepper, green onions, and celery, and saute until tender or soft. Add tomatoes and stock or water to pot. Add garlic, bay leaf, pepper, salt, and rice. Stir and bring to a boil; then reduce heat. Cover and simmer for 15 minutes. Add water if Jambalaya seems dry. Add shrimp, recover, and cook 15 minutes longer. Mix well. (Serves 6-8)